COSMIC
GAMES

COSMIC GAMES

BOOK ONE

Wilbur Woods

Podium

COSMIC
GAMES

CHAPTER ONE

The Rift

The weight of the bazooka on Max's back felt as heavy as the sins he carried with him.

Lying on the damp forest floor, wearing his olive-green camo, he sighed to himself. It was a spring morning and he was overlooking a dirt road. Max shifted his weight in a futile attempt at keeping the damned bazooka from digging into his back so much.

Technically it was an RPG-28, as the officers often reminded him. They didn't like it when Max called it a bazooka.

A torture machine would be a more apt description. It weighed a whopping twenty-eight pounds, making it the bane of Max's existence for the past eleven months, two weeks, and four days. Yes, he had counted.

"Just two more weeks," Max muttered to himself.

"Shh," the petty officer next to him hissed. Petty, indeed.

Two more weeks until the end of his compulsory military service. He would be a free man, ready to face the well-trodden path of education and a career. Ugh . . . That didn't sound particularly appealing, either, truth be told.

Become a corporate monkey for the next forty years? Or just ditch your education and languish in some dead-end job and either drink yourself to death or find a rope to wrap around your neck?

Yeah, Max wasn't exactly thrilled at his future prospects. He had tried a bunch of different options over the years and nothing seemed to click. Occasionally, he would get excited by an idea, and the feeling might even last for several weeks, but inevitably it would go away; nothing stuck with him. His family called him a "serial quitter" behind his back, as he'd discovered via a WhatsApp message that had clearly been sent to the wrong person. That had done wonders to his pride.

What pride? he scoffed.

It had all gone downhill ever since his mother died when Max was fifteen. She had always been that one person who had encouraged him. She had been a high school physics teacher and had taught Max everything about her field, hoping he would become an engineer. It never came to be. Cancer did, though.

The funeral was followed by a series of juvenile delinquent years of rebellious grandstanding in less-than-savory company. He had managed to just barely scrape his way through high school, but the grades hadn't exactly been much to speak of. No good university would take him.

At that point Max just kind of . . . gave up. His father hadn't exactly earned a *World's Greatest Dad* mug before, but after his mom died, things got even worse. He barely paid any attention to his son and just focused on work. Max felt like an unwanted roommate in his dad's home, filling up his time with video games and a series of dead-end, minimum wage jobs. The conscription mail had come every year, but Max had succeeded in putting it off, along with free counseling due to the death of a caretaker. Max got a proverbial hall pass for clinical depression. Until one day he didn't.

Being a few years older than the other kids made his time in the army less fun than it might have otherwise been, but it was still pretty decent. At least there was always a clear objective. Max always knew what to do. In the end, it was as meaningless as anything else, but it kept him occupied. What had been meaningful were his comrades. Max hadn't had friends for a couple of years, and it felt so good to be part of a community again.

If only he didn't have to be lugging a heavy-ass bazooka around on his back. Carrying the cursed thing on top of the standard-issue assault rifle made Max feel like a walking weapons rack. A constantly aching weapons rack.

Still, despite the endless purgatory of carrying a bazooka for a better part of a year, there had been some upsides. Max had lost a good thirty pounds, transforming from a pudgy guy to a reasonably fit one. Not too bad. His mind had also started to clear up. He couldn't exactly be described as depressed anymore. Just empty inside. *Progress!*

Returning to his friends, however, the sense of camaraderie from shared misery was a powerful thing. He hoped that the friendships would continue after the service.

There was Brian, with whom Max liked to spend his evenings in the barracks. He was fairly simple guy, but one of the friendliest people he'd ever met. Honest, straightforward, reasonable. The kind of person you wanted on your team.

There was also Kat. She was a badass, like most women who joined the military service. Service was voluntary for them, and so the ones who actually chose to serve were usually the tough ones. Still, there were a decent amount every year. Some wanted to beef up their resume and some seemed to simply have something to prove.

Max didn't know which camp Kat belonged to, but she sure had a chip on her shoulder. She took no shit from anybody, which got her in trouble on a regular basis.

Being attractive, with raven hair and a slender body, and with the military having a ratio of one woman for every ten guys, she got a lot of attention. Most of it unwanted.

I guess she likes spending time with me because I'm not constantly breathing down her neck. Not that she isn't pretty . . . Maybe I'll gather up enough balls to ask her out once the service is over.

Max gave a glance to the right and saw the pensive faces of his squad-mates under their green helmets. Kat sensed his gaze and gave Max a blank look in return. He smiled and turned back to watch the road.

His time in the military hadn't been all that bad. At least with all of the "hurry up and wait," you always got a lot of free time for thinking. Even now, they were waiting for a convoy of armored tanks to arrive at the road they were watching. It was part of their final field-training exercise. Max and his fellow servicemen were all carrying live ammunition, which made the whole exercise both more exciting and stressful at the same time.

Even his bazooka contained an actual armor-piercing grenade. Usually he would carry blanks or nothing at all. This was an important exercise, so he would be shooting a blank from yet another bazooka sitting next to him. What was the point of also carrying one loaded with live ammo when he would never get to shoot it? *Welcome to the army.*

His job was to shoot through a tank's armor plating after it was crippled by a mine. the odds of his grenade actually piercing the armor of a modern tank, equipped with reactive plating, from twenty yards away was around 20 percent. In those remaining 80 percent of cases, the RPG would glance off the plating, giving Max, on average, a solid 3.6 seconds before the heat-guided aiming system of the modern tanks blew him and the rest of his squad to smithereens. Max *really* hoped his country would never face conflict.

Max shuffled in place again. It was early morning and the ground was still damp from dew. The sun cast its rays through the forest canopy, painting a pretty view of golden green from the top of the hill. Things could be worse. It could be raining.

After an hour more of waiting, Max could start to hear and feel the tremors of approaching armored vehicles. Their squad leader gave a hand signal to prepare for engagement. Promptly, four tanks rolled into view from around the corner, their heavy motors giving out low rumbles. After they passed a certain point, one of the officers in charge of the exercise stood up and waved a red flag. It was a signal for the tanks to stop. The first one had hit an imaginary mine. That was Max's squadron's cue.

But something strange was happening. Even though the tanks had stopped, there was still a tremor running through the ground. In fact, the tremor was *growing*. Something was wrong. Something was *very* wrong. Then a loud, resonant sound, like the cry of an ancient battle horn, filled the air. The tremor kept increasing, now visibly shaking the ground.

"Abort exercise!" the officer with the red flag yelled. "EVERYBODY STAY DOWN!"

What the hell is happening? War? No, that can't be it. Earthquake? What is that sound?

Max looked around. His comrades were huddling to the ground, holding onto their helmets tightly. Their expressions ranged from concerned to panicked.

The battle horn sound grew louder, changing from a low rumble to a sharp, piercing whistle. Everyone gasped and put their hands to their ears in an attempt to block out the painful sound. Then, just as suddenly as it had begun, everything went quiet. Dead quiet.

And that was when the rift opened.

Above the tree line, the bright blue sky seemed to have torn open, a big black rip in space spreading wide. Strange shapes swirled on its surface, like oil on water. Then it began *pulling* at everything and everyone around it. At first it felt like a tug. Despite the shock, Max had the presence of mind to grab onto a large, nearby, rocky outcropping. But then the force of the gravitation grew into an insistent pull, finally escalating into a violent drag that managed to wrench Max off and up into midair. As he flew towards the strange black rift, he screamed in terror. He saw that everyone else around him had been pulled up as well, all now hurtling towards the blackness at an unstoppable speed. Max felt himself subsumed by complete, utter darkness.

Am I dead . . . ?

That had been quick. And relatively painless. But he was still floating in total darkness. What if this lasted for all eternity? Then Max suddenly heard a calm, robotic voice.

[Initializing Cosmic Games protocol . . .]

What?

[Assigning System Compatibility to subject #266830151 . . .]
[System Compatibility assigned]
[Assigning randomized Spawn Point . . .]
[Randomized Spawn Point assigned]
[Initializing . . .]

CHAPTER TWO

Belly of the Beast

The darkness vanished around him and Max landed face down on the ground. When he got up, he realized he was somewhere else. Somewhere else entirely . . .

He found himself in an enormous cave with high walls. The stones were black with red, glowing streaks snaking all of them, like lightning. It was a large space, practically as large as a football stadium. In the middle of it stood an unspeakable horror that let out a nightmarish roar, making Max's blood curl.

It stood a full thirty feet tall. Twisted horns protruded from its large head and steam rose from the ground in its wake. Its body was red, bulging with muscle. It had a hunch, long, ape-like arms, evil red eyes, and a slack-jawed mouth capable of swallowing an elephant whole. Jagged rows of teeth and tusks filled its mouth in discordant rows and angles. It roared again in what seemed to be excitement at the sight of the veritable feast that had stumbled into its cave.

Two hundred men and women in camo uniforms were screaming and shooting at the unholy creature in a panic. This was Max's company. The beast laughed at the soldiers shooting at it. The bullets seemed to have little effect. Then, Max noticed something incredibly strange. A green bar with a tick of red was hovering above the beast.

Is that a . . . Health bar?

Text floated in the air above the "Health bar".

[Malgaroth, Avatar of Wrath]
[World Boss], [Level ???]

What the hell is happening?

In the upper left corner of his vision, another green bar appeared. Under it, a blue bar of equal length. And under that, a green bar.

Are these mine? This can't be real.

But it felt real enough. The beast roared again and clapped its hands together, emitting a thunderous shockwave that blasted all nearby soldiers away and lifted Max off the ground. He flew a yard or so and landed hard on his back. Meanwhile, the RPG-28 landed on his chest. "Oof!" Max cried.

Then he looked around frantically, trying to find an exit. There was none. The black and red stone walls were smooth and held not a single crack, much less a crevice or a doorway. They were trapped. They were going to die.

"Get it together, Max!" someone shouted. Max turned and saw Kat a few feet away. She was on one knee, reloading her assault rifle.

With tremulous hands, Max pushed himself up off the ground. He was so scared, his mind was going blank.

"What is happening?" he asked.

Kat gave him an outraged look.

"JUST SHOOT THE THING!"

Max reached for the assault rifle cinched to his shoulder. He turned the safety off and unloaded on the beast towering in the distance. Its Health bar had gone down slightly, but it seemed the bullets didn't penetrate its skin. *How was that possible? Maybe explosives would hurt it.* Max knew that some soldiers in their company had grenades. *Should I use my bazooka?*

Max's weapon clicked empty and he unclipped the magazine. He fumbled with another one but dropped it. As he picked it up, he glanced at Kat. She screamed with fury as she unloaded another clip at the demonic thing. So fierce . . . Was she not scared?

The gunfire around them was dwindling. The monster grabbed another unlucky soldier, lifted them up in the air and grinned widely with that twisted mouth of his. He tossed the screaming soldier into its mouth and chomped down. Max grimaced.

Stray rounds of RPG-28 were hitting the beast along with the rifle-fire. The blasts seemed to momentarily disarm it and chip away at its Health bar but not to a significant degree. *What was that thing's skin made of?*

Max's weapon clicked empty for the last time. You'd be surprised by how fast you go through a clip when shooting on full-auto against a goddamn otherworldly demon from Hell. Kat's weapon clicked empty as well, and she cussed. Wasting no time, she vaulted toward a dead comrade. Max didn't recognize who he was, but the way his body had twisted by landing on the ground made him feel sick to his stomach.

Kat wasn't bothered. She slid next to the corpse and grabbed its remaining magazines and loaded her rifle with them. Impressed, Max followed her lead.

But just as the gunfire was dying down, so were the screams. The cave was a den of carnage, blood, and guts splattered everywhere. A few explosions hit the towering demon intermittently, as the result of a well-aimed grenade, but it only jerked a bit and laughed. It was a discordant, guttural blasphemy.

The Health bar above its head had turned slightly more red, but not enough to warrant hope. [**Malgaroth, Avatar of Wrath**] swiped at the ground with his massive arm and grabbed a handful of soldiers in his grip. The gargantuan demon squeezed, and blood burst out of its fist.

Max swallowed down bile as he watched in stunned horror. He knew he should act, but he didn't know what to do. With every death cry, every body hitting the ground with a sickly smack, the despair filled his mind further and further.

Having dealt with everyone in its immediate vicinity, [**Malgaroth, Avatar of Wrath**] looked around with a gleeful grin. It clapped its hands again, emitting another shockwave that blasted through the cave. It sent bodies flying, and Max huddled down behind a corpse he'd been using to steady his rifle. A mangled torso flew past him, spattering his face with warm blood. The iron taste made him sick.

Max checked his right. Kat hadn't been so lucky. She had been hit directly with a corpse that had knocked her down. Max heard her cry of pain and afterwards realized she wasn't moving.

"Kat!" Max cried out. Big mistake. The creature took note. Max was probably one of the last things still clearly alive in this pit of Hell. With a slow, leisurely gait, it approached, sadistic joy in its eyes. Its lanky orangutan-arms made the air whoosh as they swung. A veil of steam trailed behind it. As it approached, the air grew hot—almost unbearably so. Yet, Max froze. As he watched, wide-eyed, he realized he would die here. Running would do no good. Like a cold heavy rock dropped into the pit of his stomach, despair overwhelmed him. The beast reveled in his stunned fear. With two gigantic fingers, it carefully lifted Max by the neck of his jacket with two gigantic fingers. It brought him up to his face to look at him closely. The pure evil in the monster's eyes was palpable. Max couldn't breathe. The monster chuckled and opened its giant maw of protruding teeth. Breath smelling like death and brimstone assaulted Max. But it also brought him back to his senses from his death trance. He looked down, as the creature slowly lifted him higher above its mouth, clearly about to swallow him. Inside of the demonic creature's gullet, a red-hot fire burned. It called Max to action.

You won't swallow me up, you bastard!

With practiced ease, Max grabbed the cinch, slung the RPG-28 from his side to his shoulder, and unclipped the safety mechanisms, popping the lid open. Wasting no time, he fired. The power of the blast pushed him backwards, even as he continued to dangle between the beast's fingers. The rocket-propelled grenade left a trail of faint smoke as it zipped into the demon's mouth. Moments later, Max heard a muffled explosion from inside the giant. Its face shifted from glee to surprise to shock to pain, as it cried out. Max saw the Health bar plummet to full red. It wasn't as tough on the inside as outside. Suddenly a strange symbol appeared in the upper corner of Max's vision, and an urgently blinking red dot on top of it.

[Malgaroth, Avatar of Wrath] let out a bellowing death rattle as his skin started to crack. Smoldering orange veins started filling the cracks, and the steam that had perpetually surrounded him turned into black smoke. As he was being incinerated from the inside out, he dropped Max from his clutches.

A thirty-foot fall, Max thought, strangely calm and disassociated.

Time seemed to slow down. His life flashed before his eyes. It had been a short life and kind of a mess at that. He wished he hadn't wasted all that time. That he'd listened to his parents and really applied himself. What a way to die . . .

But the ground never came. It did feel like he had stopped falling, however. Max opened his eyes but could see nothing. He was floating in darkness again. An emotionless, robotic voice spoke out:

[Apologies on behalf of your Patrons, the Zoos Collective. There was an unfortunate input error made by an intern that misplaced your Spawn Location.]

"Intern . . . ?" Max said in disbelief. "Inte—WHAT THE HELL IS GOING ON?!"

[We are allowed to disclose limited information as not to provide advantage to our representatives. Everything you need to know will be disclosed in the Starting Zone.]
[Assigning customized Spawn Point to Subject #266830151 . . .]

"W-wait!"

[Customized Spawn Point assigned.]

CHAPTER THREE

Rules of the Game

Max landed on a patch of grass. He got up and looked around. He was in a forest. Definitely not the same one he had been in before all of this crazy shit had happened, nor the same country. This forest was lush and vibrant with almost-leathery-looking leaves and tall bushes. The forests he knew were mostly made up of pine trees and other conifers. No. This wasn't home. This was somewhere warmer.

But when Max looked up, expecting to see a blue, tropical sky, instead his heart skipped a beat. Forget the same country. This clearly wasn't even the same planet.

This sky was a mesh of different hues of blue, indigo, and purple. There was a sun, but it was a distant thing in the sky, looking more like an impossibly large star, much further away than he expected. As far away as it was, it still seemed to provide enough light and warmth. Max could see lightning shooting from dark storm clouds on the horizon, but they were also so far away, Max couldn't hear so much as a rumble of thunder.

When he brought his gaze down, he gasped and took a stumble backwards. In front of him was a strange creature.

The closest description he could make would be a jellyfish made of plastic. It floated in midair, its tendrils waving around eerily. Two eyes stared at Max. They were uncanny and strange. Nothing like a human's. They almost seemed . . . digital or otherwise augmented. Clear whites with black rectangles for irises. A gaze that seemed piercing and ancient. Then it *spoke*. It had that same un-lilting, robotic voice Max recognized from earlier.

[Welcome, human. Please try to remain calm. This is not a hallucination nor a simulation. We have used quantum teleportation technology to transport you to this planet, which is called "Alpha Ludus".]

Max blinked a few times and then rubbed his eyes. "At this point, I would really appreciate being told what the actual hell is going on."

[Your race has been chosen by the Zoos Collective to represent us in the Cosmic Games. You are welcome for this high honor.]

". . . Thanks?"

[Your race was facing inevitable self-extinction in the next twenty to thirty years of your measure of time and was thus chosen to be a candidate. The Zoos Collective picked your race for your tendency towards violent conflict, your extreme instinct to preserve your lives, and your proclivity for playing video games for recreation.]

"What? Is this pre-recorded? Are you there?"

[Yes. We are here.]

Trying not to hyperventilate, Max closed his eyes and took a breath. Trying to ignore his heart pounding like a panicked hummingbird, he spoke slowly and deliberately. "What. Is. Going. On? What are the Cosmic Games?"

[The Cosmic Games are a device the Intergalactic Consortium of Civilized Beings have made. ICCB for short. The purpose of the Cosmic Games is to divide limited resources fairly, such as planets with the ability to sustain life, without resorting to violence or deceit.]

"And what exactly is my role in this game of yours?" Max asked.

[You are a representative of your race. The four major factions of the ICCB have each chosen a race of beings that are in a similar situation to yours. A race of sentient beings on the brink of their own extinction. Of these four races, three will perish, as they would have if they had been left to their own devices. Their home planets will henceforth be property of the faction which chose the victorious race. Winners of the game will receive amnesty. The victorious race will be returned to their home planets, with instructions to guide their technology and civilization to a non-destructive direction.]

Sweet Virgin Mary, mother of holy Jesus Christ, this is a dream, right? I knew I shouldn't have eaten that expired pickle . . .

"R-rules," Max stammered. "What—What are the rules?"

[**The rules are very simple. As soon as only members of a single representative race are left standing, the game ends. If you are to gain victory for your species, all other three races must face total annihilation. You will fight for your right to exist.**]

Max swallowed. And swallowed again. The lump in his throat did not go away. "Uh huh . . . Anything else I need to know?"

[**There are some noteworthy stipulations. You are not allowed to cause permanent damage to the planet with nuclear weapons or similar technology. You will not physically age while on the planet if you are a fully grown adult. You will be provided a specific Framework to work within. The Framework was created to generate an equal footing to all species involved. Are you familiar with video games of the roleplaying genre, featuring elements such as Hit points, Mana, Stamina, Skills, and Attributes?**]

"Yeah . . . I'm familiar," Max said. "Adept even."

[**Very good. We will skip the lengthy explanation. You will receive a four-option prompt message in your System messages after our discussion concludes. The options will determine your specialization. They will be called Classes. Choose carefully. There are mechanics to re-specialize, but they are rare and come with conditions.**]

"How do I do that?" Max asked. "Choose a Class".

[**To access your System messages, simply subvocalize your name and "Messages". To access your Inventory, subvocalize your name and "Inventory". To access your Stats, subvocalize your name and "Stats". To access your Skills and Talents, subvocalize your name and "Skills".**]

Max tried it out and—lo and behold!—a row of messages with an insistent red dot jumping on each line opened in his field of vision. It was transparent, but he wouldn't want to ride a bike with that intruding on his vision. Max subvocalized the command again and the row of messages vanished.

[**This concludes all of the relevant information to be imparted to you. The rest is up to your resourcefulness. We are not allowed to disclose any more information at this point in the Games. But there will be further contact.**

Remember that the Zoos Collective is your ally in this. Your only ally. With that said, good luck.]

"Wait!" Max yelled. "I have questions!"

The jellyfish creature blinked out and left Max to stare, utterly stunned, at the empty space where it had been. A firestorm of emotions was swirling inside him. This wasn't real. This couldn't be real. If this were real and Max had understood correctly, some crazy, super-advanced alien race had just folded goddamn space-time or something to teleport the *entire* human race on some distant planet somewhere to participate in the Hunger Games on a gargantuan scale using some kind of video game system?

Yeah, this is a dream. A feverish, expired-pickle-induced nightmare.

Max sighed. He took stock of the situation. His weapons were gone. As were his clothes, now that he noticed. He was wearing a pure-white jumpsuit that hugged the skin. It felt kind of nice. The shoes were white too. Light ankle boots with a simple clasp buckle. They fit just right.

Good shoes, Max thought. Then he decided to have a look around.

He was in a forest. Not in immediate danger of any crazy demons, it seemed. But food, water, and shelter would be an issue he would rather solve sooner than later. Not aging sounded pretty great, but Max doubted it was a package deal that would ward off starvation. He wasn't exactly hungry now, but Max had the presence of mind to understand that could change really fast after hours of trekking in an alien forest. But before he got to that, what was this whole Class thing and this barrage of System messages he had waiting for him?

Max opened the System messages. There were five in total. He started reading them from the bottom up.

[Starter Package]
Reward: [Minor Healing Potion], [Minor Stamina Potion], [Knife, (Basic)]
[Achievement: World First: Defeated a World Boss]
Reward: [Unique Toolbox]
[Achievement: World Boss Killer]
Reward: [Class Upgrade Box]

Well, well, these could be pretty interesting. Now what's this last one?

[Compensation]
The Zoos Collective apologizes for any inconveniences resulting in your incorrectly calculated initial Spawn Point. We thank you for your patience and understanding and want to offer you compensation.
Reward: 2x [Rations], 1x [Bar of soap]

Wowww . . . So generous. Totally worth almost dying for and losing my friends over.

Finally, Max got to the final blinking red dot. On top of the pile was a message titled "Class Selection." Max opened it and four boxes with text and images.

The first box read the following:

[Combatant] Class:
Specialize in fighting for your species. This Class has limited ability to produce or utilize resources but has enhanced combat capabilities. This Class allows specialization in various forms of melee, ranged, and magical combat.
+1 Constitution per Level
+1 free Attribute point per Level

The second box read the following:

[Artisan] Class:
Specialize in refining raw materials into usable produce for your race. This Class allows specialization in various forms of work, such as leather working, metal working, or woodworking.
+1 Dexterity per Level
+1 Precision per Level

The third box read the following:

[Leader] Class:
Every enterprise needs leaders. This Class allows for creating institutions that will give members bonuses. Most importantly, settlement. But also institutions such as guilds or armies. In addition to establishing institutions, the Leader Class allows for buffing and efficiently organizing other Classes. Due to the need for dynamic leadership in relationships, this is a specialization that can be swapped out of without penalty before reaching Level 10. Additionally, applications to change your specialization into or out of the Class can be sent to the Patron faction, who will review it.
+1 Charisma per Level
+1 Wisdom per Level

The fourth box read the following:

[Laborer] Class:
The backbone of every civilization. This Class specializes in gathering resources, such as food, wood, and metal ores. In choosing this Class, you

will receive bonuses in gathering speed, inventory management, and Stamina regarding your gathering specialization.
+1 Strength per Level
+1 Constitution per Level

Max didn't even need to think about it. He barely bothered to read the rest after **[Combatant]** Class. It wasn't because every little boy wanted to be a warrior hero deep inside them. Okay maybe it was that to a degree . . .

But it was mainly the harrowing visage of that horrible demonic creature lumbering towards him. He had felt helpless. If there were monsters such as that here, Max had no second thoughts regarding the Class choice. Besides, that's what they were summoned here to do, right? To fight for their right to exist.

After he chose, it felt as if a gust of cold, refreshing wind passed through him. In his mind, he heard a voice. This one was robotic as well, but not as monotone as the one he had dealt with previously.

Level Up! [Level 1 Combatant]
+1 Constitution
+1 Free Attribute
Talent acquired: [Basic Weapon Handling]
[Basic Weapon Handling]: You now have proficiency in all kinds of basic melee and ranged-type weapons
Talent acquired: [Fighting Spirit I]
[Fighting Spirit]: Stamina expended in combat is reduced by 15%

Now then, what's inside these boxes?

CHAPTER FOUR

Maverick

It took Max longer to get the hang of using the inventory than he would care to admit. But after some mental gymnastics, he managed to get it work and to open the first box, which turned out to be the toolbox.

You have received a Unique Class weapon, [The Maverick]

Out of thin air, a monstrous revolver made of black, gleaming metal, with golden ornamentation landed in Max's lap. The thing was *heavy!* And with a barrel extending two feet in length, it was unwieldy, to boot. Max got to his feet and unsuccessfully attempted to lift it with one hand.

Okay, hard . . . Maybe two hands? Damn, that's wobbly! I think I need Strength points to manage this. Does this thing have Stats or something?

Max tried subvocalizing a few words while staring at the gun. "Inspect" finally worked. A transparent screen hovered in the air next to the weapon. When he moved the gun around, the screen followed. It read:

[The Maverick] (unique)
Indestructible
Weapon Type: Firearm
Damage: 2–4
Passive: Instead of using 50% of your Dexterity, this weapon uses 100% of your Intelligence as a damage modifier.
Passive: This weapon does not consume ammunition. Magic bullets are generated every time the weapon is fired. Firing a bullet costs 1 Mana point. You will be unable to fire this weapon if you cannot expend Mana or you are under the effect of [Silence].
Soulbound: This weapon cannot be used by anyone else.

"Infinite bullets, huh?" Max mused aloud. "That sounds pretty awesome."

He hefted up the gun and had a go at aiming it at the trees. Even with two hands, Max struggled to keep the weapon steady enough to hit anything smaller than a circus tent.

But eventually, once he was able to do so briefly, he got an uncanny wisp of an instinct that told him this would be a good time to pull the trigger. It was probably due to this . . . Talent? **[Basic Weapon Handling]**. As far as Max was concerned, this weapon was *anything* but basic, though.

Max was so lost in thought, trying to process all this new information, however that he missed the noise of the bushes quietly shuffling a few yards to his left. It was the snap of a dry branch that finally snapped him out of his reverie. Max turned and moved to the side to dodge an incoming pounce.

Almost.

His vision flashed red as a sharp, black claw swiped at him. Max took a quick glance at his hit points. Half gone. The beast attacked again. Max dodged and smacked the creature with the barrel of his gun. It was clumsy work, but it seemed to have inflicted some damage. A tenth of its Health bar had gone to red.

The beast looked like a panther, with a sleek black coat of fur gleaming in the dim light of the faint sun, and yellow eyes fixed on Max, watching him with careful predation.

Max fired at it. A miss. The panther growled and attacked again, but Max managed to deflect the claws with a doublehanded swing of the hefty revolver. This time, it didn't hurt the cat. Max fired again. This time, he clearly hit it, as it yowled and fell on its side. But there was no blood. Its skin seemed to be of the same toughness as that demon's had been. Max shot again, missing once, then hitting once. The cat yowled again in anger and pain as it leapt at Max. This time, it stayed low and reached to bite at Max's ankle. The bite drew blood. It hurt, but not nearly as much as Max thought it should have. Not that he had ever been bitten by a panther. Max shot the creature twice in the head, and it finally went limp.

Defeated Level 2 [Panther]
You gained 20 Experience points
[Achievement: First Kill]
Reward: +1 Attribute point

Panting heavily, Max plopped down on the ground next to the panther. Giving it a last wary glance, Max turned his attention to his ankle. There were clearly bite marks but no deeper or more serious-looking than you'd expect from a playful, overexcited dog.

Weird.

Max glanced at the upper right corner. The blue bar representing Mana had ticked down ever so slightly. The green bar, which Max had figured was Stamina, had dropped a bit, as well. He was still panting pretty heavily. But his Health bar . . . That was at zero! He squinted at the bar, at which point, small numbers appeared within the now-red bar. **[Health Points: 0/20]**

Now, Max wasn't the biggest RPG aficionado, but he had played his fair share to know that when your hit points reached zero, you died. He had so many questions ready for the plastic jellyfish. Or better yet, another human. Max gave a glance at the panther.

"You didn't eat anyone I know, did you?"

Great. You're talking to an animal corpse.

A transparent box appeared in mid-air, hovering above the dead creature.

Loot [Panther] (Yes/no)

"Y-yes?"

3 Cosmic Coins added to your Inventory

Huh . . . I thought I would get the typical RPG line of "Panther hide" or "Panther meat". Maybe it's because I don't have a Class or Equipment for it.

Max had the eerie sense that the panther could be interacted further with. Max decided not to and got up. There was some pain in his ankle but not enough that he couldn't stand on it.

Okay, let's take inventory. Still need to find food, water, and shelter. Preferably also people. Strength in numbers and all that. I also need to figure out The Great Mystery of The Depleted Health Points.

Max snapped his fingers. He had forgotten the other box. The **[Class Upgrade Box]**. And he had Attribute points to distribute. Doing that would help him stay alive.

Max opened the **[Class Upgrade Box]** and immediately, another prompt window took up the majority of his field of vision. Four options hovered in midair:

White Mage, F-grade (rare)
Combat healer. A Class that specializes in protection and buffing magic. Particularly adept at shielding allies and curing harmful effects.
+1 Intelligence per Level
+1 Wisdom per Level
+1 free Attribute point per Level

Ranger, F-grade
[Firearm detected]
[Changing Class option . . .]
[Class option changed]
Gunslinger, F-grade (epic)
A Class that specializes in medium-range combat. Adept at high burst damage and mobility Skills. A very potent Class.
+1 Dexterity per Level
+2 Precision per Level
+1 free Attribute point per Level

Defender, F-grade (uncommon)
A primary tank. This Class specializes in mitigating damage. Most Skills are tied to using a shield as a primary weapon.
+1 Resistance per Level
+1 free Attribute point per Level

Gravity Mage, F-Grade (rare)
Manipulator of forces of gravity. Very adept at controlling the battlefield. This magic user specializes in debuffing enemies and buffing allies. Offers high versatility.
+1 Intelligence per Level
+1 Wisdom per Level
+1 free Attribute point per Level

Damn.

This was a hard choice for Max. Out of the four, three were completely valid choices. While he wouldn't mind the thicker skin, Max wasn't really feeling the **[Defender]** Class. He had unlocked a seemingly rare Class in the **[Gunslinger]** by virtue of being in possession of a firearm. It was an "epic"-quality class and provided more Stats per Level than any other choice. As far as RPG-games went, the more Stats, the better. And since he had unlocked this powerful Class at Level One, those Stat points would have time to accrue a significant advantage.

It would obviously be tailored towards having firearm-based skills. Max almost picked it right away before realizing it was a Dexterity-based Class, which would have complicated things, as it didn't really jive with his situation of having a powerful Intelligence-based weapon in **[The Maverick]**.

That left him with the two Magic Classes. Both gave Intelligence, which would pump both his damage with his weapon and his Mana pool to keep generating bullets. Both Classes also contained something he direly needed. Max glanced at his Hit points. Back to two from zero. He wasn't exactly clear on the rules, but he was pretty sure if he had another similar encounter with a panther, he would probably die. He quickly glanced around and listened carefully.

Nothing . . . But I do need to move soon.

The [**White Mage**] Class would keep his Health topped up. It would also cure harmful effects—poison coming to mind first. He would also need to eat something soon. *Go without food long enough and those suspicious bright berries you found are going in the old mouth hole, caution be damned.*

The [**Gravity Mage**], on the other hand, could have interesting applications. Could he make things heavier? Maybe his bullets? Or make things float? That would be very cool and useful. If so, he could use almost anything as a shield. And maybe these abilities could affect other creatures? Slowing down enemies would be a huge advantage. It would make it easier to dodge their attacks, and also, most importantly, make it easier for Max to hit them.

Let's face it. My aim really, really sucks.

So while the [**Healer**] Class would most likely keep Max alive longer, it wouldn't help him deal with threats in a meaningful way. The [**Gravity Mage**] was the riskier choice, but it offered the most potential. And it reminded him of his mother.

But most importantly, the healing and protection magic was completely defensive. With gravity magic, Max could also go on the offensive. He could fight.

And that's what we're here to do, right? Fight for our right to exist.

Max picked the [**Gravity Mage**] Class.

CHAPTER FIVE

Starting Zone

[Achievement: First Class Upgrade]
Reward: F-tier toolbox
[Achievement: World First Class Upgrade]
Reward: E-tier Supply Box
[Talent Change]
[Fighting Spirit I] Changed into [Battlemagic I]
[Battlemagic I]: Mana expended in combat is reduced by 15%
Skill Acquired: [Alter Gravity]
[Alter Gravity]: Alter the weight of the targeted object to either direction for 60 seconds. Potency and length of the effect depends on your Intelligence stat and potentially the target's Resistance stat.
Cost: 10 Mana

Okay, wow. That was a lot of stuff. This skill seems interesting. Versatile. Bleh, that toolbox is probably useless though, Max thought. *But I suppose I shouldn't complain. That Skill seems awesome! It probably won't be anything to write home about for now with my low Stats, but if I manage to stay alive, it might get crazy.*

Max wanted to start moving, but first he had to assign his Attribute points, so he opened up his Character Sheet and spent two of his free points on Intelligence and one on Constitution. He admittedly wasn't a man who could shoot well, so when he did manage to land a shot, he wanted it to hurt.

Name: Max Cromwell
Class: Gravity Mage
Level: 1
Health: 11/40
Stamina: 33/40

Mana: 48/50
Alliance: N/A
Stats:
Strength: 2
Dexterity: 2
Constitution: 4
Intelligence: 5
Wisdom: 3
Charisma: 2
Precision: 2
Toughness: 2
Resistance: 2

Max finally set off deeper into the forest. He looked up at the purple sky and sighed. That would take a while to get used to. Max surmised there were a great number of things on that list. Max sighed. It would have been nice if the sky could give him some hint as to what time of day it was, but the faint sun gave no answers.

The forest was quiet. And annoyingly dense. Max soon found himself breathing a bit heavier, as he was constantly having to exert himself, pushing aside the branches of low trees and high bushes. [**The Maverick**]'s long barrel rested on Max's shoulder. The weapon had a great heft to it, but while heavy, also felt strangely comforting.

After an hour or so of trekking, Max found the edge of the forest. Wiping a sheen of sweat off his forehead, Max checked the upper right corner of his vision. His Stamina had fallen a few points, but his Mana had fully regenerated and his Health had to some degree, now resting at a comfortable half. Max figured it wouldn't have been so robust had he not put a point into Constitution.

Where the forest ended, a wild field of vegetation began.

Yeah, no. Not going in there.

Whatever was growing on this field wasn't from Earth. It was as thick and tall as a field of corn, but there were no bounties at the ends of those stalks. Just a slowly closing and opening err . . . mouth?

It wasn't exactly a mouth. It was a flower with thick, blood-red petals, which kept opening and closing idly in a steady rhythm. A mouth seemed an apt description, however, because it felt like the flower was breathing.

Absolutely, assuredly, definitely not going there. I have no idea if the mouthbreather-flowers are dangerous and who knows what might be lurking in that thick vegetation? Back to the forest, it is!

After another hour of wandering through the forest terrain, Max's Stamina had dropped by a fifth from the maximum, but his Health was back to full, which was very good, considering he had stumbled upon an interesting sight.

A figure in a white jumpsuit lay on the forest ground. It wasn't moving and was currently being dined on by two panthers.

Damn it. Do I kill them or sneak away?

In a moment of monumental foolhardiness, Max decided to go on the offense. He crept as close as he dared, while the two panthers enthusiastically munched on their hapless victim. He stopped behind a mossy rock.

Max steadied his huge weapon as best as he could manage and let loose a barrage of ammunition, firing before the panthers knew what was happening. They jumped and hunched their backs in fear and anger. Then they noticed Max with his shiny big revolver. Max had fired four more times by then. Two bullets hit the beasts.

In response, the big black cats hissed and started running towards him. Max exhaled and aimed at the one on the front. Just as it was about to pounce, sharp claws already extending towards him, Max fired his revolver once more and killed the creature.

Defeated Level 3 [Panther]
You gained 30 Experience points

The death of its comrade didn't seem to bother the remaining panther. It leapt at Max, who dodged to the side. The panther quickly turned and swiped at him with a claw. His vision flashed red and the Health bar went down by a sizable amount. But it was still robust enough.

"**[Alter Gravity]**!" Max exclaimed, and a faint red symbol flashed in the panther's face, disorienting it. The effect only lasted for a moment, however, before it attacked again.

It pounced at Max, who by that point had circled around the mossy rock. As it flew through the air, however it was clear that it had been affected by the spell, after all. Gravity clearly wasn't behaving as the panther was used to.

Max fired at it as it jumped, missing the shot but easily dodging the ensuing pounce easily. As the creature landed and turned towards Max, he was ready. He fired the panther point-blank in the head and it feel down dead.

Defeated Level 3 [Panther]
You gained 30 Experience points

Humming to himself, Max looted the two beasts for a total of ten **Cosmic Coins**, bringing his total to thirteen. What those actually were was anybody's guess, but that was a concern for future Max to figure out.

Right now, he just wanted to enjoy the sweet sensation of victory. The rush of adrenaline was fading, but it still made his senses keen. Being alive was a good thing. He closed his eyes and breathed in the rich forest air. It tasted sweet and earthy on his tongue. He ran a hand through the fur of one of the slain panthers; it was a smooth and beautiful sensation. He knelt on the mossy ground and felt the dampness on his knees and the scant rays of the faint sun gently warming his neck. Max simply reveled in being alive and having survived.

After having had his fill, he got up again and went to the half-eaten human fifteen yards away. A still expression of horror and pain was frozen on the man's face. Max wondered how many lonely corpses the planet had claimed in the last hour or two. It had to be hundreds, if not thousands. That was not a line of thought Max was keen to follow, so he steeled himself and looted the body. He was happy to find a **[Minor Stamina Potion]** but that was all.

It was time to carry on and find more beasts. And water. Max was starting to feel a bit parched. He guessed that he could always suck on leaves and moss if absolutely needed.

Actually, I should probably do that . . .

In the military service, they had taught him that even slight dehydration lowered physical and mental performance. Their company captain had made a joke about forbidding apple-juice piss. It was a pretty terrible joke, but it made the lesson memorable. Max didn't remember their exact numbers, but he figured it'd be best to not give these panthers an unnecessary edge.

Speaking of edges, that fight had been much easier. The bullets had been much more impactful. His aim still sucked, though. Fortunately, making things heavier made them easier to hit.

Easier to . . . WAIT A MINUTE!

Max lifted the big revolver and focused on it.

"[Alter Gravity]"

It took a chunk of his Mana, but it was worth it.

Max laughed in delight as he swung around, pointing the barrel in this direction and that. A blissful sense of relief spread in the overworked muscles of his shoulder and arm. Max held the weapon steady and looked through the sights at a particular leaf of a hanging branch five yards away. He fired.

"Yes!" Max cried out. "Hell, yes!"

The shot had left a charred, circular hole in the middle of the leaf.

Any further celebration was cut short as Max heard someone screaming in the distance. That had to be another human! Max wasted no time, sprinting towards the anguished cries.

After running eighty yards he found their source. Another person in a white jumpsuit had climbed a tree—a woman from the sound of it, but they were concealed by the leafy branches so Max couldn't see for sure.

An enormous black bull-headed creature was bleating angrily and smashing its hooves against the tree. It wasn't *quite* a bull. It seemed to have a humanoid body and proportions and to be bipedal, though had hooves instead of hands.

Hard to climb a tree with those. I can understand his frustration.

The thing was monstrous. Seven feet of fury and power, it was not something that Max wanted the attention of. He contemplated just slinking away, but three considerations held him in place:

If I leave that thing to continue prowling around the forest it's only a matter of time before it attacks me or someone else. Secondly, it must be worth a lot of Experience and possibly other rewards. It's clearly much more powerful than the panthers. Which would be a problem, if it weren't for the third reason: that monster can't climb trees and I have a projectile weapon.

And so Max looked around until he found a tree close by that seemed like it would be fairly easy to climb. He shimmied himself up branch by branch. It was clumsy work. Even with his now-noticeably-lighter weapon, it was still hard to climb while holding it. He went up three rungs before the branch cracked under his foot. Max's heart plummeted to his stomach as he fell; now he was dangling like a piñata, ready to be skewered. Fortunately, however, no sharp bullhorns pierced him yet, as the creature was still too wrapped up in its rampage against the woman in the other tree. Eventually, Max managed to pull himself up and resume his climb, until he was definitely out of the bull-monster's reach. He checked his Mana and, finding it sufficient, he cast the lightening spell on [**The Maverick**] again. Nothing would be more awkward than if the spell's effect ended at the wrong moment and resulted in him dropping it.

And then Max started blasting.

CHAPTER SIX

Through the Woods

T he bull-thing was *buff.* It took a lot of shooting it in its angry, frothing face to finally take it down.

Defeated Level 6 [Tauroid]
You gained 86 Experience points
Level Up! [Level 2 Gravity Mage]
You have gained + 1 Constitution, + 1 Intelligence, + 1 Wisdom, + 2 free Attribute points

Sweet, Max thought as he dropped down to loot the creature. It had thirty-three **Cosmic Coins** on its body. *Eighty-six Experience points, huh? I guess she stole the four points.*

Max waited for the woman to jump down from the branch. Upon landing, she gave Max a weak smile.

"Hey there," she rasped with a voice hoarse from screaming. Then she got up and rushed over to him, enveloping him in a hug and sobbing quietly. Max gave her an awkward pat on the back.

Finally, she let go and gave an embarrassed laugh. "Sorry. I'm a little out of it. I'm Elena. Hi."

"Hey. I'm Max."

They stood there staring at each other, neither sure what to do or say next. Max gazed at Elena, taking her in. She was short and in her early twenties. Blue eyes, puffed-up red from crying, pointy nose, with a few freckles dotting her face.

She's cute, Max thought to himself. *Also a bit defenseless. I need to get her somewhere safe.*

"Thanks for saving me," Elena said quietly.

"It's fine," Max said. "Have you seen anyone else around?"

"No. I've been in that tree for half of the time I've been here. What's going on? I mean I know *what*, but why is this happening to us, Max?"

He shrugged. "Life's funny, I guess? In that horrible 'you shouldn't laugh at it, but you can't help it' kind of way."

"Well, I'm not laughing!" Elena said, a hint of anger in her voice. "It was my older sister's birthday and I had bought her such a nice gift. Now I don't know if she'll ever see it. Or me again. Where is she anyway?"

"I don't know," Max said distractedly. "Look, we need to get going. Let's find you a fallen branch on the ground."

"Huh?" Elena said. "What do we need a branch for?"

"It will be your panther-stick. You can use it to whack at panthers."

"No way, Max," she said, tears welling up in her eyes again. "Please don't make me do that! I don't want to fight, I'm scared."

"I know," Max said. "I won't let anything happen to you. But I need your help."

She bit her lip, like a child. But getting teleported to an alien planet to fight for your life can unravel you—Max could attest to that. So although she was getting on his nerves, he felt pity for her. He'd make sure nothing bad happened to her. But he also needed to get rid of her. She would slow her down too much. He had to find others to take care of her.

"Can you do that for me?" Max asked. "Can you help me?"

Elena gave him the weakest of nods, but that was good enough for now.

"Come on," Max said. "We don't know when it's going to get dark. We need to get moving now."

Getting Elena to stand her ground against the panthers proved to be a slog. Upon encountering them, she flailed around and ended up running more than once. But at least it bought Max enough time to aim at them, resulting in quick kills. Max noticed that he took most of the Experience, but eventually Elena hit Level Two and, shortly afterward, Max reached Level Three. He considered putting another point in Constitution and another in Intelligence. He was conflicted about the former, but since it seemed to increase both his Stamina and Health, it seemed a valuable Stat. Not to mention, it provided a cushion he might need some day as a fighter. But since he didn't immediately need the Stamina and Health, he decided instead to put both of his free points in Intelligence.

Name: Max Cromwell
Class: Gravity Mage
Level: 3
Health: 42/50
Stamina: 27/50
Mana: 41/80

Alliance: N/A
Stats:
Strength: 2
Dexterity: 2
Constitution: 5
Intelligence: 8
Wisdom: 4
Charisma: 2
Precision: 2
Toughness: 2
Resistance: 2

"So, what's your Class?" Max asked as they stopped to gather a handful of the leathery leaves to suck the moisture from in order to keep them from being dehydrated.

"I, uh . . . I didn't pick any."

"What?" Max asked. "Why the hell not? It'd increase your chances of survival."

"I know," Elena said. "It's just . . . I didn't want to mess it up. I don't know what to do. I don't really get all these Stats and stuff."

Doomed. Our race is doomed.

"That's alright," Max lied through his teeth. "What do you want to do?"

"I don't know," Elena said. "I kind of like that there is a Wisdom stat. Is there a Class for that?"

"Oh, you're plenty wise already," Max muttered to himself as he stuffed a ball of leaves in his mouth.

"What do you think I should pick?" Elena asked.

"Well, you're clearly not a fighter," Max said. Elena shook her head. "I think we should find other people. We're meant to work together in this. That's why there's the Laborer Class and the Artisan Class. I think one of those would suit you."

Translation: We should find other people so I can pawn you off to some kinder soul than me. Working in a team can be great and all, but not with your useless ass, thank you very much.

Still, Max felt it right to make sure she got to safety. If there was safety anywhere in this world. He was just tired. Physically tired, most of all, but it also hadn't been the easiest day on his psyche. He still should try to lay off with the snark directed at Elena. He wasn't the only one having a bad day.

"Come on," he said. "We're wasting daylight."

It had been a long and eventful day with a lot of physical activity. Max's Stamina wasn't at a critical state, but it was getting low. He had some potions but using them before there was a true need didn't seem wise. He wondered what would happen when his Stamina hit zero. Would he pass out? Or would nothing happen as with his Health points?

Max wanted to find water—and not only for hydration purposes. Where there was water, there would likely be other people. Or at least other beasts to kill. The forest was pretty densely populated. On Earth, you'd likely not run into wildlife in the forest, save for birds and squirrels. Here, however, there were panthers and other creatures lurking about. Now that Max had a feel for how the panthers moved, plus his ability to make [The Maverick] lighter, they proved fairly straight-forward to kill when they ran into them sporadically. Max killed every one they faced, while Elena hid. She had gotten a nasty wound on her arm after her Health had dropped to zero.

They also ran into some less aggressive wildlife. Which was a nice change of pace from all the bloodthirsty panthers and, God forbid, that bull-monster. There were strange elk-like creatures around, moving in small herds of less than ten a piece. They were stocky like ponies, with furry antlers sprouting from their thick heads. Max shot one of them. The rest ran off into the depths of the forest immediately. Elena gasped but Max gave her a scowl.

Defeated Level 1 [Paldeer]
You gained 2 Experience points

"Unfortunate," Max muttered to himself.

"Why did you kill them? Elena asked. "They didn't do anything."

"It wasn't for sport," Max said. "I wanted to see."

"See?"

"See if I get any Experience."

"You killed an innocent beast for Experience?" Elena huffed, throwing up her hands. "That's just . . . Ugh . . ."

Max rolled his eyes And knelt next to the beast he had felled. He produced his knife from his Inventory, planning to dress and skin the creature and take some meat with them. He looked at the great five-hundred-pound beast on the ground. Then he looked at his dainty little knife. Then he looked at his hands. Hands which had never skinned or butchered anything wilder than a ham-burger patty. Grudgingly accepting defeat, he put the knife back in the Inventory.

"What are you doing?" Elena asked, peering over Max's shoulder.

"Nothing," Max said. "We should get going."

Whatever strange light the purple sky and faint sun provided was clearly dwin-dling, the day turning into evening. At least the trees seemed to be thinning as well. That gave Max hope. Maybe they'd find other people soon. They needed to.

Elena was tired. Hell, Max was tired too. But they couldn't stop. If the forest was dangerous during the day, Max didn't want to wander around it in the pitch-black darkness of night. He had his hammock, but Elena would not survive the night on the ground. And Max wasn't about to share. It was an ugly thought, but he realized he would rather leave this woman to die than risk damaging the hammock.

But luck was on their side that night. For just at that moment, Max realized that they had emerged from the forest, and not a moment too soon. Max looked at his Stamina bar. Four points left. Before them opened up a quiet view. A small river ran downhill under mounds of green grass and tall hay. Hay was good. Elena could hide and sleep under there. The bugs might get to her, but it would sure beat being eaten alive by a panther.

"This is fertile land," Max noted. *Coincidence? Doubt it. As much of a coincidence as having just the right monsters to fight for XP roaming the forests. Are we meant to settle and farm this land?*

"Huh?" Elena mumbled. She was pretty much walking and talking in her sleep at this point. They had been traveling through the forest for hours. The only things that had kept her awake were Max's gunfire and fear. Max had killed plenty of those panthers. Maybe seven or eight in total. He had hit Level Four and had spent his free points in Intelligence and one in Constitution, to keep him from running out of Stamina.

Then in the deep blue of night, they spotted an orange glow down the hill, near the riverbank. Max had never seen a sight so beautiful as the dancing flames flickering in the soft winds of this alien planet. He was so relieved he thought he might just cry.

Either that's a campfire or I'm a bull-monster!

Max grabbed Elena's hand. "Come, Elena. Home stretch!"

CHAPTER SEVEN

Joshua

W ho's there?" a wary voice called out as they approached the campfire. It wasn't much of a camp. A large tree grew next to the fire, resembling a sturdy, vibrant oak in the evening dusk. The group had hauled some logs and rocks to sit on, and had placed some Items nearby. They weren't much to speak of—some sharpened sticks and piles of small rocks, possibly meant for throwing. There were a good half-dozen people gathered around the fire. Most of them were asleep. One said something quietly to the other, got up, and walked over to him.

"I'm Max! And this is Elena. She's had it for today. I can't tell you how happy I am to see more people."

The man approached carefully, holding a simple hand axe to his side. He peered at Max and Elena in concern for half a moment, before his tight expression broke into a smile.

"Come! Come sit by the fire."

Max and Elena sat down on a log, next to two people who shuffled aside to make room for them. Max took a look at the group. It was a varied bunch. Most of them were adults Max's age or slightly older, men and women alike, plus two teenage boys and a woman in her sixties. All of them looked like they'd been run ragged. It had been a rough two days for everybody.

The man who had approached them with the axe in tow sat down next to Max. He looked to be in his early thirties, a tall, bearded, and hale man, with locks of medium-length blonde hair falling down from under a brown cowboy hat.

That hat must have been a box from an Achievement.

Other than that, the man wore the same white jumpsuit as the rest of the group. His brown eyes flickered in the campfire's light as he studied Max. There was intelligence in that gaze. With an inviting smile, he introduced himself.

"I'm Joshua. I'm the [**Leader**] of this sorry bunch. You guys hungry?"

"Famished," Max said, nodding weakly.

Joshua got up and came back a moment later holding two hunks of cooked meat. "Can't give you more, but hopefully this will keep you going."

Max's eyes went wide, and he snatched a piece of meat practically before Joshua could finish his sentence. Elena followed suit. Joshua gave them a chuckle as they devoured the food in a few ravenous seconds.

It was gamey and full of tendons, making it tough to chew, but Max felt like he had never had a more filling and delicious meal. Joshua watched him from the corner of his eye.

"If you're thirsty, the river's a stone's throw away. We'd have some here at the camp, but we have no containers. Can't believe we have to start over like this . . ."

"Tell me about it," Max said, wiping his mouth on his sleeve. He sighed. "Thanks, by the way."

"Yesh," Elena turned to Joshua, mouth full of meat. "Thank you."

"You're welcome," Joshua said and waved a hand. "We need to stick together in this mess, right?"

"What a mess indeed," Max said.

They talked a bit, explaining who they were and what had happened to them. A few of the other people in the group joined in, but most were too tired to bother, or already snoozing.

"So you're in the [**Leader**] Class?" Max asked.

"I am," Joshua said. "You might think it's conceited of me, but the way I see it, I'm not cut out for much else."

"I think it's an option for a reason," Max said. "We're going to need all sorts of people if we want to rebuild and defeat the other races."

Joshua laughed. "I hadn't even thought of that since that creature explained what's going on. I've been too focused on our own survival."

"You seem to be doing a good job at that," Max said.

"I like to think so too. I'm Level Four already."

"Same as me," Max said.

Joshua gave a glance at [**The Maverick**] resting on Max's lap.

"That's a mighty interesting weapon you got there. I take it you're [**Combatant**] Class?"

"Yeah," Max said, staring at the flames. Their hypnotic dance was soothing, the crackle of wood a comfort. This was the first time Max was feeling relaxed in two days. He stifled a yawn. He was tired but wanted to talk more.

"I take it you get Experience from killing stuff?" Joshua said as he tossed a log into the campfire.

"You don't?" Max asked.

"I do . . . Some," Joshua said. "But not as much as Mike. He's out fifty yards to what we think is east from here. Keeping watch. He's a **[Combatant]** like you. When we killed a panther to get that meat, he got a lot more Experience than anyone else."

"So how come you're Level Four then?" Max asked. "Did you Level Up some other way?"

"It's kind of oblique to be honest," Joshua said, scratching his beard. "I seem to get a bit of passive Experience just by taking care of these folks and making decisions for them. But I get a lot of Experience when people join the party. That's why I'm the highest Level here."

"I can see where this conversation is going," Max said with a wry smile.

Joshua chuckled again. It was a deep and resonant sound, admittedly very pleasant. "You're a smart guy. But yeah."

"You want us to join your party," Max said.

"There's strength in numbers," Joshua said. "You should sleep on it and give it a—"

"Done," Max said immediately. It was definitely the right call for now. Max wouldn't be able to do it all on his own. If he could outsource food and shelter in exchange for hunting game or helping to kill off threats, that was definitely the most effective approach to Leveling Up fast. This Joshua guy seemed genuine, and it didn't feel like Max would be killed or eaten during the night. Ultimately, it was either risking that or trying to survive on his own. Max entertained no illusion that he would last long that way.

"Well, that was easy," Joshua said. He clapped Max on the shoulder. "I'm happy to hear it, though. You and that big gun seem competent. From the look of it, you saved this woman."

Elena had slid down from the log and was curled up against it, already asleep, snoring softly.

"She hasn't chosen a Class yet," Max said and shook his head. "Maybe you could apply your leadership abilities and help her with that."

"I'll do that," Joshua said and threw another log in the fire. "What about you, Max? What do you want out of me and this group?"

"A simple transaction to start with," Max said. He watched Joshua to see how he reacted.

His smile didn't flinch. He just looked back at Max with those brown keen eyes and waited for him to continue.

"I need shelter and food. In exchange, you get protection and resources. I will go out and keep Leveling Up. I'll kill stuff and loot them. You can have whatever I don't need."

"I like that," Joshua said, nodding. "But I also need you to do watches. We don't have any **[Combatants]** other than you and Mike."

"You don't need a specific Class to do a watch, Joshua," Max said. "Me and Mike need rest to make sure we don't get killed. For now, it'd be more optimal for you to have [**Artisan**] Class people to do watches. They can sharpen those sticks or whatever they do while staying awake at night."

"Hey, that's a great idea, Max!"

"I have my moments," Max smiled. "What we used to do in the military was also just rotate the watch. Everyone gets an hour or two and then goes to sleep. It sucks, but it's better than not sleeping at all."

"That's going to be difficult without a timekeeper," Joshua said. "But I'll keep that in mind. We do that to a degree to keep the fire going. Someone also needs to be awake to hear if Mike yells out. I'm keeping watch for now. I'll wake up Marie over there when I'm too tired."

"So do we have an agreement?" Max asked.

"Well," Joshua said. "I'd prefer you were a bit more committed. What you're suggesting is kind of a freelancer thing."

Max said nothing to that; he just waited.

"But I'll take what I can get for now. I'll have time to rope you into our little family later. It'll be easier when my Charisma stat gets higher."

Max visibly flinched at that.

"I'm just joking," Joshua said, trying to contain a grin. He clapped Max on the shoulder again. "I don't know exactly how it works, but it's not mind control. Say, what's your highest Stat? Dexterity or Strength?"

"It's actually Intelligence," Max said. Joshua looked at him quizzically. "Despite my appearances, I'm kind of a wizard."

"Sounds cool, man," Joshua said. "So now that you've put a few points in Intelligence, do you feel smarter?"

Max thought about that for a moment. It was a good question. And a hard one to answer. In the few days he'd been here, he'd changed somewhat. A life-altering crisis concerning your whole species will do that. He was certainly sharper, but that could have just been down to having to survive in this environment. He didn't see himself performing any better at math than he used to.

"I guess not," Max finally said.

"My point exactly. I think it's not as straightforward as that. But we'll figure this stuff out!"

"That's great," Max said, failing to stifle a yawn this time. "Look, Joshua, I really need to—"

"Go ahead, Max. We'll talk more tomorrow."

Max huddled closer to the fire and could already feel his consciousness drifting.

"Hey, Joshua."

"Hm? Joshua asked, still sitting and staring at the fire. "What is it?"

"If you murder me in my sleep, I'm going to haunt your ass."
He just laughed. "Good night, Max."

Alliance joined: Joshua's Group
[Achievement: Joined an Alliance]
Reward: [F-tier Supply Box]

CHAPTER EIGHT

Level Up

Max woke up feeling rather refreshed. The ground was a little rough, but it had been a warm night with the fire beside him. Most of the camp was still asleep. Joshua was on the ground snoring, arm twisted at a weird angle. Only one other person was awake: a Hispanic woman in her forties, sitting on a log. She had naturally curly, long hair that was starting to get matted. Her dark eyes were currently droopy with exhaustion, a blank expression on her face. She looked up as Max approached.

"Morning," he said, offering a hand. "I'm Max."

She extended her hand. "I'm Marie."

"You look very tired, Marie."

She gave Max a weak smile. "I didn't get much sleep. Been up for a few hours, I'd guess."

"Tell you what, Marie," Max said. "You toss a log or two on that fire now. I'll go have a drink and a wash at the river, and when I come back, you're going to be snoring on the ground."

"Oh," she sighed, "I like you already, Max."

Max gave her a thumbs-up and headed for the riverbank.

It wasn't far, maybe twenty yards from the camp. Max figured it was a good place to settle. The large tree would work as a landmark, and being close to running clean water saved a lot of trouble. The bank sloped gently to a shallow, rocky bottom. Great place to gather water, once they'd figured out acquiring buckets.

Max unbuckled his shoes and enjoyed the relaxing sensation. He left them at the waterline, rolled up his pants legs, and walked into the shallows. The water was cold—not icy, but still a bit sharp. Just what he needed to wake up.

It was a nice feeling overall. He dippers his fingers in the water and enjoyed the cool sensation. The sky was purple and dark, and the distant, faint sun was barely above the horizon, just about to start its climb. A beautiful view, albeit a slightly eerie one.

After having had his fill of relaxing, he drank as much water as he could. He knew it would be a long day. It was a shame he had no containers. He had tiny glass flasks filled with potions, but Max figured they were likely too valuable to just pour out in favor of holding water in them. He decided he should mention saving used potion flasks for that purpose to Joshua, though.

Max settled on a log by the fire and fell into his thoughts. The pile of firewood had dwindled down to a few twigs and thin branches. It didn't matter. It was morning and the fire had done its job.

Max couldn't blame the people for wanting to sleep in. It had been a rough couple of days for everyone. But on the other hand, everyone needed to get their shit together like never before. Max hoped they understood that. Joshua seemed alright, although more empathetic than effective. Not that those two had to be mutually exclusive—and in a situation like this you needed both.

Meanwhile, what Max needed to do was to formulate a plan. But how should he go about it? He needed to kill as many beasts as possible. Preferably not overly dangerous ones . . . Could he just lure a bunch of panthers? Maybe use those fat pony-deer as bait? Two panthers at once, he could handle. Three would be hard, but manageable. With his current Stats and Skills, he'd rather not try his luck with four of them.

Or should he try to find those bull-monsters roaming around? They gave more Experience and **Cosmic Coins**, but they were tough. Max didn't know what the coins were good for, but it sure couldn't hurt to stockpile for when they were needed. Speaking of stockpiles, he opened his supply box from yesterday's achievement and got a [**Minor Mana Potion**]. That made his total amount one healing potion, one Mana potion, and two Stamina potions. Max considered trying to trade one of the Stamina potions for a Mana potion.

After having sat with these considerations for over an hour, making sure he had his thoughts collected for the day, he was finally interrupted.

"Morning!" Joshua called from the ground. "I thought you said you wouldn't take watches."

"Marie looked too miserable," Max said. "Plus this scored me some easy brownie points with her."

"And me," Joshua said and sat up. He rubbed his head. "It will take some time getting used to sleeping on the ground."

"I actually have a hammock," Max said, grinning.

"Bastard. Maybe I should have killed you in your sleep after all."

"There's still time," Max said and chuckled. He was rather comfortable sitting on that log, resting his gun on his thighs. "We ran out of firewood."

"I suppose that's good," Joshua said. "That will give our [**Laborers**] some easy Experience."

Max nodded and got up. "Now that you're awake, I can get going. Say, you wouldn't have a Mana potion you'd want to trade for a Stamina potion?"

A little blue bottle appeared in Joshua's hand. "Take it."

"Really?" Max asked. "Just like that?"

"Sure. We're a team," Joshua said. "But I'd like to introduce a catch."

"Spill it, dude."

Joshua got up and went to one of the flat stones that had some supplies laid on it. He came back with a haunch of panther meat.

"Thanks?" Max said.

Then Joshua went up to one of the teenage boys and woke him up.

"Sid, I got a mission for you."

"Five more minutes, sir," a groggy voice mumbled.

It took some haggling, but Sid finally got up. He was a lanky teenager with a heavy mop of hair that fell over his eyes. He gave Max a limp handshake.

"Sid here is coming with you for an excursion," Joshua said.

"Wait, what?" Max said.

"Now, come on, Max," Joshua said. "He won't slow you down. I just want him tagging along for when you get your first kills. That way, he can drag whatever you kill here and start working to get us dinner. That panther meal last night was courtesy of Sid, you see."

"Fine," Max said. He didn't like it but begrudgingly realized it was a sensible course of action. Before Max left, he told Joshua to save any potion bottles they used, as they were sorely lacking containers. With that, Max left for the woods with Sid in tow.

They walked for a while, with Sid trying a few awkward approaches at conversation. Max wasn't in the mood for it. Nothing against the kid, but he was in focus-mode. That and he was a bit grumpy from lack of caffeine. He *really* missed coffee. Max sighed to himself, trying to accept that he might never have another cup of joe again.

It was still early in the morning when they found their first prey. Or their prey found them. Regardless of perspective, three panthers pounced on them from the nearby shrubbery. Max was ready for them, however, and he cast [**Alter Gravity**] on his weapon immediately.

The same could not be said for Sid. The boy yelped and started running around, waving his arms in panic. This ended up being a great diversion for Max, though, as the panthers seemed more interested in the terrified prey. This allowed Max to focus on aiming at them, unimpeded. He killed one of the panthers in two quick shots as it tried to jump at Max.

Defeated Level 3 [Panther]
You gained 30 Experience points

Meanwhile, Sid fell to the ground. One of the panthers had swiped at him and the boy had stumbled a few paces before falling on his stomach. The panther jumped on his back, ready to tear out his throat, when a well-aimed magic bullet struck it in the head. Its brains exploded outwards. It went limp and collapsed on Sid.

Defeated Level 3 [Panther]
You gained 28 Experience points

The third panther realized it had to deal with Max before getting to the easier prey. It was bigger than the other two, with pronounced back muscles rippling under its sleek fur as it made its way towards Max.

It tried to circle around him, but he followed the beast's movements. They both stared each other in the eyes, watching every move. But the panther had made a grave mistake. It had not realized that it was not the apex predator in this situation.

"[**Alter Gravity**]!" Max yelled and sprinted to the side. The panther tried to pounce him but missed, due to suddenly weighing more than it was used to. Max shot at it, and it stumbled and growled but kept on the attack. It kept pouncing and swiping at Max, but it was clumsy and did not understand why it didn't move as fast as it normally did. It was still dangerous for Max, who had to exert himself to avoid the attacks, as they were still fast and ferocious. The big cat eventually made a swipe at him, tearing off a chunk of flesh, and his vision flashed red as his Health bar took a hit. Max was ready, however, standing his ground and shooting twice at the beast. It yowled and fell to the ground.

Defeated Level 5 [Panther]
You gained 50 Experience points
Level Up! [Level 5 Gravity Mage]
You have gained + 1 Constitution, + 1 Intelligence, + 1 Wisdom, + 2 free Attribute points
Skill Choice Available!

A Skill choice? Now that's interesting.
"Holy crap, bro," Sid said, panting as he crawled out from underneath the panther's corpse. "You killed three of them alone."

"Well, you kind of helped," Max said, chuckling as he looted the panthers. Sixteen **Cosmic Coins**. That brought his total up to eighty-four!

"I got two Experience points, bro."

"Good for you," Max said. "Okay, so now it's up to you to get these things back to the camp."

Sid cringed. "What if there are more panthers?"

"Crap," Max said. "I didn't think of that. Fine, I'll escort you out of the woods."

Fortunately, they weren't too far from the edge of the forest. Which was good, since Max was eager to see what the Skill choice was all about. Even more fortunately, they ran into a herd of those pony-deer. Max killed one of them, and the rest ran off. It gave negligible Experience, but those beasts had a lot of meat on them. Sid would need help to drag any of this back to the camp, though.

Max looked at the animal on the ground and had an idea. It wasn't based on any knowledge but rather a logical hunch.

"Hey, Sid."

"Yeah, bro," the boy answered. "What's up?

"When you get to the camp, tell Joshua that I have an idea. Tell him, we should try to use animal bladders for water flasks.

Sid made a noise. "Yo, that's gross, bro. Can they really even hold water?"

"Think real hard, Sid," Max said. "What's a bladder used for?"

"For pissing?"

"For *holding* piss," Max said patiently. "It's a container."

"Yo, I don't wanna drink piss, bro."

Max brought a palm to his face and rubbed at it. "Just—Just tell Joshua what I told you when you get back there. Make sure it's the first thing that comes out of your mouth so you don't forget it."

"You've got it, bro," Sid called out as he headed towards the forest's edge.

"Hey, Sid," Max called out.

The young boy turned.

"I'm going that way," Max said and pointed towards the forest. "So once you're done with the monsters we just left there, you're free to follow a trail of corpses heading in that direction."

"Got it, bro," Sid said and gave him a thumbs-up before he left.

Finally . . . Now what's up with this Skill choice?

Max brought up the prompt.

CHAPTER NINE

Choices

[Telekinesis I]
Gain the ability to lift an inanimate object within sight in the air and move it around with the power of your mind. The weight of the object you are able to lift, and the speed at which you are able to move it around is dependent upon your Intelligence.
Cost: 3 or more Mana per second, depending on the weight of the object.

Damn, that skill is awesome. Imagine never having to reach for the remote again. Okay, focus. *The Mana cost is pretty hefty, but maybe I could cheat it with casting* **[Alter Gravity]** *on the target before using this Skill. I could levitate a boulder or a shield in front of me for protection. I could also ambush things by sitting in wait and levitating a spear or something over their heads and* BAM! *Spear-kebab. The Mana cost makes it really situational for now, but when I'm higher-Level and sport a healthy stack of potions, I might regret not picking this up.*

Max looked at the second Skill.

[Tether I]
Magically tether two objects within sight to each other. When you release this spell, the lighter object will gravitate towards the heavier. The gravitational pull of the heavier object depends on the weight difference of the two objects, your Intelligence, and potentially the Resistance of the objects in question.
Cost: 15 Mana

Wait, this is . . . complicated. *It works on creatures, right? I could do some really interesting stuff with this. I could tether myself to something and be pulled towards it to dodge. Maybe I could even use it to climb a tree. I could also trap those panthers by pulling them up against a big boulder. While it wouldn't give me a straightforward defensive capability like lifting a shield with telekinesis, it would give me control. But if I don't know exactly what I'm doing with this, I could get hurt or mess up and die . . .*

Do either of them have a range? What are the limitations? Damn it, I wish there was a way to test them before I decide.

Max shook his head. Maybe he was overthinking it. Both would help him out, no matter what. And maybe the other choice would be available later. But maybe not . . .

Max pondered so hard, it almost physically hurt. This wasn't like deciding between chicken or fish at a wedding. This was life and death. Every decision carried a crushing weight that Max had never felt before. Regardless, he would have to choose something. This new reality was not a forgiving one. It wouldn't reward indecisiveness. So Max chose . . .

[Tether]

It may be the better choice, it may not be. But I'll live with the choice. Or . . . not, I guess."

First thing he decided to do was to test the capabilities of this new Skill. He picked up a rock from the ground and concentrated on the rock and a nearby tree trunk, five yards away.

"**[Tether]**," he said.

The rock zipped through the air and clonked a nearby tree. It wasn't at a deadly velocity, but it was fast enough to have hurt an opponent.

"Okay that could be really cool with a dagger or an arrow," Max said to himself.

He picked up a slightly bigger rock and tried it again, this time focusing on creating the tether with his mind as quickly as possible. By now, Max had learned that speed was crucial in a combat situation.

The rock flew through the air and hit the tree. It was a little slower than the first one, and if Max had to guess with his high school AP physics level of knowledge, he'd say both rocks had hit it with equal force. Enough to cause a serious bruise but not enough to break a bone.

Max looked at the upper righthand side of his vision. Fifteen Mana was a lot. It seemed to be regenerating at an acceptable rate. It ticked up from thirty-two to thirty-three as he watched the blue bar. Max figured his Mana regeneration was determined by his Wisdom stat, as it was in most games. He decided that if he was going to train with the ability, he needed to put some points in there, as much as the potential increased effect to his spells and the damage his weapon could bring from a higher Intelligence stat called to him.

So Max spent his points. He put both of them into Wisdom.

Name: Max Cromwell
Class: Gravity Mage
Level: 5
Health: 81/100
Stamina: 78/100
Mana: 53/110
Alliance: Joshua's Group
Stats:
Strength: 2
Dexterity: 2
Constitution: 10
Intelligence: 11
Wisdom: 8
Charisma: 2
Precision: 2
Toughness: 2
Resistance: 2

The next thing Max did *could* be considered reckless and stupid, but from his observations with the rocks, he was assured it wouldn't leave him horribly maimed. Probably.

He cast [**Tether**] on a sturdy tree trunk of deep, brown bark and then cast it on himself. He started skidding on his feet, plowing the soft forest ground with his heels as the tree pulled him towards it by his navel. It felt really queer. But it definitely wasn't fast enough to work as a defensive maneuver as Max had hoped.

Unless . . .

"[**Alter Gravity**]."

After having cast the spell on himself, he felt an immediate sensation of lightness. His body weight seemed to have dropped by a good 20 percent. That was also the amount of speed with which his skid towards the tree increased. And it ended with a pretty crunchy thud. Max actually lost a few Health points!

Okay, ouch*! But that's a very useful combo. Also quite Mana intensive . . .*

To his great delight, it was actually even difficult (and painful) to remove himself from the tree. Max acknowledged that his Resistance stat was piss-poor, but he doubted the panthers had much higher Stats. Besides, they were lighter than Max, so the spell would be more effective. Max suspected it wouldn't lock down one of those bull-monsters, but it would surely slow them down. And he definitely didn't want to meet them again without these tactics, since that would be a good way to get gored to death.

Max did another test, and it worked out much smoother. With a good sense of timing, he could surprise enemies and dodge attacks, by deftly sliding towards a tree or a rock—though it would require him to cast the gravity alteration spell on both himself and [**The Maverick**] before a battle started, which would be both Mana-intensive and also awkward for his personal maneuverability. Being 20 percent lighter definitely had its advantages, but Max would need to learn to move his body without tripping himself up. He used up his Mana in practicing casting the [**Tether**] spell and spent the rest of his time maneuvering around with the lightened body, until the [**Alter Gravity**] spell wore off.

He had worked up a bit of a sweat and spent ten Stamina points. Max considered it time well spent, even though he wasn't actively getting Experience. He had potions to replenish his Mana and even Stamina were they to run out. Yes, it was the right choice. There was something to be said for the brute power of just Leveling Up and the power that came with it. But with good tactics, the process of Leveling Up would be safer and faster, and it would eventually enable him to take on harder challenges which he couldn't otherwise have done without the proper preparation. Yes, this had to be the most effective approach.

Max opened his Inventory interface and chose the [**Minor Mana Potion**], which then appeared in his hand. He decided to not drink it just yet, in case he didn't find any monsters before his Mana had already regenerated an adequate amount on its own. He also resolved to make note of how much his Mana regenerated, with his Wisdom being a whopping eight and all now.

With these thoughts in mind, Max felt he was as ready as he could ever be for a wholesome afternoon of monster killing.

CHAPTER TEN

Grind

Defeated Level 5 [Panther]
You gained 50 Experience points
Defeated Level 5 [Panther]
You gained 50 Experience points
Defeated Level 6 [Panther]
You gained 60 Experience points
Level up! [Level 6 Gravity Mage]
You have gained + 1 Constitution, + 1 Intelligence, + 1 Wisdom, + 2 free Attribute points

Nice! Finally.

Four hours later and a score of panther bodies in his wake, Max had Leveled Up. He wasted no time and placed a point in Intelligence and another in Wisdom, putting them respectively at the scores of thirteen and ten. He was pretty pleased with himself. Killing the creatures had been going a lot smoother because of the **[Tether]** spell. In his last fight alone, he had tethered two of the panthers to nearby trees. As they probably weighed around 120 pounds, they had no chance of escaping it. Then, Max had just let the third panther approach and take a couple of swipes at him while he shot at it. He still wasn't sure how Health worked in this mess of Stats and rules, but he was happy to use it as a resource to save expending too much Mana. As long as Max was careful and didn't allow himself to take more than one or two swipes, his Health would regenerate before he found the next group of panthers. It seemed that like Health at a rate of an individual's Constitution's score every ten minutes. So Max would regenerate eleven Health points back soon. The same logic applied to Mana, which was a lifesaver. The **[Minor Mana Potion]** Max had received from Joshua was gone, but it had been well spent. He still had one left, anyway.

Interestingly enough, by filling the empty potion bottle with panther blood, he had acquired [**Small Vial of Blood**]. Max had no idea what use it would be but figured that he might as well store the item in his seemingly-bottomless-pocket-dimension Inventory.

Maybe it could be used for something like cooking or alchemy, Max thought as he knelt down next to one of the panther corpses. He got eleven **Cosmic Coins**, but that wasn't the point. Max produced the knife from his Inventory and slashed open the panther's throat. A trail of blood spurted out and Max brought his lips to it and drank as much as he could stomach of the warm, frothy blood.

This might be the most metal thing I've done in my life. Other than being a crazy badass arcane gunslinger committing panther genocide, I suppose.

Max's throat convulsed, but he managed to swallow the blood. He knew this was definitely not ideal. It was also gross as hell. But for now, he had to do it. Making back-and-forth trips to the river every hour or so wouldn't be efficient. And he had to be efficient. He had to prepare himself for all outcomes. Somewhere—maybe close, maybe far, but somewhere—there were millions, if not billions, of three different sorts of aliens that would murder every human on sight. Sooner or later, Max would face one eye-to-eye. When that eventuality presented itself, Max wanted to make sure he would be the one walking out of the encounter. And with that steeling his resolve, he went for another mouthful of blood.

Max wiped his mouth and coughed a bit. Truth be told, he wasn't exactly feeling like a million bucks. Blood on a mostly empty stomach would do that.

Should I keep going? I have to . . . don't I? While I can't hear a literal ticking timer, my whole goddamn species is on the clock here. Welcome to the biggest rat race in the universe. But if I'm weak from exertion, I'll just make myself easy prey. It has to be around the start of the evening now.

Max looked at the sky. Purple and indigo; dark clouds; a distant, faint sun, seemingly setting. Yup, the same as ever. Max had noticed it didn't actually get very dark on this world. The weather just stayed evenly bleak all of the time, as if the sky was bound to only gradations of a stormy, dusky night in the late summer. It had been reasonably pleasant so far.

That might change fast if one of those dark clouds starts raining down. The camp will really need to build some form of shelter soon. Okay, enough cloud-gazing. You're just procrastinating now. Make a decision. Do you continue or return to camp?

The answer was obvious. Continue the fight for survival. It had to be done. Max went for his Inventory and produced [**Rations**]. A sack of burlap appeared in his hands. It had a nice, hefty weight to it. Max scoffed at the material.

Couldn't just give us plastic, huh? This doesn't hold liquids, and they know it. But if I were to line it with cured leather . . .

Max peeked inside and let out a delighted moan. He closed his eyes and squeezed the burlap in gratitude. Inside the sack were sticks of dried meat, half a foot long, stacked in a neat row in the bottom. And some shiny, blessed, beautiful fruits! A couple of kiwis, a banana, and three oranges. And berries!

Not an ounce of mercy was shown to the contents of the poor burlap sack. Max attacked it with such ferocity that it would have scared the panthers. He ate the kiwis first. Skin and all, he'd be damned if he'd waste even a moment on cutting into them with a knife. He practically swallowed them whole, spitting out the stems and enjoying the sweetness. Dear mother Gaia of the ancient Earth, it tasted as sweet as anything ever had. Within only minutes, Max could already feel his dehydrated body being invigorated. By then, not much was left of the rations sack. He'd ravenously stuffed the blackberries and blueberries into his face almost instantly. The banana didn't last much longer. In short, Max left no survivors, apart from the dried meat.

After having had his fill, Max plopped down to lie on the forest floor. He sighed aloud and closed his eyes for just a moment.

"Oh, damn . . . I could die happy now."

Max closed his eyes and hummed to himself, enjoying a well-deserved moment of relaxation. It didn't last long. Soon enough, Max heard a bestial bellow. It was close—far too close. He opened his eyes and immediately got up, yelping in panic. One of those bull-monsters was approaching him, standing tall and muscular, twenty yards away, staring Max down with its feverish, violent eyes. It roared, fell to all four feet, and started barreling towards him, head down, horns pointed.

Max acted fast. He chose a tree to his right and tethered himself to it, instantly feeling the tug of the tree. He gave into it, running in that direction. The bull-creature rushed at him with such speed, that only a [Tether]-assisted sprint was enough to dodge the goring.

It turned back to Max, angry and confused, and started another sprint. Max fired off a couple of shots at it before he circled behind the tree. The monster hit it with such tremendous force that Max felt it in the back of his teeth. The creature was disoriented, and Max dared to fire off two more shots before he ran behind another tree.

The bull-monster soon cottoned onto his tricks, however, and this time didn't accelerate to full speed. Instead, it approached with care and tried to hit Max with its front hooves. One of them clobbered Max on the head, and his vision flashed red. In an instant, he lost a chunky portion of his Health pool, taking over thirty Damage. Max quickly tethered himself to a big mossy boulder fifteen yards away and ran towards it, shooting at the beast all the while. Not many shots hit their mark, but every little bit helped. But the beast wasted no time and chased after Max.

Max dodged the hooves as they hit the boulder behind him, cracking the stone. He just kept shooting and screaming. He knew there was no escape, so he had to give it all he had. The beast tried to crush him under both of its front hooves, but

Max rolled away and kept going. The beast kicked at him from the side and Max's vision flashed red—that was maybe another fifteen Health gone. There was no time to think. Max just kept shooting and rolling. The creature kept kicking and stomping as it bellowed in rage. Max's vision flashed red as the hooves clipped him again.

The creature then delivered another great kick, this time sending Max's Health to zero. The pain was overwhelming, exploding outwards from his ribs. Max spat out blood. He shot at the thing blindly as he screamed. It let out a death rattle and fell, partly on top of Max. He coughed out some blood.

Defeated Level 9 [Tauroid]
You gained 175 Experience points

Max could barely breathe. It wasn't just the pain. He kept coughing up blood. This was serious. A broken rib must have ruptured a lung.

Is this it . . . ? After all that big talk about fighting for the right to exist.

Max winced in pain. He wasn't dead yet. He had one more trick to try. He opened his Inventory interface and brought up a **[Minor Health Potion]**. A small vial filled with red liquid appeared in his hand. He bit on the cork and spat it out. There wasn't more than a few thimbles of the liquid and Max couldn't taste anything except for his own blood as it went down.

Max coughed again, but no blood came out this time. The pain was still there, but he found he could breathe again. His Health started ticking up and eventually stopped at **38/110**.

Good enough.

[Achievement: Survivor]
You survived a fatal wound
Reward: 2x [Minor Health Potion]

Heh, looks like I came out a winner in this transaction.

Max looted the **[Tauroid]** and received forty-five **Cosmic Coins**. After that, he crawled out from under its stinking body and looked around. He still had phantom pain in his ribs and was in no mood or condition to fight again today. What time of day was it? Sometime in the evening, it seemed, but whether it was closer to dinnertime or bedtime, he couldn't say. He shuffled slowly back to where he had left the burlap sack. It was easy enough to follow the ground where the **[Tauroid]** had trampled back to find it. After picking it up, he put it in his Inventory and pulled out the hammock. He chose a sturdy tree and set it up to sleep.

CHAPTER ELEVEN

The Field

When Max woke up, he was pleased to discover that the pain around his ribs was gone. His breathing had returned to normal, too. All three bars in the upper corner of his vision were topped up. Max felt like he had slept for a long time, but he really couldn't tell. The sky was as immutably purple and ominous as ever.

Max allowed himself a moment of relaxation and had the two strips of dried meat for breakfast. Truth be told, he wanted to eat it all, but as it was clear that salt had been used to preserve the meat, Max thought it would be prudent to save it for a situation where water was readily available. He looked at the sky again. The dark clouds looked heavy and ready to break out in rain any second now. But then again, that's how they'd looked since Max arrived here. Right now, he actually wouldn't have minded a bit of rain.

Max returned the meat and his hammock to the Inventory. It was time to hunt again.

Max walked around and collected the **Cosmic Coins** and Experience that fighting the [**Panthers**] provided. Unfortunately, it seemed that the low-Level panthers had now started to give him diminished Experience. Seemed like a classic case of video game rules. He couldn't just come back here at Level Fifty and burn the whole forest down with some crazy spell. He saw no bull-monsters and wasn't the least bit upset by that. The rewards for killing a [**Tauroid**] were significant, but the monsters posed a serious threat.

Max went over his last battle with the bull-monster in his head several times as he walked through the forest. He decided it was best to approach them with a plan of action in mind. Climbing a tree seemed like a solid strategy. If he encountered more than two, however, he would likely need to just avoid them or try to run, as unlikely as he was to survive that.

As he trekked on, he saw two shapes on the ground further ahead. From this distance, all he could make out was white and red. As he drew closer, his darkest suspicions were confirmed: these were the corpses of two people wearing the same white jumpsuit Max had on, splattered with blood and gore. They lay a few yards away from each other, faces twisted in pain. One look at them and it was clear what had killed them—a [**Tauroid**] on a rampage. Judging from the smell, the corpses were a day old at the most, as their smell wasn't yet retch-inducing. It still made Max feel uneasy, however.

This is a sight I need to get used to.

So Max looked. He watched the flies buzz around their dead bodies and the dried blood on the ground beside them. This was his new reality. Every death on Alpha Ludus would be like this. A death of pain and fear. No peaceful deathbed goodbyes surrounded by loved ones.

Max shook his head.

That's enough for now.

He looted the bodies and was very pleased to find two [**Minor Healing Potions**], a [**Minor Stamina Potion**], and a [**Minor Mana Potion**]. The latter especially pleased Max. It was clear these people had Leveled Up to a degree and had opened up Achievement boxes, but Max didn't seem able to loot the **Cosmic Coins** they had accumulated.

Probably better that way. Less of a temptation for people to murder members of their own team.

Eventually, Max reached the edge of the forest. Before him opened that same large field of thick vegetation, with those strange, red, leathery flowers at the top of the stalks he has passed through earlier. Max wasn't exactly sure which way was which, but if Joshua's camp was south, this would be the eastern border of the forest.

Max looked at the thick field before him. He had a choice to make. He could turn back towards the forest and hunt for panthers for whatever meager Experience they provided, and possibly face a [**Tauroid**] here and there, or he could venture into the unknown and evolve.

Or die screaming . . . But nothing ventured, nothing gained, right? I bet the guy who invented that phrase died screaming . . .

Wasn't this just the kind of unnecessary risk he shouldn't take? Maybe he should go back to Joshua's camp and regroup?

"No," Max said to himself.

This wasn't just about making his Stat sheet grow. This was about cultivating a mindset that would thrive in this world. This wasn't a place for indecisive cowards. He would *have* to take risks. There was no way around it. And even just facing his dread of stepping into the unknown would help him grow as a person.

So Max did just that.

The strange plants seemed to be able to sense Max as they reacted to his passage. They shuffled in place and their leaves reached out to Max and touched him as he walked by them. It felt creepy but otherwise harmless. Max pushed deeper into the field.

It wasn't long until the stalks became sparser. As it became easier to see around him, Max noticed that something was stalking him to his right side. Max gripped the black leather of [**The Maverick**] tighter and prepared himself. The field was just as dangerous as he had predicted.

Within an instant, something burst out between the stalks. It flew through the air as a red and green blur, screaming at a high pitch. Max fired at it on instinct and fell to his side dodging the thing.

Defeated Level 5 [Red Vine Stalker]
You gained 35 Experience points

Breathing heavily, Max got to his feet and took a look at his assailant. On the ground lay a strange flower-like creature. Its body was a thin, green stalk. Its arms and legs were rather long barbed vines, especially considered how small its frame was. The legs had curled up on themselves like springs, which explained their impressive speed. Its head looked like the same leathery red flowers as those on top of the nearby stalks, but with a nasty mouth, full of sharp teeth protruding outwards, as if to stab rather than chew.

Jesus, that's harrowing. So they'll jump at you, curl their limbs around your arm or neck and stab you in the goddamn face?! Nope. NopeNopeNopeNope.

Still. It was a lot of Experience for a single shot. The things seemed to not be very intelligent, at least. He could already see another one ten yards away, hiding behind a stalk, attempting to be stealthy but failing due to its red petals. Max just wished he had some form of defensive ability.

Defeated Level 5 [Red Vine Stalker]
You gained 35 Experience points
Defeated Level 6 [Red Vine Stalker]
You gained 50 Experience points
Defeated Level 5 [Red Vine Stalker]
You gained 35 Experience points
Defeated Level 4 [Red Vine Stalker]
You gained 20 Experience points

Max had traveled a bit further into the field of stalks and killed a few more of those little bastards. While it was relatively easy, it was still a pretty stressful way of gaining Experience. He had to be on constant alert, never able to be fully sure he was in control of the situation. It seemed to be draining his Stamina, but he wasn't overly concerned, considering he had a few Stamina potions.

When Max saw another set of red petals peeking out from behind a stalk, he decided to try a new tactic. He didn't want to attempt a shot at it from this range, because while his aim was getting decent, it cost a lot of Mana to keep the weapon light with [**Alter Gravity**]. Instead, he considered the possibility of tethering things to the ground. Would that work? The full gravity of this planet against anything he chose to tether? There's no way the aliens who made all this up would allow something that ridiculously overpowered.

But Max had to try.

"[**Tether**]," Max called out. The [**Red Vine Stalker**] immediately slumped to the ground and was stuck to it. It struggled desperately but was held there, like a bug caught on flypaper. Pleased with himself, he sauntered over to it and shot it point-blank in the head with a magic bullet.

Defeated Level 5 [Red Vine Stalker]
You gained 35 Experience points

Okay, that's awesome.

It clearly hadn't pitted the entire planet's gravity against the creature, or the Vine Stalker would have been instantly crushed into mush. Instead, the spell seemed to choose a concentrated spot on the ground. How big a spot? Max couldn't say, but he suspected his Intelligence stat was a determining factor in the equation.

Max delved deeper into the field, killing a few more [**Red Vine Stalkers**] with this new tactic. Once, he had a close shave when one sliced him. He took a hefty thirty Health points in damage as his vision flashed red. But when the creature entangled itself on his arm, Max jumped to the ground, crushing the creature between him and it.

They really are glass cannons, aren't they? Or should I say . . . grass cannons?

The jungle of stalks continued to grow sparser until Max approached what looked like an opening in the middle of the field. There was something large and red there, but Max couldn't see properly because of the leaves continue to blocking his line of sight. So he slowly came up to the edge of the opening. In the middle of it grew a stocky plant, eight feet in height and width, with giant leathery red petals and numerous thorny vines idly waving in the breeze.

Max took another cautious step forward. On a vine. It immediately grabbed his leg.

CHAPTER TWELVE

Vine-Mother

The vine bit into Max's ankle and he lost a few Health points. He struggled and the vine almost tripped him. Max grabbed it and shot it. The green vine blackened, squirmed, and let go. Max shook his foot in disgust. He looked at the strange plant-creature with its big, red maw of sharp teeth.

[**Vine-Mother**]
[**Local Boss**], [**Level 12**]

As with the demon giant, a green Health bar hovered above the creature. Max cast [**Alter Gravity**] on [**The Maverick**] and shot at it a few times. All of the bullets hit it. It was large and immobile.

My favorite kind of foe, Max thought, and continued shooting.

The [**Vine-Mother**] hissed angrily and its countless vine-like tendrils quivered. Some vines half-hidden under the dirt came up like snakes and struck out towards Max. He managed to dodge and duck, but one vine hit him, causing him to lose twelve hit points. Another one snaked around his leg, but he shot at it until it shriveled up.

Max saw another set of vines was approaching sneakily from the right and he ran towards the left, all the while shooting at its gaping mouth. The Boss's Health bar was noticeably going down. All of Max's bars in the upper right corner of his vision were reasonably full, albeit trending downwards, but he had a potion for every eventuality and was feeling confident.

But after firing at the creature for a while, it let out an evil high-pitched shriek. Soon enough, several [**Red Vine Stalkers**] emerged from the forest of stalks.

Oh crap . . .

Max ducked and dived and still received a nasty hit worth a sizeable amount of Health from one of the little bastards. He shot down a few and barely noticed the System messages. After having killed three of those things, he managed to get enough space to run away from the approaching vines crawling on the ground. In the time he had, he quickly guzzled down one of each potion; Mana, Stamina, Health. A little timer appeared next to each of the bars in the upper right corner of his vision. He was too busy to pay them any further notice.

He killed two more [**Red Vine Stalkers**]. They weren't as nasty when they were out in the open. After they missed their lunge, they had a hard time initiating another without a stalk to jump off of. Once they were all dead, Max focused on the [**Vine-Mother**], who screeched in anger as his bullets struck her again and again, its tentacles still quivering in the air. And then once its Health dropped to around 20 percent, something horrible happened.

Those tentacles moved.

They surged at Max like an attacking viper, curling around his every limb and torso. He took a few points of damage in the process, but that wasn't the worst of it. That was when they started pulling him towards the [**Vine-Mother**]'s hungry maw.

Max tried to struggle all he could, but the vines had a powerful grip. He would have aimed [**The Maverick**] at the tentacles, but since both his arms were entangled, it wasn't possibly. Slowly but inevitably, the tentacles were pulling him closer and closer. A harrowing cold spread through Max's chest as panic took over.

Relax . . . Breathe . . . OH MY GOD I'M GONNA DIE!

Max needed to think of something. He needed spells. Yes, spells! *He had spells!*

"[Alter Gravity]!"

A sluggish, dense feeling came over Max, like after you stuff yourself at Christmas and you just want a sofa to lie on for a few hours. His weight must have increased by a good fifty or sixty pounds. He could feel the tentacles straining against him, as his heels dug deeper into the soft ground, scraping it.

Max was still being pulled in. The gravity alteration clearly had made him more cumbersome, but it wasn't enough. He was maybe seven yards away from the mouth and he didn't expect the tentacles would just get tired and give up any time soon.

Max had to do something. He looked around for anything to latch on to, before he suddenly remembered how he had dealt with those pesky [**Red Vine Stalkers**] before. Max had no idea how well this would work, but he had to try.

"[**Tether**]!" he yelled and was pulled down on his butt on the ground. It felt like someone had dropped a large boulder on his abdomen. It was an uncomfortable, heavy feeling.

But it had stopped. The vines were strained. Max could see them straight and taut in the air, quivering with stress. Max had only precious seconds and not a lot of Mana left. With a strangled scream, he started shooting at the [**Vine-Mother**] with his right arm, which was currently being stretched by a vine.

It took a minute or so, but finally, the plant-creature let out a screech and flopped forwards. The tentacles holding Max went limp. He peeled them off and scrambled backwards. He was sweaty, shivering, and panting like a dog that had just been through the fight of its life. But he was *alive*.

Defeated [Vine-Mother]
You gained 300 Experience points
Level Up! [Level 7 Gravity Mage]
You have gained + 1 Constitution, + 1 Intelligence, + 1 Wisdom, + 2 free Attribute points
[Upgrade System unlocked]

[Achievement: World First: Defeated a Local Boss]
Reward: [Stat boost: +2 to all Attributes]
[Achievement: Local Boss Killer]
Reward: [E-tier Toolbox]

Holy shit. That's a lot of stuff! Makes it kinda worth it in the end. Apart from almost soiling myself.

Despite having all kinds of promising System messages, Max just lay there a while, breathing. He kept one eye open for the nasty little flower assassins, but he needed a moment.

I goddamn did it, didn't I, though? I earned all this stuff. I fought for my life, and I won. I goddamn won!

The rush of euphoria was *incredible*. Max reveled in it as long as the high lasted, and when he got up off the ground, had a goofy, satisfied grin on his face. Then, noticing that his trusty weapon was covered in a thick layer of dust, Max had to make do with some saliva and the sleeve of his shirt to clean off [**The Maverick**] for now.

Okay, so what's up with all of these messages?

First, Max opened the [**E-tier Toolbox**]. He wasn't sure whether to laugh or cry when the contents appeared in his hands. It was just one thing: a bucket. A sturdy bucket, made from high-quality, polished wood with a coat of resin and reinforced with an iron casing. It was as good as a bucket could get before industrialization, but it was still just a bucket, nonetheless. On the other hand, it was a container. It might not provide any added combat power, but it could make life a lot easier. And it could be used by the [**Artisans**] in Joshua's group as a model for making other buckets. For now, Max deposited it in his Inventory.

Next up, he allocated one of his free points in Wisdom. He wanted the Mana regeneration, so he could hone his tactics and understand his current and potential future abilities better. That could be best done through practice with said abilities.

Max went to the dead boss. Disgusting green ichor oozed from the bullet holes it was now riddled with. A purple tongue lolled out of its maw of spear-like teeth. Max looted it.

The Boss contained a whopping 1000 **Cosmic Coins** and four [**F-tier Gearboxes**].

Wow . . . That is so much stuff. Three boxes? I don't think this Boss was meant to be soloed!

Max had gotten lucky, and he knew it. Not when it came to the fight itself. He was rather proud of the tactics he had used. But he had been lucky to have his gravity-altering abilities and a ranged weapon. Fighting this Boss as a melee fighter or a purely offensive ranged fighter alone would not have been possible. Most likely, this Boss had been meant to be killed by a team of four. Max eagerly opened the boxes.

[Linen Hood of Wisdom (F-Grade)]
+1 Constitution
+2 Wisdom

Nice! I'm not really a hat person, but I'll take it.

[Leather Bracelets of Toughness (F-Grade)]
+2 Toughness

I haven't figured it all out yet, but I think this is one of the defensive Stats. I would venture to guess it's for physical damage, while Resistance is for magic. I'll need to test it, though, so let's not jump to any conclusions. Anyway, these are ugly as hell, but I'll take the Stats.

[Copper Ring of Intelligence (F-Grade)]
+2 Intelligence

Score! Give me that thing. Uff . . . okay, different finger . . .
The last box contained a sword.

[Shortsword of Brawn (F-Grade)]
Weapon Type: Sword

Damage: 6–10
+1 Constitution
+2 Strength

Eh . . . It would have been unreasonable to hope they're all a good fit for me, I suppose. I'll give that to someone at the camp. Maybe just give it to Joshua to make him decide. Deciding things is what his Class is about.

Lastly Max, brought up the System message for the upgrading. Immediately, a white, plastic jellyfish was floating in front of him in midair.

[Greetings, Maximillian. Congratulations for unlocking the Upgrade System! I am here to instruct you in its use.]

"You!" Max exclaimed. "I have so many questions. What does Toughness do? How does the Intelligence modifier specifically affect my Skills? How do I—"

[Apologies. I am only allowed to answer questions regarding the Upgrade System.]

Max grumbled to himself. "Fine. What is it?"

[It is a method for obtaining further strength. You will henceforth be able to use Cosmic Coins to upgrade your tools and equipment. The Upgrade System will work from Level 1 to 100. Every ten Levels will be a breakthrough Level, giving the chosen piece of equipment more power and even special abilities, depending on the grade of the Item in question. These breakthrough Levels will require special breakthrough materials.]

"So it's another power system? Like Levels and Classes?"

[Correct. In addition to new Attributes which increase with every Level and equipment gain, they will also gain properties such as increased sharpness for bladed weapons or a boost to running speed for boots at their respective breakthrough Levels. These properties or abilities vary greatly depending on the Item classification and grade.]

"I just obtained a bucket," Max said, smirking at his patron. "Can I upgrade that?"

[Certainly. But do keep in mind that if you upgrade lesser Items with Cosmic Coins, it might be considered wasteful. You can have an upgradeable Item

consume an Item that has been upgraded, but this will result in destruction of the previously upgraded Item and only 50% of the Cosmic Coins will be recovered.]

"Alright," Max said, nodding to himself. It was good to finally have something to use his pile of **Cosmic Coins** on. "Anything else I need to know?"

[**That will be all. On behalf of the Zoos Collective, we would like to add that you are performing very well so far, and we are pleased with your progress. We urge you to continue as is.**]

Max made a mock courtly bow. "I'm happy you find this monkey entertaining."

[**We hope that you will adjust your attitude into a more productive one when we are in more direct communication. But we promise to be patient. We understand that humor is a common defense mechanism of the mind in times of distress. Good luck, Maximillian.**]

Max scoffed and the plastic jellyfish blinked out of existence. With that out of the way, it was time to upgrade the shit out of [**The Maverick**] and head back to Joshua's camp.

CHAPTER THIRTEEN

Homeward

[200 Cosmic Coins spent]
[The Maverick] upgraded to +1
+1 Intelligence
+1 Precision
[400 Cosmic Coins spent]
[The Maverick] upgraded to +2
+3 Intelligence
+1 Precision
[800 Cosmic Coins spent]
[The Maverick] upgraded to +3
+5 Intelligence
+2 Precision

Nice! Feels good to have a use for these **Cosmic Coins**. *Seems like I'll be needing many more.*

He had gotten a lot of upgrades, and while it was hard to say if he felt any smarter, faster, or tougher, he certainly felt more *powerful*. It was difficult to describe—similar to confidence, but more visceral, more real. When Max hefted up **[The Maverick]** and aimed around, he could feel the heavy weapon was more maneuverable. It was easier to lift and hold steady. Max was sure his aim had improved too, but that would have to be tested, just like the increased firepower he was certain to have obtained.

Pleased with himself, Max opened the Status Screen to look at his current results.

Name: Max Cromwell
Class: Gravity Mage

Level: 7
Health: 40/150
Stamina: 65/150
Mana: 83/220
Alliance: Joshua's Group
Stats:
Strength: 4
Dexterity: 4
Constitution: 15
Intelligence: 22
Wisdom: 16
Charisma: 4
Precision: 6
Toughness: 6
Resistance: 4

Max's primary Stats were starting to look pretty impressive, with Intelligence already in the twenties. Max knew that the damage [**The Maverick**] could put out was respectable, but the real winner was the increase in his Mana pool. Not that he'd ever say no to more damage, but this fight had been a close shave. Max really needed to brush up on his tactics. He had discovered he could [**Tether**] things to certain points on the ground in a battle situation. While it had worked out this time, it wasn't exactly ideal. It was better to do his homework at night with any leftover Mana before going to bed, when possible.

Max swept a sheen of sweat and grime off his face and started heading out of the field. It was easy to find his way back the way he had come, so it took him only a short time to reach the edge of the forest.

Max had a naturally good sense of direction so would retrace his steps back to the river and then follow it back to the camp.

The walk backwards was mostly a piece of cake. Max met a few panthers and one-tapped them with a self-satisfied, almost disdainful grin on his face. Most of them gave him diminished Experience, but there were still some that gave the full amount—not that it was enough to push him forward. One might have thought a Level Eight [**Tauroid**] would have wiped the grin off Max's face, but with a tight tethering maneuver and just a handful of magic bullets from his huge weapon, the beast was felled.

That settles it, Max thought. *I am done with this forest. I need to find a new hunting ground. There is nothing left here to help me evolve.*

Mulling over these thoughts, Max traversed the forest, and almost distractedly shot a few more panthers on his way as he planned his next move. Soon enough, he saw the river and from there it didn't take long for him to locate the great oak-like tree and a group of people around the camp.

Elena noticed him first. "Max!" she called out, waving a hand enthusiastically. Max could tell she wanted to run in for a hug. He spread out his free arm to oblige. She smiled and gave him a tight embrace.

I guess she's just the hugging type.

"I knew you weren't dead!" she said, giving him one last squeeze before letting go. "Uff, you could use a bath though."

"Nice to see you, too," Max said, as he chuckled and shook his head. Then he looked over Elena's shoulder. The amount of people moving around the camp had more than doubled in two days. There were over fifteen people performing various tasks, most of them working with animal parts or wooden items. A burly man, whom Max had seen sleeping on the ground two nights before, laid down a heavy log with the help of some new person, to add to the benches near the firepit.

There was a group of three people who looked so ragged, haggard, and confused that they had to have just arrived. Joshua was taking them in with the same warmth and enthusiasm as he had done for Max that first night. Calculated or genuine, Max couldn't say, but Joshua was doing a good job nonetheless. The older man noticed Max and his smile spread wider.

"Max!" he called out. "Don't run off. I'll be with you in a minute."

Max waved a hand at him and returned to Elena. She lifted her chin and smiled at him.

"I finally chose a Class," she said. Maybe a little too proudly for Max's tastes when it came to such an elementary thing. Nonetheless he gave her a genuine, encouraging nod. "I chose [Artisan]."

"I think that's the perfect choice for you," Max said. Again, genuinely. Though he left out the part where he thought she wouldn't cut it as a leader, fighter, or a physical laborer. "How does it work?"

"Right now, we all just do whatever needs to be done. We sharpen sticks to make spears. Niles, Terry, and Vincent are [Laborers]. Also that muscley Asian girl, I think. I don't remember her name. She came yesterday. Anyway, they bring us branches, and we cut them with knives."

"That's good," Max said. "You get Experience for that?"

"Yeah. Not much, though. I actually got a bunch when I got the idea to carve seats into the logs. Look!"

Elena grabbed his hand and brought him next to one of the big logs. Indeed, it had curved, butt-sized carvings. Elena grinned proudly, waiting for Max to say something.

"Wow," Max said. "Good work. That was a really clever idea to eke out some extra Experience."

"Not too bad, huh? Have I changed that less-than-ideal first impression yet?"

Max chuckled. "You're definitely improving."

They shared a little laugh and then Joshua came up to them.

"Max!" he exclaimed as he took Max into a bear hug.

What's up with all the hugging? Oh well, it's kinda nice, I guess.

"See you around, Max," Elena called and went off to talk to someone else.

"Good to have you back," Joshua said. "Nice hat."

"Good to be back," Max said. "I see you've grown your flock since last I saw you."

"*Our* flock," Joshua corrected him. "But yes, people keep converging here. It's the nightly fires and the river. I've been getting a lot of Experience. I'm Level Six already."

"Impressive," Max said. "I've also been grinding. Decided I needed a bit of a breather here, though."

"I'm sure it's well-earned," Joshua said. "Frankly, you look like a bit of a mess."

"It was tough out there," Max admitted.

"I can only imagine," Joshua said and smiled. Then his eyes widened like he just remembered something. "Oh, I needed to thank you. The amount of meat that you single-handedly produced two days ago has kept us all fed."

"Really?" Max asked. "It was just a few panthers."

"That was the plan initially. But then Sid said that you told him they should follow your steps. I had to send out all the [**Laborers**] to carry the carcasses. Can't preserve the meat for long so we feasted like kings. I owe you one."

"I'll take you up on it someday," Max said and smiled. "How about the bladders? Did they work out?"

Joshua's smile waned and he shrugged. "It's a good idea, but we really don't have the expertise to do it. I think they need to be dried and cured like leather. But I'm no expert. We'll keep trying until we get it right, if we don't figure out other good ideas for containers."

"Speaking of containers," Max said and a big goofy grin spread on his face, "you're going to owe me another one."

Max produced the bucket that practically felt like a beacon of hope under these unusual circumstances.

"Holy shit," Joshua exclaimed.

"It's yours," Max said, offering the bucket. "Or wait. *Ours*, right?"

"Wait," Joshua quickly said and extended a palm. Then he cleared his throat. "Max, as a member of my group, will you embark on a quest to find me a bucket?"

"W-what?" Max looked at Joshua as if the older man had been struck on his head. But Joshua only smiled slyly as he stroked his beard.

"Just say 'yes'."

"Yes?"

[Quest Accepted]
Bring Joshua a [Bucket] 0/1

"What the hell?" Max asked, mouth agape, staring at Joshua.

Joshua extended his hand. "Now, give me the bucket."

Max gave him the bucket.

[Quest complete]
Reward: 250 Experience points
[Achievement: First Quest]
Reward: 100 Cosmic Coins

"Holy crap, you can give quests?"

"Yes. I got the Skill when I reached Level Five," Joshua said and threw his head back and laughed. "Damn, the Framework deems buckets pretty valuable. 250 Experience is pretty good."

"It's decent," Max agreed.

"Where did you get this, anyway?"

"That's a story for later," Max said, still staring at Joshua. "You can give quests? How does it work? Did you get anything out of this?"

Joshua focused. "I also got Experience. And obviously the bucket is now mine."

"Can we abuse this?" Max asked right away. "What if I just bring you a stick?"

Joshua shook his head. "We tried. It doesn't work like that. It has to be something that's actually needed."

"That doesn't make any sense," Max said, his brows furrowing. "What decides that?"

Joshua shrugged. "AI, aliens, magic. Who knows?"

Max scoffed. "Fair point."

"If you can think of some way to abuse the Skill, let me know," Joshua said. Max nodded.

"You should go wash up in the river and have a bite to eat. Relax and stay a while. Like I said, it looks like you've earned a bit of rest and safety. We'll talk later. I have other news to share."

With that, Joshua clapped him on the shoulder and headed towards the new arrivals. Max headed towards the river. He really could use a wash.

CHAPTER FOURTEEN

Breakthrough

The fire crackled merrily as Max stared at it, leaning back on a log. Evening was turning into night and a lot of people around the fire were openly staring at him and the great gold and black revolver he carried. He wasn't sure what kind of stories Sid and the others had told about him, but Max was pretty sure neither his deeds nor presence warranted this reverent level of fear and curiosity.

Marie sat next to Max, idly throwing a log idly into the fire.

"Going to be a cold night," she said.

"The climate seems weirdly stable."

"It is weird," Marie agreed. "But this night will be colder than the others."

"How can you tell?"

"I can feel it."

Max was about to say that that was dumb. But then again, this world was something very different to what Max had thought it to be a week ago. Who knew what was and wasn't dumb. Max knew one thing, though. While in the old days being right would have been fun, in the new reality it was more fun to have someone appreciate you and not be a wiseass.

"I hope you're wrong," Max said, but he also threw another log at the fire. They had plenty. Max caught the eye of two people on another log whispering and looking at him. They quickly turned their gaze away. Max sighed.

Marie smirked. "Don't like the attention?"

"Not really," Max said. "I don't feel like I did much to earn it, either."

"Sid has a big mouth," Marie said. "Also, you did bring a nice bucket,"

Max turned to look at her and they both grinned. Max went back to staring at the fire.

Marie tossed another log in.

"When I was seven, I was up on stage in the middle of a school play when suddenly my dress ripped. It was this nasty boy, Julio, who did it. Everybody could see my underwear. All the other kids laughed at me for weeks. I cried myself to sleep from embarrassment many nights. But my mom came to my room every night and hugged me and told me it would pass."

Max perked up a curious eyebrow and turned to look at Marie. She continued.

"Even years later when I got to high school, some girls would still bring it up. It sometimes felt like I'd never live it down. I was depressed sometimes. My mother would just say it would pass."

"Uhh . . ." Max started. "Was this supposed to make me feel better?"

Marie gestured to him to be quiet.

"Now I'm thirty-seven. And all those mean girls and that nasty boy Julio are probably dead. Now I don't feel embarrassed anymore. My mother was right. It will pass."

Max couldn't help but to laugh. Marie grinned.

"So just wait thirty years and nobody will care?"

"Maybe forty years," Marie said. "It was a very nice bucket."

They both laughed at that, before calming down. "You kept fifteen people fed another day because of your actions," Marie said. "You should be proud. Carry it. Own it."

"Is this something your mother also taught you?" Max asked.

"Ha," Marie waved a hand. "My mother was wise in many ways, but she had no pride."

Max thought of his own mother. She hadn't lived to see her boy do anything worthwhile. Max lamented that. A childish part of him wished she could see him now, know that he was a small-time hero. Would she be proud? A tear formed in the corner of his eye.

"Ah," Marie said. "The smoke is stinging my eyes, too. I should get a drink from the river."

She got up, tactfully not even glancing back at Max as she walked towards the riverbank.

Max sat there, letting his emotions swirl around in his mind. No, he hadn't made his mother proud in his previous life. He could cry over that if it made him feel better. Nothing wrong with a bit of crying. But it wouldn't do much else good. He wiped his eyes and looked over at the people sitting on the nearby logs. Max didn't even know half their names. Still, he felt responsible for them. He couldn't hold their hand, but he would hunt for them, bring them gear, and pave the way for them.

At that, a feeling rose up inside of Max like a heavy, black sludge. It was a familiar feeling, which always seemed to surface whenever Max had a good idea or a stroke of inspiration. An insidious whisper: *You can't do it. You shouldn't even bother. Who do you think you are to even bother trying?* It was a vice-like grip inside his chest and stomach. Oh, it had a name. It was called *shame.* It was called *guilt.* Those chains had been there for so long, Max had grown used to their weight. He had grown numb. But that was changing. *Max* was changing.

Now the heaviness was giving way. Something light, something noble and empowering was stirring inside him. It was breaking through those heavy shackles and letting Max's spirit fly free for perhaps the first time. That new, lighter feeling utterly enveloped Max from within. That feeling was *pride.* And it was *okay.* It was okay to feel proud. He had *earned* it.

Max sighed. He cried silently in relief. Tears delicately trickled down his cheeks. There was no System message for Experience gained or a prompt for **[Skill gained: Emotional Stability]**, but this was every bit as valuable. It was beautiful and pure and human, and worth fighting for beyond all pain and fear. Gripping the leather of his revolver, Max looked at the people around him again. Every one of them was going through indescribable hardships. Every life here had faced tremendous calamity. But all of them also had something beautiful to share. Marie, Elena, and Sid were all just regular people, struggling in this new reality. They needed people like Max. They needed fighters who could protect them. *Max* would protect them. He would. Because he could. Because they were worthy. Because human life was worth protecting. Max's chest swelled with pride and he gripped **[The Maverick]** harder.

Holding these emotions, Max eventually dozed off into a deep, dreamless sleep. And despite the coldness of the night, a powerful feeling inside him kept him warm. Max slept with a smile on his face for the first time in years.

CHAPTER FIFTEEN

Rumors

Max sat on a log, tearing at a slab of cooked panther meat. It was stringy and not exactly tasty, but it was sustenance and that was enough. Max had woken up in the morning and hunted some game for the [**Laborers**] to carry and process. After that, he had spent some time mastering [**Tether**]. Now it was around noon as far as he could tell and he knew he had to move again. There was a beautiful simplicity and sense of camaraderie in the camp that provided a wholesome life, if not exactly a comfortable one. At least not yet. More buckets would be needed.

But this wasn't the life that Max had signed up for. He still had that newly awakened sense of pride, and Joshua made him feel confident and respected. They'd talked in the morning, mainly discussing Max's explorations but also going over some ideas ranging from pit latrines to clay pottery. Being Joshua's confidant felt good. The older man seemed to appreciate his views. Earlier, Joshua had said he'd come talk to Max again once Mike had returned.

"Enjoying the meat?"

Max gave Joshua a look. He knew just how "enjoyable" it was.

"You'll need to bring some salt and pepper to us from your adventures."

"If I find any, you're out of your mind to think I'd share any," Max quipped.

They shared a chuckle.

"Speaking of adventures, you have a plan for where you're going next?"

"Actually, no," Max said. "Like I said, I don't think returning to the forest is really worth my time."

"That's what I thought," Joshua said. "Mike returned. He's washing off now, but he'll be over here in a minute. He's just returned from a scouting mission."

"Oh, you sent him out?"

"Yes. I gave him a quest to scout the surroundings around the camp. It gave him a lot of Experience. I hope he Leveled Up."

"Let's hope so," Max said. "Did you get a chance to talk? What did he find?"

"I'll let him fill you in on the details," Joshua said. "But let's say he found you some hunting grounds."

Max brightened at that. Joshua asked him questions about the panthers. How many there usually were, how sparse, what Level, and so on. Joshua told Max there were a few low-Level **[Combatants]** that had joined the group and they needed to get stronger. Max told him all that he could. In a few days, he'd become quite an expert regarding the murderous cats.

In the middle of Max estimating the panthers' average Health points, Mike approached. He was a burly man in his forties, carrying a large frame of both fat and muscle. Most of his face was covered by a black beard, thick and wiry. He gave the air of being adept at bushcraft, but his heavy breathing indicated that he'd led a mostly sedentary existence on Earth.

"Hey!" Mike offered Max a meaty hand. "I'm Mike."

They shook and Mike commented on Max being the hero hunter for the group. It was without bitterness, but Max could see him glancing at **[The Maverick]** with a quick, covetous look here and there. Max thought it was just a matter of time before someone tried to steal the weapon.

"So, what did you find?" Joshua asked Mike, who was chewing on a piece of panther meat.

"There's hills and fields far into the west. I found a tall hill and climbed it, only to see a bunch more of the same. There ain't nothing there that could threaten us."

"Any creatures?"

"Some big dogs that travel alone. Like hyenas, but bigger. Not as scary as they look. Most of 'em Level Three, and they get scared when you fight back."

"Maybe we could domesticate them," Max said.

Joshua nodded in approval. "That's a good idea, especially if someone can get a Class for it. But right now, we have to put that on the backburner."

Mike nodded and continued. "It's in the east where things start to get interesting. So, I followed the river for two hours or so, and I noticed somethin' strange. A white bridge crosses the river over there, seven miles yonder or so."

He waved a hand in the direction of the bridge.

"It's so white, it almost shines. I don't know if it's metal or stone or what. Clearly it was put there by those . . . things. So I take a deep breath and cross it. No lightning bolt strikes me down. It's a good, sturdy bridge. Maybe five yards wide. Now that's surprising enough, but the real kicker is what's on the other side."

Max leaned in closer. Mike was clearly enjoying recounting his tale and he looked at them slyly before continuing.

"Now, I thought it strange with how little sun's in this sky, but the forest over there's all green like this grass we got here."

Max thought about it and it *was* really weird. With the faint sun seemingly giving out so little light, one might think the land would be barren. But Max was no biologist, especially when it came to a planet terraformed by super-advanced aliens. Max hadn't asked questions; he had just accepted.

Mike continued, "But the place I found made sense. You know the saying about carpet matching the drapes, yeah? It was like that. I crossed the bridge and walked a bit. Not much, maybe some hundred yards. And the grass and trees ended like they'd suddenly run outta money."

"What did you see?" Joshua asked. His eyes were serious and keen.

"I stared down the cliff, and there's this valley whose ground is all dark ash. There are some squiggly trees with purple leaves, all twisted-looking and such. Just standing on the border of it, it felt wrong. There's something bad in that place. There's this heavy air, like during a storm, yeah? Smells wrong too. And I saw . . . *things.*"

Max perked up at that. "Saw what? Creatures?"

"Yeah, I think so. They were far in the distance, but a group of 'em started approaching me. I think they saw me. That's when I left."

"What kind of creatures?"

"Looked humanoid, but I can't be sure. They were all red, and when they started approaching, it scared me. That's all I know."

Mike looked uncomfortable admitting that he had felt afraid, but Max could appreciate why. *Red.* Like that monster in that cave. Were they the same things?

"Did you get any Achievements or System messages?" Max asked.

"No," Mike said, and rubbed his neck. "I think you'd get some for going in there, but I ain't going back. Not at least until I'm Level Ten."

Joshua gave Max a look.

"You want to go, don't you?"

Max only grinned in response.

CHAPTER SIXTEEN

Dreadlands

Max could see the bridge from a mile away. When he got close to it, he couldn't help but wonder about it. He was no architecture nerd, but boy, was that one beautiful bridge. It shimmered, like snow in the sunlight. The bridge crossed the river in a straight line, spanning a good twenty-five yards. The structure had no arch, as elementary architecture required, at least on Earth. The material had to be something beyond human knowledge, because the middle of the bridge otherwise would have been massively strained. Maybe the fact that the bridge was clearly made from a single block of material is what held it together. What that material was, and how it was fused together so seamlessly, Max did not know.

Max traced a palm over the banister as he stepped onto the bridge. It was smooth. Much smoother than any bridge Max had crossed on Earth. Even smoother than marble, as far as he could tell. But the texture clearly wasn't metal. It was more akin to ceramic, or crafted from a massive pearl. The whole bridge seemed like an impossible technological achievement, but then again, Max had been freaking *teleported* to another planet by entities who could turn RPG-systems into physical reality.

After Max crossed the bridge, he walked a hundred yards or so and came to a cliff, just like Mike had told him he would. Max looked down. He was standing on a patch of tall grass, but where the cliff ended and the edge of the valley started, it was as if day instantly changed to night and life changed to death. Max knelt and touched the cliffside. Dark gray, greasy dust clung to his fingers. It had a slightly sulphuric smell to it.

Max looked further down and before his eyes opened a wasteland of ash. The eternal dusk of this world seemed to thicken within the valley. Every stray boulder and lonely tree, twisted upon itself, cast a deep shadow. Bones of great beasts lay forgotten in the ground, half-covered by the gray dust. on the horizon towered a dark mountain which vomited up a pillar of thick, heavy smoke into the sky, where it joined the purple and black clouds. Clouds gathered rumbling around it and lightning struck the volcano's peak every couple of seconds. This dark desert had a heavy aura that made the air hard to breathe. Here was violence, it said. Here was death.

A cold fear made Max's stomach lurch as he looked upon it. But then he resolved to give fear no quarter. There was no room for it. He had a purpose. He needed to fight. And now he had his pride to protect. Thus resolved, Max started climbing down the slope to the bottom of the ominous valley. When he reached it, he received a System message.

[Achievement: Entered the Dreadlands]
Reward: [E-tier Supply Box]

Max opened the loot box and was extremely pleased. In the box was a **[Waterskin]**.

Holy shit!

It was an exemplary piece of craftsmanship. The stitching was tight and precise, and the leather was high-quality and well-kept. It had a faint sheen of oil protecting the leather. To Max's delight, it was full, which saved him a trip back to the river. He resisted the urge to take a sip from it until it was necessary and put it back in his Inventory for now.

The guys at the camp will be so jealous. If I make it out of this place alive. No, don't think like that. Of course you'll make it. Just be careful.

Max looked around and found "Dreadlands" to indeed be a fitting name for the place. Joshua had given him a quest to explore the area and return with information. Max had suggested that Joshua add an open-ended clause like "bring back something useful" as an optional objective, but it hadn't worked for more Experience. Ah well, it had been worth a try, anyway. Max idly wondered how he would know when the quest objective had been fulfilled as he ventured into the unknown.

After having skulked around in this desolate wasteland for over an hour, Max made some observations. Firstly, his Stamina drained faster down here. Not alarmingly fast, but fast enough to be noticeable when compared to ranging through a forest and fighting with panthers.

His second observation was that *everything* here was scary. He had seen monsters that fit into two categories. Those categories were *grouped* and *huge*. There didn't seem to be easy pickings here. There were massive hairy beasts roaming around that looked like yaks. They had black hair and sharp horns, and Max would guess their weight somewhere around six thousand pounds. They'd be a great source of meat and hides for a group who had the daring to take them down—or someone really stupid and brave who had the power to match. Despite all of his newfound confidence, Max felt like he wasn't that person today.

He had also seen some bipedal, red creatures that looked a lot like that terrible giant Max had encountered when he was first transported. Only, these creatures were small, ranging from four to five feet in height. The problem was that they were found moving or lounging in groups of at least six. Max had no idea what Level these creatures were, how many shots from **[The Maverick]** was required to take them down, nor how fast they were. From all of this, Max made his third observation: this was a great place to get yourself killed if you weren't careful.

But Max knew he had to do something. If he couldn't find a way to fight these monsters, he might as well go back to the forest. But that would mean he'd lose his *purpose* and that just was not an option. Yes, Max could return back to the safety of farming and come back later. But he had not received any "World First" achievements for simply entering the zone, and someone—very possibly someone*s*—were already here. Already grinding. And Max couldn't be sure they were even human. He had not seen any representatives from other races yet, but it was only a matter of time. And he categorically refused to allow an edge to anyone trying to outdo him.

So he needed a plan. He peeked from behind his hiding place at a group of six of those short demon-creatures. They were by a fetid pond that smelled, Max nearly gagged, even though he was a good fifteen yards away. The creatures were gibbering to each other in a chopped, quick speech, and washing themselves with and drinking from the water. Max knew he was on a timer. He didn't know the terrain and if the creatures left and went somewhere else, following them would be too dangerous. No, if he wanted to kill this group, he needed to act now. He would have to expose himself to risk. But how to mitigate that . . .

If this doesn't work, I better hope those things don't run fast.

Max formulated an escape plan involving him tethering himself to the rock he was hiding behind and just bolting straight to the edge of the valley, half a mile in the same direction. Yeah, it wasn't a very good escape plan. Max just hoped his plan of attack was better. It would cost him a lot of Mana, and if it didn't work, he was screwed. He cast **[Alter Gravity]** on his weapon and went for it.

"[Tether]! [Tether]! [Tether]!"

The demons screeched in confusion as two of their swimming friends suddenly smacked into each other and plummeted to the bottom of the pond. The four that remained at the edge noticed Max and immediately started to sprint at him. But as they ran, they found themselves being pulled towards one another and then entangled before falling to the ground. Angrily screaming, they struggled to untangle themselves from a mess of limbs.

Max wasted no time. With a sure gait, he approached the demons and shot at them with [**The Maverick**]. Despite their small, stringy bodies they were surprisingly sturdy, considering how high Max's Intelligence already was. Each of them needed at least five magic bullets to take down. They desperately tried to rise, and one pair actually even managed to. They clumsily clawed at Max, missed by a yard, and tripped over again.

Defeated Level 7 [Junior Vilefiend]
You gained 105 Experience points
Defeated Level 7 [Junior Vilefiend]
You gained 105 Experience points
Defeated Level 8 [Junior Vilefiend]
You gained 130 Experience points
Defeated Level 8 [Junior Vilefiend]
You gained 130 Experience points

Damn, that's good. Yeah, I've definitely come to the right place.

Max watched the surface of the water for a good minute. Nothing came up. Eventually, he got two more System notifications for two dead [**Junior Vilefiends**].

Level Up! [Level 8 Gravity Mage]
You have gained + 1 Constitution, + 1 Intelligence, + 1 Wisdom, + 2 free Attribute points

Exceedingly pleased with himself, Max quickly spent free points on Wisdom, as it was clear he needed to expend a lot of Mana to deal with these groups. He brought up his Stats screen and was very happy. By the next Level, his Wisdom would be inching into the twenties!

Name: Max Cromwell
Class: Gravity Mage
Level: 8
Health: 160/160
Stamina: 111/160
Mana: 185/230
Alliance: Joshua's Group
Stats:
Strength: 4

Dexterity: 4
Constitution: 16
Intelligence: 23
Wisdom: 19
Charisma: 4
Precision: 6
Toughness: 6
Resistance: 4

Max didn't want to even try to touch the water and loot the two demons that had drowned, but he did get a chunky three hundred and eighty-one **Cosmic Coins** in total from the four others. That brought his total **Cosmic Coins** count to 1191. The next upgrade for his trusty revolver would require 1600 coins, which wasn't that many dead **[Junior Vilefiends]** away. Of course, he could upgrade other Items, like his ring or his hat, but Max had always been a greedy gamer. Upgrading **[The Maverick]** represented pretty much a permanent upgrade, whereas the lesser Items would eventually be switched for more powerful ones. This was an urge that Max had to temper. This was not a childish game for cool min-maxing. This was real life with some serious stakes. After the next upgrade on his ornate hand cannon, he promised himself he would upgrade the lesser Items to increase his chance at survival.

With that, he hefted **[The Maverick]** on his shoulder and continued his exploration. At this rate, Level Ten was close.

CHAPTER SEVENTEEN

In the Valley of Shadow and Death

It was hard finding suitable prey as most of the [**Junior Vilefiends**] were in large packs and, while Max figured he could take out another two small groups before running out of Mana, he'd rather keep a safety net for himself. He sat down to have a drink from his new flask. It was full of cool, fresh water. It had a slight leathery taste to it, but that was fine by him. He had a portable water container now and that was worth gold in this world. Max glanced to his left. The edge of the valley was roughly a mile away. He'd dare not venture further before learning more. It was reasonable to suspect that most of the stronger monsters would dwell deeper in the Dreadlands. Max took another swig as he leaned against a rock as warm as the dust-covered ground. Max attributed it to the towering volcano on the horizon. He wondered what terrible monsters prowled near it. For now, he would settle for the ugly impish fiends he already knew. They gave a substantial amount of Experience and **Cosmic Coins**. Max suspected he wasn't supposed to be able to kill a group of them alone. He based this off the fact that there were several dead bodies here and there in white jumpsuits. For one reason or another, none of them had any loot. They must have used their potions. Still, they had died. Max wondered what Level and Class they had been.

But Max was doing quite well for himself, overall. With [**Tether**] being such a powerful and versatile ability, he hadn't only managed to kill a group, he had *destroyed* one in seconds.

Max smiled to himself. If he had had any second thoughts in the back of his mind about choosing [**Gravity Mage**], they had been thoroughly abolished by his latest encounter. While the Mana cost to [**Tether**] enemies to each other was substantial, Max was starting to get to a point with his Wisdom and Intelligence where the cost wasn't prohibitive anymore. He was effectively regenerating two Mana per minute. With [**Tether**] costing thirteen Mana with his Mana-talent, Max would just need tactical breaks to make sure he wouldn't run out in a critical situation. He also still had to cast [**Alter Gravity**] to [**The Maverick**] to actually be able to shoot accurately. Having had a slight bump in Strength and Precision did help, but it wasn't enough for now. He also needed to be mindful of having enough Mana to always be able to cast [**Alter Gravity**] and [**Tether**] to himself for a quick escape. He had tested making himself lighter around Joshua's camp and had noticed that he could run faster with it, and more importantly, run faster for longer. Max wasn't sure exactly how fast the [**Junior Vilefiends**] were in pursuit, but he was sure he'd find out sooner or later. And he'd better have *some* contingency for that inevitability, no matter how shoddy.

With his Mana mostly regenerated, Max got up and peered around to decide on the direction to head towards next. He stopped dead in his tracks when he noticed that only five yards away was one of those massive yaks. It was staring at Max with an incredulous look on its face, as if trying to understand what it was seeing. Max swallowed. He wanted to run, but every instinct inside him was screaming for him to stay still. The great creature barreled closer and made a rumbling noise. It sniffed at Max and stared down at him with its dull-seeming eyes. At least it wasn't an aggressive predator. That didn't mean it wouldn't leave Max a broken mess on the ground like a hippo or a bull might do if you caught them in a bad mood.

The creature blew out a gust of stinky breath through its massive snout. It gave Max a sniff and snorted before turning away. Max let out a long-held breath. His heart was hammering like a woodpecker on caffeine. As calm and cool as he might seem compared to other people he'd met here, this beast was in a league of its own. Being in a fight with someone just two inches taller than you can be intimidating. But staring into the eyes of an unpredictable animal thirty times your size put things in perspective. Max fell to his knees as he watched the lumbering beast's backside. He willed his legs to turn back to bone and muscle from the quivering jelly they'd become and got up. He would need to go and hunt more prey. Whether these animals were docile or not, Max would grow stronger and hunt them. They had enough meat to feed the whole camp two times over and hide enough to make a goddamn tent out of.

After having avoided a trampling and a heart attack, Max was feeling lucky and he went to find some more suitable enemies. He found a group of [**Junior Vilefiends**] feasting on a corpse. It appeared to be a baby yak. It was hard to be sure with all the blood and guts, but the corpse was the size of a car. Max quickly surprised them by tethering two pairs of them together and the fifth one to the carcass. As Max approached, he also noticed a humanoid figure approaching. It *was* a human! Someone else was farming here! It was a man in his late thirties. His white jumpsuit was gray with dust and ash. He had clearly acquired some additional equipment, wearing sturdy boots, gloves made of leather, and shin guard made of some sort of metal. The shin guards chinked rhythmically as he sauntered closer, a black shafted spear resting on his shoulder.

Max was surprised and delighted, but first he needed to deal with the demons. He shot the four quickly. But he wanted to observe the final one. Max released the tethering, and without wasting any time, the monster snarled and lunged at Max. In a few sharp movements, it was on him, slashing with those sharp claws attached to its long monkey-like hands. Max's vision flashed red and he was only half-surprised to lose twenty-eight Health. Another claw came in lightning fast and stabbed him in the stomach. He was punted backwards and as soon as he landed, he patted his stomach to assess the damage, which was minimal. It felt so strange to have taken an attack that should have left a fatal wound and to find it only marginally hurting. Losing another thirty Health was alarming, though. These things were fast.

Max ran towards the carcass and the [**Vilefiend**] followed, slashing at Max's back one more time before they reached the dead yak. Max tethered the demon to the giant body and promptly killed it.

These things would rip me to shreds in seconds if I didn't have the proper tactics. I lost almost ninety Health by just dealing with one.

The Experience and **Cosmic Coins** made up for the increased danger, however. Max was very pleased how easy this new monster type was to kill, as long as he approached them when they were preoccupied.

"Interesting ability you got there," a confident drawl announced. "I cannot imagine why you let that one take a chance at you."

The man got within ten yards and looked at Max. He scanned his clothes and stopped for a moment to look at [**The Maverick**]. Then he focused on Max's face with his hale blue eyes and held the stare, searching, unblinking. There was a hint of humor there, but it was laced with something violent.

"Hello there," Max said. "I just started exploring the area. I wanted to test how these things move."

The man nodded sagely and carried on speaking. His drawl had a dreamy, distracted quality, as if the man was thinking of something else as he spoke. "Wise. Even wiser to not give them a chance. They are fast buggers."

"I noticed," Max said. He was getting uncomfortable. Despite the aloof tone, the man's gaze was disturbing. Max didn't like the vibe he was giving off. This man was clearly dangerous. It was obvious in the easy poise with which he held the black-shafted spear. It was the casual drawl in a hellscape like the Dreadlands, but mostly it was those cold blue eyes that started at him without any emotion. Max wondered if he would have to fight him.

The man didn't say anything. He just stared.

"I'm Max. What about you?"

The man shook his head, amused. "There is no need for names."

"What do you want?" Max asked.

"Well, when I first saw you, I was waiting for you to die, so I could pick up that mighty nice gun you got there. But that does not seem to be happening any time soon."

There was no hesitation, no apologetic smile. Just the stare.

"The weapon's Soulbound to me," Max said. "You can't use it."

"Pity," the man said. "You could be lying, of course."

"Then why not just try to kill me?"

"Messy," the man said simply. "Also, I would rather not take my chances with the Tribunal."

"The what?"

The man gave Max a quizzical look, his first display of emotion. "Oh? You don't know? Seems like you didn't ask our patrons enough questions."

"Huh? I did ask some."

"Clearly not the important ones. You did not ask what becomes of a man who kills another man here, or you would know that any act of murder is reviewed by our good patrons. Apparently, if the deed is deemed unjust, there is punishment involved."

It would not have crossed Max's mind even in a million years to ask something like that. Nonetheless it was valuable information. Assuming it was true. The fact that the man had even asked that question confirmed to Max what kind of a person he was dealing with here.

"But as to what I want . . ." The man continued and thumbed the shaft of his spear as he thought. Then he cast a sly glance at Max and grinned. "Oh, that is a complicated question."

"Well, I'd like to carry on hunting," Max said and took a tentative step back.

"Then carry on, my friend," the man drawled.

It felt instinctively wrong to turn his back to this man, so Max kept glancing back every few steps. The strange man made no movements; he just kept staring. Once Max got far enough, he started walking towards him. When Max stopped, he stopped, keeping a good sixty yards between them.

The next forty minutes were *extremely* uncomfortable as Max searched for prey. He would rather be fighting another **[Vine-Mother]** than have this weirdo skulking behind his back.

Finally he found another group of **[Junior Vilefiends].** There were eight in total. Six of them had formed a loose circle around the other two, who were engaged in a full-on brawl. They slashed and punched and kicked at each other, moving quick as snakes. The ones forming the ring laughed and cheered and conversed in that fast, clipped language. If one of the combatants was pushed against the wall of the ring, the others would push them back into the fight.

Max had been watching them from the top of a small hill. The stranger was behind Max, staying out of sight of the demons, leaning against his spear.

Max wasted no time. He knew how to do this by now. He used [**Tether**] four times and ran towards them, shooting the closest tangle. Before he even got close, a black-shafted spear flew past him in a blur and hit the area where the monsters lay and struggled on the ground. Six of the demons blasted into gore as the spear pierced their bodies. It *thonked* on the ground fifteen yards away from the monsters, twanging upright on a crack in the ground it had made.

CHAPTER EIGHTEEN

The Stranger

Max got a whopping 208 Experience from those eight kills, which had cost him over fifty Mana. He looked blankly at the carnage of exploded red bodies as the Stranger jogged up to the corpses to loot them.

"Wh—" Max spluttered. "What the hell, man?"

The man turned to look at Max and smiled coldly. "You have a good ability. But mine is better. It is called **[Shatter Toss]**."

"I don't care about your stupid ability! Why are you following me?!"

The man picked up his spear. It seemed undamaged by the throw. "Is it not obvious yet? To prevent you from Leveling."

"What the hell is wrong with you? Why would you do that?"

The Stranger shrugged. "I don't like sharing."

"What?!" Max was fuming. He wanted to shoot this guy, Tribunal be damned. *Just breathe. Just breathe and—I'M GONNA SHOVE THAT SPEAR SO DEEP UP HIS ASS HE'S GONNA BE SPITTING SPLINTERS!*

"It's clear you're not going to die here, unless something unexpected happens. So, in order to make you leave, I'm going to steal your Experience."

Max groaned. Now he really considered killing a fellow human. He realized that he'd been naive to not anticipate something like this, but his own perspective had shifted so massively, so quickly. They all needed to work together to survive. This Stranger was strong, as much of a bastard as he was. Humanity needed people like him.

"We should work together. We'd both Level Up faster," Max said.

The Stranger gave a meaningful glance at his spear had landed, the ground around it shattered like ceramic. "I told you. I do not like sharing."

"Fine," Max said, trying to sound reasonable. He barely kept his voice from trembling with fury. "I'll just go two miles in that direction, and you can go two miles in that direction. There's plenty to go around for both of us."

"Now, that is very reasonable," the Stranger said. "Too bad I'm not."

Max tried to keep his poker face. He could feel his face involuntarily twitching. Of course there would be people like the Stranger in this new reality. The leash of society was cut, and the assholes could run rampant. It angered Max to no end. What was he supposed to do?

Max gave the Stranger a dark look. The hale blue eyes stared back, emotionless, but for a hint of amusement. The sensible thing was to leave, come back later, and hope not to run into this man again. But that was also the wrong thing to do. Max knew it. He had only just discovered his new principles, his new sense of pride and purpose. Being sensible now would betray them and Max would be weak and lost again.

No. He refused to backslide. He would not yield to bullies. He would fight for his right to hunt on these grounds.

"Then let's go find some prey," Max said, still locked in a death glare with the Stranger.

The Stranger laughed. It was a hollow, joyless thing. "I knew I could count on you. No, you're not the quitting type. You are a fighter. Respectable, but unwise."

"We'll see," Max growled.

Max was growing frustrated. Twice now, he'd successfully sneaked up on a group of [**Junior Vilefiends**], and efficiently tethered them, only to have the Stranger snatch most of his Experience away with his ridiculous spear-throwing ability. A part of him whispered that he should quit and try again later, that this was a waste of time.

NO! That is the old, weak me. I won't quit. I can't quit.

But he had to think of something. The spear flew fast but not faster than the eye could track. The second time the Stranger had thrown it, Max had tried tethering it to the ground, but it was too fast and had too much momentum to be slowed down by his spell. The Stranger always stayed back and threw the spear when the tethering was done. He could throw it a good seventy yards. Extremely impressive, Max admitted grudgingly. He must have had a Strength-based build.

Nothing here I can tether his shot to . . . No ceiling, hmm . . . Maybe I could lure a group next to a hill and try to steer his spear at that.

It would be complicated to pull off as well as risky. He would have to delay the [**Tether**], which would give the demons time to take swipes at him. And if he failed to lure them in, they would kill him.

Max sat on the ashen ground, lying against one of those squiggly barren trees. He took a sip from his flask. The Stranger stood a few yards away, like any travel companion waiting for his friend.

"Might I have a drink?" the Stranger drawled, politely as ever.

"You're serious?"

The Stranger shrugged. "Doesn't hurt to ask."

"I don't even want to share a goddamn planet with you, much less a drink."

The Stranger smirked at that and just went back to watching Max.

"How do you even survive out in this desert without water?" Max asked.

"Maggots," the Stranger said.

"W-what?"

"There are caves, with large, strong maggots. Easy to kill, very squishy."

"Jesus."

"Oh, I think this place is as far out of Jesus's reach as any place ever will be," the Stranger mused. Then he nodded to himself. "Good place."

Max scoffed at that. "What Level are you anyway?"

"Eleven," the man drawled and looked at Max for his reaction. He didn't seem disappointed at the dumbfounded expression on Max's face.

"How is that even possible?"

"You may have a mighty powerful gun on you person, but I have something better."

"What?" Max asked. "That spear's special?"

"This? Just a regular spear."

"What is it, then?"

The Stranger laughed mirthlessly. "I'm an insomniac, son. While you were napping and playing with whatever friends you must have made, I was killing things. Have barely slept a blink since I got here."

Level Eleven, huh? I'm so behind. The Level Ten boost must be a pretty decent one. He probably got that spear skill from that. I guess I've slacked a little bit around Joshua's camp, but I thought I was doing well. I need to get rid of this guy and storm on, full speed. He's surprisingly talkative, but I'm not picking up on anything I could use to solve this problem. Think, Max, you just need to prevent him from throwing that spear or make him not want to follow you.

Having rested, Max got up and started to move. The Stranger followed twenty yards behind him. It seemed he really wasn't going to kill him. At least there was that.

It wasn't long before they found another group of [**Junior Vilefiends**], who'd recently killed a pair of humans and were now feasting on them. Max grimaced before finding a hiding spot behind a rock to observe them. He needed to do something differently this time. The Stranger hid behind another rock, still not actively sabotaging Max.

Wait . . . There's something there.

Max became lost in thought to the point that eventually the Stranger grew impatient. Rather than waiting any longer, he threw his spear at the group, killing four of the monsters instantly. The two others clocked where the spear had come from and started sprinting towards the older man. Max had to act, or he would get no Experience at all. Knowing he had Health to spare, he simply ran in front of them and used **[Tether]** on them. Max killed one with five quick shots to the head, but after just a single shot at the other one, a rock flew at it with crushing speed, blasting half of its skull off. In total, Max had gained 160 Experience.

"Could be worse," he grumbled to himself. He shot a vicious glance at the Stranger, who was idly tossing a rock up and down on his palm as he sauntered towards the spear he had tossed.

"I used these to kill things before I got the spear," the Stranger drawled as he passed Max.

Max looked at the spear. He had just realized he could tether it to something like a hillside or a large boulder and then bolt off as the Stranger struggled to yank it out. But there were issues with this plan. This guy had a physical build with probably an emphasis in Strength, Dexterity, and Constitution. Max wouldn't get far and his Stamina was probably lower than the Stranger's, which would potentially enrage this already-dangerous man. Another issue with the plan would be that when Max ran out of the spell's range, it would most likely immediately cease. Max hadn't tested it, but it was fair to assume so. He knew, however, that whatever he did, the spear was key.

Spear . . . Sabotage . . . Okay. Wait! Yes! That could work. Just need to get lucky with the monsters.

CHAPTER NINETEEN

Freedom

It was getting late. The dark purple sky with its eternally faint sun hadn't changed much, but Max had gradually learned to read its various nuances. Although the planet was in a constant state of dusk, this was definitely an evening dusk now. It generally got colder towards the evening, but this wasn't noticeable in the Dreadlands as the nearby volcano made everything warm. Max was almost tempted to grab some shut-eye, but it was far too dangerous here. He gave a glance at the Stranger following him and scoffed. He probably slept in a maggot cave or something.

Let him follow. I have a plan now.

Soon afterwards, Max deliberately passed by a group of **[Junior Vilefiends]** as if he hadn't even taken notice of them. And just as Max suspected he would, the Stranger clearly got curious.

"Giving up already?" he called out.

"Can't you just give up?" Max called back.

"Negative."

Suit yourself . . .

It took considerably less time for Max to find what he was looking for. He grinned to himself as he prepared. This was still going to be hard. He would need great timing. He would need to be fast.

Please let this work.

The skinny little demons didn't notice when Max approached them from behind. They were too focused. Max was still a good twenty yards away and the Stranger was another twenty yards behind him. Max resisted the urge to glance back. He couldn't let the Stranger think that anything was amiss.

Then, Max took a deep breath and yelled,

"**[Tether]**!" At that, right on time, the Stranger's spear whooshed past him, a few yards to the right. It flew over the entangled **[Vilefiends]** right to the side of the prey they had been preparing to attack. A giant yak.

The great beast roared in anger and pain and turned to look for the source of this attack. It noticed the Stranger. Max turned to take a look and was delighted to see the "Oh shit!" written all over his face. The great yak bellowed and started charging towards the Stranger.

It trampled the [**Vilefiends**] and Max was pleased to discover he'd gotten exactly half of the Experience, 415 in total, given killing the demons clearly hadn't even been on the yak's mind, focused as it was on barreling towards the Stranger. He was already running.

Max's face split into a grin so wide, it practically ached.

Freedom.

Not wasting any time, he jogged over to the pile of crushed [**Vilefiends**] and looted them for exactly 500 **Cosmic Coins**. Then he did something rash and unplanned that almost surprised himself: he took the Stranger's spear.

Even if he survived the yak and came after Max, he would have a harder time stealing his Experience by just throwing rocks.

Max watched the giant yak chase the Stranger further into the horizon. Then he focused. He chugged a [**Minor Stamina Potion**] down, leaving him with just one more for a rainy day. But he didn't think twice about using one now. Max didn't know if he'd just gotten rid of the Stranger permanently or if he had just bought himself some time. And if it was the latter, it was time to grind!

Oh, one more thing.

[**1600 Cosmic Coins spent**]
[**The Maverick**] **upgraded to +4**
+7 Intelligence
+3 Precision

Ok, *now* it was time to grind!

Max reveled in his freedom, so thoroughly energized by having outsmarted the Stranger, he felt he could hunt all night and morning. Max stored the spear in his pocket-dimension Inventory. He was slightly surprised that trick worked, as his trusty revolver couldn't be placed there, a constant source of inconvenience, but it was likely due to the Soulbound property of the unique weapon.

All in all, things were looking up for Max. He had potions, he still had a trickle of water and some of that beef jerky and even one more [**Rations**] if needed. As cumbersome as [**The Maverick**] was to carry, Max continued to run around, seeking out [**Vilefiends**]. Max killed two groups in the first hour and Leveled Up.

Level Up! [Level 9 Gravity Mage]
You have gained + 1 Constitution, + 1 Intelligence, + 1 Wisdom, + 2 free
Attribute points

Max wanted to put both free points in Constitution, because he would need them now to elongate the grind. Upgrading his weapon had already given him a nice, chunky amount of Intelligence, and his Wisdom score was enough for his current Mana expenditure.

That could change if I get a new ability at Level Ten, though . . .

With that, he decided to put one point in Constitution and one in Wisdom. He took a quick look at his Stat screen before continuing. He had no intention on wasting a single second unnecessarily.

Name: Max Cromwell
Class: Gravity Mage
Level: 9
Health: 180/180
Stamina: 99/180
Mana: 158/260
Alliance: Joshua's Group
Stats:
Strength: 4
Dexterity: 4
Constitution: 18
Intelligence: 26
Wisdom: 21
Charisma: 4
Precision: 7
Toughness: 6
Resistance: 4

Throughout the following night Max cleared out several more groups of **[Vilefiends]**. His mastery of **[Tether]** had become so fine, he was now managing to connect targets almost instinctively. During that critical moment when he'd tethered the Stranger's spear, he'd come to a realization about the spell. It had just *clicked.*

This epiphany let Max preserve Mana by using **[Tether]** in creatively timed attacks. Instead of tethering the two closest targets, he would use two targets to sandwich a third. They would usually get out of the squeeze eventually, but not before Max had peppered them with enough magic bullets to finish them off. Max grinded through the night, chugging down his last Mana and Stamina potions as he went. Time passed in a haze. His body ached and felt fatigued, but he kept going, regardless. It was early in the morning and the faint sun was just beginning its climb to the sky when Max finally Leveled Up.

Class upgraded from [Gravity Mage] E-grade to [Graviturgist] D-grade
Level Up! [Level 10 Graviturgist]
You have gained +1 Constitution, +2 Intelligence, +2 Wisdom, +2 free Attribute points
Skill Choice available!
[Skill System unlocked]
[Additional System message: Your patrons attempted contact. Leave Dreadlands to ping them back.]

"Finally," Max whispered through parched lips. He was out of potions and his water flask was empty. He had never felt as wrung out as this. He had given the hunt his all and the fruit of his labors were sweet. A part of his mind still urged him on, to strike while the iron was hot. To go deeper into the Dreadlands and find new foes to test himself with and to Level Up further. Sometimes listening to that part of one's mind is necessary. But sometimes you have to listen to your body and be reasonable. This was one of those times. He didn't want to become one of the numerous half-eaten corpses on the ashen ground. Max turned and started to walk towards the edge of the valley. It was time to return home.

Home . . . ?

CHAPTER TWENTY

Aftermath

Without noticing, Max had ventured deeper into the Dreadlands than he had intended to. He'd gotten so caught up in his excitement over outsmarting the Stranger that he'd been careless. He could still see the edge of the valley, but it was further away than he felt comfortable with. He started towards the border, hoping he would reach the area around which he had descended, near the bridge.

Along the way, he passed between some high hills, like large domes built from ash, which formed a passage that was clearly trodden often. The hills had a few crevices within them and Max cast wary glances at them. Who knew what was lurking there? The Stranger had talked about giant maggots living in some of the caves.

Max's instincts told him to steer clear, but his curiosity won out when he spotted freshly-dried blood near the entrance of one. He snapped a branch off of one of the twisted trees nearby. It was a wonder the bone-dry thing was even still alive. Then Max threw the branch towards the bloodstains and tethered it, so it would be certain to land.

As fast as a blink, something horrible surged out of the cave, crossing over ten yards in half a second.

It had a green, bulbous body with dozens of skittering little legs, like a caterpillar and no eyes on its face; there was no room for them, just a horrible round maw of sharp teeth that could cut a man in half, and sharp pincers around it to keep hold of the prey. It was so large that, although it had extended outwards, its rear end was still within the cave. The thing smelled almost as ghastly as it looked.

Nope. Nope. Hell, nope.

Max simply shot at the thing and screamed. It wasn't a wise thing to do, but the adrenaline rush was too strong for him to react any other way. It tried to wriggle backwards to its cave, but it was too slow.

Defeated Level 9 [Foulworm]
You gained 300 Experience points

On top of a generous 258 **Cosmic Coins**, Max also got a box when he looted the terrible beast.

[F-grade Material Box]

"That's interesting," Max said to himself. "Is this a rare drop?"

He decided to figure it out later. He was at the end of his rope, and he still had a long way home. He looked at the dead monster lying on the ground.

That Stranger ate *these?*

Without wanting to think about it any further, Max started making his way out of the valley.

It wasn't a half a minute after Max had climbed up from the valley and finally again found himself standing on soft green grass for the first time in what felt like ages that the plastic jellyfish appeared.

[Greetings! Exemplary performance as ever, Maximillian!]

"Uh, just Max is fine."

For half a beat, the device or being said nothing, as if unsure whether to comply or not.

[Very well, Max. You are among the first fifty people out of all races to reach Level 10. An Achievement was given to only the first person, but this is commendable nonetheless.]

"Thanks," Max said. "Are you here to pat me on the head?"

[We are here to instruct you on the Dreadlands and Skill System. Let us start with the Dreadlands. You are clearly already adept at surviving within it. There are, however, some things you must know.]

"Can I move during this? I'm really thirsty, and I need to get to the river."

[You are allowed to move, but that will break the barrier that repels acts of aggression. If you move, you are at a risk of being attacked and we will not be allowed to intervene.]

Max scoffed and started to make his way towards the river. "I'm sure it will be fine."

[Allow us to explain while you travel. The Dreadlands are what could be called a "neutral zone." While the starting location you were spawned in was designated for only humans, the Dreadlands are different.]

"Wait. Different how?"

[Another race, the representatives of Kiritus Corporation, are working to acquire the plentiful resources from the same area. The Dreadlands are a crucible created for conflict.]

"Oh, crap. So there's aliens prowling around on top of strong monsters? Wait. I thought there were four races? You only mentioned one. What's up with that?"

[Yes, for now you will only deal with a group of equal size to the Kiritus Corporation's representatives. You are only inhabiting a relatively small island. Think of this as a single-round elimination tournament. If you manage to exterminate the representatives of the Kiritus faction, all surviving humans and the resources they have acquired will be teleported to another area, where a group of representatives who have also won a round will be pitted against you. The setup will be similar. You will again have a neutral zone to fight over.]

"Now that sounds like some good reality TV," Max quipped as he walked towards the riverbank. "So how many enemies do we have here? What else is in the Dreadlands other than a lot of Experience?"

[We will disregard your barbaric comment. As for the Dreadlands, there is a high amount of processed resources in the area, such that you would not be able to access without appropriate technology and processing facilities. For example, planks and manufactured metal components such as nails. These will not only provide use to representatives, but also allow for fast Leveling for [Laborer] and [Artisan] Classes. The further into the Dreadlands you go, the more dangerous the monsters, the higher quality the various arms, armor, and usable material you will be able to obtain, and the higher the chance you will run into representatives of other races, which will most likely result in mortal combat.]

Max dipped his face in the flowing river as soon as he was able to kneel by the edge. The cold water felt incredible. It refreshed him, giving him that little boost needed to fully process everything that was being said here. Once Max had lifted his face and started pawing the water into his mouth, the creature from Zoos continued.

[Slaying other races is highly recommended for [Combatants] as it will provide a lot of Experience points as well as each defeated opponent's gear and supplies. Engaging in combat with the other races will also increase the chances of your obtaining skills that are related to combat between sentient humanoids. An example of one such skill would be the ability to sense the presence of nearby enemy races.]

"That does sound powerful," Max agreed. He hadn't been in combat with anything but monsters, but having an ability that would prevent the likelihood of him getting caught with his pants down sounded perfect.

[We understand you are under the effects of physical exhaustion, so we will be brief. Let us move to the second topic: The Skill System. Having reached Level 10, you are now able to upgrade your skills and, under certain circumstances, learn new Skills entirely, a topic we alluded to in the previous discussion. You might learn Skills pertaining to the environment you inhabit. For example. a person spending a lot of time underwater could eventually learn [Underwater Breathing], if they use the Skill as often enough and/or as innovatively as you have done with your spell [Tether]. There was actually a heated debate over giving you [Tether II] outright as you hit Level 10. However, we eventually agreed this is technically against the rules, and thus you were rewarded with something appropriately fitting within your next Skill Choice.]

"Don't I get a say in it?" Max asked. "It's my life, after all!"

The creature paused again. It gave Max a strange sense of pleasure to have the ability to make this otherwise so composed and robotic a thing a little flustered. Or so it seemed.

[Ask . . . you? What a highly unusual request. To involve the subject in the decision. Counter-intuitive . . . No way to prevent bias in such a primitive being.]

"Hey, you're right. No big deal. It's just a decision about me. About my survival. But just in case it happened to be possible to ask what I think next time . . .

I'm just tossing it out there as a suggestion," Max said, as sweetly as he could manage.

[**We will take this conversation under review and discuss the possibility of changing this protocol in the future. For now, do you have any other questions . . . Max?**]

Max sighed as he filled his waterskin and empty potion bottles. "What is the reward I got regarding my Skill Choice?"

[**Because of your exemplary tactical prowess with [Tether], a relatively elementary ability that you were able to use with numerous variations, we have manipulated your Skill Choice to give you an ability akin to [Tether] which is quite rare and powerful for Level 10. You are, of course, free to choose what you will, but it is advised that you accept this ability.**]

"Isn't this cheating or something? Aren't you not supposed to help us?"

[**We assure you, this was done considering all stipulations, rules, and laws. We filed the necessary documentation for this to be allowed. It was not viewed kindly by the other three factions, but the consensus was clear: You deserve this reward, Max.**]

"Well, I'll take what is given. Thanks, I guess."

[**You are welcome. The Zoos Collective, pick out promising individuals to help if possible and necessary, as all the other factions do. While you have waged your own combat, we are engaged in what you humans call a "paper war".**]

"Wait, all of you factions are out there lawyering against each other?" Max couldn't help but laugh. What was this crazy fever dream (and if this did turn out to be a dream after all, Max promised never eat another pickle before bed in his life)? "You're all filing motions to some judge left and right to get advantages using loopholes, while trying to deny the other factions from doing the same?"

[**It is more complicated than this, but you have understood the spirit of the matter. We are all bound to not use violence or deceit, so this is how we must do battle. It is the least barbaric way of combat that the ICCB has devised.**]

That's kind of tragic. Even super-advanced beings use proxies for war and try to push each other into legal landmines.

[This is all highly irrelevant. What it comes down to is that we are trying to increase the odds of you surviving and winning. Do you have any other questions?]

"What happens if I kill another human?"

[Each act of murder will be reviewed in the Tribunal. If the circumstances, both moral and physical, are standard, only the Zoos Collective will perform an internal investigation. If it is a mass genocide of their own species or the situation is unusual, the whole ICCB will review the case. The punishment for such a deed will be individually determined, depending on the circumstances.]

"What is it usually? Give me some ballpark idea. Are we talking execution, a time out, loss of experience?"

[We are not allowed to disclose such information.]

"I kinda figured. Thanks anyway."

[Do you have any other questions?]

"I suppose that's it for now," Max said. He wasn't feeling particularly curious or pensive at the moment. His high from the victory and hunt was waning. He wanted to get back to Joshua's camp and just collapse.

[Until we speak again.]

And with that, the plastic jellyfish blinked out of existence just as quickly as it had appeared. Max wondered idly if it was a hologram. He decided that naked leprechauns from the seventh dimension could have been singing it into existence with magic for all he cared. All he wanted to know right now was the nearest place he could sleep.

After a trek that felt like an eternity, Max finally got to the camp, already bustling in all of its morning chores. It had grown again and had now expanded to two firepits around which there were all sorts of knickknacks. And hides, strung on wooden racks to be cured! Max saw panther hides and some big brown hides that were probably taken from those pony creatures. *Sweet!* He'd ask about them when he woke up. He saw a few familiar faces and gave them a tired smile and a hand-wave. Joshua came up enthusiastically to greet Max, but with just a few words he let him be. Max had just enough energy to set up his hammock on two even branches of the great sturdy tree before he hopped in and fell asleep almost immediately.

CHAPTER TWENTY-ONE

Fruits of Labor

A slight trickle of rain pattering against the tree leaves woke Max up. He could tell it was evening, as the two fires had already been lit casting a pillar of smoke towards the sky, and people were sitting around it, many with a piece of leather or wood in their hands, trying to improve their Levels.

Either it hadn't been raining for long or the tree had soaked up most of it. Max felt a little damp but not uncomfortable. He yawned and stretched, enjoying the gentle sway of the hammock. A bird resembling a crow looked down at Max from a higher branch and croaked as if asking a question. A heavy blanket of dark purple clouds covered the sky, not letting any of the faint light of the sun through.

Despite how comfortable Max felt in his hammock, he knew it was time to move. There were fifty other people who had reached Level Ten around the same time as him. Max knew that not all of them would be human. Just off pure logic alone, only 25 percent would be, on average. Then subtract the bad eggs like the Stranger, and suddenly a sense of urgency flooded Max's mind.

But now he had a perfect opportunity to multitask. He would do his Skill Choice before getting up form his cozy hammock. And so he opened up the appropriate System message, which started blinking red as soon as Max looked up to his right.

[Telekinesis I]
Gain the ability to lift an inanimate object within sight in the air and move it around. The weight of the object you are able to lift, and the speed at which you are able to move it through the air is dependent on your Intelligence. Cost: 3 or more Mana per second, depending on the weight of the object.

Huh. The same skill choice that I had earlier. A much more reasonable pick, now that I have the Mana to use it effectively. But let's see what the Zoos guys gave me.

[Gravity Pulse I]
**Send out a wave of gravitational energy in a cone ten feet wide, throwing back
anything in its path and causing damage proportional to your Intelligence
modifier. The closer the object(s), the more potent the effect.
Cost: 15 Mana**

*Solid spell. This would keep nasty stuff off me in a pinch. It'll also cause direct
damage, which is interesting. I could blast a whole group of* [**Vilefiends**] *with this at
close range and hurt them all.*

[Additional option added]
[Gravity Well I]
**Create a sphere of condensed gravity within thirty feet of where you are.
Objects within its range will be pulled towards it, depending on their weight,
their Resistance and your Intelligence modifier. You can exclude objects such
as yourself from being pulled at will.
Cost: 30 Mana to cast and 3 Mana per second to maintain.**

Okay, this spell is very cool. It's like casting [**Tether**] *on a whole area! I could set it
on a group of* [**Vilefiends**]*, and they'd all get pulled into it. It is costly in terms of Mana,
though. But as opposed to tethering all my targets individually, it'll at least break even,
and possibly do even better. It doesn't seem quite as versatile as tethering, but I'm sure I
can figure that out. Hell, it's not like I can't use* [**Tether**] *after picking this up anyway.*

Max chose [**Gravity Well**] and immediately jumped out of his hammock,
pulling it down after himself and gathering it into a messy bundle and depositing
it into his pocket dimension Inventory. When he retrieved it later, it would come
out neatly packaged, which still blew his mind.

Max picked a spot in midair to test his new ability. It created a translucent,
ethereal sphere, five feet in diameter, that looked as if waves of hot air had been
condensed into a swirling orb, five feet in diameter. It immediately sucked up half
the leaves of a nearby bush, which clumped around its invisible core. Max took a
shot at the spinning mass of leaves. A magic bullet blasted through them, tossing
up dirt on a nearby hillside.

That was easy! My Precision isn't that *high!*

Max shot a little off on purpose, and the bullet still clipped the bits of flutter-
ing leaves. He then shot again towards the edge of the core, but that one just missed
and struck the hillside.

Max's Mana was draining pretty fast, but he still managed to run some tests,
such as throwing rocks of various sizes and at various speeds at the [**Gravity Well**].
At one point, he even let himself be sucked up by it. When he got close enough,
he was almost yanked off his feet. He struggled to escape the pull, which felt like

a powerful cyclone dragging him towards it. He focused on controlling the properties of the spell, forcing the vortex to alternate between pulling and pushing and locking it in a stalemate until he ran out of Mana.

Afterwards, he sat down and took a drink from his water flask, at which point Sid approached him, holding a big chunk of meat.

"Yo, dude. What the hell is that?"

"It's a water flask," Max said, trying not to look too smug. "Want a drink?"

"Hell yeah, bro," Sid said, an excited grin on his face. "Take this beef, bro. It's for you."

With a grin of his own, Max gratefully accepted the meat and started gnawing down on it. This was no stringy panther meat. This was a rich and fatty, full of flavor and juice, which ran down his chin as he ate, but he couldn't care less. He let out a small moan as he attacked the slab of meat.

After half of it was gone, Max sighed and let the rest drop onto his lap. Sid gave him back his flask and grinned. "Good, yeah?"

"What is this beautiful sorcery?"

"It's [**Paldeer**] meat, bro," Sid said. "Spiced with my special sauce."

"Okay, that sounds wrong."

Sid laughed. "No, no, bro. It's a Skill I got when I Leveled Up to Five. It's called [**Food Preparation**]."

"Huh," Max said. "How does it work?"

"It's kinda weird," Sid said and scratched at the stubble on his chin. "I just . . . decide I'm going to use it when I start making food, I start using Mana, and it just makes the food better and more filling. You feel me, bro?"

"Damn," Max said. "That's pretty useful. So you're going to be the camp chef?"

"Yeah, bro!" Sid said, excitement lighting his eyes again. "It feels good to be useful. It's sweet having people smile at you and thank you. I never had that before."

"I kind of know how you feel," Max said and nodded slowly. They shared a moment of camaraderie and understanding. Yes, it felt good to be useful. Valuable. To have a purpose.

Max lingered a moment longer and then he got up.

"I need to go see Joshua," he said and clapped Sid on the shoulder. "You're doing good work, Sid."

"Hey, bro," Sid called to Max's back. Max turned. "You ain't gonna leave us, right?

Max shook his head and smiled. "I don't think I will. In a way, I need you guys as much as you need me."

"Rise and shine," Joshua said and got up as he saw Max approach. He had been sitting on one of the logs, which had now been skillfully carved in terms of both comfort and aesthetics. "You slept for a long time."

"Needed every minute of it," Max said. "Good to see you."

"Likewise, friend."

Friend? I like that.

"I had a bit of an adventure, actually," Max said. "Let me know when you have a minute."

"I'll make a minute for you," Joshua said as he sat down. He gestured for Max to do the same.

Max told him what he had seen and experienced in the Dreadlands. He told him about the monsters there, about the nature of the place as far as the Cosmic Games were concerned. They discussed the Stranger at length, but Joshua could not give him any useful advice about what to do if the madman were to return. Max also asked for another quest for the sword he had obtained from [**Vine-Mother**] and the Stranger's spear. There were other [**Combatants**] in the camp, and most of them unarmed. The Framework seemed to judge the weapons as reasonably valuable, as they provided 150 Experience each. After Max finished telling his tale to Joshua, the exploration quest's condition was also fulfilled.

[**Quest complete**]
Reward: 300 Experience points
[**Quest complete**]
Reward: 500 Experience points

"Oh, this quest system of yours is really nice," Max said.

"Tell me about it," Joshua grinned. "It's been helping everyone Level faster, me included. I'm Level Nine now."

"Ten is going to be a good one," Max said and briefly explained what was to come with the Class upgrade and the Skill system.

"So have you figured out anything new about the quests?"

Joshua shook his head and accepted the flask from Max. "There is a limit to how many I can give to a single person. One at a time. Also the quests have to be things that are actually needed. I gave the artisans a quest to craft wooden spikes and spears for defense and for the hunters, but eventually I just got a System message in the line of "[**Quest requirements not met**]". It's also weirdly particular about the needs. Like what, we needed forty-eight wooden spikes, but forty-nine were too many? It also works the other way around. That bucket you found has been really useful. But we didn't *need* it."

"Seems like the System is fairly straightforward," Max said. "If it's something useful, you can give a quest for it. If something stops being useful, you can no longer give it as a quest."

"But how can the System know what's useful and what isn't?"

Max shrugged. "Magic."

Joshua laughed. "Alright, maybe that's what we should be thinking about."

"What we should be thinking about is this [**F-grade Material Box**] I found on my adventures," Max said and brought up his Inventory Menu. Of course, Joshua didn't see any of this, but that didn't dampen his enthusiasm.

"Another adventure, another prize, huh?" What's inside?"

"Let's find out," Max said and opened the box.

[You have obtained 15 planks (F-Grade)]

CHAPTER TWENTY-TWO

Resource Question

Fifteen planks materialized in Max's lap. He and Joshua both yelped, attracting the attention of other people nearby. The planks were three feet long and of crude but sturdy make. On a closer look, they were definitely cut to be two by four.

"Ho-*ly* crap," Joshua whispered reverently. "You got these from the Dreadlands?"

Max nodded. Joshua stood up, an enthusiastic fire in his eyes.

"Lily, come over here," Joshua called. "Martin and Bill, you too."

A young girl of maybe fourteen stood up from a nearby log and came over. She had a sullen but focused look in her eyes. Max didn't know what had happened during the time she had been here, but she had clearly been forced to grow up before her time. She was promptly followed by a burly man in his forties, the white jumpsuit straining against his beer belly, as well as a third man, thin and wearing a pair of spectacles with broken lens on his grim face. Max had never seen any of them, but when they looked at him, a flash of recognition was visible. They all nodded to him respectfully. Max smiled and nodded back.

"Look at this," Joshua said, pointing to the pile of planks around Max.

"Is that . . . ?" The burly man looked at the cut wood and rushed to Max, picking up one of the planks. Where did you get these?"

"A supply box I got in the Dreadlands," Max said.

"Dreadlands?" the man asked as he inspected the plank, before turning back to Max. "Sounds ominous. I'm Bill. You're *that* Max, right?"

Max gave Joshua a glance. He smiled. "I guess I am."

"Keep this up and you'll be a folk hero," Bill said and went back to inspecting the plank.

The other man approached, hand extended. "I'm Martin. Nice to meet you."

They clasped hands. Martin had very dry palms. His eyes were steady and his voice monotone. There was an air of formality about him. "What do you want us to do with the planks, Chief?"

Chief, huh? Well, why not . . .

Joshua grinned excitedly. "That's what I called you for. We need to decide how to best use these planks. Are there any more, Max?"

Max shook his head. "No."

"Pity," Joshua said. "Well, I know what kind of quest to give you next."

"I don't know how to get more of these boxes. I think they're a rare or an uncommon drop from the monsters."

"Hey, Max," Bill said. "What's the difference between rare and uncommon?"

"In video games 'rare' is usually more valuable and . . . well, more rare than uncommon. Like, in this world the gradation system is based on letters. These planks came from an F-grade box. I'm no expert, but these look basic. They're crude work, right? No sanding done, no resin coat or anything. D- or C-grade planks would probably have those. I have no idea what an A-tier plank would be like. Hell, it could be indestructible or something."

"I hear you. Well, I am an expert, and I say these are indeed crude work," Bill said. Max gave him a quizzical look. "I worked at a sawmill, like my daddy before me. Know a thing or two about wood. So you're saying you can't bring those planks back consistently?"

"That's the gist of it," Max said. "The box could have contained many other things than planks too, for all I know."

"Damn it," Joshua muttered. Everyone turned to him. "Well, it's not like we couldn't use other things, but we could *really* use more of these. Mainly for shelter. This rain is going to give at least some people the sniffles or worse."

"Fifteen planks is not enough for a shelter, Chief," Martin said.

"Was just about to say that," Bill said.

"We need to figure out what's the best way to use them, then," Joshua said.

"Without nails, we have limited options," Martin said.

"That's why little Lily is here," Joshua said. He got down on his knees to be on eye-level with the girl. "Lily, do you think you could fashion nails out of bone?"

The girl considered and then whispered, "Yes," as she nodded.

"That ain't gonna work, Chief," Bill said. "Bone nails are gonna be too brittle."

"It could work from a theoretical standpoint," Martin said.

Bill let out an exasperated sigh. "Listen, you egghead, you wanna waste Lily's time on the off-chance the nails might work from a 'theoretical standpoint'?"

Joshua watched them but got nothing more out of Martin except for sullen muttering. "What do you suggest, then?"

"Depends on how we use this stuff," Bill said. "But there's wooden pegs we can use for fastening. Or rope or sinews, what have you."

"You agree, Martin?"

The spectacled man let out a quiet deliberate cough. "If no nails are available, yes I suppose it is the best option."

Bill groused but said nothing.

"What do you think, Max?" Joshua asked.

Max threw his hands in the air. "Don't ask me. I just kill stuff."

They chuckled and went back to debating how to get the best use out of planks. When she wasn't being directly addressed, the girl kept quiet. Mostly it was Bill and Joshua throwing the ball back and forth, with Martin joining in, usually to object to something Bill had said. Max watched them and smiled to himself. Definitely worth protecting. He wanted to get back out there.

Soon. Stay a while. Enjoy the peace. Take it in.

". . . Which is why you should give them to me!" Bill shouted, stomping his dirty white boot on a log.

"Y-you, you?" Martin spluttered. "You're just a . . ."

"Just a what?" Bill roared. "Say it, Martin."

"Listen," Martin said. "I was an architect. You don't know anything about structural load or—"

"Look around you, Martin! We're living in the woods, eating half-raw meat and sleeping on the ground. The hell is your fancy degree good for?"

"Look, guys," Joshua said, loudly "Maybe you two could share it."

"I already have woodworking skills," Bill said. "I should have them."

"So do I," Martin said. "I have **[Precision Cutting]**."

"Well, we ain't needing to do cuts on these planks!" Bill went on, waving his hands in a wide arc. "We can't both specialize in wood!"

"Actually, I think you can," Max said. Their argument had gone on for a while, and Max was grateful to finally somehow be able to interject. Everyone turned to listen. "You're going to get Class upgrades at Level Ten. I skipped mine because of a rare box I got, but let's say you're now **[Artisans]** with skills related to wood-working. So you'll likely get a Class like **[Carpenter]**."

"A carpenter?" Martin said in mild outrage. "But I have a degree in—"

"Sod off with your degree, Egghead," Bill said. "So, we'll both be carpenters. That's the problem."

"You didn't let me finish," Max said. "Later you'll get a specialization in your Class. I started off as a **[Combatant]**. I probably should have gotten the **[Mage]** Class at Ten. But since I already had a specialization, I just got an advancement in that. By that logic, you'll get a choice later down the line. Maybe at Level Fifteen or Twenty. And even if that's not the case, I know for a fact that you'll start gaining Skills depending on what you do at Ten. So one of you can specialize in making tables and stools, and the other one shelter and storage. We'll need both."

"Hmph," Bill said, crossing his arms. "I can see why everyone speaks so highly of you. You're alright, Max, you know that?"

"Thanks," Max said, smiling and nodding.

"That still doesn't solve how we should distribute these planks," Martin said.

"You know you're really stupid for someone so smart," Bill said. "Didn't you listen to Max? We'll work on these planks together, damn it. We'll argue about how we specialize while we do it. Come on."

With that, Bill slapped Martin on the shoulder with a meaty hand so hard that the skinnier man's glasses bounced up and down on his nose. He muttered something as he adjusted them but gave a resigned smile. They went off with the planks, leaving Joshua and Max sitting on the log with the silent girl.

"So we don't need the nails?" the girl asked with a faint voice.

"No," Joshua said. "But we should use animal bones more, now that I think about it."

"We could make goblets from the skulls," Lily said.

"That's kind of badass," Max said and gave her an encouraging smile. She flinched at the eye contact but meekly smiled back.

"You guys are morbid," Joshua said and chuckled. "But that does sound like a good idea. But we would need something to plug the holes of the skull. Maybe clay?"

"If you find clay, it might just be easier to make containers from that," Max said.

"Oh, we should definitely find clay," Joshua said.

"I think—" Lily started. She looked at them as if making sure she had permission to speak. "I think I would like to work with clay. I could make cups and plates and . . . Normal things. To remind us . . ."

"That would be great," Joshua beamed at Lily. "You'll be our clay specialist, Lily."

Lily gave Joshua a shy, appreciative smile.

"Don't we need high temperatures to work with clay?"

"Not necessarily," Max said. "We made little clay cups in art class at school. We just left them to dry, wrapped in paper towels."

"Well, we won't have paper towels any time soon, but that sounds promising."

"Hardened clay would probably be better. We sadly can't do much with open fires other than cook," Max thought. "If we could build an oven . . ."

A few cogs turned slowly in Max's head.

"Oven! Bricks. We could make clay bricks!"

Joshua caught on right away. "Bricks! Genius! Shelter!"

They went on excitedly for a while, running through all the possibilities. The excitement was infectious and even Lily got caught up in it, coming up with some ideas herself. Joshua gave Lily a quest to find clay and then called other people to join her in the search. That left Joshua and Max alone.

"Any more tricks up your sleeve?" Joshua asked.

"I think I'm out for now," Max said.

"Keep 'em comin'," Joshua said. Then he fell silent for a beat and gave Max a pensive glance. "So, when are you going to leave again?"

"As soon as possible," Max said immediately. "I'll need potions and food with me."

Joshua looked down and let out a little laugh. He wasn't surprised at all. "You'll get them. Bring back something nice."

"I will."

"At least say hi to Marie and Elena before you go." Joshua said. Max nodded at that. "You sure you don't want to stay any longer?"

A pang ran through Max. Of course he would like to stay. To share ideas with Joshua and eat the meat Sid cooked. He looked at the people around. Elena had brewed tea from some herbs and was circling around and handing it out. They were all tired. It was still raining. All things considered, it really sucked. But they had each other and you could see it in their smiles as they talked with each other.

This is what's good in humans. And it's worth protecting. And I will *protect it. Proudly.*

Max lifted his head up high and smiled. Genuinely. "I'm sure."

CHAPTER TWENTY-THREE

Back to the Dreadlands

Max wiped the blood off his mouth after he finished drinking from a [Vilefiend]'s neck. One flask of water would only last so far if he was going to be venturing further into the Dreadlands. There had to be fresh water, since the further into the wasteland he went, the taller the twisted, squiggly trees got. But the water could just as well be underground. Or maybe the stinky, sullied water the demons drank is what made the trees twisty. If there was no accessible fresh water, it would be hard to venture deep alone, at least with only one flask and a few thimble-sized potion bottles of water.

The blood tasted foul, but it wasn't poisonous. He filled up an empty potion vial with blood and carried on. He had been slowly inching deeper into the Dreadlands, still killing mostly [**Junior Vilefiends**] but he had also found two [**Foulworms**] in a fissure and a cave. No loot boxes of any kind so far, but Max did get a [**Minor Mana Potion**] from one of the worms. As ugly and menacing as they were, they were an easy kill.

Max was getting tired and hoped to find another cave with one of those repulsive worms again. He would take a page from the Stranger's book and sleep in one of those caves. He wouldn't go as far as to eat the worms, though. At least not yet.

Max knew he wasn't far from the edge of the valley—maybe two or three miles. But he couldn't see the edge of it. It was a windy day and gusts of ash were thrown up, making visibility low and his thirst high. Despite the adverse circumstances, even without finding a water source, Max figured he would survive for two more days.

Max found two more groups of [**Vilefiends**] before reaching an ominous-looking cave. Killing the [**Vilefiends**] was a piece of cake now with [**Gravity Well**]. Max didn't even bother to approach them carefully and unseen. He would just walk up to them, they would charge at him, and he would cast the spell. They were so light that a well-placed spell would leave them dangling helplessly in the air. Unfortunately, it seemed that after hitting Level Ten, they offered significantly less Experience. After finishing off a group of eight, Max only received 450 Experience, half of what he was used to. It was still a decent amount, but Max assumed the Experience needed for Levels would grow on an exponential scale.

Max was feeling sufficiently exhausted as he dragged a **[Vilefiend]** corpse to the cave entrance. He tethered the dead demon to a spot by the cave, and immediately afterwards, one of the worm monstrosities sprung out of the cave's mouth. With its caterpillar legs skittering around, its mouth closed around the **[Vilefiend]** and its pincers locked it in place. Max had been expecting both the lunge and the devouring, but it still scared and disgusted him. It wasn't difficult for him to shoot at the horrid creature until it stopped squirming.

Defeated Level 9 [Foulworm]
You gained 300 Experience points

At least these things still give me the full package.

Since the five-hundred-pound horrid worm was fully out of the cave, there was enough room in there now for Max to sleep. It would be risky, but he would need to take it. The cave smelled so nasty, Max immediately felt bile rising up. He held it in, looking around. A smeared pile of yellow goo was the most likely culprit for the eye-watering stench.

Worm poop? Holy baby Jesus Christ, hallowed be thy name, why does my existence contain alien worm poop?

Max brought several handfuls of the gray ash from outside to cover the yellow goop. Max wasn't sure if it actually reduced the reek, but at least he felt a bit better about it. Then he placed all his potion bottles full of water and blood at the entrance and covered them with ash. It wasn't much of an alarm system, but it was better than nothing. With that, Max curled up in the least objectionable corner of the **[Foulworm]**'s domain and fell into a restless sleep.

A short while later, Max woke up. Groggy and thirsty he pawed around him for the water flask. He could not have slept long. Or if he had, the sleep wasn't exactly restful. Max figured it was probably a case of both. Regardless, he got himself up and prepared to delve deeper into the Dreadlands.

As he continued on, he noticed a steadily thickening smog beginning to grow around him. The twisted trees grew taller and closer together, and in addition, there were strange gray and red spires reaching to the sky, varying in height from ten to thirty feet. As far as Max could see through the smog, the structures were coarse and porous in nature. When he got closer to them, the air got hotter and it seemed the smog was coming directly from their many holes.

While that was curious, the smog was proving dangerous to Max, as it was becoming increasingly difficult to see where he was going. He became constantly on edge. He avoided any sudden changes in the terrain, mainly because he worried a worm might ambush him from a hidden hole.

And then there were the screams. Blood-curdling, whining screams could be heard from various directions every minute or so, like whales calling to each other across a vast ocean. But this was no distant and benign ghostly song. This was a malevolent, high screech that raised up every hair on Max's body. The resonant cries cut through the air, and Max wasn't sure he wanted to find out what could make such a sound.

But then something else drew Max's attention. The smog was irritating to breathe in and seemed to drain his Stamina faster than the Dreadlands generally did. But eventually, Max noticed the smog becoming more transparent and more . . . fragrant?

This is steam, isn't it?

The scent had earthy and metallic notes to it; suddenly the fumes felt rich and invigorating to breathe in. Max inhaled deeply as he followed them to their source. After a short walk, he encountered a field of small pools of green, still water, idly steaming.

Holy shit! Hot springs?

This was a volcanic area, after all! Max approached carefully and touched the water with the tip of [**The Maverick**]'s barrel. He carefully let a drop of water drip on the back of his hand. Hot, but not scalding. Kneeling at the edge of the pool, Max tentatively dipped two fingers in the water and tasted it. Earthy, metallic, a side note of sulfur.

Yes! Goddamn, yes! This is drinkable! And hell yes, I'm taking a soak, thank you very much for asking.

The pool was probably three or four feet in depth and looked safe enough. Max cast [**Gravity Well**] in the middle of it, just in case. These were the Dreadlands after all. But no flesh-eating monsters were caught in his spell, just a massive of swirling green water. Satisfied, Max put his gun down by the edge of the pool and jumped into the water, jumpsuit and all.

One might have found this foolhardy, but Max had to be prepared to make a quick escape if necessary, and he'd be damned if he'd have to run around naked until he found something else to wear. Secondly, his jumpsuit was so grimy, he would be hard-pressed to call any part of it white anymore. It might as well get a soak while Max did.

The hot water felt *amazing*. Having been constantly sweaty, wet, tired, you name it, since getting to Alpha Ludus and only having been able to wash himself in a flowing river, this was as close to Heaven as he could ask.

Max let himself enjoy the soak for a number of minutes before he finally steeled his resolve and scrubbed the grime off of him, even giving his matted hair its first proper wash since he got there. Yes, it had been itchy. No, there would be no further discussion about it.

Max got up and immediately drank half of his flask empty. It felt wise to leave some to dilute the mineral-rich water. It was definitely drinkable, unlike the nasty water that was abundant in the outer rims of the Dreadlands, but it could make him sick if he drank too much. But this was still a huge win and it bought him more time to explore.

Just as Max had filled his flask, he heard another one of those aggressive screams. Max looked up and flinched in horror. The sound had come from a towering creature half-shrouded in steam. It was right across a couple of pools, only ten yards away.

CHAPTER TWENTY-FOUR

Firehole

Its height was nearly as formidable as its scream. It was twelve feet tall on all fours, with thick arms supporting its massive, hunched back, and had a face like nothing Max had ever seen even in his most messed-up dreams. A giant insectoid, it had four sharp pincers protruding from each corner of its mouth, Which was dripping with saliva, and several black eyes dotted its head.

Max couldn't help it. He screamed. He grabbed his gun and flask. Then he cast a **[Gravity Well]** at the creature's general direction and bolted. The monstrosity gave a slow start but picked up speed as it got out of Max's spell's range. Max canceled the spell.

Max sprinted away into the smog, firing his gun behind him. The creature followed Max, lumbering behind like a tall shadow in the thick smog. Max turned a tight left and ran between the formations of those porous spires. The insectoid followed him, only slowed down by having to barrel through the structures. Rubble rained down on Max's hood and back, the crashing of stone on the ground sounding like thunder behind him as he ran. Max saw a cave ahead. The spires were thinning and the creature was closing in on him. Max cast another **[Gravity Well]** and ran towards the cave. If there was a worm waiting for him, then so be it. At least he had a sliver of a chance.

The creature was just a few yards away when Max leapt inside the cave headfirst. He could feel the swish of air behind him as the monster swiped at where Max had just been. It let out one of those terrible screams and bent down and tried to spear Max against the wall with one of its claws. It missed by a foot.

Max scrambled deeper into the cave, and the monster attacked again. This time, however, it didn't have the reach. That didn't stop Max's stomach from lurching, though. Max almost sat down to recoup himself, before he realized to his great horror that the giant insect monster had started digging at the cave's entrance. It was very motivated to get dinner.

NopeNopeNopeNopeNopeNopeNope.

Max looked around the dark cave in a growing panic and saw that there was a tunnel leading towards an orange light. He took a final glance towards the dozen emotionless eyes staring at him as the cave's mouth crumbled and the creature pushed its head and front claws inside. The four curved pincers at its mouth snapped at the air, way too close for comfort. Max yelped and scampered towards the orange light. He kept crawling as the ceiling gradually lowered until the cave sloped downwards. Behind him, another crazed scream shook the cave. At this point, Max was beyond caring to know what was happening behind him and how close the flesh-eating aberration was. He just kept crawling downwards into the claustrophobic darkness, only a faint orange glow to guide him. Max crawled long enough for his heart to stop thrumming, for the depraved screeches to stop shaking the cave, long enough to feel the sweat on his body grow cold. Finally, he gasped and collapsed, breathing in the warm, dry air. It was harsh and made him cough, but he breathed in deeply regardless. He was alive and that alone was one hell of a rush. He laughed, and it echoed somewhere down towards the orange light.

Well, I'm sure as shit not turning back. I don't even have the space to do it. I'm not gonna back up blindly into that horror's mouth. So, as always, there's only one way: Forward.

Collecting himself and letting the jittery high of the adrenaline settle down, Max ventured towards the orange light. It eventually started to glow brighter and stronger, as the air got hotter. It was a veritable sauna inside the cave. Max was no geologist, but this was surely related to the volcanic activity in this area. Was he about to reach the end of the tunnel and fall into molten lava? Maybe. *Still beats being eaten alive by a giant demonic cockroach thing.*

Well, fortunately he didn't fall into the lava, but as it turns out, there sure was a lot of it. Max found himself looking down into a large room with a black platform in the middle and two black stone bridges extending to it from opposite sides of the room. Other than that, *yup*, mostly lava.

The lava gave the room dark red glow. There were also lit torches by the doors.

Torches?

Max had a choice. He could wriggle his way forward and drop down on the platform, but he'd have to toss [**The Maverick**] down first. He wasn't exactly fond of that idea, but he was short on options. His ornate revolver clunked down on the platform. There was nothing for it now. The only thing worse than turning back now would be turning back without his weapon. He shuffled himself to face the other way and dropped down.

It was a drop of ten feet or so, even from a dead hang. Max was scared. If this didn't work out like he thought it would, he could end up with two broken ankles. He closed his eyes and let go. To his great relief, however, he was alright. Red flashed in his vision and he lost twenty Health, but that was it. Absolutely manageable. He picked up his trusty revolver and looked around.

First thing Max noticed was that he wasn't feeling that heat anymore. The black stone platform emanated a soothing coolness around it. He was still sweating, but considering he was in a room full of lava, he could have just as easily been fried like an egg on the platform. Now he just had to pick a direction. While there were some symbols above the doors leading out of the room, it wasn't in a language Max recognized. He chose one at random and went through it to a hallway. The hallway was also lit with torches, the sleek black walls giving off the same cooling feeling. There was something here keeping the proverbial water running.

But who? The demons? That didn't feel like the right answer, but what did Max really know about this world. He tried moving as stealthily as possible, softening every footstep with conscious care. They sent off faint echoes traveling towards the darkness, regardless. Max chose a right at an intersection, which led to a path upwards. Then another right. He crossed another platform bridge and took another path up. He deemed up was probably best. He didn't know what he was dealing with and he wanted to make sure there was at least a chance of an escape if shit hit the fan.

When Max approached another intersection, he heard a pair of footsteps approach. Instinct taking over, he quickly went to the right through a pair of double doors and then closed them behind him. Way too loudly.

Crap. Well, they probably would have noticed anyway. Think fast.

The footsteps approached the doors.

"[**Tether**]," Max whispered, binding the doors to each other. Deciding that would have to do, he ran through the platform room to the other door and tethered that one behind him as well. The corridor went downwards, but Max was out of options now. He came to a T-section and chose right. Again, it went down, but this was no time to turn back. Lost in a maze of high black walls and endless intersections, Max cursed his luck. What had he gotten himself into?

Max eventually arrived at a large hall that held all sorts of tools and tables. It looked like some strange underground office space. Or a lounge. There was a desk and beside it, a huge pile of the same shining black rocks Max had seen everywhere.

They had a mining operation here. Why did it stop? Where did everyone go?

As if on cue, Max heard a loud cry in the distance. Clearly not human, but close enough. Curiosity got the better of him and he followed that sound. When he walked further into the gloomy light that the sparse torches provided, he heard more voices, all of them joining each other in a discordant cacophony. It sounded like a battle. There appeared to be shouting, banging, and the roar of flames. Max jogged towards the sounds, passing half-finished meals of some glowing green grub and giant pickaxes tossed aside in a hurry. He followed the sounds until he reached a vast atrium, lit not only by hundreds of torches but flying fireballs as well.

CHAPTER TWENTY-FIVE

Obsidian Dwarves

It was hard for Max's brain to process what exactly was happening. Everything was a blur of black and red and orange and shouting and flying stones and fireballs. Max crouched instinctively next to a hunched black form. It was a dead . . . something.

Max took stock of the situation. There were three dozen stout black creatures with shiny bald heads shouting and getting in formations. They used hammers and pickaxes and threw big, sharp rocks with leather slingshots. They were shouting frantically to each other, scattering and regrouping like trained soldiers. All of them wore brown leather overalls, except for three who wore loose robes and were weaving elaborate motions in the air and chanting in a low rhythm. The flaming giants were throwing fireballs, some of which exploded in the air while others hit the bald creatures. Six of the giants had come up from the magma surrounding the edges of the room, and the obsidian dwarves were doing their damnedest to keep them in the lava.

They were nine feet tall, and hot magma dripped off of them as they lumbered. They would scoop some off their bodies and mold them in their hands like snowballs and throw them at the fighting dwarves. Oftentimes it would explode in the air above the formations, blocked by an invisible shield, but sometimes it did so within a formation, throwing the stout creatures in all directions as they screamed in pain.

Max didn't know how friendly the shiny black creatures were, but it probably wouldn't hurt his chances if he helped them. It was that or try to find his way out of this obsidian maze and hope he wouldn't be caught intruding. So he cast [**Alter Gravity**] on his revolver and started blasting at the fire giants, but it seemed to have little affect. The closest giant did notice Max immediately, though, so he must at least have dealt more damage than the slingshots and throwing hammers. The molten creature peeled a glob of magma from its arm and threw it at Max.

"[Tether]," Max said without thinking and the glob flopped over like a flimsy paper plane. That's when *everyone* in the room noticed him. The shiny black dwarves started talking and pointing and one of the formations moved towards him, shields raised, concern in their strange eyes. Another fireball flew at the group approaching Max and broke through a shield in the air. Max quickly tethered it, and it struck the ground near the dwarves. It exploded violently but only glanced some unfortunate members of the formation. The shocked dwarves jumped and looked frantically back and forth between Max and the giants. Max saw the robed figures making hand gestures and talking fast and loud. They pointed at Max and the sizzling ground where the fireball had landed. The creatures seemed to reach a consensus, and the obsidian men went back to attack the fire giants.

Well, first contact made. Could have been a lot worse. I didn't get thrown into the lava.

Max kept shooting and tethering the fireballs. With Max's help, the obsidian dwarves found their second wind and fought harder than before. The giants were sturdy and the fight went on for a long time. Max had to chug down a Mana potion, but finally they felled one, then another within just seconds.

Defeated Level 16 [Magma Titan (Elite)]
You gained 721 Experience points
Defeated Level 18 [Magma Titan (Elite)]
You gained 338 Experience points

Their bodies fell with a shudder and splash, the stone floor sizzling under each landed corpse. The remaining giants roared in fury at the sight of their fallen brethren.

A third giant turned towards Max and let out a deafening roar. Max could only hear the ringing in his own ears by the time the beast approached him. Some of the obsidian dwarves attacked it as it emerged from the lava, but it swatted at them with a flaming fist and sent them flying.

Then it threw a glob of magma at Max, but he was already running away. Max knew **[Gravity Well]** wouldn't work well, as it hadn't slowed down the giant insect monster before. He needed to do more.

More! *That's it! Well, it might not be, but try or die.*

"[Gravity Well], [Tether], [Tether], [Tether], [Tether]."

First, Max cast the well of gravity at the giant's feet. It clearly slowed the giant down, and it looked down at its own feet in confusion. Then, Max used this time to spam **[Tether]** until his Mana only had a trickle left, just enough to maintain the **[Gravity Well]**. Then, Max tethered the titan's every joint: knees, hip, elbows, neck. Eventually, the colossus curled up into a molten ball and stopped moving. It still struggled against the spell, but it had clearly been defeated.

The obsidian dwarves attacked it immediately and relentlessly. While their picks and hammers had been accurate and nasty when thrown, they were downright devastating when wielded with powerful hacks and strikes against an immobile target. Their black, shiny muscles rippled as they gleefully beat the creature until it finally let out a death rattle.

Defeated Level 16 [Magma Titan (Elite)]
You gained 721 Experience points
Skill Upgrade: [Tether II]
Achievement: First Skill Upgrade
Reward: [E-tier Supply Box]

The remaining **[Magma Titans]** were livid. In their great fury, they threw globs of magma and splashed at the lava, but when a fourth of them stumbled, clearly hurt, they had a quick exchange of roars. All the while, the dwarves threw stones and hammers and spells at them. Angry and hurt, the giants started moving to the back of the room, submerging themselves deeper and deeper into the lava until their heads dropped underneath and just like that, they were gone. They were driven back to wherever the hell they came from.

And with that, every remaining beady eyeball in the room turned to Max. There were still over twenty of them left alive and they surrounded him quickly, pushing in uncomfortably close, while talking to each other excitedly in rumbling, low voices. Some of them raised a pickaxe or a hammer towards Max, more scared than aggressive, but their brethren slapped them in response. The robed figures approached last, using slow dignified steps. The other obsidian dwarves gave way as they came to stand before Max, regarding him with wary curiosity.

"Uggubimimurshubuggimumu," one of them said.

"I'm sorry, what?" Max said and let out a nervous laugh.

The creature that had spoken waved a hand. "Borogorossibamoghibbimu?"

"Ehh . . . That sounded like a question," Max said. "But I can't understand anything you're saying.

"Ibossomigurruboto," the creature said amiably and waved a hand towards the door that Max had come from. It seemed like they wanted to leave.

Max raised a finger. "Just one second."

He went to loot the two molten giants and was stunned to receive 3015 **Cosmic Coins.** Not only that but he found two **[E-grade Material Boxes]**.

"Score!" Max yelled out and pumped a fist in the air. The creatures behind him got spooked and a few of the most nervous ones raised their weapons again, before they were also slapped. They departed when Max came back.

Max didn't feel exactly safe, surrounded from behind and in front by the obsidian dwarves as they walked through the dim corridors. Still, the creatures seemed more like curious children than man-eating monsters. Max hadn't counted out being eaten just yet, but he liked his odds well enough to not sweat overly profusely.

They took a series of turns and passed some of those platform rooms until they reached an ostentatious hall. It was filled with giant hanging drapes of red and black, trimmed with heavy gold rope. To the sides were life-sized statues of these people, only made from jade, gold, and some shiny electric blue metal Max couldn't name.

On the floor was spread a giant red and gold carpet that extended the whole room's length, some thirty yards. There were a lot of these obsidian dwarf people in the room, maybe two hundred or so. They were sitting on long tables, holding drinks, eating food, and discussing.

Among them, large tortoises, the size of dogs, with red skin and black shells, were eating scraps on the floor. Most of their shells were studded with various glittering gems, as if whoever owned them wanted to show off their wealth.

At the end of the room, on a dais carved from stone, five thrones stood high. They were made of that electric blue metal, adorned with gems and gold trimming around the edges. Various fluffy furs lined the seats and handholds.

Five shiny black dwarves sat on these ridiculous seats, dressed up at least as extravagantly as their gaudy chairs. They were shrouded in expensive silks and satins of myriad colors, and gemstones and gold hung from every inch. They regarded Max imperiously, but with badly veiled curiosity as they into dug their pockets for extra rings and necklaces to adorn themselves with before Max was presented to them.

Max was brought in front of them and they gazed on him from their thrones and muttered in their strange rumbling language. Then one of them stood up, holding a gilded staff, studded with a fist-sized ruby. It glowed and flickered like live flame. He looked Max in the eyes with an ancient gaze, deep and keen.

"Can you hear me, Flesh-Thing?"

CHAPTER TWENTY-SIX

Kingly Gifts

There was a slow, rumbling voice inside Max's mind.

Yes? Max thought. *I can hear you.*

Very good, the voice inside his head said.

He gaped at the shiny little man, who smiled back. He turned to the one in the middle. He was the most ostentatious of the five, wearing a three-pronged crown made of that electric blue metal. It swayed dangerously as the king nodded in acknowledgement. Then he addressed Max at length in the strange, rumbling language these people used. By some spell cast seemingly by the one who was standing up, it was instantly translated directly into Max's mind.

Welcome to our home and hearth, Auspicious Stranger. You stand in the Hall of a Thousand Glorious Facets before the Five Kings of Avarice. I am High King Morogostoborikkut. We thank you for helping to repel the attack of the [**Magma Titans**] *and, in doing so, saving the life of one of the crown princes, Prince Kommorotustik, nineteenth in line for the throne.*

Max stared in mute shock the whole time, his brain refusing to work. A stout obsidian dwarf, who Max may or may not have noticed previously, bowed before him. Max didn't know what these people considered polite, but he bowed back just in case. The High King seemed to be pleased by this and he gave Max a dignified nod before speaking again.

You are one of the Children, are you not? Those cast out from the Heavens by the gods? We have not seen flesh-kin come to our realm for two centuries. Does this mean gods conduct these games for you to win back your favor with the Heavens?"

Max was still confused, but he decided to just roll with it. He tried to explain what had happened to him and the whole human race as best he could. He spoke aloud, more so to make sense of the whole thing to himself, than for any other reason. The standing man kept nodding and then announced to the crowd what Max had said.

Fear not, Auspicious Stranger. I am as magnanimous as I am rich, and you will not be ill-treated, even if your people were cast from the Heavens."

"That's not—" Max started but the standing man sharply shook his head and the High King looked outraged for having been interrupted. Max cringed to himself and bowed deeply.

Hm. For having saved my great-great-grandchild, each of the Five Kings will present you with a gift. You may choose one and let the Great Records show which of the kings had the most wealth to give away!

With this announcement, the whole hall burst into cheers, stomping their feet and banging their tables in excitement. The High King clapped his hands and five adjutants approached from the edges of the room to consult with their kings in rumbling whispers. Afterwards, they promptly left through a side door.

Sit and rejoice, Auspicious Stranger! Your courage has brought you the friendship of the kings! While we wait on our treasures to be bought, enjoy our mead and our meat!

With that, dwarves bustled over to Max from all directions, one of them seating him in a stone stool, another placing a small, single-legged table in front of him, and the rest bringing various food and drink, until the table was so overstuffed, a small platter of roasted mushrooms clattered to the floor.

Max bowed again to the kings. He eyed the food with suspicion but decided it was too impolite not to try. The first thing he went for was the steel flagon on the table. He emptied it in two gulps. It was a thick, frothy beer that had an aftertaste to it which reminded Max of moss. It was the most delicious thing Max had ever drunk. It was so hot underground and he had been having such a hell of a day, that he hadn't realized just how parched he'd been. The flagon now empty, Max sighed audibly and burped, slamming the flagon back on the table.

This clearly pleased the High King. He let out a boisterous, rumbling laugh and the whole hall joined him as sycophantically as one might imagine. Immediately afterwards, Max's flagon was filled again and he was thirsty enough to drain half of it down in practically one gulp.

The food consisted of strong-smelling meats, mushrooms, something that might have been boiled moss, and some really ugly fish. Max tried the meat which was spicier than he usually cared for, but at the moment, he didn't care. It was food and he was famished. He didn't know where his next meal would be. Hell, he didn't even know if he would ever get out of *here* alive. So he sweated bullets, coughed and ate, while the kings watched him with rapt attention on their shiny, stone faces, their various expressions showing a range of glee, curiosity, and pensiveness.

Max shoveled the last of the mushrooms into his mouth just as the treasures were being brought into the room. The court gasped as the sight of them. Max's eyes bulged when he saw what was being offered.

First, the King of Taxes, Brumuroggorum, will offer up his treasure!

The court cheered as an aide picked up a cloak. To have described it as gaudy would have been like calling the Statue of Liberty a garden gnome.

It shimmered with a thousand gemstones as the aides came towards Max and put the cloak on his shoulders, pinning it with a thick jade clasp. The shoulders were padded with fist-sized emeralds and on top of the gemstones studded upon every inch of the cloak, golden raindrops hung and chinked merrily as Max moved around in the ridiculous thing. He bowed towards the King of Taxes and unclasped the cloak, taking it in his hands and inspecting it.

[The Mantle of Ministers]
Indestructible
+7 Resistance
+7 Toughness
+22 Charisma
Passive: Increases the effect of your Charisma regarding all your [Leader] skills by 15%
Active: Once a day, make a person below your stature forget an inconvenient fact. This person must be your subordinate in some manner.

Dear god, this is powerful. In all the wrong ways. If Machiavelli's Prince ever wanted something tailor-made . . .

Max did his best to hide his disgust as he gave the cloak back to the aides. The King of Taxes did not look pleased, but he stayed still. The crowd murmured. The High King laughed.

Never has a gift been rejected so quickly! Our Auspicious Guest clearly saw instantly what a cheap rag was offered to him. Let us see if the King of Commerce, Gorobitukkimoshul, can offer something more interesting!

The item on the next trolley was a giant gilded Swiss Army knife. Max picked it up with both of his hands. It weighed so much, he almost dropped it.

[Pocket of A Thousand Tools]
Indestructible
+10 Strength
+10 Dexterity
+10 Constitution

Passive: Increase the yields or effects of all activities that yield [Laborer] experience by 50%
Active: Will always pull the correct tool for the occasion.

Max saw there was a spring mechanism to the side of the giant golden brick. Max pushed it down until something clicked. A stick sprouted from a hole, a compass at the end of it. Max let out a dry chuckle.

Yeah, I'm lost alright. Now, I don't know the full capabilities of this thing, but it looks VALUABLE. If it could turn into a shovel or a spyglass when needed, I could find a great deal of use for it. Maybe it could even be turned into a water filter. And even if I decide I don't need it, the guys at the camp could get tremendous use out of it. This thing alone could kickstart our ability to develop technology at the camp. It could give us an edge that no one else could beat. If we could use it to produce things like industrial glue or weld things together or . . .

Well, Max wasn't sure of all the potential applications, but they were plentiful, to say the least. Max bowed deeply to the King of Commerce and put the prize back on the trolley.

"Oh ho! Our guest liked this one! He managed to summon an otherworldly tool used in the Heavens for who knows what kinds of miracle work. He might think he wants this one, but he has not yet seen my gift. Behold!"

The High King's trolley was the largest and, while the others were made of some black metal, the High King settled for no less than gold, studded with tiny diamonds. Whatever was on the trolley was hidden underneath a heavy silk blanket, weighed down by emerald tassels. The aides revealed what was under the veil with a skillful flourish.

It was a statue made of that strange bright blue metal. The court *oohed* in unison. Clearly the alloy was valuable. Max went closer to inspect the statue. It was the shape of a nondescript humanoid. It had longer legs and a slimmer torso than these obsidian dwarves, so it could have even passed for a human, which is probably why it was being offered as a gift. Max tried to inspect it, but got . . . nothing.

This is . . . Just a statue?

As valuable as it must have been, Max had no interest in lugging the world's most pompous paperweight through the Dreadlands. He quickly turned to bow to the High-King, who got up violently and snarled angrily, bearing a gilded sword.

CHAPTER TWENTY-SEVEN

A Choice of Kings

The whole court gasped as the High-King boomed.

THIS IS A GRAVE INSULT TO MY PERSON AND I WILL NOT—
What is it, Durumurammagorstorus?

The translator had turned to the High King and was now whispering a rapid stream of words in his ear. The High King sheathed his sword and Max let out a long breath. Then the High King turned to Max and bowed to him, Max immediately reciprocating. Then he proceeded with the ceremony.

I apologize for my hotheadedness. It is my only weakness. King Durumurammagorstorus has just told me that the Auspicious Stranger explained to him that he is a humble member of a simple gatherer society and a statue of pure Truesilver would be too grand a gift for his stature. He says he would dishonor my glory by accepting such a kingly gift, being so low of stature himself. In my exceeding gracefulness, I accept the forfeit!"

The court cheered and Max tried to look as humble as he could. He took a glance at the translator, who gave the slightest shake of his head in response.

You're welcome, Flesh-Thing. You can repay me by choosing my gift. But if you choose not to, you will owe me a favor.

Max didn't know what choosing a king's gift would entail, but the man had just saved his life, possibly while risking his own by lying to the High King. And as seemingly civilized as the obsidian people were, they were clearly unpredictable and it wouldn't hurt to have an ally. The High King addressed the court again.

*Next to display his wealth is Durumurammagorstorus himself, King of Treasures! Can he offer something better than the [**Pocket of A Thousand Tools**], which our guest expressed keen interest towards. Let us see!*

A black samite veil was lifted and on the trolley was revealed a . . . sack. Granted, it was a beautiful sack made of purple silk with golden embroidery adorning it. Max went up to the trolley and looked inside. Within it were thumb-sized marbles, colored in hues of white and gold. Max picked one up and inspected it.

[Celestial Illumination Pill]
D-grade cultivation pill
Effects: ???
Level requirement to consume not met.

A bold choice by the King of Treasures! Not as flashy as the other gifts have been, but certainly a kingly gift of exceeding value. A thousand cultivation pills of this grade could buy a palace!

Max didn't know what these "pills" were for or how useful a gift this might be to him, but he felt he would have to pick it nonetheless, as much as the giant golden Swiss Army knife called to him. He bowed to the King of Treasures and moved to the last trolley to make a perfunctory final performance.

The last item, presented by the King of Finance, was revealed to be a gorgeous ivory hunting bow that came with a leather quiver of silver scrollwork. In the flickering light of the room's myriad braziers and torches, the bowstring seemed to glitter like gold. Max picked up the bow and inspected it.

[Hydra Slaying Bow]
Weapon type: Bow
Damage: 52–104
+13 Dexterity
+13 Precision
Passive: Deals 25% extra damage to all Lizard creatures.
Active: Once per hour, the bow can be strung without an arrow. It will fire a magical arrow, always resulting in maximum damage.

Powerful. It deals pretty much double the damage I'm able to with [**The Maverick**]. *And that's without any Attribute points considered. Not really useful to me, though.*

Max bowed to the last king and let the High King hype up the audience for the climactic moment, at which point Max was supposed to step up to his chosen trolley. Max let the dramatic tension gather, both for the benefit of the court as well as to make sure he had made up his mind. He really wanted the [**Pocket of A Thousand Tools**]. It would provide immense value to his community and help them build faster than any rival Max could imagine. But choosing that treasure meant he would also owe the King of Treasures a favor. He could always betray him, but seeing as the king could apparently read his mind, it didn't seem like a wise idea. Thus, Max decided and finally stepped towards the beautiful purple sack of pills. The court cheered. The King of Treasures stepped towards the edge of the dais and bowed to the court and finally to Max, while flashing a meaningful look to him. Max bowed back.

After the court proceedings had adjourned, Durumurammagorstorus, King of Treasures, had taken Max back with him to his chambers. Once they had reached his ostentatious estates of gold, glamor, and glitter via the obsidian mazes, they walked into his study, and the king told his aides to leave.

Now Max was standing in this refined space, with beautifully carved stone furniture and bookshelves of ornately carved wood. Carpets worth fortunes covered the floor of white marble.

The King of Treasures rummaged through his notes and books without so much as glancing at Max. Finally, he found what he was looking for. He pulled up the corner of one of the carpets and spread a circle of salt on the floor. Then he clapped his hands and the salt circle glowed blue. The obsidian dwarf motioned for Max to step into the circle.

With some reservations, Max complied, hoping that he wouldn't turn into a stout rock person. After a moment, however, Max sensed nothing out of the ordinary.

Then Durumurammagorstorus spoke.

"Can you understand me?"

Max's eyes went as wide as saucers. "Holy crap. Yeah, I understand you."

"Very good. As you may have picked up on, I Am Durumurammagorstorus. Please just call me Durum. You chose wisely."

"Yeah . . ." Max said. "What are those pills anyway?"

"All in good time," Durum said. "You'll thank me on your knees for them later, I can promise you that."

"So, who the hell are you people?"

"Now that is an astute question," Durum said. "If I said we are not natives of this planet, what would you say?"

"I'd say that's crazy," Max said and laughed. "That would mean . . . Wait, does that mean what I think it means?"

"It means our race was a contestant in this game you're engaged in."

"But that's not possible," Max said and sat down in the circle. It had been a long day. "The Zoos guys said that once the game ends, three races are extinct and the winning race will get to go back to their planet."

"And yet, this planet is full of all sorts of people, clustered in small communities or cities. Most of the ancient ones have devolved into beasts, though. We believe we are a rather recent addition to the planet's fauna."

"But that contradicts what the Zoos guys said," Max said.

"And you believed them?"

"They said they can't use deceit," Max said.

"And you believed them?" Durum said and shook his head laughing drily.

"And you're saying you know the truth?" Max asked, skeptically.

"Yes," Durum said. "No. Well, some of it. I have theories and I have educated guesses."

"Doesn't sound like much to go by,"

"It's better than lies," Durum said sharply. "Here is what I think. I think my people are the descendants of a race that won the games but refused to return to their planet."

Max blinked dumbly. "But why? Why would you not want to return after you won?"

Durum clasped his hands behind his back and started pacing in front of Max. "Another good question. One that I cannot answer with verifiable fact, only speculation. The reason why you're here is because I want to uncover the truth."

"The reason I'm here is because I got chased off by a giant insect monster," Max quipped.

Durum gave him a sharp look.

No jokes. Got it. Yikes, what a grouch.

"I can still read your thoughts, you know."

"Yeah, I don't think I like that," Max said.

Durum shrugged.

"So what do you need me for?" Max asked.

"My people used to live deeper underground," Durum said. "I'm not exactly sure what drove us out of there. Now the way in is trapped and we possess no tools or magic that can be used to break through."

"But I do?" Max said. Durum nodded.

"Your description of the fight with the [**Magma Titans**] matches what the miners told us. You can use gravity magic. This is a rare branch of magic. With it, you can help us get in and lead the expedition to the ruins."

"Just hold on for a second," Max said, growing increasingly annoyed at being bulldozed by the king. "I have my own problems. I need to be Leveling and gathering resources, to make sure my people survive."

"I see," Durum said. "I did save your life, though. It would be a shame for that to have been in vain."

"Are you saying you'll kill me if I don't comply?" Max asked.

Durum made a disgusted face. "What kind of a brute do you think I am? Of course not! But the High King will have your life the minute you leave my protection."

"What?"

"There is another cog spinning in this clockwork," Durum said. "I have wanted to launch an expedition to search the ruins and try to pry open the entrance before.

But I haven't had the political pull. Every time, the High King has thwarted my attempts. But you chose me in the gift ceremony."

"And that was a big deal?" Max asked, arching an eyebrow.

"A huge deal," Durum said. "It gave me enough political power to make some splashes. That leaves you in a very unfortunate position, however."

"I'm not sure I follow," Max said.

"The High King is no fool. He knew he was giving you a useless gift that you would immediately turn down. This way, he had an excuse to kill you. He didn't think I would lie for you, and now that I have, things are . . . complicated."

"Why would the High King want to kill me?" Max asked.

"He is the High King," Durum simply said. "He is the biggest fish in the smallest of ponds. He does not want me making splashes, and he knows I will need you, both for influence and for your abilities. The High King fears what change might come from opening the ruins. And he fears the Wrath of Heavens from poking into the history of the 'gods'. Zealous fool."

"By 'gods,' you mean—"

"Of course I mean the beings that teleported your race here," Durum snapped impatiently. "The High King has had his view of reality distorted, and the potential for new information and treasures could upset his status as the High King. To make it all go away is as simple as just killing you."

"So if I just try to leave, I'll be assassinated?"

Durum gave him a grim nod.

CHAPTER TWENTY-EIGHT

Insights

S o, unless I help you, I'm getting bodied by the High King," Max snarled. "How convenient for you."

Durum spread his hands. "I did not get to my current position by not stacking the deck in my favor."

Max glowered at Durum. Durum gave him an apologetic smile.

"Listen, Max. This will be worth your while. The ruins will be full of powerful monsters and potentially valuable artifacts. I am already rich. More wealth won't increase my influence. All I want is the records. The lesser houses of my liege will want the riches, but you will get your share."

Max grumbled. It didn't sound bad, but he didn't like being used.

"Help me, and I will have enough power over the High King to save your life," Durum said.

"You could have your people escort me out of this place right now and I could go off on my merry way."

"I could," Durum simply said.

"But you're not going to?" Max said.

"I'm offering you an opportunity to grow. If you can succeed in this, you will profit more than by running away from what you refer to as 'giant insect monsters'."

"Okay, you do make a good point," Max admitted. "But I don't like the way you're doing it."

"I don't need you to like it. I'm your king, not your friend."

"I don't do well with authority," Max said.

Durum chuckled. "Make yourself useful to me and you might find yourself befriending a king. That could be a valuable boon for you, Max."

"I'll do it," Max said. "You don't leave me with a choice, but I'm on board. If this expedition will make me stronger faster, you don't even need to hold an axe over my head."

"I like to hear that," Durum said. "And it will. You have my word as a king. If you pull this off and I gain my goals, there is another reward at the end of all this on top of all the loot and Experience."

"Oh?" Max said, perking up. "Like what?"

"I will teach you what those pills are and how to use them."

Max scoffed. "Fine. So how do we do this?"

"For you, it is a simple matter," Durum said. "You will be assigned chambers in my estate. You will be provided with appropriate food, and you will rest and wait. And you will *not* leave the chambers."

"For how long?"

Annoyance flashed on Durum's face. "As long as it takes me to prepare the expedition. I will not go myself for obvious reasons. I will have this language spell imbued into an amulet and given to one of my aides who will lead the expedition. I will grease the wheels and pull the ropes. It should not take long."

Max made a face. He did not like the idea of waiting in a room for an undetermined amount of time doing nothing. He should be out there killing things.

"I see this does not please you." Durum said. "Don't worry, I will have you suitably preoccupied."

"I'm listening," Max said, crossing his arms.

Durum went to a beautifully carved stone chest and opened it. It was full of potions of all kinds. Durum picked a purple one out of the stack, then came back over to Max and handed it to him.

[Potion of Greater Mana Regeneration]

"Do what it says," Durum said.

"Thanks?" Max said. "Which is?"

"Drink it," Durum said. "I will have more brought to you. I want you casting spells in your room until you're sick of it."

"Why? To increase my Skill Levels?"

"Those won't hurt," Durum said. "But what I want you to do is to get intimate with the spells. Feel the shape of them. Feel the Mana inside your body and in the spell."

Max scratched his head. "I have no idea what you're talking about."

"That's why I am giving you so many potions," Durum said. "Just do as I say. It is preparation for when you're able to ingest the pills I have given you."

"Fine," Max grumbled.

Max had been escorted to a simple, but beautiful room. There was a stone bench and table, a pool of warm water in the corner, and a bed. A BED! It was a beautiful four-poster with a soft mattress. Max fell upon it immediately and sighed. He would sleep in a bed tonight. Indoors, even! He would have curled up under the satin sheets immediately if he knew he had then time to spare. But he didn't. He had to practice *feeling* the Mana of his spells, whatever the hell that meant. He had a crate of those purple potions waiting for him, and a pile of black leather balls in another crate. Durum had asked him if he needed training equipment, and heavy balls had seemed appropriate. The room was spacious, but it wasn't exactly a gym. It was large enough to move the balls around it, but small enough that they would still likely hit something. Fortunately there wasn't much to break.

Before Max delved into "feeling the Mana", he wanted to look into the Skill Upgrade on [**Tether**] he had gotten. Max went up to his notifications and brought up the relevant one.

Skill upgraded to [Tether II]
You can now alternate between attraction and repulsion between targets. The ability now ignores a portion of the target's weight and Resistance stat. Mana cost increased to 20.

"Hot Damn!" Max said to himself. "This opens up a whole new world of possibilities. Let's see how it works."

Max picked up one of the leather balls and raised his arm out straight. Then he tethered the ball and the palm of his hand in a repulsion bond. The hefty leather ball shot out of his hand and thudded half a second later into a wall. If aimed at a regular human, the ball flew fast enough to cause injuries. Of course, a human augmented with the Framework would only take some Damage from it.

It works like two magnets of the same charge. Really powerful magnets. Now, the offensive capabilities of this upgrade would be awesome, if I didn't already have a gun. But I'm sure I can think of some ways to use this to hinder enemies.

Next, Max opened his boxes from the fight with the [**Magma Titans**]. First in line was the supply box. It provided Max with [**Rope (E-grade)**], which he was quite happy with. He hadn't had a desperate need for a rope so far, but he was sure it would come in handy eventually. Next up was the [**E-grade Equipment Box**] which could be exciting or useless to him. Well, even if it was the latter, he could still give it to someone in Joshua's camp.

[Quiver of D—]
[Firearm detected . . .]
[Changing reward]
[Gun holster of Fine Leather (E-grade)]

+3 Precision
+2 Dexterity

Max was *elated*. Carrying [**The Maverick**] had been extremely cumbersome. Its status as a Soulbound weapon meant he couldn't even tuck it away in his pocket dimension Inventory. That effectively made him one-handed. But this would change everything. There was a thick leather strap attached to a holster. Max slung the thing over his shoulder and stuffed his weapon into it. It was a little small, but with some wiggling and struggling, he managed to get [**The Maverick**] in there snuggly enough to fasten a buckle against the grip of the weapon. The end of the barrel was left hanging around Max's butt. While it was a clumsier setup than one might wish for, it was a vast improvement over having to carry the damned thing everywhere. Max sighed in relief.

Although he was desperate to go to sleep at this point, first he practiced more with the repulsion effect of his upgraded [**Tether**] spell. He tethered two balls together and watched how they interacted. He tethered a ball and a spot on the wall and tried throwing the ball at the spot. It flew back and hit Max on the shoulder, costing him a few Health points.

He went on like this until his Mana was spent. Then he decided it was time to chug one of those purple potions and try to "feel the Mana."

The potion was very powerful. It immediately started ticking Max's Mana up at a rate of two per second. He didn't know how long the effect would last, but he had a stack of them, which meant he could be casting one [**Tether**] every ten seconds for a very long time.

At first. Max didn't really understand what he was supposed to do.

Feel the Mana? What is this hippie shit?

He kept tethering the balls in various ways and chugging the purple potions. He was brought food and drink at some point along with another crate of those potions. Max took a break to replenish and continued.

He noticed his Stamina was ticking down and the exhaustion was kicking in. He slammed down a [**Minor Stamina Potion**] just to keep going for a little longer. Just to see if he'd figure something out.

While there was a certain "feel" to him choosing which objects to tether and whether to use repulsion or attraction, he didn't know where to go from there. Max decided to just focus on that feeling and to see if anything happened.

After spending somewhere between two to three hours of casting, Max had certainly improved his command of [**Tether**]. It was now second nature to him to cast almost as fast as he could think. It would be very useful tactically. But as to any new sensations regarding "feeling the Mana"? It was hard to say. He felt like he could feel the Mana depleting as his bar went down. That was a new sensation. Before, when Max had cast a spell, his only indication of doing so was the blue bar in the upper corner of his vision. Now he had some faint feeling of casting it.

Max was encouraged by this and thought he was probably heading in the right direction. He would ask Durum next time he got a chance. But for now, he was way too tired in all sorts of ways to go further. Max dragged himself to that sweet soft bed and fell into a dreamless slumber almost immediately.

CHAPTER TWENTY-NINE

Mana Negotiations

Max woke up feeling refreshed like never before. Having slept probably for around twelve hours, he truly felt like a million bucks. Being able to sleep indoors in a real bed without imminent danger hanging over your head made quite the difference.

Max got up and found himself smiling properly for the first time in a while. Who wakes up smiling?

Max decided it would do him no good to waste this exuberant energy and so he ate breakfast quickly and got to casting **[Tether]**. Upon starting, Max realized that he noticed the Mana expenditure much more acutely. That's what a good night of sleep will do for one's ability to process and learn.

While focusing on the feeling of expending Mana, Max wanted to also get a feel for the spell. He took a leather ball in both hands and tethered it to a wall. Then he held the ball at a distance where there was a strong pull but not enough to prevent him from keeping hold of the ball.

He shifted around, taking a few steps backwards and to the sides, to try to get a feel for it. Feel for what specifically? Max still couldn't put his finger on it, but he was starting to get some sort of an idea.

Max closed his eyes and sat down with the ball and tried to sense the tug of the spell. Then he let the spell go and spammed **[Tether]**, trying to get a feel for what happened when the spell was cast. How was the tether between objects formed?

Max meditated on this question for a long while. Durum's aides came to check up on him and left him food, but Max paid them little mind. He was absorbed with figuring out the nature of the spells and Mana, now that he knew what he was looking for. Well, he didn't know exactly. But he followed his intuition; it was definitely leading him somewhere.

Durum came by later, wearing the enchanted amulet, and told him that the motion to mount the expedition had gone well. It would require some bureaucracy and cashing in old favors and gathering up volunteers to get them on the move, but it wouldn't take long. They exchanged a few words and Max asked Durum for advice. He refused to give any, claiming that Max had to figure it out himself. Max asked for a crate of Stamina potions and it was delivered to him shortly after Durum had left.

Enjoying the abundance of resources, good food, and comfortable lodgings, he delved deeper into the study of Mana. He must have cast **[Tether]** several hundreds of times. It didn't provide him with a Skill Upgrade, most likely because he wasn't using it in combat nor doing anything creative with it. But the training was still making him more proficient, as he was now able to make a tether lightning-fast, practically without even thinking about it. Max was eager to try it out in combat, and he had a feeling that time would come soon enough.

As for the research into Mana, it was harder. Max had definitely begun to feel things and, while he couldn't name what he had learned about Mana, it was getting ingrained into his body. He could feel the Mana leaving his body every time he cast **[Tether]**. On top of that, he could sense a sort of a *string* between the tethered objects. It wasn't anything visible, but it was clearly there. It gave him an intuitive understanding of how much tension existed between the objects. When he held a ball in his hands, he knew just how fast it would fly towards the wall just by trying to sense the string. Once he was sure the string was indeed there and he could sense it at will, he would get a notification.

[??? Unlocked]
Level requirement to use not met
[Talent unlocked: ???]
Level requirement to use not met

Max sat down on the stone floor and started to laugh. All this work for *that*? This had to be what Durum had made him work towards. Max didn't know what it was, but it had better be good once he met the Level requirement. Maybe Durum would actually tell him more now. Max wondered what Level he needed to unlock whatever he had just gained. Fifteen? Twenty?

Max decided it was a good idea to pocket the remaining potions. There weren't too many, but he'd take what he could. The purple Mana regeneration potions were clearly especially valuable. He tallied up what he had before putting them in his Inventory.

4x [Potion of Mana Regeneration]
5x [Stamina Potion]

Max wondered what grade of potion the stamina ones were. Clearly higher than the minor versions he had been using so far. These new ones always restored him to full Stamina.

The next hour or so, Max spent his time learning to draw [**The Maverick**] from the holster as fast and smoothly as he could. It was clumsy work, and he needed to twist his torso to get it out. But if he wanted to be hands-free, learning to draw fast might just save his life. Max hoped it would never come to that, but he knew failing to prepare was preparing to fail. It was tedious work, but when the stakes were his life, Max found himself highly motivated. He would have continued the practice further if Durum hadn't eventually entered with his aides.

"Hello, Max," Durum said and took a glance at the empty potion crates. "I see you have been hard at work."

Max gave him a nervous chuckle, but Durum just smiled knowingly.

"Have you learned anything?"

"I have," Max said. "I unlocked a bunch of stuff, but I have no idea what they are."

"You unlocked something already?" Durum asked, surprise lacing his rumbling voice. "This was faster than expected. Very interesting."

"What is it that I was training for? How will it be useful?"

"It is another layer of the Framework," Durum said. "Maybe even the main layer. It is the reason the Attributes and Abilities exist."

"I don't really understand," Max said.

"I don't expect you to," Durum snapped impatiently. "Just know that it is useful for you to learn this. When you unlock the System and retrieve the necessary records and manuals from the ruins we need, I will teach you more."

"You're telling me less than you know," Max grumbled.

"As is my prerogative as a king," Durum said. "Now, the preparations are done. The expedition is scheduled to leave in an hour. My aide Rulgumarogommos will lead the expedition, and you will be second in command, Max."

Max didn't know what to say to that, so he bowed. The king reciprocated.

"We will prepare you with a few more supplies to add to those potions you intended to steal," Durum said, and a smile tugged at the side of his shiny black lips. It seemed the Kings of Avarice could appreciate a little opportunism. "Grab anything you need and come. Oh, and one more thing, Max, before I give this amulet to Rulgum."

"What is it?"

"As your king, I order you to come back alive and bring me the records."

Max chuckled. "Yes, my liege."

CHAPTER THIRTY

Ruins of the Ancestors

With Durum leading them and Max walking three steps behind with the aide, they arrived at a large room with one of the seemingly ubiquitous obsidian platforms overlooking lava. On the other side of the room were giant doors wrought of stone and metal. The metal had numerous scuff marks and chips taken out of it, clearly as a result of having survived various violent attempts at opening the doors.

Durum said some words to the people gathered. Besides the thirty or so obsidian dwarves who were going to be delving the ruins with Max, there were around two or three hundred people packed tightly together. The platform heaved and bobbed underneath them, but the aide, Rulgum, assured Max it was stable. That didn't stop him sweating bullets, but he had no choice but to deal.

After giving what sounded like a quite ceremonious speech, Durum turned to them and touched the amulet on the aide's neck.

"You had better not let me down now, Max."

Max nodded. He was pretty sure it would work. Mainly because they had come here earlier and had actually managed to almost open the doors. But of course they had had to slink back to Durum's estates afterwards, making sure nobody had seen. And delivering a shiny speech before performing a stunt such as opening the doors to the ancient secrets of your ancestors was just good politics.

Max walked up to the platform's edge. There was a rectangular stone slab almost buried by the lava. It was most likely some white or gray stone, but it was hard to be sure, as it shone with an orange gleam, heated by the lava.

Max started casting [**Tether**].

He cast several spells to the front of the slab and attached them to the platform he was standing on. Then he cast some repulsive tethering to the back of the slab, from both the opposing wall and the slowly swirling lava itself. Max didn't actually see the tethering points, but it seemed like it didn't matter, now that he had a more intimate command of Mana in general.

The giant stone slab started moving. Max chugged down a Mana potion and kept casting [**Tether**]. The stone slab slowly started sliding towards the platform's edge. As it did that, the giant stone and metal doors creaked and began to open. Everyone in the audience gasped. Max chuckled to himself as he cast elaborate hand signs and gesticulated like a classic wizard. None of it was necessary for him to cast [**Tether**]. It was just some added flair that Durum had requested of him.

When the giant doors finally swung open all the way, uproarious cheers filled the chamber. Durum smiled and waved a hand heavy with gleaming rings and bowed to Max, who reciprocated the gesture.

With that, it was time for their expedition to leave. The obsidian dwarves spent some time checking their packs and other gear. They had no access to the pocket dimension Inventory, despite most of them having Stats. In fact, all of them had Stats and Attributes, as these were the finest warriors of Durum. They were very low-Level and weak individually as far as Max was concerned, but he definitely appreciated any help given.

As they stepped inside, the first thing Max noticed how precipitously the temperature dropped only ten yards from where they had started. It was also pitch black in there, the faint light from the room they'd left already too far away to have any impact. The group lit their torches and moved forwards, quietly, anxiously. On the floor were broken bits of stone and bones black as night.

"Are these the bones of your people?" Max asked Rulgum.

"Yes," he replied quietly.

They didn't talk much more for the next hour. Everyone seemed wary and on edge, as if the environment itself were exerting a sort of psychic pressure upon them. Max was sure that everyone felt it. There was a *dread* to the place. Intermittently, they heard some distant voice, almost like a faraway lamentation. Max didn't know what it was, but he sure didn't like it.

An hour later, they started to hear skulking around them, faint echoes of soft steps on stone and tiny rocks falling. They inserted their torches into various cobwebbed sconces on the walls. Rulgum ordered a group to enter rooms one at a time. They steeled themselves before stepping into the unknown. They checked five rooms, and all were clear. But the dread was growing. There was something *bad* here.

"Why did your people leave this place?" Max asked.

"It's not clear," the aide said. "Not even King Durum knows, and he is the highest priest of knowledge among our kind. It is believed that the ruins were overtaken by lava, or that the Heavens brought a plague down upon them."

"There are a lot of bones on the ground," Max said. "Maybe it was a plague."

Max paused for a moment and then continued, "Rulgum, whatever horror came upon your ancestors, do you think it's still down here?"

There was worry in Rulgum's eyes. "I don't think all of us will be leaving this place alive."

When they reached the sixth room, they finally encountered something. As soon as the first dwarf entered, something let out a horrible shriek and jumped at him, his scream swiftly turning into a gurgle.

Seconds later, the ugliest thing Max had ever seen emerged from the doorway.

It had two bulging yellow eyes, bloodshot and wild, set on an elongated rat-like face, sharp, black teeth protruding from its mouth. It was skinny and probably only five feet tall of gleaming black obsidian, ominously hunched over. To the trembling dwarves it must have seemed like a nightmare, but for Max it was just another creature to dispatch. He didn't hesitate. He tethered the creature to the doorway and started blasting at it.

It screeched and pulled itself away. Despite being hindered by the spell, it was clearly extremely strong, as with the same motion, it also slammed two dwarves against a nearby wall. They groaned but had survived. Max kept his distance, and blasted it, while tethering it again to a spot on the wall. The dwarves poked at it with spears and threw hammers and shot arrows at it. Eventually it let out a final groan and fell on the dusty floor with a thud.

Defeated Level 10 [Twisted Wretch]
You gained 150 Experience points
Achievement: [First Player Kill]
Reward: 3x [Health Potion]

All of the dwarves looked at each other in shock. Max approached the dead creature. As he did, he received a prompt to loot it and was surprised to receive 208 **Cosmic Coins**. But what was really strange were the System messages. This had been . . . a player?

It didn't have a name. It easily could have just been any other monster Max had killed. Was the System mistaken or was this . . . ?

Max looked at the hideous, twisted body on the ground and then at the dwarves looking after their wounded. Both had the same gleaming obsidian skin. Not much else was alike. Their statures and faces were all drastically different. Max produced a knife from his Inventory and stabbed at the monster's palm. The skin was as hard as expected. Not as hard as obsidian stone, or Max would probably be missing a finger, but hard like hard candy. It took some wiggling and sawing with the knife to get into the flesh. If humans had to fight these guys without Stats and with only primitive weapons at their disposal, they'd take a beating. These guys had natural armor.

Eventually Max got through the skin and flesh to find what he was searching for. It confirmed his suspicions. He called Rulgum to his side.

"Look," Max said. "Black bones."

It was as if the aide's glossy obsidian skin went a shade paler at the notion. Somehow these twisted monsters were related to the dwarves.

Max didn't understand what Rulgum told the other dwarves, but they seemed very distressed. They muttered to each other and argued with the aide. Eventually, Rulgum got them back in line and they continued on.

Max was lost in thought. He wasn't concerned with the Achievement he had attained. He was concerned with the one he hadn't gotten. He hadn't gotten the World's First Player Kill. Somewhere out there, people were already murdering each other. It could have been just a single event, it could have been a couple, it could have been death by the thousands.

The numbers didn't matter. What mattered was the reminder that this wasn't a game. This was serious. This was a fight for the survival of Max's species.

CHAPTER THIRTY-ONE

Gauntlet

Max roared as he kept shooting at the horde of monsters crowding the hall-way, adrenaline rushing through his system. They clambered over each other, claws raised, screaming and rushed towards the line of dwarves. Their hordes seemed endless. Ever since they had killed the first, it was as if the ruins had awakened. First, there had been distant cries that seemed to have an almost questioning tone. Then other voices joined in, creating a discordant chorus seemed to grow increasingly bloodthirsty and ominous. And the cacophony started to grow closer and closer until finally it seemed to explode upon the expedition.

It was a massacre. Max could keep most of them at bay with **[Gravity Well]** and the stragglers could be slowed down with **[Tether]**, but there were too many of them. Max had already drunk a **[Potion of Greater Mana Regeneration]** and now he found his trusty revolver clicking empty for the first time ever. It was an insignificant sound in itself. Just the faintest of noises. But the significance of that empty click made Max's blood run cold. They were being overwhelmed.

Max was no coward. He chugged down a Mana potion and raised his arm again. It trembled. This wasn't fear. This was despair.

"We need to fall back!" Max shouted to the aide.

"WE HOLD THE LINE," he shot back. "IF WE TURN, THEY WILL HUNT US DOWN LIKE ANIMALS!"

Four obsidian dwarves had already been ripped to pieces. Max had already Leveled twice, so dense was the stream of horrors that poured towards them.

Max allowed himself a glance backwards between shots. Still no screeches or sounds of movement. It seemed that at least they wouldn't have to fight on two fronts. They would eventually be overrun. He could attempt to flee, but return-ing alone with no prize probably wouldn't bode well for him either.

"CHARGE!" the aide bellowed and twenty obsidian dwarf warriors raised their shields high and drove the enemy backwards. Max could release his

[Gravity Well] since the enemy had no space to push forwards. They scrambled at the shield wall, claws raking metal and stone. Horrible, bulging yellow eyes gleamed with murder as they screamed in relentless rage.

Then a resonant wail carried through the corridors, and everyone froze.

Max tried to move and fire **[The Maverick]**, but he found that he couldn't. He was frozen still, holding his weapon high up in the air. In the upper-right corner of Max's vision, a symbol of some strange status message appeared. Max couldn't say what it was.

The wail came again. A lonely, sorrowful wail from somewhere far away and from an indistinct direction, like the underwater call of a humpback whale. High and low notes mixed in an eerie cacophony of distress. It sounded like something was dying of sorrow somewhere dark and lonely.

The status started flickering. The yellow-eyed monsters began to recover. Instead of attacking the dwarves again, however, they gibbered to each other, horror plain to see in their giant yellow eyes. Whatever made those sounds, they seemed to be familiar with it. They pushed each other backwards and slinked back into the darkness, completely forgetting their previous prey.

All of the dwarves and Max slumped on the ground a moment later. The debuff was gone and they could move again. Max noticed his Stamina was drained to zero. As when his Health dropping to zero hadn't resulted in his death, losing all of his Stamina didn't make him pass out. But it did cause him *extreme* lethargy. It was physically painful to even keep his eyes open. There wasn't much he could see in the barely lit hallway, but he knew if he let his eyes close, he would immediately lose consciousness.

He rolled on his stomach and tried to push himself up off the floor. It was about as productive as trying to jump up towards the sky to reach the sun. It was simply not happening. His muscles strained and Max tried to fight the pain, but it was no use. His body was useless. With great effort, he produced a **[Minor Stamina Potion]** from his Inventory and brought it to his lips. He sucked the tiny bottle dry and saw his Stamina rise by one hundred points. As if by a miracle, suddenly his mind was capable of feeling something other than pain and fatigue, and his body worked. He was still breathing heavily, and his clothes were soaked with cold sweat. He needed a break and he was pretty sure the dwarves could use one too. Max went up to them and fed them sips of **[Stamina Potion]** as well.

It felt bad using up such valuable resources, but this was no place to be stingy. He needed these people to get out of this hellhole alive. Besides, the potions were courtesy of King Durum. If he ever made it out of this place in one piece, Max was sure he could ask for more.

"We need to fall back," Max said to Rulgum after they'd gotten all of the dwarves up. The dwarves had potions on their person as well, so Max had only needed to spend two.

"You don't understand," the aide said. "If we return empty-handed, our king's pride and station will be weakened."

"Is that more important to you than your own goddamn life?!" Max asked, slamming a fist into the wall.

Rulgum looked at Max with a steady gaze. "Yes."

That was all he said. Max sighed. All of these people were willing to die before admitting defeat and they had dragged Max into this mess. Max cursed himself, these damned ruins and these damned dwarves. They would need a special kind of luck to make it out of this place alive.

They had almost been overwhelmed by the [**Twisted Wretches**] and there was something here that was so sinister that it made those horrible twisted creatures mortified. Max had no idea how they could defeat whatever it was that had wailed through the corridors and stunned a group of over twenty warriors.

But for now, Max could only do his best. He brought up his Stats and spent all of his free points on Intelligence.

They needed raw firepower to get through this nightmare. Max was head and shoulders above anyone else in the expedition in terms of combat prowess and Damage capabilities, and it wouldn't hurt to capitalize on that fact.

Name: Max Cromwell
Class: Graviturgist
Level: 12
Health: 210/210
Stamina: 101/210
Mana: 13/380
Alliance: Joshua's Group
Stats:
Strength: 4
Dexterity: 6
Constitution: 21
Intelligence: 38
Wisdom: 27
Charisma: 4
Precision: 10
Toughness: 6
Resistance: 4

Max had noticed that his [**Tether**] spell was doing some heavy lifting. Maybe it was his increasingly higher Intelligence or his newfound understanding of Mana or both, but it could now hinder very strong opponents, such as the black wretches of this ruin. These monsters were brutally strong, and they made short work of the frontlines of the dwarves, if they got clean hits in.

It was expensive to keep casting in an all-out brawl like this, when there were so many targets, but Max was happy to see his power increase. No human or human-like alien could escape his spell if it came to that. At least not one with the same Resistance stat as these monsters.

That made Max realize that he would really need to do something about his defensive Stats if he were going to fight the other species in the future. Who knew what kind of spells they would have at their disposal?

Focus. You need to get out of here alive first. What can you do to make sure that happens?

"We need to rest," Max said. "At least a few hours."

The aide looked at him, not particularly pleased. Then he looked at the men slumped against the stone walls and lying wounded on the floor. He gave Max a curt nod. "Let us find an easily defensible room."

With that. they nodded in agreement and gathered everyone up and found themselves a place to rest and lick their wounds. Despite barring the door and keeping careful watch, none of them slept easy in the darkness.

CHAPTER THIRTY-TWO

End of the Road

Max napped lightly, just enough to stave off exhaustion. He couldn't sleep. He wouldn't. He needed to think of a way to keep them alive in this mess. He eventually devised a plan and finally allowed himself a wink of sleep. When he woke up, he went over to Rulgum, who was keeping watch at the door.

"Hear anything?" Max asked as he sat down.

"Just some skulking around and sniffing," Rulgum said. "They know we're out here somewhere, but as feral as they are, they don't really check door by door."

"Lucky for us," Max muttered. "How do you want to proceed?"

"We move deeper into the ruins, checking one room at a time. Something valuable is bound to come up."

Simple man, simple plan.

"What if we get overwhelmed?" Max asked.

Rulgum gave him a disgruntled look. "Then we fight like last night."

"We would have died without that wailer in the distance," Max said. "We need a more tactical approach."

The aide let out a long string of rumbling mutterings that Max didn't catch.

"I'm assuming you have one, or did you come sit here just to annoy me?"

"Last time when we got attacked, we just held our ground," Max said as patiently as he could muster. "This left us open to an attack from our back and—"

"Did we get attacked from the back?" Rulgum asked. "No?"

Max closed his eyes and bit on the inside of his cheek.

"Lucky thing we didn't," Max said a little more coldly than was necessary. "But to add to that, the corridor we held ground in was wide and several of them could come up and attack us."

"Just get to the point," Rulgum said.

"Every time we move forward, we need to have a defensible room behind us to fall back into. One person with a torch should stay behind everyone and mark the door towards which we all immediately head when we see enemies."

Rulgum regarded Max with a thoughtful, discerning look. It wasn't entirely hostile but it also wasn't exactly friendly.

"This is a cowardly way. And it will take a very long to make progress."

"I'd rather be slow and cowardly than dead," Max said. "We can't bring anything valuable back to your king if we are all dead."

The aide scoffed. He gave one last cold look to Max, before giving him the faintest of nods. "Fine."

With the change of tactics, things began to go swimmingly. Not only did they not have to resort to desperate last stands, but nobody died, despite the slew of **[Twisted Wretches]** they killed as they approached. Half a day in, Max had already Leveled Up again. Not only that, he got his first Skill System upgrade.

New Talent Obtained: [Player Killer I]
[Player Killer I]: When in combat with other player species, increase all Attributes by +5.

Useful. This is a start in terms of building defensive capabilities against the other species. I assume it also works against these enemies. It's not much, though I'm sure I'm still very vulnerable. I think it would be easiest to find gear with high defensive Stats. Maybe there's some down here.

He put the free points from Leveling Up into Intelligence instantly, pushing the Stat to forty-one. The expanded Mana pool helped him feel secure about using **[Tether]** liberally to trap the wretches against door frames in order to block the way from their comrades as the dwarves hacked and stabbed them to death. Defending the small rooms worked wonders not only in terms of decreasing casualties but also the morale of the expedition. It was clear to the dwarves that this had been Max's idea and they smiled and bowed to him as they walked past him during their breaks.

Another thing that increased the morale of the expedition was the prodigious amount of gold and jewelry discovered in the rooms. It seemed like the ancestors of the obsidian dwarves had been just as avaricious as their descendants. The expedition cheered in excitement every time they found glittering statues and chests full of diamonds, until Rulgum snapped at them to be quiet. But from the glint in his eyes, it was clear he shared their excitement for the found treasure. Max had half a mind to tell Rulgum that they should take this treasure back to their king and return later with a reinforced expedition. He knew Rulgum wouldn't like that and he knew why. If they went back, other kings would prepare expeditions to clear the chambers. They had a unique opportunity to clean the ruins and take the most valuable things. And to find the most valuable things, they would need to delve deeper. So they went onwards.

The feeling of dread was still there. While the threat of the [**Twisted Wretches**] had been mostly neutralized, it was still a nerve-wracking experience to traverse the darkness. The ever-so-faint wail was to be heard from time to time, but it wasn't close enough to inflict that stunning status effect.

They had been checking rooms for the better part of a day before they came across a crossroads leading in four different directions. The one going forward had a wide stairway leading to giant double doors. Max needed to use [**Tether**] to pry open the doors. Inside was a study akin to the one King Durum had in his estates. It was dusty and dark, but there were dozens of half-melted candles on little desks and on the walls that they promptly lit. There were twenty bookshelves in the room, ten on each side of the room in neat rows. Max went over to one of the books. The pages fell like snow off a roof when Max picked it up, pushing up a small cloud of dust at his feet. The book contained simple pictures of the obsidian dwarves and some symbols, along with rows of text he couldn't read.

The dwarves of the expedition murmured to each other excitedly as they picked up the books and showed them to each other. They might have found something they were looking for. The problem would be choosing which books to bring out.

They had carts made of wood and metal that they pulled along. In them were potions, food, and other useful things, such as rope and torches. And, of course, some choice pieces of gold and jewelry they had gathered. All of them were emptied at the order of Rulgum, while other dwarves brought the old tomes to the center of the room and started sorting them out.

Max was happy they seemed to have found something valuable, but he was feeling anxious. This was going too well. He went to the double doors to keep watch, as he was of no use in choosing what literature to bring back.

He watched the dark corridor and let the dwarves work. Their bustle in the flicker of candle and torchlight was making too much noise in Max's opinion. He wanted to close the double doors, but that would cut off any time for warning. They'd be finished if they tot trapped in the library room, as the potential swarm of the wretches that could come from three directions would be too much to defend against.

But that was not what mainly worried Max. They had been in a desperate situation with the monsters before and they had survived. More troubling was that they hadn't heard a sorrowful wail in the distance for a long time.

"We have found what we are looking for," Rulgum came up to say to Max. "The king will be pleased."

"So we can leave?" Max asked immediately, not taking his eyes off the corridor.

"Yes," Rulgum said. "We will fasten the cargo to the carts and proceed. Have you seen anything?"

"No," Max said. "Nor heard. That's what worries me. Why is the wailer silent?"

"Surely it has delved so deep in the ruins that we cannot hear it," Rulgum said, waving a hand dismissively.

As if to prove Rulgum wrong, the wail suddenly pierced the darkness and filled the corridors, its cold, harrowing notes crawling inside the library and freezing everyone in place. Max noticed he couldn't move and his Stamina had been cut in half. The eerie wailing came closer and a faint white light was beginning to reach the crossroads in the corridor.

Max watched the debuff timer tick down as the light shone brighter and brighter as the long still seconds passed. Eventually, the immobilizing effect of the debuff relented. Max turned to Rulgum.

"We need to go," Max hissed. "Right now."

Rulgum nodded and everyone scrambled to push out of the door as fast as they could. As soon as they got out of the library, the source of the shining light turned the corner. Max looked up at the tall, white figure and screamed.

CHAPTER THIRTY-THREE

Siren of Despair

Max's scream was cut short by the wail of the creature that emerged. Max found his Stamina drained and his movement completely restricted. He could only watch in horror as the creature approached.

It was white and tall, maybe eight feet in height, and its whole body shone with a cold white light. From every inch of its torso protruded hands as white as pearls, with red claws clicking against each other. The creature's long white hair descended to its skinny, feminine legs. But the worst was its face. It had no nose, no ears, no eyelids. Just perpetually open hollow sockets, within which just a single speck of white light could be seen on each, inhuman and dead in every way, and a toothless, black blasphemy of a mouth, lipless and hanging loose as if broken, all the way down to its pallid chest. Its hollow eyes looked at the dwarves in a childlike curiosity. One of the creature's many hands reached towards one unfortunate dwarf and grabbed his arm. She plucked it off like a berry from a stem. There was no scream of pain, just a slight tremble as a fountain of blood sent echoes of faint pattering on the ground.

The lanky creature hummed to itself as it continued to pluck off the dwarf's limbs one by one. Then the creature climbed on top of him and its gaping mouth made a terrible rasping sound, like the weak, ragged breath of a dying person. It went on for half a minute and when she was done, all skin, flesh, and blood from the dwarf had been sucked out. Only black bones remained.

That was when the debuff ended, and chaos ensued. Many of the dwarves started running, but Max raised **[The Maverick]** and shot at the horrible creature.

[Siren of Despair]
[Dungeon Boss], [Level 30]

A few magic bullets hit the horrible creature, and it lost a surprisingly large amount of Health for a Boss. Before Max could attack again, the Siren wailed again in that sorrowful, lonely note, and they all froze and lost Stamina.

This Boss is just going to stunlock and eat us one by one. The Stamina drain is really bad. Eventually the thing won't even need to wail.

It ate another dwarf and to Max's great horror, all the Health he had cost the Boss had been restored. Her Health bar was back to fully green, but that didn't stop her from ripping another dwarf to pieces.

The Siren's ended before it could devour the dwarf it was working on. The dismembered obsidian dwarf let out an indescribable scream of fear and pain, and it made Max's heart grow cold.

Max wasted no time. He chugged a **[Stamina Potion]** and tried to tether the monster to a wall. It was instantly pulled against the stone, clearly struggling against the gravity of the spell, but either due to its Level or innate Resistance stat, it wasn't fully locked down.

And either way, it didn't prevent the monster from wailing again, rendering everyone immobile.

It repeated the trick twice, devouring four more dwarves. Max tried to shoot at it again, but all the Health was recovered as it sucked in the lifeforce of each helpless victim.

There were little over ten dwarves left around Max. They were as terrified as he was, and every few seconds of freedom they got between the creature's cursed wails, they used for scrambling for a desperate escape.

Max's mind was being overwhelmed by panic. He desperately tried to think of something. Any physical movement he could manage was dreadfully slow and painful. He needed another Stamina potion soon. He could still use spells. They only required him to speak the spell aloud. Maybe Max could use **[Gravity Well]** and hope the thing got pulled in for long enough for them to escape.

Another wail. Max dropped **[The Maverick]** and tried to block his ears. He had no Stamina and every movement was agonizing. It didn't work. Nothing worked. Seven dwarves eaten. The shining creature got closer.

In the next interval, Max drank a **[Stamina Potion]**. It topped up his Stamina, but in only two more wails, he would be down to zero again. Max knew he needed to do something and fast. Anything. He needed to find some wiggle room. So he cast **[Gravity Well]**.

The good news was that the spell did slow the Siren down enough so that it wouldn't have time to rip the limbs off its next morsel if it wanted to. Max felt lucky to notice the spell was still active even after the wail. He was fully immobilized, but the spell did what it was supposed to. Max was losing Mana, but he still had a decently healthy pool left.

The bad news was that the **[Siren of Despair]** tilted its head and looked towards Max with those blank, inhuman eyes. It approached him, the dozens of hands upon its body twisting around excitedly, grabbing the air in violent fistfuls.

When it got to him, it grabbed a leg with one of its pallid hands, ready to rip Max apart from limb to limb. But the **[Gravity Well]** had slowed the Siren down just enough.

The debuff relented and Max could move.

In an instinctual panic, Max shot at the arm grabbing his leg and it let go. The creature sent out an angry screech of pain, and then it opened its maw wider for another one of its stunning wails.

Max didn't think. He just acted on instinct. He targeted the upper and lower jaws of the creature.

"**[Tether]**!"

Its lower jaw slammed shut so hard the creature actually lost some Health. It stood up straight and tried to wail, but only a muffled high sound came out. Its many hands clawed at its shut mouth, but they could not pry it open.

Max scrambled backwards away from the grabbing hands and started shooting. It took a laughably low amount of bullets for a Boss. Every bullet took off a clearly visible amount of Health. The siren clawed at its jaw in fury until its lanky, frail body collapsed on the floor.

Defeated [Siren of Despair]
You gained 5000 Experience points
Level Up! [Level 14 Graviturgist]
You have gained + 1 Constitution, + 2 Intelligence, + 2 Wisdom, + 2 free Attribute points
Achievement: [World First: Defeated a Dungeon Boss]
Reward: [C-grade Equipment Box]
Achievement: [Dungeon Boss Killer]
Reward: [D-grade Supply Box]

Max knew he should be impressed. That was a shitload of experience. He knew he should go and loot the Boss. There must be a ton of goodies on its body. He knew all of this intellectually, but emotionally he wasn't quite there yet.

He just looked at its blank eyes and myriad arms. The arms had stopped grabbing and squirming and the dim white light of the eyes had been snuffed. A sheen of cold sweat covered Max as he breathed heavily and stared at the monster.

Max's mind noted idly that the dwarves had gotten up and were talking amongst themselves quietly. It took them less time than Max to recover. In a minute or two, they were all standing in a row in front of Max, Rulgum at the helm, and they bowed to Max in unison.

"Our king will hear of this," Rulgum said, his tone now soft and reverent, whereas before it had been clipped and annoyed. "I will see to it that you will be rewarded for saving the expedition and our lives."

Max nodded in a distracted manner. He was still staring at the creature. "Thanks. I need defensive Items or supplies my people can use to build a community."

Rulgum bowed to him once more and then went back to organizing what was left of the expedition. They put the bones of their comrades in the carts and when they were ready, they stood in wait for Max.

Max got up and looted the [**Siren of Despair**].

10x [D-grade Equipment Box]
8000 Cosmic Coins

Damn, that's a whole ass armory, Max thought to himself. On some level he was excited, but it was a distant feeling, something he wasn't quite ready to process after the experience he had just had. But he did make a point of reminding himself to go through these boxes, keep what he needed, and upgrade it with the massive stack of the currency he had accumulated. Max checked his Inventory and saw he had 23,516 **Cosmic Coins.**

The rest of the Items will go to the people in the camp. I have a feeling I'll have a lot of stuff to bring. We'll need to sort out the quest business with Joshua.

Thinking about all the things he had just gained for himself and the people back at the camp brought him back to reality. Max cast a last glance at the empty eyes of the Dungeon Boss.

Yeah, don't need expired pickles for nightmares anymore. I wonder if someone at the camp has the [**Psychiatrist**] *Class?*

He chuckled to himself. It was going to be alright. He would carry this. He was strong enough. He had to be. There was no choice. This was just another milestone. Another level of deep fear experienced. Now that he had, what fear was there left to rattle him?

Max was sure he would find out eventually. But before crossing that bridge, he would focus on doing what he could best. Shooting stuff, looting stuff. It was time to get back to King Durum.

CHAPTER THIRTY-FOUR

Return to the King

As soon as their ragged expedition shuffled out of the great stone doors back to the realm of the obsidian dwarves, they were met by an entourage of thirty dwarves all armed and armored, standing in two neat groups. At the main door lay a dead dwarf in a pool of blood.

This was no welcome committee waiting for them with open arms and smiles. All of the thirty dwarves waiting for them wore tight expressions, their dark eyes seemingly prepared for violence.

"These are the High King's men," Rulgum whispered to Max. "The dead man is Dormoguddumukun, a messenger of ours. He was supposed to wait here and deliver a message to King Durum when we arrived."

"So that's how it is, huh?" Max said grimly and immediately drank a [**Potion of Greater Mana Regeneration**] and muttered to himself, casting [**Alter Gravity**] on his revolver and himself.

One of the High King's men stepped forward and addressed Rulgum. As he listened, he began to tremble with suppressed fury.

Max didn't understand what was being said, but he understood very well what was going on. And he would have none of it.

"Tell them to lay down their arms and I will spare them. I have nothing against any of these individuals. But if they choose to fight for their treacherous Thief-King, I will show no mercy."

Rulgum turned to him, wielding an expression of horror and respect. He regarded Max for a moment longer, before he turned to the High King's captain and told them what Max had told him.

Their captain barked out a nasty laugh and many of his men joined him in it. That was all Max needed to justify action. He stepped forward and tethered the captain to a spot on the ground before him. The captain skidded there, flailing his arms around and yelling.

When the captain came within reach, Max butted him in the face with [**The Maverick**]. A strange sensation passed through Max, as if the weapon had enjoyed it very much.

The captain fell, and Max peppered his face with magic bullets, until the Framework gave him a notification.

Defeated Level 10 [Soldier of the High-King of Avarice]
You gained 200 Experience points

The last of the High King's men's laughter had died. Max gave them a dark, challenging look. They would take nothing from him. They had not faced the unspeakable horror that had almost slaughtered Max and who had gone with him. The High King deserved nothing of this loot, and Max would do whatever it took to protect what he and the expedition had earned for themselves. Still, Max hoped the theatrics of killing the High King's captain would be enough to fend the rest of them off. He didn't want to spill blood in vain. These were people, after all.

But that wasn't meant to be. The second in command shouted something, and Rulgum barked at his tired men to form a line. Not a single man remaining of the expedition would die on Max's watch. They had faced the horror with him. He would protect them.

Max cast [**Gravity Well**] near the other group of fifteen men. He cast the spell beyond the ledge of the platform, over the glowing magma. Six dwarves were pulled into the core of it; two skidded over the ledge and died instantly. Max let the spell go and the other six were dropped.

The other group further from Max charged at the expedition. Max cast several [**Tethers**] at the charging line and they all stumbled and fell, some bouncing off of each other due to the force of repulsion, hitting the other fighters, some tangling with each other, sandwiching other members. Max shot a few rounds in there with [**The Maverick**] but the expedition jumped the rest of them, screaming in incoherent anger as they hacked the High King's men to pieces.

What was left of the group closer to Max had almost reached him. Max cast [**Alter Gravity**] on himself, followed by a repulsion [**Tether**] next to where he stood. He hadn't tried this trick before, but he knew it would work as intended, because of his study of Mana and the nature of the spell.

Max blasted off fifteen feet away, skidding to a stop next to the expedition's carts. He kept shooting, tethering, and skidding about. The smartest of the High King's men changed targets from Max to the dwarves from the expedition. Those were the ones Max shot down first.

When there were only a few of the enemy left, Max tethered them down and shot them one by one, until not a single one of the High King's men were left breathing. All of the enemy died struggling defiantly, none of them cowering or begging. Not that it would have mattered. Max had given them a chance to back down. Now he had let a darkness in, which cooled down only when the last of his enemies lay dead. The amount of Experience Max received in total was over four thousand.

Level Up! [Level 15 Graviturgist]
You have gained +1 Constitution, +2 Intelligence, +2 Wisdom, +2 free Attribute points
[Cultivation System Unlocked]
You are now Quartz-Level Cultivator (lesser)
+5 to all Attributes
Achievement: [Cultivator of the Heavenly Arts]
Reward: [F-tier Cultivation Pack]

[Cultivation path choice available]

[??? Unlocked] - > [Quartz Meditation Technique: Basic Mana Cycling]
Level requirement to use met

[Talent unlocked: ???] - > Talent: [Mana Instinct I]
Level requirement to use met
[Mana Instinct I]: All cycling techniques are 5% more effective

Max was almost overwhelmed by the amount of notifications. But beyond that, something in his body awakened. It was like water made of light flushed through him, making every cell inside of him shimmer with excitement and power.

His muscles convulsed and when he tried to breathe, it was like drawing in cold mountain air after swallowing a packful of mints. So fresh, so cool, so acute that it physically hurt. The sensations flushed over him, until the only thing that was left was a slowly pulsating sense of Mana coursing inside him. It had a familiar sense, a flavor similar to the intimations of the nature of Mana he had gotten from training with **[Tether]**.

After settling down and adjusting, Max looked at the carnage before him that he himself had created. Conflicting emotions struggled within him.

All these things I've unlocked . . . I feel so empowered. I don't know what all this means, but this is better growth than I could have ever imagined when I stumbled down that cave. If I were to face that giant insect monster again, I wouldn't even flinch. I have changed down here.

Rulgum talked frantically to his men. Something about getting word to King Durum immediately to bring reinforcements. Max barely listened. If more of the High King's men attacked, he would deal with them.

You need to be hard, Max. But don't become a monster. These people are not the enemy. The petty High King is not worth a breath. What matters is what King Durum can give me and my people. I'll need to learn what I can here, return to Joshua's camp, and go hunt the enemy.

It wasn't long before a slew of men came into the room like a stream of stout, shiny obsidian. Max was relieved to see Durum, taller than the rest and dignified as befit his station.

He said something in his tongue that Max could not understand. Max asked Rulgum to give the amulet to Durum, and the aide bowed to Max and did as he was bid.

"My dear subjects," King Durum said in almost a tender voice. "Is this all that is left of you?"

Rulgum fell on a knee and bowed his head, as he told King Durum what had transpired. The king turned to Max in surprise and then looked at the corpses scattered around the room in their pools of cooling blood.

"Max," Durum said as he turned back, "it seems you have taken it upon yourself to protect my people with your life. That is the very sense of the word 'heroic'."

Max bowed. "Thank you, my liege."

"But this mess you have just created . . ." Durum waved a hand. "I suppose it was necessary. I can even turn this into our advantage . . . Yes . . . This could be my chance . . ."

He muttered to himself, steepling his fingers full of rings as he thought. Then he snapped out of it and looked at Max with excitement in his eyes.

"We must act quickly now. My men will escort all of you back to my estates. You will be fed, bathed, clothed, and treated with the utmost respect. Then we shall have a wake for our fallen men, and I will reward each of you as I see fit. After that, I will have an audience with the kings and you will all testify. Let us waste no time and go now!"

CHAPTER THIRTY-FIVE

Heavenly Cultivator

Max was sitting in the room he'd been using previously when King Durum suddenly entered with a small entourage at his back. The king took a look at the two assassins lying face down on the ground.

"Looks like the High King sent his regards," Durum said dryly.

Max gave him a humorless chuckle.

"Rulgum told me in detail what happened in the ruins," Durum said. "Your actions have indeed been beyond valiant."

Max craned his neck down in a respectful bow.

"There will be rewards fitting your deeds," Durum said. "I did not want to discuss them right after the wake. I felt that was the right time to reward the other men. They crave simpler rewards. But now I have time for you. Anything in particular that you want?"

"I want many things," Max said immediately. "But right now I need information. I unlocked this 'Cultivation' system and it seems you prepared me for it. I want you to tell me everything I need to know."

King Durum smiled slyly. "Yes, I could sense your body has changed. Well, your patrons will explain the workings of the system probably as well as I know for now."

Max felt a pang of disappointment. He had been hoping he'd gain an edge here.

"But," King Durum said, "after a cursory reading of some of the books that you recovered, I know there is a lot of advanced knowledge hidden in these musty tomes. I just need time to read them. Time I don't have now."

"Because of the mess with the High King?" Max asked.

"Precisely. But this mess will work to my advantage if I move adroitly. Funnily enough, the mess with the High King is intimately related to the knowledge you have retrieved."

"Huh? I'm not following."

King Durum smiled. Seemed like he was having a great day. "Many of the books you brought back have detailed descriptions of Cultivation techniques. Our ancestors might have even developed a Way."

Max gave him a puzzled look.

King Durum waved a hand. "Something I'll explain to you later."

"Later" this, "soon" that. Kings sure make easy promises.

"The reason why the High King wanted your life and the books was so he could maintain the status quo. He is the High King. If some other fledgling king, like me, would discover something that would upset the balance of power, his comfortable life would be in jeopardy."

"Makes sense," Max said.

"But I want to take our people further. I want to teach them the old ways and enjoy the Heavenly gifts. But it is hard for our people. You might have noticed that we are physically very weak when compared to you."

"You really are," Max admitted.

"Most of us have lost the Framework. All kings and their bloodlines carry it, and our kin is able to Cultivate. It is a rare gift, which is why you were rewarded so heavily by saving a seemingly insignificant member of royalty. He must pass his bloodline."

"Wait, are you saying the Framework is an actual physical thing?" Max asked, suddenly alert.

"Yes," King Durum said. "As far as we know, all of our ancestors used to have it. In the golden days, everyone would have a Class and everyone would Cultivate with the Heavenly Arts. But over time, our bloodline diluted, and now only few possess the Framework and thus the ability to Cultivate."

"How is the Framework relevant to Cultivation?" Max asked.

"I do not know for certain," Durum said. "But I do know this: teaching Cultivation to a person without the Framework results in two different outcomes— either nothing happens or their body is destroyed."

Max nodded. He was eager to hear more, even though none of this was directly useful. But it did change his perspective. His Stats and Abilities were . . . etched into his DNA? How did that even work? Why did the aliens go through all of this trouble? Just to make it a fair contest?

Maybe. What do you know about alien logic?

"So, what is this Cultivation?" Max asked.

"It is harnessing the spiritual energy of the universe," Durum said. "There are endless names for it, but the Framework translates it as Mana."

"So, it's just a new layer to the Framework?"

No," Durum said, spreading his hands, clearly enjoying the conversation. Max glanced behind him at the aides and guards. They were shuffling their weight on their legs and doing their best to stand straight and still. "The Framework is simply training wheels. Or . . . maybe a vehicle for Cultivation. I do not know. I am eager to learn more from the books you have recovered."

"So my Intelligence stat doesn't mean . . . intellect?"

"No," Durum scoffed. "It is a representation of your ability to understand the spiritual power of the universe. I don't know why the Framework translates that Stat as 'Intelligence' for you. How stupid. For my people it is called 'Spirit Power'."

"Makes sense," Max simply said.

It's probably Intelligence because it's that in all the games, isn't it?

"Now, let us make a simple analogy to help you understand how Cultivation works. Let us say you started with two points in Strength. Do you have four or more now?"

"Yeah, I do," Max said.

"Your score has doubled, but your physical strength has not, has it?"

"I wish," Max said, chuckling dryly. "I think I am a tiny bit stronger, though."

"That sounds right. I think around fifty Strength is needed to double the baseline strength of a species. But with fifty Strength, a medium-Level Cultivator using a [**Path of the Body**] can shatter a tree trunk with his fist. With one thousand Strength, a medium-Level Cultivator could shatter a mountain. But a god-Level Cultivator could shatter a planet with just five hundred Strength."

"So Cultivation is a multiplier?" Max asked.

"Yes and no," Durum said. "It is not that simple. It is also a matter of control. A Class like your Gravity Magician is a way for a low-level Cultivator to give form to the universal spiritual energy. But a god-Level cultivator can simply manipulate the pure energy itself, essentially manifesting his will into reality."

"Manifest reality . . ." Max said distractedly, trying to comprehend. "This is all kind of . . . a lot."

"There is a lot of theory around it," Durum said. "I don't expect you to understand it all immediately."

"So what *is* Mana exactly?" Max asked.

"Mana is the baseline. It is the One. It is the Endless Heavens. It is beyond this game of yours and beyond the Framework. It is the consciousness that created existence."

"So is it God?"

"*God?* Not gods . . . ?" Durum asked quizzically. "The translation is . . . No. Gods are just powerful Cultivators that play with a planet. From what I understand about this ICCB you have told me about, I assume playing with a planet like that is illegal. But I do not know. Just know this: Mana is the endless beginning and the beginningless end. It was here long before ICCB and it will be here long after they are but dust and memories. Mana is the lifeforce of the body and the consciousness of the mind. It is life, but at the same time it is death, in a perfect paradox, perfect cycle. And this is what you must study."

Max blew out air and rubbed his face. "Sounds like I will need a patient teacher . . ."

Durum nodded amiably like a kindly godfather. "I will teach you more later. I can at least give you the basics after I have studied the texts of my ancestors. But let us focus for now. I still need things from you. I will reward you for your heroics in the ruins, as promised. You have already made a friend in a king. But now I ask for more help."

Max regarded him for half a moment. He could refuse, he sensed it. It would upset Durum, but there would be no trouble for Max. He could just go back home to the camp and figure out his next move. But no. His instincts told him he wasn't done here just yet.

"As long as I get more rewards."

Durum laughed heartily. "You speak with such open greed. Just like my people. Just like a Cultivator. I like you, Max. Very well. We shall help each other further."

"What do you need from me?" Max asked.

King Durum gestured towards the dead assassins on the floor. "Testify against the High King for me."

Max laughed. [**The Maverick**] seemed to share his mirth. "I would have done that for free."

Durum gave Max a serious look. "You will?"

"You agreed to cough up something good, so not any more," Max said and grinned.

The king scoffed, but it was in good humor. He was rich and he needed Max.

"Tell me what to say and do, and I'll do it," Max said. "Meanwhile, you tell me where to start with this Cultivation business, so I have something to fill my time while you do your politics."

"Very good," Durum said. "I will teach you the basic theory of cycling techniques. You can practice with that and use the pills I gave you."

"Sounds good to me," Max said.

"I will need some time to set up an audience with the five kings and to prepare the case. Even though you seem perfectly capable of dealing with threats of the High King, I will set up a guard and have your food tasted for poison."

"Oh, how fancy," Max smirked. "I've never had a food taster."

King Durum was confused by the offhand comment, so he opted to bow to Max. "Now then, let me teach you about the flow of Mana within your body . . ."

CHAPTER THIRTY-SIX

Paths to Many Roads

Max sat on a tiny stone table, eating food that had been promptly delivered after Durum had left. The king had gone over the Mana cycling technique to Cultivate Max's spirit and taught Max what to say in the trial against the High King.

He had also gone over the different Cultivation paths Max would have to choose from.

"There will be a few paths available for a warrior such as yourself," Durum had said and cast a glance at [**The Maverick**]. "I will not tell you what to choose. But I think it would be wise to choose a path that compliments this magnificent weapon of yours."

That was all well and good and Max was eager to start cycling, but before doing that, he wanted to make an inventory. First of all, he had gained four Levels in the ruins, which meant all kinds of free Attribute points to distribute. He'd do that before starting the cycling.

Secondly, he had over 23,000 **Cosmic Coins**. Not a paltry sum by any means. The next upgrade for [**The Maverick**] would cost 32,000 coins. By that logic, the next one would be sixty-four thousand. He had enough coins for a +7 upgrade on his trusty weapon.

You did promise to upgrade other gear, you crazy min-maxer. This isn't a game, as you well know. You've stumbled from one mortal danger to another, and Lady Luck's been there waiting. Don't tempt fate.

Maybe one upgrade on [**The Maverick**] would be appropriate. The rest of his coins, or at least a part of them, he could use to upgrade the gear he would get from the loot boxes dropped by the Dungeon Boss. Max was pretty pleased with himself for not having used any coins on the inferior gear he had acquired so far. Not that it wasn't stupid, but you can't help but smile when you get away with something.

He could open the boxes now, but he wasn't sure which would be a better play in terms of Joshua's ability to grant quests. He could open all ten of the boxes now and receive his lot. With luck, it would be four Items or even more. Then he would have Joshua give him a quest for six pieces of equipment.

But he could also have Joshua give him a quest for bringing ten loot boxes and then take whatever stuff he could use for himself anyway. That should result in more Experience for both Max and Joshua.

So, save equipment boxes for later, check.

Max did open his **[F-grade Cultivation Pack]** and **[D-grade Supply Box]**.

The supply box contained five **[Mana Potions]** for which Max was very pleased. Out of all the potions, those were definitely the ones Max always ran out of first. He still had some of Durum's Mana regeneration potions but more certainly wouldn't hurt.

Next, he opened the cultivation pack. In his palm appeared a stack of pearl-white coins. A few of them spilled to the floor and rolled away. Max cursed and retrieved the strays.

Then he settled back on his seat and inspected one.

[Lesser Spirit Coin]
Consumable: Contains a small amount of Spiritual Energy. Used for attempting to advance a Cultivation stage.

Another question to add to the pile I'll shove in Durum's face when he makes the mistake of admitting he has some time.

Max counted a total of ten of the coins before he put them in his Inventory. He thought this whole Cultivation business was very confusing, but the way Durum had described it made it seem extremely powerful, when built on top of the Framework. Not to mention him being a . . . Quartz-Level Cultivator? Whatever that meant, it seemed to be a good thing. It had given him a boost of five for all Attributes, which was nothing to scoff at. Max was especially pleased with getting some points in Toughness and Resistance.

Next, Max spent his free Attribute points. He had six to spare and decided on an even split between Intelligence and Wisdom. He had half a mind to just pour it all into Wisdom, but with the fat stack of potions in his possession, he figured it wasn't needed for now. Besides, having a higher Intelligence meant more potent Damage and Abilities, which would save Mana in its own way.

Constitution was definitely being left behind, but Max was still hoping he would find Items to rectify the problem. He went over the math of how many shots of **[The Maverick]** he could take with his Health pool. Four, five tops. Max didn't like those numbers. His weapon was powerful, but who knew what the enemy had at this point?

Regardless of the many things in need of improvement, Max smiled when he looked at his Stat sheet. It was starting to look bulky.

Name: Max Cromwell
Cultivation stage: Quartz (lesser)
Class: Graviturgist
Level: 15
Health: 290/290
Stamina: 290/290
Mana: 540/540
Alliance: Joshua's Group
Stats:
Strength: 9
Dexterity: 11
Constitution: 29
Intelligence: 54
Wisdom: 41
Charisma: 9
Precision: 15
Toughness: 11
Resistance: 9

Now all of the easy stuff was out of the way. There remained one more thing before he could start working on that cycling technique in conjunction with the big bag of pills Durum had gifted him when he had first arrived here. According to Durum, each **[Celestial Illumination Pill]** would increase the efficiency of his cycling by 50 percent for an hour. So that was a thousand hours of increased cycling speed. From how Durum had explained the cycling technique worked, Max was not looking forward to those thousand hours. Cycling of Spiritual Energy sounded a lot like meditation, something Max had started and given up a hundred times in his old life. Meditation was *boring*.

But before all that there was a choice to make. Max brought up his System messages. The annoying red blink had been going on for quite a while. Time to bite the bullet and make another choice based on very limited information, that would affect his life and, by extension, the lives of all of the people in Joshua's camp. *Totally no pressure.* At least Durum had given him some pointers on what was to come.

[Cultivation path choice available]

You may choose a singular specialization for the way in which you choose to pursue the Heavenly Arts. This choice is permanent and will alter the

fundamental structure of the Spiritual Energy of your body, mind, and soul forever. None of the abilities from other paths are completely locked off to you. A Cultivator of Mind will still be able to Cultivate the Body. But the weight of the specialization is substantial. Choose carefully.

[Path of Spirit Pact Cultivation]
Choose a creature to form a Spirit Pact with. You will share Spiritual Energy with one another for life, seeing and sensing with each other's bodies and accumulating a shared well of power one could not achieve alone.

[Path of Martial Body Cultivation]
Concentrate your Cultivation to enhance the capabilities of the corporeal body. Acquire enhanced strength, speed, and endurance beyond natural limitations of the body.

[Path of Celestial Weapon Cultivation]
Focus on an exclusively martial path. Channel Spiritual Energy through your weapon and bind your life force with them. This Path is a balance of Body and Soul Cultivation. Strong in neither, weak in neither.

[Path of Soul Essence Cultivation]
Enhance the pure Spiritual Energy produced by your soul. Acquire superior spellcasting abilities by extending the reach and potency of your Spiritual Energy outside your physical body.

[Path of Heavenly Craftsman Cultivation]
Acquire peerless genius within creative pursuits. Infuse objects with spiritual energy to enhance their properties.

[Path of Ascended Mind Cultivation]
Gain insight into the hearts of men as well as beasts. Gain abilities such as sensing the emotions of others, getting flashes of foresight into the plans of your enemies, and concentrating your Spiritual Energy to receive boons of luck from the Heavens.

Well, that's a lot of choices, Max thought. *But how am I supposed to choose based on such limited descriptions?!*

Max tried to inspect the choices further in an attempt to glean more details. None were given. Why the Framework of the Heavens or whatever the hell all this was wanted him to make such an important choice practically blind was a very good question. Max suspected it had something to do with boldness. It was bold to act decisively in the face of the unknown and there seemed to be a reward at the end of that . . . If one succeeded.

Max could sense a hint of emotion or something like it from [**The Maverick**] again. It was excitement and . . . *fear?*

It was basically a choice between [**Path of Soul Essence Cultivation**] and [**Path of Celestial Weapon Cultivation**]. While the Martial Body path would certainly have its uses, that wasn't exactly how Max was built right now. Cultivating his Soul Essence would allow for more powerful manipulation of Mana, resulting in more potent spellcasting, as the description said. It felt like a no-brainer, and Max almost chose it, if it weren't for Durum's advice.

It was a hard decision to make. Should he lean into the versatile gravity magic he had acquired or the special weapon he possessed? The path of weapon specialization seemed to still have an affinity towards Cultivating magical ability. It also appeared to have some alignment towards physical abilities, which could be detrimental in terms of build efficiency. Although having a more durable body sounded appealing to Max. It was time to find and fight the other species, and Max would need defensive capabilities.

[**The Maverick**] almost physically vibrated with emotion. It was a strange sensation, an insistence. Like a dog barking at you and going in little circles, clearly wanting to tell you something.

Both Durum and his weapon seemed to have a clear opinion on what should be chosen. Was that the right choice? What would be the implications?

I can't just sit on the fence forever. I will never have enough information or rationalization. I just have to decide. Indecision is death in this new reality.

Max chose [**Path of Celestial Weapon Cultivation**].

CHAPTER THIRTY-SEVEN

He Awakens

A strong sensation like a fever passed through Max's body. It was followed by a surge of power and he could feel some strange energy gathering in the middle of his chest. It swirled around and started pulsating like a second heart, a faint but consistent pulse. From the nexus of energy, Max could feel Mana spreading all over his body, filling him up like a cup. He could feel the power being spread very thin. This must have been due to him being a beginner-Level Cultivator. Max had a gut instinct that if he advanced on the path of Heavenly Arts, this feeling in his body would grow stronger.

But what really startled him were two things. First was the System message.

Adjusting subject to [Path of Celestial Weapon Cultivation]
Error . . .
Existing Soulbind detected
???????
???????
[Path of Celestial Weapon Cultivation] rejected
. . . Computing . . .
New Cultivation path discovered
[Path of Divine Soulbond]

What the . . . ?

The second thing that startled Max was the voice.

"Finally!" a voice from seemingly nowhere announced. It was a self-satisfied and dignified voice, not in the least afraid of letting itself be heard. "I thought you might actually shit the bed with this one."

"Who's there?"

"They call me 'The Maverick'," the voice announced. "An apt name, as far as I'm concerned!"

In slack-jawed astonishment, Max turned the gun in his hand. It looked exactly like it always had. Black with gold ornamentation and a sturdy leather grip, made of fine rough leather.

"Quit that gaping," Maverick said. "You're embarrassing us."

"Nobody can see us," Max said, shaking his head at the whole situation. "Wait, how the hell can you see?"

"How should I know?" Maverick answered, as if Max was asking a completely stupid question. "Magic. Spiritual power. Voodoo shenanigans. Call it whatever you like."

"So, you talk now?" Max said. "Is this going to be a thing?"

"It is going to be *the* thing!" Maverick said, exceedingly pleased with himself.

Max rubbed his face. "Dear Zeus in heavens, please help me . . ."

"It's going to be great!" Maverick went on enthusiastically. "You'll be my side-kick and we will go on epic adventures! We will—"

"Look," Max cut in sharply. "I'm sure I'll grow to appreciate your glib non-chalance, but there are going to be serious situations coming up. I'm gonna say this right out of the gate. When it's a serious situation I want no bullshit from you. Are we clear?"

Maverick was silent for half a beat. There was a grudging respect to his airy voice when he spoke again. "Fine. As long as you recognize your position as the sidekick of this team."

Max shook his head. "How the hell are you even sentient?"

"I suppose it is a product of my inherent awesomeness," Maverick said.

Max stared at it, quizzically.

"You're no fun, you know that?" Maverick said and somehow huffed. Apparently magical guns don't need lungs to huff. "I don't know much more than you do. We're going to have to wait for our gracious patrons to explain some things. I'll ask the questions."

"The hell you will," Max said.

"Fine," Maverick said. "We'll share. But you really should listen to me. I have no idea how you've managed to scramble around and keep yourself alive, but it can only be a result of an absolutely divine stroke of luck. As further proof of your miraculous luck, you now have *me* as a companion!"

"You talk a lot," Max said glumly.

"One of my numerous gifts to the world."

"I'm sure the world rejoices . . ." Max muttered.

"You just wait!" Maverick said happily. "Your friends are going to love me!"

"I'm sure they won't be able to contain themselves," Max said. "But listen. As interesting as all this is, we will have time for this later. We'll ask Durum or the Zoos what happened. Now I need to get in on this cycling technique."

"Right," Maverick said, surprisingly all business-like. "Despite my numerous talents, I'm not sure how to do this, but I am distinctly awesome, so it will not take long to learn."

"You . . . What?"

Maverick sighed. "You are sometimes so slow, Maximillian. If we are to become the best of the best, better than all the rest, we need to work together."

"But you're a gun," Max said.

"And you're a monkey," Maverick said. "That didn't stop you from pulling off miraculous stunts. Now, shut up and go over with me how to do the cycling technique, so we can get to work."

He can cycle . . . ? Wait, he does have a nexus of Spiritual Energy inside of him. I can sense it as well as mine. I seem to share a soul with this wacky bastard.

"You *do* share a soul with me," Maverick said. "And that means I can hear what you're thinking."

Max sighed. "Oh great . . ."

Max had taken a **[Celestial Illumination Pill]** and started working on the cycling technique. It was simple and straightforward, but straining. It involved rhythmic breathing combined with imagining pushing and pulling the Spiritual Energy of his body up from his toes to the top of his head, and repeating that over and over again. Simple, but surprisingly hard.

Maverick had huffed about how difficult it was for the first fifteen minutes, making it challenging for Max to focus. He had snapped at the weapon and told him what to do again, and he seemed to have listened this time, since he had been quiet since.

After an hour, the pill's effect waned. It was quite clear the moment it happened. While the cycling had been arduous before, after returning to baseline, it became downright sluggish. It was like trying to push liquid cement up and down his body. Max got up, stretched his limbs, and moved around a bit. Then he drank some water, popped another pill and started cycling again. 999 hours left to go.

After a few more hours of (blessedly) silent work, he finally started to make some progress.

Leveled Up Quartz-Level Cultivator (lesser) to 1
+1 free Attribute point
Leveled Up Quartz-Level Cultivator (lesser) to 2
+1 free Attribute point

Okay. We are starting to get somewhere. This is weird but kind of exciting. I would have definitely been more motivated to meditate on Earth if the gains would have been this tangible.

Max took another break. Maverick was blessedly silent for whatever reason. Max enjoyed a glass of wine the dwarves had brought him an hour ago or so. It was akin to white wine but green in color. It tasted pretty vile, truth be told. Max wasn't much of a wine person to begin with, and the swill that the dwarves made was definitely not designed for human tastes. But he enjoyed the relaxation the alcohol provided, so it was worth it.

Leveled Up Quartz-Level Cultivator (lesser) to 3
+1 free Attribute point

"What the . . . ?" Max turned to look at **[The Maverick]**, which he had placed on the stone dining table.

"Are all humans this lazy, or do you just have a particularly unfortunate configuration of genes?" Maverick called from the table. "I can't believe I'm having to do all the work here."

"Wait, you can *actually* cycle?" Max asked, striding up to the table. "I thought you were just putting on airs."

"Of course I can actually cycle," Maverick huffed. "It wouldn't do for my pride to make my sidekick do all the work, as much as I enjoy the pained scrunch on your face when you try to concentrate."

"I don't scrunch my face," Max protested.

"Ah right, of course you don't," Maverick said. "Just like you don't snore."

"I've never snored," Max said but with a quiver of uncertainty in his voice.

"Oh, Maximillian," Maverick sighed. "Why lie? You know I don't sleep. I hear everything."

"You . . ." Max said. "What did you say?"

"I said you snore. And that I don't sleep. Try to keep up, sheesh."

"So you can use a cycling technique while I'm sleeping?"

"Seems hardly fair for me to exert myself while you're snoring," Maverick huffed. "But theoretically, yes."

"That sounds . . . Very promising." Max said, his mind racing with the possibilities. He—*they* might have gotten very lucky with this path they'd chosen.

"Mind you, while my awesomeness is everlasting to say the least, this cycling technique does seem to put a strain on me," Maverick admitted.

"So you won't be able to cycle through every night?"

"My word," Maverick huffed. "What am I, a machine?"

"Well, technically . . ."

"I'll do what I can, as I'd hate to be left lying around, collecting dust for an eternity if you happen to die," Maverick said in a high, haughty voice. "It'd be terribly boring."

"I can imagine," Max said, sincerely. That sounded like a purgatory of the worst kind. Then he smiled to himself and thought of something. "I guess we'll just see how impressive you are next morning."

"Oh, worry not, my trusty sidekick," Maverick said. "You won't be impressed—you'll be *astounded!*"

CHAPTER THIRTY-EIGHT

High King's Favor

Max and Maverick cycled for a while, obtaining Level Five in **(lesser) Quartz-Level Cultivation.** When Max woke up in the morning, they were Level Seven. This, of course, resulted in endless boasts by Maverick, which Max discovered couldn't be quelled by weary praise. Thankfully, it had waned by the time Durum came to them.

The king was notably surprised by Max's gun suddenly turning sentient. Durum seemed pensive and clearly annoyed over what had happened. He seemed to agree with Max that **[The Maverick]** had turned out *too* sentient for his tastes.

Unfortunately, Durum couldn't provide much useful information regarding their situation, but he was quite pleased with the speed at which Max had acquired Levels in Cultivation.

Afterwards, they went over what Max needed to say when he testified at the imminently upcoming trial. Max didn't feel particularly nervous about the whole ordeal. Regardless, screw the High King and huzzah for Durum. So, Max would help him.

For most of the trial, Max just stood and waited. He was called to speak twice, and magical amulets forged to communicate with Max were given to the five kings and the adjutants who acted as the lawyers. Max said his lines and kept his mouth mostly shut when the High King's representative tried to bully him into giving flustered answers. When the sentencing was carried out, the High King's glare at Max could have melted lava. He was to step down from his position as High King until deemed worthy again. Max was personally aghast that the former High King wasn't stripped of his estates and status completely. When he suggested this to Rulgum, who sat next to him throughout the proceedings, the aide looked at him like he'd completely lost his mind. To strip a king of all his possessions was a punishment so severe, there was no crime so vile to justify it.

Afterwards, the court voted for the next High King. For his success in the ruins and seemingly deft politicking, Durum was chosen. His grin shone like a hundred suns across the room. He swore an oath to only steal from the government as much as he deemed just and not an ounce more.

Max ate and drank his fill during the feast that followed. The party started so soon after the proceedings that Max had a sneaking suspicion it had all been theatrics and the arrangements had already been made ahead of time. He didn't care. He was seated at a place of honor on a long, beautiful table on top of the dais. Many ugly looks were cast at him, presumably from the supporters of the former High King.

As unpleasant as the wine was to Max's palate, it tasted like victory nonetheless. The food of the dwarves wasn't exactly to his liking, but the new Max of the planet Alpha Ludus would eat his piehole full every time the chance presented itself. This was not a place to be a picky eater.

[The Maverick] had been quiet for most of the time, only deigning to comment if he had something particularly insightful to say. Max suspected he didn't like Durum, and the feeling was mutual. Despite the explosive entrance his companion had made when he had become conscious, it appeared he could sit quiet and still too. That was definitely a point in the gun's favor. But he was sometimes also just . . . not there. Maverick had claimed he didn't sleep, but Max could sense his soul, and intermittently, it was as still as a pond. Max wondered about that.

Max also noticed he could feel Maverick cycling Spiritual Energy from time to time. In fact, ever since yesterday, his sense of Spiritual Energy and, more importantly, the bond between Maverick and him had strengthened. He could not sense Maverick's thoughts as apparently the gun could his for some reason, but he could feel his presence and Max had an instinctive feel for when particular emotions were evoked in Maverick. For example, he could tell whenever the gun decided that something it said was particularly clever.

Leveled Up Quartz-Level Cultivator (lesser) to 8
+1 free Attribute point

Eventually High King Durum walked over to him. The excited babble of the court died down as they had another royal spectacle to observe.

"Max," he said in a voice more deep and resonant than before, as if he had suddenly found more confidence with his higher status. He spread his arms and gave Max a dignified bow. Max wiped his mouth, then got up and bowed as well.

"My liege, High King," Max said in his most courtly manner. Hearing his new title clearly pleased the king. Durum almost unconsciously touched his new crown made of that strange electric metal.

"You have proven yourself an ally most valuable," Durum said. Max bowed again. "I am a just king, and I will reward you handsomely. What would you have, Max? Ask, and, if it is in my power—within reason—I will give it to you."

"Might I ask two things, honored High King?" Max asked, his head still bowed.

Durum stared at him for half a blink, before bursting out into laughter. Next to him Rulgum translated what Max had said to the crowd and they roared in laughter just the same.

"Max," Durum said, smiling at him. "I name you *Dwarfmind*. You are an honorary member of my people now. You share our endless greed, and we respect that. What are these two things you want?"

"First thing," Max said and bowed to the court and then the High King again. "I thank you for the title *Dwarfmind*. My avarice can never be as deep and true as yours, but you do me great honor."

This was translated and the crowd clapped.

"As my first reward," Max continued, "I would ask you to teach me more of the ways of Cultivation if you can spare the resources and time as High King. You are wise and I have much to learn from you."

Durum was pleased by this request. It was a public endorsement of his prowess in Cultivation as well as a reminder that they had recovered something valuable in the ruins.

"Indeed we have recovered many of the secrets of our ancestors from successfully delving the ruins!" Durum announced to the court. They cheered. "My people are going through the books we recovered, and another expedition is being planned to recover even more of what was lost. This will usher in a new golden age! WE WILL BE RICHER THAN WE COULD HAVE IMAGINED!"

The crowd roared. Max smiled to himself when he looked at the pure pleasure on Durum's face as he waved a hand so stacked with glittering rings that it seemed like it should have sprained his wrist. The next favor Max was about to ask was a big one, but he was sure if there ever was a time to ask it, it was right here and now.

Eventually, the applause calmed down and Durum turned back to Max. "And what would be the second favor you had in mind, *Dwarfmind*?"

"I'm glad you asked," Max said and smiled.

CHAPTER THIRTY-NINE

He Returns

When Max came back to Joshua's camp with fifty obsidian dwarves in tow and a talking gun, to say the little community was surprised would be an understatement.

"Max!" Marie exclaimed as she saw Max approach. "What is all this?"

"This is good news," Max said, smiling at her. "And it's good to see you."

"The dwarves are good news," Maverick said. "But I am the *great* news!"

"Who said that?" Marie asked, looking around.

"It is I, the Maverick!"

Marie gaped at the weapon. "Your gun talks."

"My human talks too," Maverick said. "Pleasure to make your acquaintance."

"L-likewise?" Marie said, still looking at the gun on Max's holster quizzically.

"You'll get used to it," Max said wearily. "Well . . . you might . . ."

"It's good to see you too, Max," Marie said. "I hate to say, but I am surprised every time you come back. It is dangerous out there."

Max gave her a dry laugh. Then he looked her up and down. And at the camp. There were definitely more people here. The camp had spread out in every direction, and Max could no longer see every distinct face. But he got the general picture.

Everyone was clearly ragged, exhausted, and depressed. A few people were on the ground wincing in pain as their bloody bandages were being swapped. The bandages looked a lot like the fabric the jumpsuits were made of. That meant . . .

"What happened here?"

Marie sighed. "We have been fighting off attacks. The monsters are becoming stronger and more aggressive. They've attacked the camp twice. We've managed to fend them off, but a lot of people got hurt and worse . . ."

"I'll cull them," Max promised. "Or drive them off if they come again. I plan on staying a bit longer this time."

Marie brightened at that. "That would be great for the camp. But Max, what is this retinue?"

Max looked behind him. Fifty dwarves stood there in disciplined formation. At their head was one of the lesser aides of High King Durum, a young dwarf named Vurukoggonomonnar. He was keeping his head slightly bowed, the magic amulet for communication hanging from his neck.

"These are the obsidian dwarves of High King Durum. He is a new friend. He promised to help us build shelter."

Marie peered behind the dwarves at the carts upon carts lined with bricks made of hefty black stone. Max had been told that some of the dwarf [Artisans] had Skill to produce lava that could be placed with great precision. It would be used to line the bricks.

Marie turned back to Max. She looked at him like she couldn't process what he had just said. "They'll build us what?!"

The dwarves were preparing the ground of the campsite for building when Joshua approached. When Max had gone to meet up with Sid, the boy had promptly fed him and disclosed that Joshua had been out on a hunting trip to learn how it was done. Max appreciated his brand of leading from the front.

"Max!" Joshua exclaimed. He was as tired as the rest of the ragtag camp. "What on earth is going on here?"

"I'm not sure that expression works anymore," Max said, smiling smugly. "I managed to bring something very nice home this time."

"I can see you sure brought *something*," Joshua said, looking around. "What is going on? Who are these people?"

"They're subjects of my friend, a dwarven king," Max said, trying his best to contain his feeling of overwhelming smugness. "They brought us useful Items and they'll build us shelter."

"Items . . . ? Shelt—What? Max that's amazing!"

"I think so too," Max said and grinned. The dwarves were almost ready, just waiting for Max to give them the signal to start. But he needed some business done with Joshua before that.

Joshua knew what was up. He turned to Max, also smiling excitedly. "This is exactly what we needed. It hasn't been easy around here. This quest will give us both so much Experience!"

They brainstormed some variations of what the appropriate wording for the quest should be, so that it would include both the tools Max had brought along with him as well as the houses that were about to be built. Eventually they decided on the best phrasing they could come up with. The Framework seemed to be very intelligent in picking up on intended meaning.

"Max," Joshua said, "acquire shelter and tools for the camp."

[Quest Accepted]
Bring the camp shelter and tools
[Quest complete]
Reward: 20000 Experience points
Level Up! [Level 16 Graviturgist]
You have gained + 1 Constitution, + 2 Intelligence, + 2 Wisdom, + 2 free Attribute points
Level Up! [Level 17 Graviturgist]
You have gained + 1 Constitution, + 2 Intelligence, + 2 Wisdom, + 2 free Attribute points

"Holy shit," both Joshua and Max said in unison. Then they looked at each other, as if to make sure that had just really happened.

They laughed in disbelief. The dwarves and people around looked at them curiously.

Max clapped Joshua on the shoulder.

"Come. I'll introduce you to Vuruk. You can decide where you want to place these shelters."

It was a busy afternoon of arranging the layout of the camp. There was enough material for ten little stout black bunkers of obsidian stone, according to Vuruk. The **[Artisans]** who could create and manipulate lava even made a smooth floor for each of the buildings.

Each could house eight to ten people in total, depending on how uncomfortable you wanted to be. That was almost enough room for everyone in the camp, but Max suspected there would be fights over sleeping places.

They could have tried doing something creative with the piles of black bricks the dwarves had brought, but Max, Joshua, and Vuruk all agreed that it was better to build something that the dwarves already knew how to do well.

Joshua ran around the camp telling people how to best use the new buildings and how to use the space between them, as there were nice sturdy walls to build on. They could put logs and vegetation on the roofs and create little canopies between the buildings. That would mean everyone would get some form of shelter from the weather on bad days. Fortunately, most days didn't seem to be particularly rainy or windy, but when it happened, it was sure to be unpleasant.

The dwarves worked fast, and many of the **[Artisans]** and **[Laborers]** of the camp helped. Sid and a couple of other cooks had prepared the meat that Joshua's hunting group had brought back.

Shelters hadn't indeed been Max's only trick. He had also requested that High King Durum provide his people with simple tools and containers, including a big cooking pot. Durum had laughed and told Max that he would have given him his weight thirty times in gold if he had asked, and all had wanted were cups and spoons.

"Throw gold at a drowning man, and ask him how valuable it is," Max had said. "If I ever barter you for gold, Durum, know that I am either mad or a king myself."

Max couldn't exactly tell which evoked more joy, the shelter or the tools Max had brought, but the camp's depressed mood was long gone by the time night fell and the stout little houses were done.

People were laughing and having animated conversations. Some of the kids and teenagers were even dancing in turns as the others clapped. The stew tasted like a delicious treat to Max, after having had the displeasure of dwarven cuisine for the last days, but to Joshua's camp used to half-cooked meat and raw berries? The hot stew was an absolute banquet.

Sid and the other cooks received almost as much praise as Max did. Max grinned when he saw a flustered teenager receive a kiss on the cheek from some girl his age after he'd given her a second serving.

"So these are your minions?" Maverick asked Max when the commotion had finally quieted down. The dwarves had returned to their homes, with a promise from Max that he would return to Durum soon. Now Max was sitting on a log in front of a fire, as he always liked to do. Joshua, Marie, Elena, Sid, Bill, Lily, Martin, and many others were gathered around.

Joshua sat next to him, laughing, and Max flushed and groused.

"Stop calling them that," Max snapped. "They're my friends."

"So they can't be my minions, then?" Maverick asked, clearly considering the possibilities.

"What do you need minions for?" Max asked exasperated. "You're a gun. You don't have any needs."

"I am a person!" Maverick said in indignation. "I have all the needs of a normal person. Need for expression. Need for conversation and company. Need for continuous adulation . . ."

Max groaned.

Joshua leaned in closer. "If you're a person, what is it that you want, Maverick?"

Maverick hummed thoughtfully as he considered the question. "Well, I need to take care of Max. That lost little lamb couldn't find his way out of a wet paper bag without me."

"How do you even know what a paper bag is?" Max asked.

"I can sense your thoughts," Maverick explained. "And your dreams. Boy, you guys would be surprised by—"

"Okay, next topic!" Max interjected.

Maverick huffed. "I also *want* to not get interrupted when I speak, but I guess we can't have it all, can we?"

There was laughter all around and Max could sense Maverick was pleased.

"Shouldn't we go over the Items I've received?" Max asked Joshua. "What about the attacks? I could check the perimeter."

Max was about to get up, but Joshua placed a hand on his shoulder. "Let's worry about that tomorrow. Have another bowl of stew."

"I'll grab one for you, bro," Sid said and got up.

"Fine," Max said. "Thanks, Sid."

Joshua squeezed him on the shoulder before letting go. "You're going to stay a bit longer anyway now, aren't you?"

"I am," Max said. "I might as well Cultivate here, and I need to make sure I have a home to return to when I come back from my next adventure."

"Home," Joshua mused. "I like that. I suppose the camp is starting to look like home."

"I can't believe we have houses now!" Elena said excitedly. "Max, you keep outdoing yourself."

"They're barely houses, but I thought they'd help . . ."

"Barely houses?" Marie scoffed. "We barely had two sticks to rub together before. Next thing we know, you'll bring us a bathtub and blankets."

"I wouldn't be surprised," Bill said. "Max is a hell of a lad. Too bad he's got that yammering gun now, though."

"I'll yammer you to the ground!" Maverick said. "Max, let me have a go at this guy. He's fat—he'll move slow. We can take him on easily."

Max ignored Maverick. "What did you guys do with the planks, Bill?"

"After a bunch of arguing," Bill said, casting a glance at Martin, "we decided to make tables for Sid. The boy needs a bunch of space to prepare food for this whole lot, and it's better if there ain't too many chunks of dirt in the meat."

"Good choice," Max said. "I got another material box. We'll see what—"

"Tomorrow!" Joshua and Elena said in unison. Max relented and let out something between a sigh and a laugh. Sid came back with a bowl of still-warm stew for Max. It tasted like a place he belonged to.

CHAPTER FORTY

Simple Stuff

It hadn't been easy for Max to convince the others to let him sleep in his hammock on the great oak-like tree. A lot of the people had insisted he have his own room in one of the ten houses, but Max had refused their kind offer. He was perfectly happy sleeping in his hammock, although he did have to admit to himself that, after the soft beds he'd grown accustomed to, courtesy of Durum, it did take a bit of getting used to.

Regardless, Max woke well-rested. He noticed they had gained a Level in Cultivation, bringing them up to Level Nine. Max had told Maverick he didn't expect him to work with a cycling technique that night, since he had been lazing off. Maverick protested that he would get much too bored during the night if he didn't do something and that he needed to show Max what hard work meant. They argued idly as Max washed in the river nearby.

Today would be a big day. Yesterday's little revelations were definitely something Max had enjoyed, and admittedly needed. It was good to be back on track. Despite all of the fine things Max had brought, people were still scared and wounded and Max would need to deal with that.

Fortunately, he still had all sorts of things to help the camp with. He had one **[C-grade Equipment Box]** and ten D-grade ones. Max was very curious to see what kind of equipment the C-grade box contained. If it didn't have an item Max could use, he would probably cry a bit.

He also had two **[E-grade Material Boxes]** to give to Joshua after receiving the appropriate quest, as well as quite a few free Attribute points to distribute. He was sitting on them, as he wasn't sure what would be the best build for him. Maverick had told him that the only option was to dump everything into Intelligence, because that would make *him* more powerful. Max had decided to not ask his advice after that.

There was one thing bothering, Max though. He had gotten a notification that the patrons had wanted to contact him when he had Leveled Up to Fifteen. Max assumed that was because they wanted to instruct him with Cultivation, but due to some rule, they hadn't contacted him within the Dreadlands, where Durum's kingdom was located.

But now that Max had come back, the Zoos Collective had made no attempt at contact. Max had even double-checked the notification to see if he could prompt the plastic jellyfish to appear somehow but to no avail.

That was inconvenient—because Max had questions—and worrisome, because after having asked about it yesternight at the campfire, Max was told that other people were being regularly contacted by the Zoos. For now, Max could only wait.

"Morning, Elena," Max called as he approached the short woman, who was hunched over a makeshift table made from a stone slab on the ground, working on something. "What are you doing?"

"Paste," she said distractedly before she turned. "Oh, good morning, Max. I'm not used to you being around yet!"

"I hope you'll make some progress with that," Max said and squatted down next to her. "I plan to stay for at least some days."

"I'll believe it when I see it," Elena said and nudged him. "Joshua says you're the impatient type."

Max let out a chuckle. "I suppose I am. What kind of paste are you working on? Smells fresh."

"It's a healing paste for the wounds," Elena said. "I found this plant that's like aloe vera. I'm using it as a base and trying out other herbs and berry juice and stuff like that to see what works best. I'm done testing this one and it seems to work pretty well."

"How do you test it?"

"On myself, of course," Elena said as if it was obvious and peeled up her sleeve. She had thin little cuts that were scabbing at various rates. The higher cuts were clearly healing more cleanly. "That third concoction I tried was really bad. See, it's still irritated. *Not* doing that one again . . ."

Max had to just nod and appreciate the commitment. Maybe his first impression of Elena had been wrong. Or maybe she'd just been in shock like any person would be in the situation Max had found her. Now she was being helpful and proactive. That was what Max was all about, so he couldn't help but appreciate her efforts.

"That is really cool, Elena! I'm really impressed."

She blushed and averted her eyes. "Oh stop it. It's just a little healing salve."

"And who knows what it will be in a week from now?" Max said and rose up.

"Maximillian, is this what you humans call 'flirting'?" Maverick asked.

"No. What's wrong with you?" Max snapped at him. Elena giggled. "This is called having a normal conversation. Please take notes, so we might have one someday. Please."

Max and Elena exchanged a few more words before Max went off to find Joshua. The camp had grown large enough that you couldn't immediately tell who was who from afar anymore. But Joshua was still wearing his signature brown cowboy hat, so Max found him easily enough.

"Morning," Max called as he approached. Joshua was standing with Martin next to one of the black stout houses. They both turned and smiled—Joshua brightly and invitingly, Martin shyly.

"Max! Good morning. Come join us, we're tossing some ideas around."

Max went up to them and looked at the space between two of the bunker houses, which the other two men were staring at.

"You guys are figuring out how to use that space?"

"You catch up quickly as always," Joshua said.

"The question is not how we should use it," Martin said. "We're agreed that we should build a back wall and a roof in the space between the walls of the buildings. The question is the limited availability of materials."

"I do have a material box, just so you guys are aware," Max said.

"We'll get to that," Joshua promised. "But one box probably won't be enough to give us enough of anything to make use of all of the spaces."

"How about the idea with the clay bricks?" Max asked.

"Lily found clay, but the deposit is unfortunately quite far away," Joshua said.

"And her attempts so far at creating adequate-enough bricks have not been successful," Martin said.

"Give her time," Joshua said.

"Yeah, Martin," Max said. "Think how hard this new reality is on us. Then imagine you were experiencing it as a kid."

"I know, I know . . ." Martin said and sighed. "It is hard. That is why I have a 'stick up my ass' like Bill likes to say. I don't deal well with stress. I'm a mess."

"You're our mess, though," Max said. Martin gave him a tired smile.

"Maximillian," Maverick chimed up. "Is this what you humans call flir—"

"JUST WHY!? Why do I have to deal with this?"

Max hadn't been much use in the conversation about architectural decisions. He had mostly been nudging Martin in this direction and that with ideas. Eventually he felt he had exhausted his usefulness and went on his way, telling Joshua to look him up when he had the time.

Max was burning to open the boxes and see what was inside. Maverick had fallen quiet. It—or rather *he*—did that from time to time. He claimed he didn't need to sleep, but even when Max had called him, he hadn't answered. For a revolver needing attention more than gun oil, that was strange. Max decided that he'd ask about it, when the gun decided it was time to make his next oh-so-clever statement.

Max wandered around and exchanged greetings and a few words with people he didn't know. They thanked him and told him if he ever needed anything, all he had to do was ask. All the usual. Max's heart swelled with pride, and the smiles he gave them were genuine.

He was still a little uncomfortable with the attention, but he certainly appreciated it. These were the people who gave him purpose. The normal people who just needed a roof over their heads, food in their bellies, and each other.

Max would do his best to provide for them, so that they could flourish and build. That was something Max couldn't do. But he could fight, he could protect, and he could bring them what they needed. And he had. Success tasted good.

Eventually, he ran into Marie, who was inspecting a rack made of sturdy sticks and a tanned hide. She softly ran a finger over the leather and stood there contemplating. Then she did the same for the other racks in the same row.

"How's it going?" Max asked and approached with a smile.

"Oh, hello, Max," Marie said. "Very good. These leathers seem to be my best work so far."

"So you've taken up working with leather?"

"Oh yes, I think it's very interesting. But I do wish we had the internet or even manuals on how to do this."

"Yeah, it's rough having to reinvent the wheel," Max said as he came to stand next to Marie and look at the leathers. "But these look good."

"Yes," Marie said. "I tried a few times, but the leather never worked out. Then this one guy—Richard, was his name I think—told me I need to soak the leather in boiled bark. There's tannins or something in them that does something to the leather."

"I guess that's where the word 'tanning' comes from," Max mused. "So now it works?"

"Yes, I know they succeeded, because they gave me a prompt and Experience. These two pieces here are true **[F-grade Cured Hides]** and these four here? **[F-grade Cured Leather]**."

"Very good!" Max said. "There are so many useful applications for leather. We still use leather items on earth."

"Yes, that's what excites me," Marie said. "I can make things and be useful like you."

Max turned to smile at her, but she turned away, almost bashfully.

"I meant—" Marie said, "—what you do is amazing. I can't do that. But I want to make beautiful things that will help people."

"I think you're on the right path," Max said, ignoring Marie's awkwardness. "What Level are you?"

"I'm Level Nine. I think it's on the higher end for **[Artisans]** in the camp. Only Elena and Joshua are over Ten. And Mike too, I think. But he is injured."

"I saw him yesterday," Max said. "He looked very tired."

"He got an infection from one of the wounds," Marie said. "But Elena's salves saved his life."

"I didn't know Elena had been developing so quickly," Max said. "Is she trying to obtain some sort of a **[Doctor]** Class?"

"It would be amazing if she did," Marie said. "But to me, it feels like she is more of an apothecary. I was going to say pharmacist, but I'm not sure that's accurate on this planet."

Max grinned. "Who knows? Few more Levels, and she might have a fully-functioning laboratory."

"Next thing we know, you'll bring us a sack full of beakers," Marie said and they grinned at each other.

"Not the first thing on my list," Max said. "I saw that Elena cobbled together a pestle and mortar."

"She was absolutely gushing about it this morning," Marie said, smiling fondly. "You sleep late, by the way."

"I do," Max said and rubbed at the back of his head. "But I have other good qualities to make up for it."

"You sure do," Marie said. "Now shoo, I need to get these leathers down and start working on them. Lily made me a stack of bone needles, and Sid is getting good at keeping the sinew intact for me."

CHAPTER FORTY-ONE

New Rules

Max left Marie and continued taking in the camp, which was admittedly turning into a village. Max tried to prompt Maverick, but the gun was quiet. Max considered it was possible the prickly weapon could be sulking, but as far as he could tell, he hadn't done anything to provoke him. The gun just seemed to go offline sometimes.

Max was heading for the oak and to sit down and eke out some more cycling technique before Joshua found him.

"There you are," he said and gave Max an easy smile. "It's starting to get harder to locate people. I wish I had a Skill that could tell me where the people I need are!"

"You know, I wouldn't be surprised in the least if you got one soon enough," Max said.

"Here's hoping." Joshua said. "How do you like the camp?"

"I was just thinking it could be called a village soon enough."

"That would make me a village leader. Maybe it would give me new Skills, so I could be of more use."

"I think you're useful enough," Max said. "You've managed to keep a lot of people alive and working for a while now."

"I'm not sure how much of a hand I have in that," Joshua said, in almost half a mutter. "But you are partially right."

"Is something bothering you?" Max asked.

"No—well, yes," Joshua said and cast almost a shy glance in Max's direction. "Do you think I'm a good leader?"

"Where is this coming from?" Max asked.

"It's the guys from the hunting group I was with yesterday. They're a group of tough guys. Good men, I'd say. Taking well to adjusting in this new world."

Max thought of the Stranger and wondered what exactly Joshua meant.

"They're very good at hunting by now," Joshua carried on. "So good, in fact, that I was of no use during the hunt."

"I suppose they let you know that?"

"Loud and clear. The leader of their bunch, Brian, told me he had talked with the Zoos, and they would give him a Class change, if he wants one."

"That's good, I suppose," Max said. "You shouldn't be the only [**Leader**], since the community is getting so big."

"Exactly what I said," Joshua said. "But he responded that he wants to be the chief and that I should step down. His men agreed, and they weren't very nice about it."

"They tried to scare you?"

"They succeeded," Joshua said. "They're a bunch of serious guys. They told me that I should do the wise thing, so no accidents happen in this dangerous, new world we've found ourselves in."

Max shook his head. Of all the petty bullshit . . . People should work together. But Joshua clearly had things in hand. That Brian guy just let his ego run so fast and loose he couldn't think straight anymore.

"I'll deal with them if trouble comes along," Max said. "You have my word."

"They're serious guys, Max," Joshua said. "I think some of them are itching for a coup and don't mind cracking a few eggs to do so."

Max remembered the horrible Dungeon Boss in the ruins. The clawing hands and the way it casually devoured the life force of a person in one gulp. Even after victory, the terror of it all still haunted him. He chuckled at the notion that these guys were "serious".

"I don't think you have anything to worry about, Joshua. There are new rules in this world. I'll support you as the leader."

"You sound awfully sure that's enough," a brusque voice cut in, and a tall man of strong build came over to stand next to them, and behind him a group of six hunters. Most of them held crude hand axes and sharpened sticks, but one had a proper spear, which Max recognized to be the one he'd taken from the Stranger. Their clear leader had a sword at his belt, which Max suspected to having belonged to him as well.

"I don't believe we've met," Max said.

"Brian," the tall man said and offered a hand. Max took it. The man gripped him tightly..

Like a caveman . . .

"I'm Max."

"Oh, I know," Brian said. "You're starting to get a reputation. Nice houses you brought us."

The way he said "us" had a nasty undertone to it. Max decided he didn't much like this guy.

"Maybe we could get to know each other later?" Max suggested, as politely as he could muster. "Joshua and I still need to talk."

"Is it private?" Brian asked, his voice dripping with faux innocence. "Or is it about the camp business? Shouldn't I be included?"

"Should you?" Max asked, ice in his tone.

"Hey, what's that supposed to mean?" one of the thugs behind Brian said.

Brian raised a hand. "We talked about this, Rob. Just let me talk."

Max was getting impatient. "What is this? What do you want?"

A flash of anger passed over Brian's eyes, but he controlled himself. He looked at Joshua. "Looks like you told him something to give him a less-than-charitable impression of me. Did you tell him what you did the last time those panthers attacked?"

Joshua let out an awkward chuckle and gave Max a glance.

Brian nudged at Joshua. "I suppose he told you I want to be the leader."

Max nodded. "He did."

"And why shouldn't I?" Brian asked and turned to his group. "Who was it that protected this village during those last two attacks? Huh?"

His men gave a cheer. Brian's voice rose.

"Who fought for you all? Who bled for you? We were at the helm of the attack, while Joshua here threw rocks with the women? *This* is who should lead us?"

Now Max understood what was going on.

"You should take the [**Leader**] Class," Max said. "You'll make a great captain for the [**Combatants**]."

"Yeah, I sure would," Brian said, still talking loudly. "But why should I take orders from *him*?"

"Who the hell cares who's taking orders from who?" Max snapped, finally losing his patience. "What are you? Dogs? Kids playing in a sandbox, fighting over who gets the coolest toy? You goddamn child, just look at the situation we're in! Does it look like the people of this camp need a warrior to lead them? Or do they need someone who can gather people together? Someone who can help them work and grow together? Are you really so stupid that you don't understand that you don't have those skills? I don't want to believe you're evil, so that leaves stupid."

Brian gnashed his teeth and fury flared in his eyes. He laid a hand on Max's shoulder and squeezed it as he came to loom over him with all of his six and half feet.

"You will think carefully what you say next," Brian said in clipped tones. "There are new rules here. Rules of the jungle."

Max regarded him with a disdainful sneer. "Remove the hand."

That made Brian only squeeze harder. He leaned in, his face so close to Max now, they could kiss. "And what if I don't?"

Max looked the man dead in the eye and said a single word: "[**Tether**]."

Brian's head hit the ground faster than anyone could say "What the hell?" The man grunted, more from surprise and anger than pain, although Max suspected he lost a few Health points.

One of Brian's thugs was foolish enough to swing an axe at him. Max dodged the swing without needing to make use of any Skill. It was a clumsy motion, and much slower than anything Max had contended with lately. Max cast [**Alter Gravity**] and two [**Tethers**] on the man, who immediately afterwards flew towards one of the bunkers with a meaty thud.

Max didn't need to have gone so far. But he felt it necessary. It was necessary to show them it wasn't the rule of the jungle here. It was *his* rule.

The other four hunters left looked like they were waiting for Max to fight them. They stood, weapons ready but clearly scared. Max ignored them. Instead, he squatted down to Brian struggling on the ground.

"I think you've misunderstood the situation here," Max said. "I'm not sure what you wanted, and I really don't care."

Brian tried to say something, but with his lower jaw glued to the ground, he could only growl and sputter.

"You have exactly two choices, Brian," Max said. "You either play nice, or you play somewhere else. You can take your men and anyone foolish enough to follow you and set up your business wherever if you don't like the way Joshua does things. Understood?"

Max released the tethering and Brian grunted. He rubbed his chin and cast a baleful glance at Max but said nothing.

"Am I . . ." Max said, drawing out the words, ". . . understood?

Brian stared at him, but Max gave no inch. He stared back, letting the man know he couldn't care less if he never saw him again. Max was sure they were good hunters. Max was sure humanity needed them. But if they were going to be trouble, this was not the place for them.

Not that Max let that show. And to his surprise, something softened in Brian's stare. He cast his eyes down and nodded. Then he turned to Joshua and also gave him a curt nod, a tad ruder than the one Max had received.

"I'll take the boys out and get us some more meat for the evening, Chief."

Joshua gave each of the six hunters a nod. "Thank you, Brian."

CHAPTER FORTY-TWO

Victor's Spoils

Joshua gushed at Max so much, it embarrassed him, but Max couldn't help but smile, regardless. It felt good to stand up to bullies and brutes. And besides, he had done the right thing. That felt good, in and of itself.

Joshua certainly had weaknesses as a leader, as any person would, but he was earnest and wanted what was good for everyone. Max could trust him to at least try to do the right thing, and that was enough for him to vote for Joshua. And to Max's great fortune, he was in a situation where his vote happened to cast a long shadow. And he would be damned if he wouldn't leverage that.

Dwarfmind, huh? Speaking of that, I really need to find time to Cultivate.

But that time wasn't now. Now he was sitting with Joshua and a bunch of other people at the logs. Joshua was giving a little speech about Max's daring adventures, and he made Max recount some of the tale.

Max wasn't as good a storyteller as Joshua, but people seemed interested enough, which was, of course, flattering. He stumbled with his words a few times, but people only smiled at him kindly. Max had never felt anything like that before. It was good. Not that he protected the others in the camp for smiles and approval, but it sure didn't hurt either.

Even Brian and his men nodded along as Max spoke. Joshua had stopped them before they left to hunt with their proverbial tails between their legs and asked them to join the little gathering.

Joshua and Max had agreed that Brian and some of his men would do well with the new equipment the camp was about to get. Max would have personally rather given Mike most of the Items that he himself couldn't use, but Mike was still out of commission.

"Max, please bring the camp eleven equipment boxes," Joshua declared, in an attempt to make a quest of it.

That didn't work. It was probably because Max couldn't take the boxes out of his Inventory. He could only open them in the Inventory menu, and the Item within would materialize in his lap.

Max whispered an idea to Joshua, who cleared his throat, a little embarrassed. "Max, please bring the camp eleven pieces of equipment."

[Quest received]

"That did it!" Max said and started opening the boxes.

The Experience had been quite substantial. Each of the D-grade Items was worth 250 Experience, and the C-grade Item had been worth 500. That gave a total of 3000 Experience to Max. Not bad at all.

Max didn't know how much Experience Joshua got from these quests, but he told everyone that he just Leveled Up and they cheered. That put Joshua at Level Fifteen, if Max wasn't mistaken.

The momentary look of concentration on Joshua's face confirmed that guess. He must have gotten a lot of notifications. He'd talk about the Cultivation business later and would probably end up giving him a handful of **[Celestial Illumination Pills]**. They were valuable, but Max had so many that it'd be a good idea to give them to people who knew what they were doing.

Max was extremely happy that he had been greedy with his **Cosmic Coins**, as there were several Items that Max was planning to claim for himself. But first, they'd distribute the Items he couldn't make use of.

To the good fortune of the camp, not all of the equipment was combat-related. There were two pairs of good leather gloves that gave Stats in Precision and Constitution, which would be very useful for pretty much any non-combatant. The people of the camp must have made a world record in callused hands by now. Nobody complained, but for some jobs, you definitely wanted gloves.

There was also a hammer with a proper metal head, looking very much akin to the ones used on Earth. Not something you'd choose for battle, due to their lack of reach, but definitely useful for nailing things in place—for example, pegs in the ground. It also gave bonuses in Strength and Precision, but people were more excited about its utility.

Along with all of that was an apron made of smooth leather that gave five Dexterity and four Strength. He gave that one to Bill, who had taken up building defenses against the panther attacks. Next up were two weapons, a bow and a battle-axe, which he gave to Brian to give to his men.

Brian wasn't exactly over his humiliation yet, and Max wondered if it was a good idea to give him more weapons, but he had to trust Joshua's judgment in this. It felt like Brian was being more careful now, and the thanks he gave seemed genuine. But time would tell.

The rest of the Items were Max's to keep, all of them useful to him in varying degrees. There were four D-grade Items on the ground for him and one C-grade Item folded on the log as carefully as he could. He went over them one more time.

[Necklace of Insight (D-grade)]
+4 Intelligence
+4 Precision

It was a thin chain with a white bauble attached to it—a paltry trinket compared to the ones he had seen with the obsidian dwarves, but the Stats would be useful.

[Ring of Sturdiness (D-grade)]
+5 Constitution
+2 Resistance
+2 Toughness

This is so nice! It's exactly *what I need. This would probably suit someone with a* **[Tanking]** *Class best, but as long as I'm flying solo, I'll make good use of this bad boy.*

Wondering how many rings he could wear in total, Max picked up the next Item.

[Sash of Prowess (D-grade)]
+3 Constitution
+6 Precision

Max liked this one. It was a light silken waistband that was easy to cinch around him. The Stats weren't exactly ideal but definitely useful. The Precision was starting to rack up, and it did make maneuvering **[The Maverick]** easier. He could control enemies with his Abilities, but when it didn't work well or he was in some other sort of tight spot, this was sure to come in handy.

[Boots of Careful Steps]
+5 Wisdom
+2 Precision
+2 Constitution

Upgrade! I definitely appreciate the Wisdom boost. These white ones that came with the jumpsuit are excellent. It's probably best to give them to someone in the camp. There'll surely be a use for them.

That left only the last Item. The folded purple-and-black robe made of soft, light material. Max's first C-grade Item. And it was a head above anything Max had gotten so far, barring [**The Maverick**] of course.

[**Robes of Shadowsilk (C-grade)**]
+6 Constitution
+9 Intelligence
+3 Resistance

This is so good . . . It's almost on par with the treasures from the five kings! Those must have been B-grade Items. The [**Pocket of A Thousand Tools**] *could have been an A-grader, even. This doesn't have any additional effects, as B-tier Items and above apparently have. But I can upgrade it with my* **Cosmic Coins**.

"Hey," a miffed voice called. "If you plan on upgrading this dirty rag to ten before me, you have another think coming."

Max chuckled. "Well, good morning to you. Where were you?"

Maverick yawned. "That's a good question. I believe the world is notably ready for my fulgurant presence."

"Fulguwhat?" Max cocked an eyebrow. "So you were . . . sleeping?"

"Sleeping has such a pedestrian ring to it. I would like to think of it more like resting, or hibernating."

"Why?" Max asked.

"After the initial burst of excitement wore off, I became increasingly tired. I think I need to get used to being sentient. It's hard work. You wouldn't know."

Max gave him a look. "You don't think I'm sentient?"

"Barely," Maverick said. "But you get the job done by carrying me around to exciting new places."

Max just shook his head. "Well, now I'll be even better at it thanks to all these new Items. I suppose we should also spend the free points from Cultivation."

"All in on Intelligence," Maverick said immediately. "Trust me."

"You know we're going to eventually run into people from other species?" Max reminded him. "We need defensive Stats too."

"Best offense is a good offense," Maverick said.

"Don't you mean best defense?"

"Not if you blast them up so quickly that you don't need defense."

"That sounds great on paper, but things can get very messy, very fast."

Maverick huffed. "Fine. Do as you see fit. But put at least *some* points in Intelligence. Heavens know you need some . . ."

"That's not what the—ugh . . ."

There were some amused chuckles around him. Most people were busy sorting, wondering, and arguing about the new Items Max had given them, but a talking gun was admittedly quite an attraction. Max could sense Maverick enjoyed the attention.

Max turned back to Joshua for the little ceremony to continue. There were still two [**D-grade Material Boxes**] for him to turn over. After that, he was looking forward to finding some quiet place to Cultivate for a bit. As much as he appreciated the people around him, he needed some space.

CHAPTER FORTY-THREE

Twin Cultivators

The material boxes contained fifteen [**Sheets of Linen Cloth**] and six [**Coils of Rope**]. The people gathered around actually cheered when they saw those Items materialize in Max's hands. While they'd been excited about the tools, they were downright ecstatic about the materials. Max could hardly blame them.

The sheets of cloth were quite large—maybe three feet in span, and six feet in length, akin to a single-bed bedsheet. Not only was there a slew of potential uses for such material, but it would provide a substantial boost in Experience to any [**Artisan**] working with them.

The rope was sturdy and of reasonable length. While it would have no clear application in providing Experience, it would certainly be massively useful in fastening things, or for making traps for hunting.

And the Experience was quite nice. For the two quests Joshua gave for both sets of material, Max got a total of 3400 Experience. That pushed him over the edge.

Level Up! [Level 18 Graviturgist]
You have gained + 1 Constitution, + 2 Intelligence, + 2 Wisdom, + 2 free Attribute points

Max had equipped all of his Items and decided to spend his many free points in a mix of Constitution, Intelligence, and a dash of Wisdom to round out the numbers. He put the excess in Resistance. Max figured he would most likely be more vulnerable to magic-based attacks, as he could avoid physical attacks with some care and foresight. Max looked at his Stat screen and smiled to himself. He had come a long way since entering the realm of the obsidian dwarves.

Name: Max Cromwell
Cultivation stage: Quartz (lesser)

Class: Graviturgist
Level: 18
Health: 540/540
Stamina: 540/540
Mana: 750/750
Alliance: Joshua's Group
Stats:
Strength: 9
Dexterity: 11
Constitution: 54
Intelligence: 75
Wisdom: 55
Charisma: 9
Precision: 27
Toughness: 13
Resistance: 17

With all of that done, Max decided to excuse himself and find a nice comfy patch of grass under the oak. It was time to Cultivate.

"You know I'm kind of miffed," Maverick said once they had sat down and Max was about to pop one of Durum's pills. He halted the movement just in time.

"Uh huh," Max said.

"As my sidekick, I feel you are able to Cultivate faster than me," Maverick said. "I don't want people thinking you're pulling more weight than me in this team of ours."

"I don't know what to tell you, Mav," Max said. "I'm using these pills and you're not."

"First of all," Maverick said. "Never call me 'Mav' again."

"I'll stop the moment I never hear Maximillian out of your voice-hole again."

"Hmmmm. I will consider that. In the meantime, give me one of those pills."

"Huh?" Max asked. "To do what with?"

"To cycle, you dunderhead," Maverick said. "I have a soul. I can cycle Spiritual Energy. What's the problem?"

"You don't have a mouth or a digestive system to start with?"

"Pffft. Who needs that? It all seems very gross anyway. Just put a pill in one of my bullet chambers. What's the worst thing that could happen?"

"You know I faced a horrible screaming monster made of hands that sucked people dry," Max said with a lopsided smile. "I thought that was the worst thing that could happen. But then you started talking."

They argued some more, before Max relented and flicked open [**The Maverick**]'s cylinder. It was squeaky clean and even seemed to sport a faint sheen of oil, which made the gold shine. Max had to admit that it was a beautiful gun.

Then he felt his companion's smugness in their Soulbond and resolved to never think something like that again.

The pill fit in the chamber well, leaving a little wiggle room. If it didn't work, Max could just pop it out of there and use it himself. But if [**The Maverick**] could use it, it would really cut down the time they needed to spend cycling with the pills.

"Just make sure you don't fall asleep if you consume the pill," Max said.

"Please," Maverick said with a note of hurt in his voice. "What kind of buffoon do you take me for?"

It turned out magical guns *could* consume [**Celestial Illumination Pills**].

Who knew? Max thought when he fed a pill into each of the chambers of the revolver's cylinder. Max really hoped Maverick wouldn't just go limp in the middle of cycling, but it wouldn't be the end of the world if one pill was wasted. Still, Max would rather not waste them. Who knew where it was possible to get more from.

Leveled up Quartz-Level Cultivator (lesser) to 9
+1 free Attribute point
Leveled up Quartz-Level Cultivator (lesser) to 10
+1 free Attribute point
Leveled up Quartz-Level Cultivator (lesser) to 11
+1 free Attribute point
New Talent Obtained: [Twin Souls Cultivator I]
[Twin Souls Cultivator]: When both parties of [Path of Divine Soulbond] are using a cycling technique simultaneously, the effectiveness of the technique is increased by 10%

"We are amazing!" Maverick declared.

"Shh," Max hissed. "Talk when the pill is done working."

Maverick grumbled something, but Max wasn't listening. It was amazing, and he could actually feel a slight hastening of the Spiritual Energy inside of him. It moved slightly faster, slightly smoother.

It was still sluggish and difficult to move the energy, but the Levels did help. Max was a little surprised Level Ten didn't do anything special, but then again Cultivating was a lot faster than Leveling. It would be a good idea to stay in the camp and Cultivate as much as was feasible to rake in the easy free Attribute points.

Once the pills were finished, Max grinned. The grin was intended for Maverick, but it didn't matter that Max wasn't facing him. The gun could sense it through their bond.

"That new talent we just got is excellent," Max beamed. "We'll just have to see how well you can handle being awake."

Maverick did his best to stifle a yawn. He didn't *need* to yawn, did he? What was the point of stifling one?

"I am a bit tired," Maverick admitted. "But I can keep going. At least for one pill. Maybe two."

"What do you think about Cultivating during the night, while I sleep?" Max asked.

"If I'm awake and terribly bored, I have to, don't I? Otherwise, I increase the chance of you getting killed for being too weak."

"Do you want to use pills for it?" Max asked. They still had a massive pile left. "Do you think it's a good idea?"

"Despite my numerous gifts, math is not my strong suit," Maverick admitted. "Fortunately, I am in a position to delegate such tasks as hashing out the math to my trusty sidekick."

In other words, Maverick didn't want to take responsibility for the decision. Max was fine with that. He wasn't sure what was the right answer. Of course, the most optimal course of action would be to only use the pills when they were both using a cycling technique. They would get much more efficiency out of the pills that way. But how many Cultivation Levels were they forsaking in the short term if Maverick had to cycle with basically half the speed at night? If he could cycle for even three hours per night, that would rack up pretty fast.

And those racked up Levels would mean more Stats. More Stats meant a higher chance of survival. That was good. But more Stats complicated the equation of efficiency even further.

More Stats meant more opportunity to find loot, even Cultivation material. More Stats meant more monsters killed, which turned into more Experience and **Cosmic Coins**. Max wished he had a calculator or an Excel sheet to type in all the numbers and compare. But it seemed that being inefficient in this situation (at least on the surface) would yield more gains overall.

Of course they could just huddle up in the camp and consume their **[Celestial Illumination Pills]** with maximum efficiency. But at the same time, there would be members of other species going out there in the Dreadlands and putting themselves in a position to advance beyond Max's reach. Max could not allow that. He didn't have all the time in the world. This was a race. The one who held the advantage got the spoils.

"Use them," Max said. "But you better make sure you don't fall asleep mid-cycling."

"Don't need to tell a Cultivator genius like me twice," Maverick said. "Say, I think I could still go on for an hour or two, if you still have juice left in you."

The challenging tone did not go unnoticed by Max. He grinned, excited at the prospect of being able to enjoy the peace of Joshua's camp while also growing stronger at the same time, with relatively little effort.

Just as they were about to pop another set of pills, the horrified screams began.

CHAPTER FORTY-FOUR

Under Attack

These panthers were definitely different to what they were before. Max couldn't tell if they were even the same species, or if the ICCB had changed the spawns.

They were larger than tigers, their heads hanging at an almost-relaxed angle, jaws wide, ready to snap the heads right off of necks whole. They wore protective silver collars around their own necks that extended down their spines by half a foot. Their sleek, black bodies rippled with muscle as they prowled and pounced around, arousing panicked yelps and screams of pain around the camp.

Their roars filled the night and as one noticed Max, he felt a lurch of fear in his stomach. He mastered it fast. He had seen worse than overgrown cats.

The panther lunged at him, two-inch claws extended. Max instinctually tethered himself against the oak and slid backwards enough to dodge. Then he made another tethering between the panther and the tree, but a repulsive kind this time. The beast was strong, but it was as if it were fighting against a mighty wind in its attempts to reach Max. Max shot at the creature, and it yowled in anger. Then another cat lunged at him. This one got on top of him and bit Max on the face.

It was a harrowing experience. Max's whole head could fit in its mouth. His vision flashed red and he lost over sixty Health. There was more shock than pain, but Max still yelled, as adrenaline rushed through his blood.

An emergency **[Gravity Well]** was conjured behind the cat, and a repulsive **[Tether]** between Max and the face-eating cat propelled it into the swirling mass of gravity.

Max released the other **[Tether]** keeping the first cat struggling. It was as dumb a beast as Max suspected, and when it pounced, the **[Gravity Well]** pulled it in from midair.

Both of the cats got tangled together and they yowled in anger, fear, and confusion as Max blasted the life out of them with **[The Maverick]**.

Defeated Level 11 [Mutated Panther (???)]
You gained 240 Experience points
Defeated Level 10 [Mutated Panther (???)]
You gained 210 Experience points

What a crummy amount of Experience for fighting such powerhouses! They're nasty for their Level. And what is that question mark business?

Max heard a nasty rip of flesh and a gasp somewhere nearby.

Who cares about the Experience? I need to help my people. These beasts are dangerous!

Max killed a third panther. He had come too late. The mutated cat fell next to its prey, a young guy in his twenties like Max, his throat now a fountain of red.

Max gave a regretful sigh, but he had to keep moving. He ran around, having used **[Alter Gravity]** on himself and his weapon. He moved like a machine, pulling panthers away from the hapless people and peppering them with bullets.

As fast as they were and as violent the damage caused by their claws and fangs, they died fast. Max's Intelligence was helping him pack a serious punch. The **[Tethers]** *yanked* the enemies off their prey and only a few bullets were enough to finish off most of the beasts.

Maverick laughed maniacally and taunted the panthers as their attention veered from their prey to their hunter. Max was so focused, it was like he was in a trance. He could barely hear the screams nor Maverick's taunts.

He bobbed, weaved, tethered, pushed, pulled, created space, and killed. It was a berserker rage born of need. The need to protect. The need to smite anything daring to hurt his new home and family.

Max passed Brian and two of his men struggling with two panthers. One of them had a deep gash in their arm. When Max came to them as a whirlwind of magical bullets, their hard faces yielded in relief. Max had the presence of mind to nod before he continued.

Defeated Level 11 [Mutated Panther (???)]
You gained 221 Experience points
Defeated Level 11 [Mutated Panther (???)]
You gained 218 Experience points
Defeated Level 10 [Mutated Panther (???)]

You gained 196 Experience points
Defeated Level 12 [Mutated Panther (???)]
You gained 271 Experience points

And so on, and so on. Somewhere in the blur of battle, Max had consumed a **[Potion of Greater Mana Regeneration].** How many did he have left? Wrong question. How many *panthers* were left? Right question.

The last stragglers were prowling by the black bunkers. People had wisely gone inside, the bravest and strongest fighting at the doors. A few corpses lay scattered on the ground, eyes fixed somewhere the living could not see. Their ripped throats and bloodied clothes only deepened Max's rage. He shot every single panther, until the sounds of battle stopped.

All that was left were soft whimpers, calls for help, the rattle of torch fire, and the distant howl of the wind. Max looked at the bodies on the ground. He only hoped that he wouldn't recognize any of the faces.

Still, this was a victory, and a big one at that. This pack had been formidable.

Max went around and looted most of the panthers for their **Cosmic Coins.** He got a little over three thousand in total. There was more to be looted, but he figured some should be left for the others. Who got them wasn't his business, though. He wanted to find Joshua to see if he needed help. Or Elena, since she had some healing ability.

Most of all, Max wanted to discover what was behind these panther attacks. Was this something cooked up by the ICCB to propel their growth? Or was this an attack by some enemy species?

It felt more like the latter. Could someone have a Class to control beasts? Having control over so many beasts of relatively high Level sounded unlikely, but maybe there were roundabout ways of getting these results. Max was sure there were Classes and Cultivation paths to provide just the means for an attack like this.

But if this was an attack by the enemy, why didn't they join the panthers in the attack? While the casualties were clearly over a dozen, maybe even as high as twenty, this had only made the rest of the camp stronger and had resulted in plenty of resources.

If I hadn't been here, they would have been all dead. Joshua, Elena, Sid, Marie . . . All of them would be on the ground.

This had been an attack to destroy them. It was just lucky that Max had been here. It couldn't have been the ICCB. They wouldn't try to obliterate a community like this.

Of course there was a third option. It could just be pure chance.

Max gazed at the dead and those mourning them. He could only hope nobody he had known had been killed. But he didn't feel sorrow nor despair. What he felt was an overwhelming anger spurring him into action.

I will NOT let this happen again. I will protect these people.

Tricks of the ICCB? An enemy attack? Goddamned pure bad luck?

Regardless, one thing was sure. Max needed to go back into the forest and find out what was going on.

CHAPTER FORTY-FIVE

Aftermath

A heavy, somber silence had enveloped the camp. Only the muffled sounds of work could be heard, such as a few grunts and one or two calls for someone to come help lift something. The cries of the wounded and of those who had lost someone had died down. No one spoke. No words were needed. No words could describe the loss.

Joshua was talking with Elena and making sure she had everything she needed to tend to the wounded. She was crushing something with her makeshift pestle and mortar as she listened to him.

Joshua had assigned as many helping hands as Elena could use. While the death toll was high, there was also a score of wounded people. When you added those to the people in shellshock or catatonic with grief, the functional working force of the camp had to work twice as hard.

There was a group of people on their knees ripping apart the jumpsuits taken from the fallen. They were making bandages.

Marie was among them. She gave Max a grim nod, and he reciprocated.

When Elena noticed Max, her eyes welled with tears. He gave her a sympathetic smile. She jumped on him, hugging him tightly.

"If you hadn't been here," she said through choked tears. "There were so many. I . . . I . . . Thank you, Max."

She let go.

"I'm glad you're okay," Max said. He squeezed her once more on the shoulder.

She mustered a brave nod and turned back to Joshua. "Please send a group to find me the herbs. I'd go myself but . . ."

"Don't worry about it," Joshua said. His voice was steady and his expression calm. Behind his eyes, however, there was an anger similar to Max's. He could see it. "Walk with me, Max."

They turned and Max followed Joshua, who strode along with long, determined steps. "I can never repay you. This attack was unlike any before."

"You don't need to repay me," Max said. "I did what I'm here for."

"That's . . ." Joshua's voice lost its steel of his voice. "I'm very glad you're on my team. If you hadn't been here, I think we would have all died."

"How many did we lose?" Max asked.

"Twenty-one people."

Twenty-one people. Twenty-one people who had been ripped away from their lives, forced to survive with next-to-nothing. Tired, hungry, aching. Brought into this world, and for what? Just to end up slaughtered.

Max knew he had done his absolute best in their defense. There was no scenario where he could have saved more of them. But it still stung him. It still angered him. He'd get stronger, and he'd find out what had happened. And then he would make goddamn sure it wouldn't happen again. He would protect everyone.

"I need to get out there," Max said.

Joshua gave him a wary glance. "What if these beasts come again?"

"That's what I need to go out to prevent. Whatever is causing this, we can't let them have the time to prepare another attack."

"You think this was an attack?"

"I'm almost certain."

"The panthers have simply evolved," Joshua said before they stopped in front of a group of people who were simply hanging their heads, doing nothing. "I think it's just a way for the aliens to speed up the game."

"Maybe," Max said quietly. "But that's not the full story."

Joshua instructed the group to first get some water for everyone with every pot, bucket and pan they could find and then go help those who were processing the panther meat. They all got up with empty eyes and slow steps. What they really needed here was a [**Psychiatrist**]. These people would have to find a way to deal with their trauma without the guidance of a professional, which was a worrying prospect.

Maverick was awake, but uncharacteristically quiet. He seemed to have at least some measure of tact, which Max could appreciate right now. This was no time for flippant quips.

The weapon stopped cycling Spiritual Energy, which it had been doing. He gave Max a sort of a mental nod and went back to cycling. Max decided he might not be all that bad after all.

Joshua and Max walked along and came to where the panthers were being processed. Some of the skilled [**Laborers**] were separating the meat, intestines, hides, and bones, while [**Artisans**] came to collect and work those parts further.

Sid already had a large pot being prepared for cooking. His other arm was secured in a makeshift sling that was spattered with blood. It didn't seem to slow him down. His single working arm seemed to have the speed of two. He seemed to be perpetually cooking. He had to. Regardless of their still having meat from the previous hunt, they could not let these resources go to waste. Max wondered if it would ever be possible to preserve meat for later use. He knew it could theoretically be dried and salted, but salt was scarce so far.

Sid noticed them, wiped sweat off his face and gave them a tired little smile. Joshua and Max came closer.

"You holding up the fort, Sid?" Joshua asked.

"We got everything under control, Chief," Sid said. "I got my pack of bros and sisters to sort this meat out. Will probably have to throw some of the intestines away."

"Have some taken to the fishing spot. They could still work as bait."

"You got it, Chief," Sid said. Then he turned to Max and nodded to him in appreciation. "You really saved our asses, bro. You got good timing."

"That I do," Max admitted. "I'm glad you're okay, Sid."

"Don't worry about me, bro," Sid said, about to turn back to his work. "I'll cook you up a nice proper steak. On the house. Or the camp. Or whatever, bro. But you got it!"

"Thanks, Sid!"

Max and Joshua continued on, Joshua organizing the camp, and Max assessing the damage and what he should do. Well, it wasn't so much what he should do as when he should leave.

He knew he shouldn't waste time. He didn't have enough information. For all he knew, the camp would be suffering an attack in the next few days. Other smaller attacks had happened in that timespan. But they'd only been tests of defense. This had been the real thing. It could have cost whatever entity was orchestrating the attack a great deal of resources.

Leveled Up Quartz-Level Cultivator (lesser) to 12
+1 free Attribute point

"Good job, Maverick," Max muttered to himself. Joshua gave him a look, but Max just shook his head. He had talked about his Cultivation path with Joshua in scant detail, but now was not the time to get into it.

"So you're off somewhere again?" Joshua asked with a tinge of hurt in his voice. "I could use you around here. For moral support, if nothing else."

"You'll do just fine," Max said. "I'm more useful to you and everyone else out there."

"I suppose . . ."

"Besides, I'm not going far this time. Just to that forest over there to find out what's going on. This could be a short trip."

"I hope so," Joshua said. "You'll need supplies with you? Potions?

Max shook his head. "Keep them. You guys will need them here more than I will."

They exchanged a few words before Max excused himself. Joshua was busy and he didn't really need him there. Max decided he would go set up his hammock and get some sleep. Tomorrow could be a long day.

He would need to spend these free points from Cultivation and his massive stack of **Cosmic Coins**. Then he would get a good meal and leave first thing in the morning. Maybe a new Boss had spawned. Whatever it was, Max would take care of it.

CHAPTER FORTY-SIX

Sharing

Max woke up to a somewhat normalized camp life. As always, he overslept as far as the community was concerned. But the sleep had been productive beyond just providing him rest, as Maverick had been active during the night. There was a red dot in the System notifications in Max's field of vision. He checked it, although he knew what it was.

Leveled Up Quartz-Level Cultivator (lesser) to 13
+1 free Attribute point

Max sat up in the hammock and looked down at the camp. People were bustling about, doing all sorts of tasks, some of which were new ones, thanks to the supplies Max had brought them. For example, the camp now had an abundance of containers, so half a score of people were going back and forth to the river to fill as many containers for the day as possible.

There was, of course, a sense of melancholy to the camp. They had survived and won last night but at a high price. Many faces seemed lethargic and crestfallen. Max could only thank the fates that none of the people he had grown to care about had been hurt.

Max returned the hammock to his Inventory and went to the river for a wash, waving a hand at various people who were hollering at him. When he got back and took a bowl of fish stew from one of Sid's cooks, he noticed Lily sitting on the ground, eating. Max sat next to her.

Lily had been away last night, practicing using clay at the site she had found. As far as Max knew, she stayed there all day, every day.

"Good thing you were there," Max said. "It got messy last night."

"I heard you saved a lot of people," Lily said and gave him a little smile.

"I suppose I did," Max said. "That's what I'm good for. I could never do what you do. I heard from Marie that you're working at the clay deposit daily."

Lily nodded. "It's actually been a little complicated."

"How come?"

"Because I can make a pretty good cup or plate by this point, and I always bring one or two home when I return. But not everyone's been happy about me just grinding the Levels and not bringing back everything I make. Most of my stuff I leave to the site."

"Oh," Max said. "You're power-Leveling."

"Uh huh," Lily said. "I was big on mobile games on . . . on Earth . . ."

Her gaze turned glassy for a moment, but she shook herself out of it.

"So I feel like I know what I'm doing. I think it's better for me to power-Level now and then create something *actually* useful later."

"So now that I brought back a bunch of cups, plates, and pots, that's a weight off your shoulders?" Max asked.

Lily brushed her black hair off her face and smiled brightly. "Exactly! Thank you. And now I also have models to work with. You keep saying you don't do much other than kill stuff, but honestly, I think you're great."

She blushed a little and gave him a shy look. Max smiled.

"You're doing great too," Max said. "Keep doing that power-Level thing. The more people that can really appreciate that this is sort of a game, the better for us."

"Yeah," Lily said. "I'm taking notes from you."

"What Level are you anyway?"

"I'm Level Fourteen," Lily said.

Max turned to her, eyebrows raised. "Really? You're almost on par with Joshua. That's impressive."

Lily gave him a gentle smile.

Max produced the sack of **[Celestial Illumination Pills]** from his Inventory. He scooped up a handful and waited for Lily to understand. She put down her bowl of fish stew and cupped her hands. Max poured about twenty pills into them.

"What are these?" Lily asked.

Max smiled knowingly. "You'll really appreciate those once you hit Fifteen."

"You unlock a new thing at Fifteen?"

"Oh, a big thing," Max said. "These will help you Level Up faster."

"Wow. Thank you, Max," Lily said and gave him that shy smile again. "You know, you should see Elena. She's gotten a lot of Levels lately. I think she's either Thirteen or Fourteen. If you have any more of these to spare, give some to her. Or if you don't, you can take these back and—I mean, I would like them but . . . I just . . ."

"Don't be silly," Max said and chuckled. "I already gave them to you. Keep them."

"Thanks," she said demurely.

Max poured the rest of the fish stew down his gullet. He wasn't the biggest fan of fish, but he wasn't one to complain. Food was food. They were a long way from hamburgers and ice cream, no matter how fast Sid Leveled Up.

"I'll go see Elena," Max said and squeezed Lily on the shoulder as he got up. "Thanks for the company."

"See you, Max!"

Max went off to find Elena. He could spare another handful of pills, as there was a massive amount of them still. Not that he should use them frivolously, but for dedicated power Levelers like Lily or Elena, it would be worthwhile. If Elena were to become a [**Doctor**], [**Apothecary**], [**Alchemist**], or the like, it could literally save Max's life one day.

Elena greeted him with a tired smile. If she had slept, it hadn't been for long. Max offered her a bowl of fish stew, after having asked Sid's crew if she had eaten anything this morning.

Her exhausted eyes lit up. "So considerate. Thank you."

Max shrugged. "I try."

"Try too hard, you mean," Maverick quipped.

"Can't you cycle or something?" Max snapped.

"I was going to, but your interactions are very interesting," Maverick said.

"What's cycling?" Elena asked.

"I'll tell you in a minute," Max said. "May I sit?"

"Of course."

"You look like hell," Max said as he came to sit down on a rock next to her. She was observing her patients, who were in varying states of unconsciousness.

"Feel like hell too," Elena said. "I suppose this place is a hell of a sorts."

"Sometimes," Max said. "But when I look at what people have built here, it feels amazing sometimes too. We'll pull through this."

Elena gave an uncertain nod between spoonfuls of stew.

"Thanks to people like you," Max said. "Lily told me you've been really pulling your weight and then some. What Level are you?"

"I'm a Level Fourteen [**Herbalist**]. Leveled Up just tonight," Elena said. There was no pride in her tone. She just stated it.

"That's really good!" Max said. "You're almost as high-Level as me."

"Huh," Elena said between spoonfuls. "I thought you'd be higher."

"I'm Level Eighteen," Max said. "At Fifteen, you unlock a system that's a good idea to spend some time with. It relates to that cycling thing Maverick and I talked about."

Max explained the basics of the Cultivation System to her and gave her a handful of pills. She protested at first, before Max showed her how many pills he still had left in the purple sack. Once Elena was convinced and willing, she asked Max if she could break some down.

Max shrugged and said that he'd trust her judgment; they were her pills now, anyway. After finishing the bowl of stew, it was obvious Elena could barely keep herself on her feet anyway.

"Go sleep for two hours," Max said.

Elena shook her head vigorously. "I can't. I need to look after them. If they move in their sleep and a wound rips open, it'll be bad."

"I'll keep watch. If anything happens, I'll wake you up. Sleep close. I'll give you exactly two hours."

"You're too much of a softie," Elana protested. "You'll just let me sleep till the cows come home."

"What the hell is this expression?" Max asked. "Did you grow up on a farm? People still say that?"

"I don't know. Don't tease me!"

Max let out a laugh. "Anyway, I'll give you two hours, not more."

"How can you tell the time?"

Max smirked. "These pills? Their effect lasts exactly two hours. I'll cycle with Maverick for two hours and then spend some time with my **Cosmic Coins** and Attribute points, and then I'll wake you up. How's that?"

Elena sighed. "Oh . . . That's . . . Good night, Max."

That was all she said. She gave Max one last grateful smile and put down her bowl of stew. Then she walked a few paces and found a spot on the ground to lie down, falling asleep almost instantly.

Max popped a **[Celestial Illumination Pill]** and gave Maverick one. It wouldn't be as effective as usual, because he had promised to keep an eye on the wounded. Still, this would be a good opportunity to eke out a Level or two before heading for the woods.

CHAPTER FORTY-SEVEN

Last Minute

Fortunately, nothing bad happened while Max was keeping watch. And he made excellent progress, to boot.

Leveled Up Quartz-Level Cultivator (lesser) to 14
+1 free Attribute point
Leveled Up Quartz-Level Cultivator (lesser) to 15
+1 free Attribute point
Advancement to Quartz-Level Cultivator (greater) available

Max immediately went to his notifications and opened the advancement message. Therein was a simple Y/N prompt, asking if he wanted to advance at the cost of Five **[Lesser Spirit Coins]**.

Absolutely yes.

It felt like a cold winter breeze passing through every vein in his body. His mind tingled with cold, almost like brain freeze from eating ice cream too fast, but not unpleasant. It felt invigorating, finally concentrating around his solar plexus, where his soul apparently resided. He could sense Maverick going through the same sensations.

Advanced to Quartz-Level Cultivator (greater)
+5 to all Attributes
[Quartz Meditation Technique: Basic Mana Cycling] -> [Quartz Meditation Technique: Advanced Mana Cycling]
[Achievement: First Soul Advancement]
Reward: E-grade Cultivation Box
[Achievement: World First Soul Advancement]
Reward: C-grade Cultivation Box

Oh damn, I didn't think I'd get a World First here. C-grade stuff could be huge.

"Yes, my trusted sidekick!" Maverick bellowed, startling some of the patients lying down nearby. "We are at the forefront of peak performance! We are the Alpha and Omega! We are the good, true and beautiful! We are—"

"OKAY!" Max cut in. Then he hissed an angry whisper at Maverick. "People are looking. Can you please be reasonable for two minutes?"

Maverick huffed. "Won't even let me enjoy my spoils of war. I'll have you know—"

"Will you pipe down if I spend some **Cosmic Coins** on you?"

"Oh, yes, please."

"Okay . . ." Max thought aloud. "How should we do this? We got 26,515 **Cosmic Coins**."

"Give it all to Papa."

"Please never refer to yourself as 'papa' again."

"I kind of like it," Maverick said cheerily.

"I bet you do," Max muttered. "I could upgrade you some. It might even boost your ability to Cultivate, who knows?"

"Oh, I am absolutely positive it will. Come on!"

"I could bring you up to +7 . . ." Max thought aloud.

"Do it. Dooooo it."

"But that would cost over twenty-two thousand coins . . ."

"Oh, but ever so worth it, wouldn't you agree?"

"But I do want to upgrade this awesome robe I just got."

"I will shred that rag while you sleep."

"I will eventually get better things, of course . . . As nice as the robe is, it's only C-grade."

"While I am special-absolute-godlike-bonanza-grade."

"While I am stuck with you," Max agreed.

[3200 Cosmic Coins spent]
[The Maverick] upgraded to +5
+9 Intelligence
+4 Precision
[6400 Cosmic Coins spent]
[The Maverick] upgraded to +6
+11 Intelligence
+6 Precision
[12,800 Cosmic Coins spent]
[The Maverick] upgraded to +7
+13 Intelligence
+8 Precision

"YESSSSS! I FEEL THE POWER! I HAVE BECOME DEATH, THE DESTROYER OF WORLDS. TREMBLE AT MY FEET! COWER IN DESPAIR!"

Maverick went on for a while. Max gave up. People were going to look. There was no helping it. Max zoned HIM out, deeming it wise not to mention Maverick's lack of feet. Instead, he needed to decide what to do with the remaining 4115 **Cosmic Coins**. It wasn't exactly a decision based on careful analysis and math. It was simply a gut feeling. Max went ahead and put all of them in his new robes.

[100 Cosmic Coins spent]
[Robes of Shadowsilk] upgraded to +1
+7 Constitution
+9 Intelligence
+3 Resistance
[200 Cosmic Coins spent]
[Robes of Shadowsilk] upgraded to +2
+7 Constitution
+10 Intelligence
+4 Resistance
[400 Cosmic Coins spent]
[Robes of Shadowsilk] upgraded to +3
+9 Constitution
+10 Intelligence
+4 Resistance
[800 Cosmic Coins spent]
[Robes of Shadowsilk] upgraded to +4
+10 Constitution
+10 Intelligence
+5 Resistance
[1600 Cosmic Coins spent]
[Robes of Shadowsilk] upgraded to +5
+10 Constitution
+10 Intelligence
+7 Resistance

Okay that's enough for now.

He still had a thousand coins and change left, but Max figured he'd rather save them for now. Spending them on the D-grade Items he would end up giving away felt wrong. He could, of course, consume them for most of their **Cosmic Coins**, but that would mean one less perfectly good Item for the camp.

After all that, Max spent all his free Attribute points. He had seven points to spare from the Cultivating and he decided to round out his Constitution and Intelligence. They were both useful Stats and rounding them out made him happy. The rest he used on Toughness and Resistance. Being able to round out Toughness was a happy coincidence.

After that, Max brought up the Stat sheet to admire it for a moment. He had made such good progress. Yes, these were rough times for the community, but right now, Max felt like nothing could stop him. He would fix things for these people.

Name: Max Cromwell
Cultivation stage: Quartz (greater)
Class: Graviturgist
Level: 18
Health: 600/600
Stamina: 600/600
Mana: 850/850
Alliance: Joshua's Group
Stats:
Strength: 14
Dexterity: 16
Constitution: 60
Intelligence: 85
Wisdom: 55
Charisma: 14
Precision: 37
Toughness: 20
Resistance: 27

Max wished he didn't have to wake up Elena, but he really needed to go. She muttered something incomprehensible and tried to doze off again. As difficult as it was, Max steeled himself and shook her awake.

"Hey," Elena said, sounding beyond grumpy. "Thanks."

"You sure?" Max asked, smirking and quirking an eyebrow. "You don't sound grateful."

"Shouldn't you be out there adventuring or something?" Elena asked.

Max got up. "I should, but first I'll bring you some water."

"Thanks," she said weakly. "I still kind of hate you right now. I was dreaming of cake."

"Was it cheesecake?"

"Yes . . ."

"In that case, I understand your deep ire," Max said. Elena chuckled softly behind Max as he went to grab a jug of water.

Max was finally back out there, hunting. It felt good trekking through the woods, feeling that special kind of alertness that Max only felt when he was out adventuring. Dried leaves crumpled under his foot, and the forest air was fresh and fragrant. The weak sun cast a few rays through the canopy, and the faint sounds of birds and little critters shuffling in the bushes gave a feeling of serenity to the atmosphere.

The time he had spent in the camp had been precious. It was a delight to eat Sid's cooking and to be admired and respected by the people there. But the longer Max stayed, the louder *that* nagging feeling got. It wasn't that Max felt like he didn't belong there. No, that wasn't it. He actually felt a strong sense of belonging when he spent time with the people of the camp, Joshua especially. First, Max hadn't been sure if Joshua was being sincere with him. He was nice to everyone. But eventually Max came to feel that they shared a deeper bond. Joshua was a friend. And a good one at that. And the camp was home.

But that nagging feeling was always there. The best thing he could do for the community was to stay away from it, and that feeling was complicated and it hurt. But it was the right thing to do. It gave him pride. It gave him purpose. He was at the forefront of the fight for humanity's right to exist. To be out here, dealing with threats and bringing home resources in a way that others couldn't—that was *his* job.

Brian and his fighting men had asked Max if he needed them to collect any animals he happened to kill. Max said it wasn't needed. He didn't want them around, even though they seemed to be more docile and respectful now after their showdown with him. But they genuinely weren't needed. There were more-than-enough panther corpses from the attack to be processed.

Speaking of panthers, it wasn't long before he ran into more of them. Max was walking along when he heard rustling from a nearby bush. And this clearly wasn't a squirrel or similarly small critter moving around. This was something careful, quiet, and *big*.

A black shape growled and pounced at him. Max dodged, but his vision still flashed red. Forty Health gone. He turned and took another swipe and then a third. There was another panther behind Max. They had ambushed him with a pincer attack. Losing over one hundred Health in a matter of seconds gave him a flash of panic. Maverick sent a flash of emotion, telling him to cool down and focus.

Max instinctively tethered the beasts to each other. They growled with frustration but somehow had the presence of mind to untangle themselves and get back on their feet. Max shot at them. They were slow, but they approached him in perfect synchrony. Max cast a repelling **[Tether]** to himself and one of them.

That messed up their formation, and they yowled as they fell to the ground, on their sides. Max finished them off.

Defeated Level 12 [Mutated Panther]
You gained 280 Experience points
Defeated Level 12 [Mutated Panther]
You gained 280 Experience points

Max knelt and looted them for their **Cosmic Coins**. These were the same mutated, larger panthers that had attacked the camp. They even had the spine-protecting silver collars.

But what they didn't have was the **(???)** in the System message as when Max had killed the earlier ones. Why? What had the question marks meant?

Max produced a **[Minor Health Potion]** and drank it. It almost restored him to full Health. Maybe it would have been more prudent to let his Health naturally regenerate, but these monsters were smart and ferocious enough to warrant it. If the ambush had been done by three or four panthers, it could have been a real problem.

Max knelt on the forest floor and filled the little potion vial with panther blood. He would give the vial to Elena. Maybe she could get some use out of it. Then he wiped his hands, got up, and brought a hand to **[The Maverick]** resting in the holster at his side. He would need to be ready for anything.

CHAPTER FORTY-EIGHT

Following the Map

Max delved deeper into the forest, holding a very peculiar map. There were three types of monsters. There were the old **[Tauroid]** that had gained some Levels but had not undergone an evolution, making them essentially harmless, as Max could shoot them dead with a single bullet.

But his only interest in the map were the panthers. There were two kinds: the normal ones and the ones with the (???) at the end of the System message. Whenever Max killed another set, he went in the direction they had come from.

Max dispatched a good fifteen of them before night fell. His Stamina was still healthy, and his expenditure of Mana was so minimal that it wasn't even a consideration. The panthers were vicious, but with a little care and foresight on his sight, they weren't an issue.

He still wanted to keep going. He wondered if his advancement in Cultivation was giving him more energy. It did seem like that at first guess, but he didn't want to jump to any conclusions yet. He didn't want to end up in a situation where he had stayed up all night and would then have to face whatever was causing the attacks in a sluggish state.

So when the first signs that he was growing fatigued started to show up, Max decided to lean into them, instead of soldiering on, his typical modus operandi.

Instead, he set up his hammock and went to sleep.

After what could not have been more than five or six hours, Max woke up, feeling adequately rested. Maybe the advancement had actually done something to his body. He did feel more . . . *acute*, somehow.

It was hard to describe, But he seemed ever-so-slightly more alert. A little bit stronger, a little bit faster. His sense of Mana in his body was especially keen. Max felt good. Great, even. It was as if whatever change he had undergone yesterday with the Cultivation stage advancement had solidified itself during his sleep. He felt *powerful.*

He got up and put the hammock in his Inventory. It seemed that Maverick was sleeping again. He hadn't even Cultivated during the night. Funnily enough, Max actually missed his ridiculous remarks at the moment. He could feel Maverick's soul thrumming as it rested. It felt more potent too. Max smiled to himself, knowing the gun would be excited to feel more powerful once it woke up.

It didn't take long for Max to find more mutated panthers. They were easy pickings for the most part. Max racked up the kills and followed his map. Everything was going swimmingly as the panthers moved in packs of two mostly. Except for when they didn't.

Now, Max saw four of them approaching. They came at him from the direction he'd been heading. The panthers with (???) in the System messages were getting more prevalent. Max saw them from afar, which was a lucky break, because if he hadn't, they could have caused him serious trouble.

The four panthers moved in synchrony, walking side-by-side. When they noticed Max, they split into pairs and vanished into the bushes opposite to each other.

Max looked around. There was a sturdy tree behind him, some five yards away. Good target to use for tethering himself for evasive maneuvers. There was a thick bush in front of him and to the right. He was almost certain the other pair would jump at him from there. A well-timed **[Gravity Well]** should do the trick. As for the other group he—

The pairs attacked in perfect synchrony. Max executed his half-baked plan in half a blink of the eye. Two of the panthers were caught swirling in the air by the **[Gravity Well]** at the same time as he slid towards the tree behind him.

One of the panthers missed, and the other clipped him with a claw. Max lost twenty Health. Not too bad.

But they attacked again, and even when Max tethered them, they managed to keep moving, as he had observed before. They pounced on him and ripped at him. His vision flashed red several times, and as he used a repelling **[Tether]** twice on himself, he shot at them, creating a third repelling **[Tether]** on the ground where they stood, pushing them even further away. Max gritted his teeth and shot again at the pair. They fell. When Max went back towards the two he had left swirling in the air, they were gone.

Damn it. Where are they?

Max huddled up against a thick tree branch, **[The Maverick]** at the ready. He listened and made his best effort to use all of his senses. He gave a quick glance at his Health Bar. Over two hundred Health lost. A big chunk of his Mana gone, too. These panthers weren't pulling their punches.

Max waited and looked around, listening for the faintest crunch of dry leaves or the crack of a fallen branch. Nothing. Just the sounds of the forest. Had the two panthers . . . retreated?

Surely not. Beasts couldn't do that, right? But these were intelligent beasts, that much was clear. Max carefully moved towards where he had used the **[Gravity Well]** on the two panthers. They weren't waiting in the bush. That was good. He searched the ground for track marks. He thought he saw a paw print or two leading away, but it was hard to tell.

But it did look like there were some faint marks on the ground in the direction the panthers had initially come from.

He sat down for a moment, drinking from his waterskin and eating the rest of the dried meat he'd been holding on to since almost the start of the games. As he ripped at the tough meat with his teeth, he listened and watched, in case the panthers were still sneaking around. Nothing happened.

Max noticed that the panthers weren't the only things that had changed. The forest had grown. It was much thicker, and Max could swear it spanned a further distance in every direction now than before. It hadn't crept towards the river, but who knew what the reason for that was.

When he was finished with his meat, he carried on. Still a little wary that he might get jumped by the two missing panthers, he continued to tread carefully. But nothing happened. Where had they gone and why?

Curiously enough, no more panthers appeared. He was sure he was going in the direction that the trail of panthers had led him. Had the missing panthers warned the others about him? Were they preparing for some mass attack elsewhere? While his mind wanted to initially brush the thought off as preposterous, he had to admit that he was in a pretty crazy reality, and the panthers clearly had some intelligence.

He carried on, keeping **[The Maverick]** at the ready. He hadn't felt the need to cast **[Alter Gravity]** on the weapon for now. The extra Strength from Cultivation advancement helped, of course.

But he had also developed a surprisingly toned right arm, since arriving at Alpha Ludus. His whole body overall had undergone some distinct changes. He had gained better muscle definition and tone over his whole body, but the right arm definitely stood out, even compared to the left one.

Those gains weren't Framework-related, But that didn't stop Max from smiling to himself. He'd really come a long way in many a way since arriving here.

Abruptly, he sighted a panther thirty yards ahead. That immediately snapped him out of his musings. Max prepared, his mind focusing. The panthers never moved alone. There would be some in the bushes nearby. They could—

This panther was acting very, very strangely. It sat down and tilted its head, tail swishing behind it, almost as if in impatience.

When Max approached, it only looked at him with those lamp-like yellow eyes and sniffed the air. Max came closer, still wary of the myriad possible traps that could be sprung on him. But if this was a trap, it was a stupid one.

Max stopped a good fifteen yards away. The panther sniffed the air again, turned and looked over its shoulder at Max.

It wants me to follow it?

The panther yowled, definitely impatiently this time, and it walked a few paces, watching back over its shoulder to see if Max followed.

Wary as he was, Max was also curious. He kept his distance, and when the distance grew too large for the panther, it sat down, licking at its paw, waiting for Max.

Max followed it for a while, until he came out of the woods into an opening. A little stream trickled nearby, next to a cave that let off a foul stench. A panther cub peeked out of the cave, before its mother came out and snatched it from the back of its neck and carried it inside. In the middle of the opening was a large boulder, a mossy giant, reaching up to ten feet high in the air.

Atop the boulder, smiling in that easy, slow manner of his, eyes giving a twinkle of mischief, leaning on a spear, stood the Stranger.

"It's been a while," he drawled. "Has it not, Max?"

CHAPTER FORTY-NINE

Unhappy Reunions

You!" Max exclaimed. "What is going on?"

"Oh, a long story that," the Stranger said. "First of all, I must applaud you on your deft performance in escaping me."

"Can't say I regret that," Max said. "You weren't particularly cooperative."

"Not one of my strong suits," the Stranger admitted. "But I learned a great deal from our previous encounter."

"I really hope it explains what's going on here," Max said darkly. "I really don't appreciate what I *think* is going on here."

"Don't get ahead of yourself, my friend," the Stranger said and smiled. "Enjoy the moment. Listen to my story."

"It had better be a good one," Max growled.

The Stranger merely smirked.

"Now, you chasing me away by using a wild beast gave me a fun idea. An idea for poetic vengeance. You see, I wondered what would have happened to you had I died. Would you have been judged by our patrons? Or was this a potential loophole? I'll save you from the details of how I tested my theories. Suffice it to say, it *is* a loophole."

"Vengeance . . . ?" Max's brain tried to piece it together, but a part of him just couldn't believe it. Eventually, however, it clicked. "*You!* You're the one attacking the camp!"

"Ding, ding, ding," the Stranger said and clapped slowly. "Winner winner, chicken dinner."

"Just to get back at me?" Max asked, a dark storm gathering behind his voice.

"Why not? You took my spear and my fun from me," the Stranger said. "So I asked myself where could I hit you that would hurt the most. You were nowhere to be seen in the Dreadlands, smart little adventurer that you are. And I couldn't figure out a way to thwart your growth."

Max looked around. There were a few panthers lying on the grass, watching Max idly. Maybe three in total. And the cub and the mother in the cave. There could be more inside for all he knew.

"But I knew you would have friends somewhere, being such a little Boy Scout. It didn't take me awfully long to find them huddled up by the river. Being an emaciated, weak, lost traveler, they took me in with open arms. I like people. I really do. So trusting, so generous."

Max snarled at the Stranger but said nothing. He would let him talk. He needed to think. *Four or more adult panthers . . . and the Stranger, who is . . . who knows how powerful currently?* Max hoped he'd become stronger than him, being a higher-Level Cultivator, but he wasn't sure.

"I ate their food and listened to their stories. It did not take long to ascertain that I had come to the right place. Oh, how they adore you, Max. The Bringer of Buckets, the hero, the protector. I did not really understand why they held you in such high esteem, or how they'd come to the conclusion that you were some sort of a protector. I think you're just like me."

"I am nothing like you," Max spat. The Stranger tutted and wagged a finger.

"Now, now. Listen to my story first," the Stranger drawled on. "So I wanted to prove them wrong, of course. You are no protector. You are a lone hunter, just like me.

"And so I started testing things. I came to this forest and found rather strong panthers here. I wondered if the beasts in my starting region had also grown stronger. Most likely. Now, my first attempt was to have a panther get interested in me, then wound it, and then run from it until I found one of the lovely fools of your community wandering about."

Max glared at the Stranger.

"It worked perfectly," the Stranger said. "The panther found easier prey and immediately killed some fool picking for mushrooms. I got no notification, no divine judgment, nothing. So I escalated my research, but I will not bore you with the details. Eventually, I developed a talent called **[Animal Friend]**. It's a very exciting ability. Allows me to communicate with animals and have a Charisma bonus when dealing with them."

I'll start by consuming a **[Potion of Greater Mana Regeneration]**. *I could retreat into the cave, and hold the entrance, but I have no idea how many panthers there are. I should assume at least six. I could run around, gather them, tether them to each other, and then use a* **[Gravity Well]**.

"My bond with the beast allowed for further, more intricate communication with the other panthers. She basically works as a liaison or a translator, if you will. Then I started feeding them stories of the evil village that attacks and eats panthers. Technically true, and their simple beast minds lapped up the story without blinking. The rest was just a question of organizing the attacks and teaching them to work together. They learn surprisingly fast, these beasts. Mighty interesting creatures. They're also ruthless, which is a trait I like about them."

"I'm sure you guys have a lot in common," Max said, buying time to refine his battle plans. It was hard to focus on that, while keeping his rage in check, but he managed. "You can control a pack of panthers? Just like that?"

"I wouldn't say control," the Stranger said. "I can give them suggestions and ideas. I can control the matriarch to a degree, but it is more of a negotiation on some days. However, by now, I have learned what makes these little cats tick. Sometimes they allow me to teach them. I've tried little raids on the people working in the clay deposit. That little girl is always there, but she is too damned fast and careful. I must say I am a little upset that you killed all my well-trained pets."

Lily. No. You will not take her!

"So you've been goading the panthers to attack the camp?" Max asked, spitting the words between his teeth. He gripped his revolver. He was ready to kill the Stranger at this point. Tribunals be damned. If he didn't kill him, he would just continue doing what he was doing and more good people would die.

"Precisely," the Stranger said, clearly pleased that Max caught on. "I even Spirit-Bonded with that matriarch in the cave you saw. It is my Cultivation path."

So, he is at least Level Fifteen. That doesn't surprise me. Question is, if push comes to shove, will he attack me, or only use the beasts for fear of the Tribunal?

"I did not actually know you had come back from your hunts," the Stranger said. "I thought it would be fitting that the protector returned to a mangled wreck of a home, utterly destroyed."

"Why!?" Max spat out. "You could be doing this against the enemy! Against the *real* enemy. You could be useful. You could be what humanity needs right now. Instead, you play these sick, petty games!"

The panther on the rock growled. The Stranger didn't look happy about Max's outburst either, but whatever little emotion flicked on his face, it was gone as soon as it had appeared.

"You call it petty, I call it justice," the Stranger said in a tone darker than before.

"And I call it stupid!" Max shouted. "Don't you understand what's at stake here? Go hunt the enemy!"

"Who said I won't?" The Stranger said, almost offended. "That was my plan for after I have taught you your lesson."

"What goddamn lesson!?"

The panther got up and hissed, baring its teeth. The Stranger tutted again.

"To never cross me again," the Stranger said, looking down at Max. "If you steal a finger from me, I will take an arm from you."

"You," Max said from between his teeth, "won't take a single thing from me anymore! EVER!"

Max unholstered **[The Maverick]** and blasted a volley at the panther by the Stranger's side.

CHAPTER FIFTY

Ultimatum

Max would have found the brief moment that the Stranger's complacent smile broke into an indignant snarl delicious, if he had had the time to savor it. Max shot the panther next to the Stranger with a few well-aimed shots. It died with a pained yowl and Max ran ahead to look into the cave's mouth. The matriarch came out and hissed. The surrounding panthers all hunched their shoulder blades and started prowling towards Max, their eyes gleaming with deadly intent.

Max cast [**Alter Gravity**] on himself and his weapon. Then he moved even further away from the Stranger, who clearly hesitated. Perfect time to chug down a [**Potion of Greater Mana Regeneration**]. The other panthers were prowling towards him, but both the Stranger and the matriarch stood still, watching.

He doesn't want to risk the Tribunal. Coward. Well, all the better for me.

The panthers came from both sides, three approaching him from both sides of the rock. This was going to be easy. The panthers had no element of surprise.

In quick succession, Max cast two [**Gravity Wells**] at both groups.

The Stranger gasped in frustration and immediately went over to help the panthers out of the spell. He moved *fast.* He lunged at the panthers like an American football player, arms outstretched, and pushed them out of the range of Max's spell. In the process, he almost got pulled into the swirl himself, but he either had enough Resistance or bodily strength to wrench himself free. Max released the spell.

While all of this was going on, Max shot at them. The Stranger took a bullet. A face of utter shock and outrage stared Max down. At that moment, Max knew without a shadow of doubt that only one of them would survive to face the Tribunal.

Max used two simultaneous **[Tethers]** on the big mossy rock to propel himself backwards as he shot at the tangled mess of panthers on his right, still swirling and yowling angrily in the **[Gravity Well]**.

The move backwards gave him just enough time to dodge a spear throw from the Stranger. He had run towards his spears faster than a professional sprinter as Max used another set of tetherings to maneuver towards the panthers trapped in his spell. He shot at them, killing one. He didn't release the spell, as it forced the Stranger to find a better angle, while Max deliberately positioned himself so that either the big mossy rock, or the three panthers in the air were shielding him.

Then the mother attacked. She swiped at Max twice, and he instantly lost fifty Health. Max turned and used a repelling **[Tether]** instinctively, pushing the panther away. By then, the Stranger had found a better angle and thrown the spear. It struck Max and propelled him four yards away. He fell on the ground, clutching the spear in his hands. It hadn't pierced skin, but it still hurt quite a bit. One hundred Health gone like that. Then the mother panther and the other three free panthers jumped on him.

They got a few swipes in before Max used another **[Gravity Well]**. Another forty Health gone. And the Stranger ran at him. Max threw the spear away into the woods with a **[Tether]** repelling it from his hand. It flew in a beautiful arc for a good fifty yards.

The Stranger produced a knife from his Inventory. In the meantime, Max quickly chugged down a **[Health Potion]**.

The Stranger came at him with the knife, attacking fast as a viper, but Max slid away with a **[Tether]**, shooting at him a few times.

The Stranger was shocked, possibly by the damage **[The Maverick]** had caused so quickly. Max wasted no time. He used **[Tether]** on the Stranger and the ground to hold him still, and he kept shooting.

The Stranger was fast, though. He broke free from Max's spell and went to free the panthers. He tackled the group of four, but Max managed to impede him with a **[Tether]**. Still, two of the panthers broke free. They immediately attacked Max. Max shot at them, while the Stranger ran behind the big rock, presumably to drink some potions.

Max managed to kill the two panthers attacking him and to drink a **[Mana Potion]** but in that time, the Stranger had freed all of the remaining panthers. One psychopath and four panthers left.

The four panthers came at him from two sides again, Max used tetherings to the left in order to steer his enemies to all come at him from the same direction. Only the matriarch and Stranger reacted quickly enough to avoid it. The other three panthers were caught in a new **[Gravity Well]**.

Max shot at the Stranger, who moved in swift jerky moves from side to side to avoid being hit. Meanwhile, the matriarch prowled closer and pounced at Max. He repelled the attack with a **[Tether]** and alternated shots between the Stranger and the trapped panthers. He managed to kill two more of the panthers. He released the **[Gravity Well]** and cast multiple **[Tethers]** to stay out of the Stranger's reach.

His Mana was starting to get low. The Stranger got in range and swiped with a knife. He was brutally strong. Another thirty Health gone from just a knife. Now, both his Health and Mana were in the two hundreds. But the Stranger was breathing heavily and slowing down ever so slightly as well. So was the matriarch. They were expending Stamina. The Stranger took time to chug down a potion, presumably Stamina. Max took the time to use one too. But he had to choose: Mana or Health. No Mana would result in no Health. He chugged down another **[Mana Potion]**.

Still, the Stranger was too fast. If Max didn't zip around with **[Tether]** and shoot at him, the Stranger would always be at his heels. But if he did, the panthers would be able to get a jump on him, taking swipes. But Max could move reasonably fast without a tethering, due to the **[Alter Gravity]** still affecting him . . .

Max alternated between targets to keep them off of him, eventually managing to kill the last panther, other than the matriarch.

The Stranger was too focused and angry to care, but the matriarch yowled with anger and took another swipe at Max. He lost another thirty Health. Max tethered the beast to the big rock. Max took a few shots at it before the Stranger charged him. Another twenty points of Health gone. Max was starting to feel pain. Only a little over one hundred Health left.

Max repelled the Stranger away, but despite the potency of his spell, the Stranger was just too strong. He doubled down, which kept the man away. It cost him a fair chunk of the Mana he had left. Max could only do a few more tetherings now. But it gave him enough time to kill the matriarch.

Level Up! [Level 19 Graviturgist]
You have gained + 1 Constitution, + 2 Intelligence, + 2 Wisdom, + 2 free
Attribute points

"You'll pay for that," the Stranger snarled and charged again. The knife pierced Max in the abdomen, and his vision flashed red. There was pain. Almost paralyzing pain. The knife was lodged in his lung. Max coughed, and the Stranger pushed him down. Wild eyes and a rictus grimace of anger stared down at him. The Stranger pulled the knife out, and Max gasped. He struck again, and Max instinctively blocked him with a hand. The knife cut right through his palm. The pain was blurring his vision.

Maverick woke. He sent a strong pulse through his soul to Max, which brought some clarity back. He only had Mana for two [**Tethers**]. It wouldn't be enough. Even if he could get the Stranger off of him, the man was so strong, he would break free from the tethering.

Maverick sent another pulse of Spiritual Energy through Max. His vision became clearer, and he noticed he had a sliver of Health again. And a bit more Mana.

"Suspend this fool, Max!" Maverick said in a sharp tone. Max knew immediately what it meant.

The Stranger had climbed on top of Max ready to strike again. Coughing up blood, Max rasped, "[**Tether**]!"

Max cast multiple times. Three repelling [**Tethers**] yanked the Stranger up to dangle in midair over him. A look of horror dawned on the Stranger's face. He threw the knife, but Max lifted up his useless arm and it glanced off the shoulder, cutting as it went. A minor scratch compared to his lung situation.

Max raised [**The Maverick**].

"Yes," Maverick said coldly. "You were a fool to oppose us."

"Please!" the Stranger said, desperation in his voice. "I promise, I will—"

Whatever else he had to say was lost in the sounds of gunshots echoing through the forest opening. It took but a couple before the Stranger's eyes lost focus and he went limp in the air.

Max turned to his side, throwing the Stranger's body on the ground further away. He sighed. Dropping [**The Maverick**], he took out a [**Health Potion**] with his good hand. His body resisted the liquid, blood mixed with the potion, but Max swallowed it down. His breathing became a little easier. His hand was still damaged, but it no longer felt like he was drowning in blood.

With a weary motion, Max got up and picked up [**The Maverick**] again. Just as he did, a plastic jellyfish appeared in midair in front of him.

"Max?" Maverick asked.

[Hello, Max. You will now be immediately transported to the Tribunal. Apologies for the inconvenience.]
[Initializing relocation . . .]

Max felt fear lurch inside of him. Maverick caught onto that.

"Max?" the gun asked. "Are we in trouble?"

[Initialization complete.]
[Relocating . . .]

CHAPTER FIFTY-ONE

The Tribunal

After coming out of the floating darkness Max had already become accustomed to when being teleported by the Zoos, he fell to a floor made of a strange white material. Max got up and looked around.

He was in the corridor of some futuristic craft. Every surface was smooth and white, and a single tube snaked across the ceiling above him, pulsing with some green energy. Max approached a nearby window and looked out.

"Is that . . ." Max trailed off.

[That is the planet Alpha Ludus.]

The Zoos representative hovered next to Max.

[Remain calm. You are on a vessel of the ICCB. You are here to partake in a Tribunal.]

"I know it was against the rules!" Max stammered. "But he attacked my village! He was using a loophole. If I hadn't done it, dozens of humans would have died!"

The Zoos representative turned to Max, but from the look in its digital eyes, it seemed like it was . . . distracted?

[We did not realize you had an encounter like this.]

"Wait, what?" Max said. "That's not why I'm here?"

[We do not have the time or interest for any squabble you had with the person you killed. We are sure you acted in the best interest of your species. If you did not, we will have to overlook it this time.]

Well, that was a relief. He wouldn't even get a slap on the wrist. Wait, if he wasn't here because of the Stranger, what was happening?

"Why am I here then?" Max asked.

[**You are here to be reviewed regarding your Cultivation path. The Framework has acted out of accord, and we must inspect your situation and decide how to proceed.**]

"Isn't me getting a good Cultivation path a good thing?"

[**We certainly think so. The Zoos Collective is pleased by this serendipitous event. However, this Tribunal is not held within the Zoos Collective. This is a Tribunal concerning all the four major factions of the ICCB.**]

Max gulped. It probably wasn't a good thing he had somehow attracted the attention of all of the four factions. His heart rate increased, as stress flooded his body. What kind of trouble was he in exactly?

[**It appears that your cortisol and adrenaline levels are rising. Would you like a sedative?**]

Max was still looking out at the planet hanging in space. It was the first time he had ever been in outer space, he realized. *Obviously. What kind of a normal Earth person goes to space? Other than an astronaut, I guess.* But the notion didn't excite him as much as it probably should have. The stress was overloading him too much.

"Uh, I'm good, thanks."

[**Very well. Note that the Zoos Collective has taken a special interest in you. We make sure to protect our interests. You will be returned to the planet shortly. We can all but guarantee this.**]

"I really hope so."

[**We should get inside. Please be completely honest. But do not mention the murder of your fellow human in the Tribunal. It might complicate things. They will be sure not to ask anything regarding that. They will only want to know about your Cultivation.**]

Max nodded at that. Maverick stayed quiet, but Max could sense a strength in his soul that he still found surprising. It definitely gave him comfort. He didn't have to face this Tribunal of super advanced, probably hostile alien creatures alone.

Max was standing on a round rink of a platform floating in midair in the middle of the room. The room was dimly lit, and he could hear a faint high-frequency buzz. While the Zoos' plastic jellyfish floated in the air next to Max, the other species of the ICCB were around Max.

One of the species was swimming in a ring of green gel that went around the platform. They were frog-like creatures with no hindlegs, just tails for swimming. They each had four arms, with at least ten little fingers at the end of each, webbed by a thin layer of blue skin.

The second apex species of the ICCB looked like tiny gray men—baby-sized at barely two feet of height. A dozen of them lounged on top of the gel, watching Max with unblinking, completely black eyes. Their little mouths spoke in a strange, fast gibber, as if someone had sped up human speech three times over.

The fourth species was the most unsettling of all, and it explained where the buzzing sound was coming from. A swarm of oversized green flies was flying overhead of Max, many tiny tendrils drooped from where their mouths would have been expected to be and, rather than legs, they had pincers to grab things. They took turns flying by Max's head to look at him closer. A waft of rotten meat assaulted Max's nostrils every time they did that, but he resolved to endure without complaint.

Super-powerful Cultivating house flies? Why can't aliens just be like humans with blue skin or something?

The flies made a sound that cut the air like a knife. Max flinched and covered his ears. The fly currently moving its mouth tentacles stopped and turned to Max. It waved one of its appendages in an offhand manner and Max received a System message.

Talent obtained: [Thousand Tongues Master]
[Thousand Tongues Master]: You understand any language of any sentient being.

Holy crap. He just casually gave me an insane talent because it was convenient for him. Just how powerful are these people? Also, the Framework works outside of the planet! Which does confirm what Durum said. My Stats are somehow ingrained in my DNA.

"Do you understand me, human?" the talent-giving fly asked. The ripping metal sound of its vocal chords still cut the air and hurt Max's ears. The Zoos representative cast a translucent barrier around Max.

"I am Azzzhtik'Likzirrruk. I will be leading this Tribunal. You will address me when you speak unless otherwise specified. Now, you have been summoned before the Tribunal of the ICCB for investigation of your Cultivation path. Start by explaining what has transpired and what you know about your path. I am addressing both of you. Talk."

Wow, this fly guy is a prick, Max thought as Maverick enthusiastically went into an explanation of his awakening to sentience and what he had experienced since.

Max told his story next, with a lot less flair and embellishment than what Maverick's story had contained. Regardless of this, there wasn't much discrepancy between the stories, except for the issue of Max's competence, which Maverick found lacking on multiple occasions in his story.

The little gray men began to chatter amongst themselves. Even though Max could understand their language, they spoke so fast, it was hard to make out the words. The air was filled with the sounds of ripping metal as the fly-people conversed, and the frog-like creatures burbled to each other within the gel, creating little drifting bubbles of air.

"Enough," Azzzhtik'Likzirrruk said. "So, it is true. You have unlocked a new path."

"How powerful is this path exactly? What are the limitations? What are the advantages? Can we assure it is definitely stronger than any of the other paths as the postulation suggests?" one of the grays asked, gibbering slowly and carefully, to make sure the other species understood.

"It is not clear yet," the largest of the amphibian creatures in the gel announced. His voice penetrated the thick gel and echoed throughout the room. It was a burbling but potent sound.

"We are only working with what the Zoos have disclosed," Azzzhtik'Likzirrruk said. "Everything seems to match what the other parties have said. We have no reason to suspect deceit or omission of critical information. For now."

The Zoos jellyfish stirred, its robotic voice filling the audience:

[It is clear that the advantage this path provides is less than your catastrophic projections have let us believe. This weapon, while sentient, needs sustained, intermittent hibernation time.]

"Who is to say that is not simply a temporary hindrance?" the leader of the frog-people said. "If the limitation is lifted, the weapon will be able to cultivate while the human sleeps, thus resulting in an accelerated growth that no other competitor can match."

"Yes. Precisely," one of the grays piped up. "They will eventually reach a stage of Cultivation where sleep is barely needed. Provided they acquire the resources, they can both Cultivate ceaselessly and utilize this talent they have acquired which increases their cycling technique efficiency if they cultivate simultaneously. How can any of my representatives compete with such an advantage?"

"Need I remind the Kiritus Corporation of Subject #511962, the wielder of absorption magic and their unique way of Cultivation?" Azzzhtik'Likzirrruk asked coldly. "Would you like to re-examine said case with the Tribunal in light of your stance regarding this human's advantage as unfair to compete against?"

"Thank you for reminding me, honored Azzzhtik'Likzirrruk," the gray said. "Let the records show that I will withdraw my previous statement as hasty and unjust."

"Let the records show," Azzzhtik'Likzirrruk said.

"What if there are other benefits?" the frog-person asked, its fat lips curling into a frown. "Cultivation changes the body fundamentally. What if this weapon changes in an unpredictable way?

"Yes," another of the fly-people buzzed. "That is likely. The best course of action is to kill this human and compensate the Zoos Collective."

[That will not happen,] the Zoos jellyfish said, calm as ever. **[The Zoos-Collective is willing to spend an inordinate amount of veto power on this human.]**

"That course of action narrows down further outcomes," Azzzhtik'Likzirrruk said. "What does the Zoos collective suggest?"

[We are willing to allow compensation for other major factions. An [F-grade Equipment Box] **to all representatives of the other races. The Zoos Collective will incur the cost entirely.]**

This caused a massive uproar from all of the other species. Max watched the barrier's wall shake and flicker dramatically. He was way over his head here. Cold sweat dampened his neck.

I really should have taken that sedative. At least I won't be killed. Maybe.

Maverick sent a pulse of emotion. This one was difficult to read. It meant something along the lines of Maverick having suspected all along that he was peerlessly awesome.

"This is an insulting offer," one of the grays gibbered once the room settled down. "You would offer trash as compensation. Almost a third of the population no longer has any use for an F-grade Item."

"Agreed," the frog said, his voice echoing throughout the room. "We suggest that we be allowed to disclose information of this new path to the whole population."

This caused another thunderous cacophony of shouts, and Max sighed and sat down on the ground. He was clearly going to be here a while.

CHAPTER FIFTY-TWO

Golden Goose

The apex faction representatives of the ICBB argued. And argued. Then they had a break and Max was offered "human food". He was excited at the prospect, wondering what kind of treats that might entail. When he was escorted back to his room, there was a pile of carrots and a bowl of oatmeal waiting on a table. Max let out a little laugh and sat down to eat. Not exactly the feast he had hoped for, but he wouldn't turn down a free nutritious meal. Maverick lamented at great length at not being able to taste things. Max told him he was being rather dramatic over a couple of carrots, which resulted in the weapon sulking.

After finishing his meal, he returned to the audience chamber to listen to yet more arguing. They intermittently examined his soul and his Spiritual Energy as well as Maverick's.

They had scribes making notation and functionaries bustling around Max, taking measurements with devices of various shapes and colors Max could not have even imagined before seeing. But any interest he had in that was drowned out by the incessant arguing.

". . . and if the weapon reaches autonomous function? Or transmutes into an automaton, or similar complete sentient entity?" one of the grays demanded.

Maverick's soul thrummed with excitement at those notions. Max admitted he was intrigued himself. He had had no idea what kind of an advantage their Cultivation path could be. Apparently, it was a big deal.

[Ridiculous proposition,] The Zoos representative said calmly. **[Has there been any indication towards such evolutions? If not, is this not but mere conjecture and projection?]**

"And who is to say you don't know more than you're letting on and are deliberately downplaying the issue?" the leader of the frogs croaked in his resonant burble.

The jellyfish turned to the amphibians and said in a note louder than Max had heard before, **[You would accuse us of deceit?]**

The frog creature hesitated.

"Enough," Azzzhtik'Likzirrruk said. "Does anyone else have input that can be considered useful?"

There was some negotiation between the parties, but eventually, silence fell. Azzzhtik'Likzirrruk took this as a cue to continue.

"If not, I will issue a ruling. Subject #266830151, also known as Max Cromwell, will not be removed from the games, nor will his status as a player be altered."

A chorus of angry shouting, croaking, buzzing, and metallic screeching filled the air.

"Silence!" Azzzhtik'Likzirrruk snapped. "As compensation, as suggested by the Zoos Collective, each of the hurt parties will be offered the choice to obtain this new Cultivation path for themselves, should they desire it."

"How ridiculous!" the frog leader cried out. "To postpone Cultivation until you find a piece of **[Unique]** equipment?"

"Or," Azzzhtik'Likzirrruk screeched loudly, cutting the frog leader short, "you may issue a population-wide quest to eliminate subject #266830151. Considering the approximate value of this **[Path of Divine Soulbond]** relative to the other paths, the reward can be as high as an A-grade Item or supplies of equivalent value."

"Surely an S-grade item would be appropriate," one of the grays lounging on the green gel suggested.

"I concur," the frog creature said.

"Do you want to use veto power on this matter?"

"Yes," both parties answered immediately.

Dear Lord Odin in Valhalla, wake me from this nightmare. A bounty on my head? AN S-GRADE ITEM BOUNTY?!

"Very well," Azzzhtik'Likzirrruk said. "Let the record show both parties used veto power here. The record should also now state which hurt party chooses which compensation."

"Kiritus Corporation chooses to issue a bounty," one of the grays said. "My representatives are in the same initial arena. The choice is obvious."

"Forkkrof Syndicate also chooses to issue a bounty." The frog creature raised a hand inside the green gel. Neither he nor the other amphibians in his party were happy about this ruling. They all regarded Max and the Zoos jellyfish with open hostility.

There were some fast slashes of screeching metal in the air as the fly creatures conversed. Max couldn't make out but a few stray words of what they were saying. Finally, Azzzhtik'Likzirrruk spoke.

"The Swarm has decided to inform the population of the chance of a new, more powerful Cultivation path."

The leader of the Forkkrof Syndicate laughed openly. "Good luck trying to find a fool willing to postpone Cultivation until they find a **[Unique]**. They'll either power up too slowly or die trying."

"The incompetent ones will," Azzzhtik'Likzirrruk said. "But there are 2,779,000,000 Asbanti left in the population. We only need two to succeed in order to accrue an advantage. What's a few million lives for a weapon like this?"

The offhanded way the fly creature of the Swarm spoke chilled Max.

What's a few million lives?

It wasn't even a comprehensible number of people. And to be so nonchalant about it! Max tried to reason with himself. This creature was probably thousands of years old, and it had seen species bite it by the trillions. It didn't make him hate the ugly flying thing any less.

[Does this conclude the proceedings?] the Zoos jellyfish asked. **[We would like to transport our representative back to the Games.]**

"Adjourned," Azzzhtik'Likzirrruk said. "Take your human."

[Follow us, Max], the jellyfish said in its placid voice.

Max found himself again in the forest opening he had been picked up from. The dead pride of panthers lay scattered around the area, and the Stranger's limp body lay on the grass nearby.

The Zoos Collective's plastic jellyfish had followed Max. When he turned towards it, the robotic voice immediately began talking.

[That went better than expected. We are pleased.]

Max bristled. "I didn't do anything wrong! And now I have a massive bounty on my head."

[Yes. That is a regrettable turn of events. But your advantage is substantial. If you wield it properly, you should be able to fend off coordinated attacks.]

"Hey!" Maverick snapped. "We didn't ask for this mess. My sidekick and I don't need a target on our backs! Since it's not our fault we're in this mess, we need compensation."

[Regretfully, the Zoos Collective is not allowed to give further help. We ran over the rules in 316 iterations, trying to find a loophole. It is in our best interest that you not be eliminated.]

"Then give us information," Max said, trying not to frown. He was still angry. But he had to believe the Zoos guys. If it were up to them, they would have probably kept Max's advantage under wraps. It was just a shitty situation. Sometimes life sucked.

[We have prepared some information that we have deemed legal to disclose. This will be woven into your introduction to Cultivation, with which you have already acquainted yourself. Please sit down.]

Max was taken aback by the jellyfish's request. Previously, the Zoos Collective had had no regard as to whether Max was tired or dying. They were polite, surely. But now they were almost considerate. They had even fed him! The oatmeal sat nicely inside Max.

[The Zoos Collective urges you to prioritize Cultivation as long as you can provide materials for advancement. Levels and Cultivation work in tandem, and both seem equally beneficial, but it is not so.]

The jellyfish paused as if to give Max time to digest. Max wished he had a pen and paper. Or better yet, a smartphone.

[But survival is of the utmost importance. You should also continue killing creatures and looting them. Creatures above Level 15 have a chance of dropping Cultivation material. You will need [Spirit Coins] for the initial Levels, and later on, rare materials relating to your path. We cannot fully predict which materials the Framework will deem necessary for you to advance.]

"Didn't you create the Framework? You can't look under the hood to see what's going on?"

The jellyfish was quiet for a while, as if going through some internal negotiation.

[We cannot disclose to you details of the origin of the Framework. Know only this: the initial Levels of Cultivation with the help of the Framework are mostly mechanical in nature. Simply get your body attuned with Spiritual Energy through cycling techniques and advance using [Spirit Coins]. The later advancements will require spiritual insight.]

"What kind of insight is that? You mean like the training I've done to get a more intimate sense of Mana?"

[Precisely. You have had good fortune. This is why your advancement in the Heavenly Arts has been remarkable.]

Max thought about that. He had gotten a World First achievement. While he liked to think he had worked hard on the Cultivation—and of course Maverick being able to sneak in extra Levels had helped tremendously in sharing the workload—he was surprised nobody had done it better. Had the Mana training that Durum had put him through helped him that much? Max felt queasy thinking how hard cycling Spiritual Energy to everyone else must be, because it was a strain and a half on him.

[We suggest a regimen of Cultivating as far as your resources will take you, using that gathered power to acquire more Cultivation resources and to repeat the process. If possible, challenge some Bosses for further equipment upgrades. But an emphasis on Cultivation will be the most beneficial.]

Max nodded, eyes on the ground, watching the grass sway idly in a gentle breeze. The faint sun cast a little warmth on the back of his neck. Everything had been going so well. But now he was in deep shit again. The deepest shit he had ever been in his life. He had the entire population of two species against him. The grays and the frog-people were probably issuing their system-wide messages right now. One way or another Max's fate was being determined as they spoke.

[One more thing, Max. We would like to make a request of you.]

That was unusual. It snapped Max out of his thoughts. *Request?* Max felt like he didn't have much of any say in anything when dealing with his patrons.
"Sure?"

[We have observed that you have poured a substantial amount of resources to improving the circumstances of your fellow tribemates. We ask you to act more selfishly in the interest of your self-preservation. You will need to take the bounties put on your person seriously. The other species will come after you. And they will be organized. That is a unique opportunity for growth. And one you must be ready for.]

Max ruminated on that for a while. What they said even struck Maverick as being significant. The two of them reached an unspoken but deeply felt understanding. They resolved to overcome this. They resolved to win. Max would continue running at the forefront. Maverick would be by his side, and they would outfight anything thrown at them.

Max would earn humanity its right to exist. And that journey would start with himself.

CHAPTER FIFTY-THREE

Cultivation and Tools

After Max looted the panthers, he sat down by the Stranger's corpse. Maverick asked him why, but Max shook his head. It had been a token gesture on Maverick's part, anyway. He could sense what Max felt. Regret? No. Grief? Absolutely not. He felt no remorse nor horror over the Stranger's death nor his part in it. In fact, he was upset over how little murdering another person had affected him.

It needed to be done.

Maverick's soul resonated in agreement.

The sun was setting in the distance. The faint light it gave off had not much warmth left. The air was growing cool, and Max pulled his robe tighter around him. He regarded the corpse beside him with cold eyes.

No. He wouldn't be burying the Stranger. But he would remember him. This was a lesson. It was hard accepting that people like this existed. People who would just choose destruction for no good reason. The Stranger had known what he had been doing, and he had done it anyway. It had been pure and simple malice, even at the potential expense of his and his whole species' existence.

Max would not give behavior like this any more of his precious time. His mind returned to Brian and his gang of thugs. Those were posturing fools. They would test their limits, but they could be put in line. Max had done well to do so. But the Stranger had not been such a person.

Max would not be soft again. He would not negotiate. He would remove anyone who threatened the human race as the Stranger had.

"Wow, that's pretty dark," Maverick remarked. "I always considered you the comic relief of our endearing little duet."

"I'll do what's right," Max said. "That is all."

"And you'll just . . . decide that?" Maverick said and whistled.

"Got a problem with that?"

"I'm actually impressed," Maverick chimed in. "You're finally taking notes from me."

Max chuckled and shook his head.

"Do you think they'll allow you to do that?" Maverick asked. "To just remove people you don't like?"

"People I don't like," Max cracked a wry smile. "You make it sound so flippant."

"Ah. I suppose you haven't learned enough from me after all," Maverick lamented.

"But yeah, I do think they're just going to let me do that. The Tribunal system for our species is only Zoos business, unless something crazy happens. Me removing a few bad eggs won't attract the attention of the ICCB."

"You're confident they won't punish us."

Max smirked. "I'm their golden boy now. Their big advantage."

"*We*," Maverick corrected, a hint of annoyance in his voice. "I feel like you're letting this get to your head already."

"Our little jellyfish patrons will lose face if I die. They'll do everything they legally can to provide us with advantages. If we kill a few assholes, I doubt they'll blink twice."

"I like it!" Maverick exclaimed. "So we can do what we want?"

Maverick's voice rose in excitement. "Oh, we're going to be bad. Next time you rough up that Brian, let me do the talking. I just can't wait to show him who's who and what's what."

"Let's try to keep each other from going completely psycho, yeah? We're the good guys, remember?"

"Fine," Maverick huffed. "But can't we also be the cool guys?"

"I've never been one, I guess."

"Well, you're lucky I am here to teach you!"

Max got up. "Oh, great."

"Oh, great, indeed! We're finally leaving this stinking corpse," Maverick said. "Now, are you thinking what I'm thinking?"

Max smirked again. "You know I am. Let's go Cultivate."

When he got back to the camp, Max was blunt and brief. The people were still licking their wounds, but overall, things had apparently normalized. As much as Max could tell at least. It wasn't like he had spent a lot of time in the camp, after all.

He found Joshua and told him that the threat had been dealt with. Joshua had all sorts of questions, but Max cut him off. He had no time for this right now.

"Max," Joshua asked, "is everything alright?"

"I—I'm fine," Max said.

"'Fine' can mean many things," Joshua said dryly. "Did something happen?"

"I'll tell you about it later," Max said. "Let's just say I'm suddenly very busy."

"Busy?"

"Later, Joshua."

"Right, right," Joshua said. "Do you need anything?"

"Just peace and quiet. I'll take one of the houses and Cultivate there."

"Cultivate? Yeah, of course."

"I'll leave it by the time I need to sleep. I just need a place where I won't be disturbed."

"You've got it, my friend," Joshua said. He clapped Max on the shoulder. "Do you need anything else?"

Max smiled. "Not now. But I have a request."

"Anything," Joshua said immediately.

"If anyone happens to get their hands on **[Spirit Coins]**, I really need them right now."

"I think you've done enough for our little camp to get something back from us in return. I'll spread the word."

"Thanks, Joshua." Max said. "I'll see you later."

Max had been waiting for this. It was the moment where he finally got to open his Cultivation loot boxes. Max didn't have great expectations for the E-grade box, but he was hoping for **[Spirit Coins]**. The other one would be C-grade. That could be a spectacular prize at this Level. First, Max opened the **[E-grade Cultivation Box]**.

A strange contraption appeared in front of Max on the floor. It was a criss-cross of thin, silvery rope that formed a star in the middle of the round formation that the thing created. The rope was attached to a smooth strap of black leather that formed a circle around the star.

Cultivation Treasure: [Mana Focus Formation (E-grade)]
Enhance ability to focus longer on cycling techniques while sitting in the ring.

Okay? That seems . . . useful? Is this like coffee? Or motivation? How does it work? I guess I'll find out.

[C-grade Cultivation Box]

What appeared in Max's lap was an ornate box made of wood. When Max opened it, he couldn't help but feel disappointed. What was inside were . . .

[Candles of Aspect Attraction]
Used to attract the main Aspect of the user.

They were beautiful candles. Made from clearly high-quality wax, deep purple in color, and trimmed with bright red scrollwork. They were each easily over a foot in height. Max closed the box.

"Maverick," Max said. "What is this?"

"Scented candles?" Maverick asked sardonically. "How the hell should I know?"

"Are these supposed to be useful?"

"Probably," Maverick said. "Or maybe they're for relaxation. According to your memories, some people were big on scented candles."

"These are from a C-grade box," Max said. "They have to be useful. We will need to ask Durum about them. He might know what an 'Aspect' is."

"Bleh, fine," Maverick said. "That king thinks he just knows everything, doesn't he?"

"He knows more than us, that's for sure."

Maverick said nothing to that. Max could feel a hint of sulkiness emanating from his soul.

"Well, that's a worry for another day. I'm not going to lie, I'm annoyed at this C-grade treasure not being something life-altering."

"At the right moment, a scented candle can be life-altering," Maverick mused.

"Piss off."

"Well at least we have this . . . pentagram thing on the floor," Maverick said.

"That's more like a Star of David," Max said. "But with a lot more points."

"How was I supposed to know that?" Maverick huffed. "I'm just a gun."

"A gun who likes to pretend he knows everything."

"Shush. Just step into the formation and stop slacking off."

Two **[Celestial Illumination Pills]** later, it happened.

Leveled Up Quartz-Level Cultivator (greater) to 2
+2 free Attribute points

"Two free points?" Max wondered. "Don't mind if I do."

"Since I put in half the effort here, it's only reasonable that half the points go where I want," Maverick announced.

"Let me guess. Intelligence?"

"Oh, yes," Maverick said almost ominously. "MORE POWER! MORE—"

"Okayyyyyy . . . We still have some of this pill left to cycle with."

Max concentrated once more and cycled. They exhausted the pill's effect in fifteen minutes. In wordless agreement, the two of them simply ingested another set of pills and barely missed a beat with their cycling.

The formation tool clearly helped. It made it possible for Max to not lose concentration, even when stray thoughts tried to enter his consciousness. He could brush them off easier and stay focused on the cycling. It was like the tool helped his mind stop fighting the exercise. While the effects where subtle, it was definitely noticeable. Max could only imagine how useful this would be the more tired he got.

But even with all the tools and advantages at his disposal, Cultivation was still damn hard.

Max was dual-cultivating with Maverick, using **[Celestial Illumination Pills]** and his new Cultivation treasure, but they had only accrued a single Level in two hours. It was probably fast as hell when compared to others at this Level. Not that anyone seemed to be at the higher Quartz Level yet.

Granted, Leveling his Class was getting slower too. Max still wanted to get to Level Twenty in the near future, as it most likely entailed a substantial upgrade in some regard. But the allure of Cultivation kept him sitting still and eating pill after pill. As far as he knew, he was still the world's best at it. He had the fortune of stacking up advantages and if he had the patience, he would stay the world's best at it.

This would not only satiate his ever-growing pride but could possibly mean further World First achievements.

"Don't fall asleep on me, Maverick," Max said. "We aren't stopping for a while."

"Bah," Maverick said. "The way I see it, it's *you* who'll be begging for a break once your will runs out."

Max gave him the spiritual equivalent of a shoulder punch. Then they fell back into a focused cycling rhythm.

Leveled up Quartz-Level Cultivator (greater) to 3
+2 free Attribute points

"Ugh . . ." Maverick sighed. "I'm not saying I need a break. I am merely suggesting that you look like you need one."

Max didn't say anything. He just hung his head. He was so tired. Two hours had passed and they had gained another Level. It was as if Max's head was a fuzzy cloud. Stringing two thoughts together was an exercise in futility.

"It is getting late," Max admitted. "We could sleep a few hours and continue."

"By few, you mean ten hours right?"

"We don't even need eight anymore. Let's sleep for four or five and continue."

"I need coffee," Maverick sighed.

"You've never even had a cup."

"I have whiffs of your memories. You used to love coffee."

"Addicted" was a more appropriate word for it. Not for the first time, Max wondered if he would ever have a cup again. Probably not.

"Let's go talk to someone who's going to take the night watch, so they can wake us up."

"In the morning, right?" Maverick asked, his voice thin with discomfort. "I know you oversleep."

"You know what they say," Max mused. "New headsman's axe hanging over my head, new me."

CHAPTER FIFTY-FOUR

Christie and Plans

They woke up early to a gentle shake. A woman in her early thirties looked down at Max with curiosity. Max hadn't even let go of [**The Maverick**] in his sleep.

"Morning," Max muttered.

"If you want to call it that," the woman chuckled. She had a throaty, confident voice. "I can't believe you wanted to voluntarily wake at the ass-crack of morning."

"No choice," Max said, rubbing his eyes. He had a bit of a headache, but that was to be expected. "I need water."

"Brought you some, darling," the woman said.

"Wow, good service," Max said.

The woman let out a rich laugh. "Least I can do. I'm Christie."

Max grabbed her extended hand. It must have been soft and delicate once; now it was calloused and toughening.

"I'm Max."

"Oh, I know who you are, darling."

"I suppose you do, but it's polite."

"Like taking up a hut for yourself, so that ten people have to sleep outside?" Christie asked with a smirk. She was a beautiful woman, with full lips, intelligent eyes, and sleek black hair that had been pulled back into a ponytail.

Max hadn't realized he'd done that. "I wasn't . . ."

"Relax," Christie said. "Nobody is blaming you for that. The way I see it, these are your huts and you can decide what goes on with them."

"Nah," Max shook his head. "They were a gift. I'm just pulling my weight and adding to the pile like everyone else. But I suppose I did need one for now. And tomorrow."

"You're pulling more than your weight, darling," Christie said and put a hand on his shoulder. "The way I see it, you're pulling us all forward."

"Thanks. I like to think I do."

She smiled at that and just looked at Max, squatting next to him. Max waited to see if she had anything else she wanted to say. Max didn't want to be rude, and he would entertain her for a few minutes if he had to. But what he really wanted to do was get back to Cultivation. It was going to be a long day, and he needed to start now.

Christie's eyes narrowed as she looked at Max, and then she smiled. "Alright, darling. I'll leave you to whatever you're doing here. Call me over if you need any help."

"Thanks, Christie."

"I'll see you around."

She got up and gave him a little wink before sauntering off in long, confident strides. Max wondered what her story was. She seemed to handle this new reality with more poise than most people.

"I can't believe she didn't even say a word to me," Maverick huffed. "After all, it is I who brought all these good things to this community. You're just the pack mule."

"She was probably intimidated by your awesomeness, so she talked to the pack mule."

"Ah, yes," Maverick said, completely lapping it up. "That must be it. Ah, but I have such magnanimity for the hearts of maidens. If she only knew what a disappointment you are compared to me."

"Yeah, I'm sure she'd love you . . ." Max said between gulps of water from the black stone jug. He put it on the floor and got into a comfortable position, sitting cross-legged with his back against the wall. "Let's start."

They popped their pills and got to work. The cycling might have been ever-so-slightly smoother than it was yesterday, but it was hard to tell. Focusing was hard. It couldn't have been more than four or five in the morning, and Max was still groggy and annoyed. By the great god Anubis, did he miss coffee . . .

Whenever he found himself drifting off, he reminded himself that there was a massive bounty on his head, chased by billions of creatures. Yeah, that was a pretty powerful motivator.

Leveled Up Quartz-Level Cultivator (greater) to 4
+2 free Attribute points

Maverick gave a cheer at that, but even he was too tired and strained to go on a megalomaniacal rant. Max could have actually used his peppy attitude now, but he would have to do without.

But it was hard work. Pushing the Spiritual Energy up and down inside his body was starting to become something Max was practiced at, but now that he had obtained a higher advancement Level, it was like someone had sneaked in and racked in heavier weights.

That made Max really happy with all the tools he had. His new cultivation treasure on the ground was perfect for this stage of his advancement. The [**Celestial Illumination Pills**] were a powerful advantage, not to mention that he was pretty much advancing at *over* double the speed, combining Maverick being able to cycle and their [**Twin Souls Cultivator**] talent.

Regardless of all this, Max was starting to feel greedier and hungrier for something that could make the progression faster. Strong as he might be, he had a mountain to climb. He needed to be stronger than anyone he faced. And preferably by a large, comfortable margin.

With these thoughts at the back of his mind, Max Cultivated ceaselessly and tirelessly. By noon, Max could hear the distant bustle of the camp outside, but nobody came to bother him, for which he was grateful. That enabled him and Maverick to push out another Level.

Leveled Up Quartz-Level Cultivator (greater) to 5
+2 free Attribute points
Talent Upgraded: [Twin Souls Cultivator I] -> [Twin Souls Cultivator II]
[Twin Souls Cultivator II]: When both parties of [Path of Divine Soulbond] are using a cycling technique simultaneously, the effectiveness of the technique is increased by 20%.
New Talent obtained: [Natural Mana Affinity I]
[Natural Mana Affinity I]: You have a basic ability to wield Mana.

"Nice!" Maverick said. "Upgrades!"

"That improved cycling system is nice," Max said. "We'd really benefit from getting a better cycling technique. We should visit Durum soon. Maybe he can give us pointers."

"That greedy king will want something in return," Maverick said. "I don't trust him."

"I trust him enough," Max said. "But you're right. If we go there, he won't just give us handouts. Still, we need him. He could also tell what the hell that [**Natural Mana Affinity I**] thing does."

"I vote 'no'," Maverick said. "And my vote as the leader of this duet should count more."

"Well, it's either that or trudging along like we've been doing . . ."

"Well . . ." Maverick considered. "Maybe I did judge the king too hastily."

"We should go there. Maybe today or tomorrow. I don't think it's the worst idea to keep pushing today. Then we'll have a break from all of this tomorrow. Go kill a few monsters and meet a king."

"That does sound like a plan," Maverick said. "Hey, what's this new sensation?"

Max raised an eyebrow. "What sensation?"

"You don't sense it?" Maverick said. "I suppose you are rather slow on the uptake sometimes . . ."

"Just tell me what's going on," Max said, not even trying to hide his exasperation.

"It's like I have Mana ready to use at my fingertips," Maverick said.

"You don't have—"

"I know," the gun said impatiently. "Look. It feels like . . . I can almost . . ."

A loud bang echoed in the hut. A magical bullet cracked the wall and ricocheted a few times, pinging around Max, who covered his face.

"Goddamn it, Maverick!" Max yelled. "What the hell was that?!"

"That was *awesome!*" Maverick exclaimed in triumph. "Finally, I'm getting some agency. Soon enough, I won't need you to carry me!"

"I'm not sure if I dread or eagerly anticipate the day you sprout little legs."

"If I don't receive the ability to soar through the air majestically, I want my money back."

"What money?"

"Unimportant," Maverick said. "What we need to do is wrap this up and go to the dwarves to see if Durum can tell us how we can upgrade me further. I can just tell this is only the beginning."

"Upgrade you?" Max asked.

"Imagine all the augmentation I could have!" Maverick said cheerfully. "Maybe I could have a rocket launcher. Or two—no wait—three barrels!"

"Yeah, I am definitely starting to dread the day . . ."

"Oh! Oh! And a laser sight! I need a laser sight!"

"I need a break," Max said, grabbed Maverick and went outside. "And lunch."

"Oh! A detachable lunchbox for my minion!"

"Wait, I thought I was your sidekick, not a minion."

CHAPTER FIFTY-FIVE

Uncultivated Cook

They managed to push two more Cultivation Levels that day, until they both finally had to lie down on the floor. Neither was going to admit to the other that they couldn't carry on, of course, but they didn't have to; they could sense each other's souls.

Max looked up at his upper corner. He had only two hundred Stamina points left. Concentrated Cultivation seemed to drain him faster than a full day of adventure. Max wondered if pumping up his Constitution would be a good idea. If he had to suddenly protect the camp from another attack, he could be drained pretty low. Smart use of potions could help with that, but those were valuable and scarce.

Max sighed contentedly, as one does after finishing a day of hard work, and emptied the rest of his water jug. Christie had checked up on him and been gracious enough to refill it.

When they got out of the stout little bunker, Max noticed it was late in the evening. The faint light of the sun was gone by this point. The heavy purple clouds hung overhead as ever. There was a certain beauty to them.

Max gave one last glance back at the bunker.

"Oh, you have to be kidding me," Maverick groaned. "You're not seriously suggesting we have another go at it now?"

"Our lives are at stake," Max said.

"Your life, maybe," Maverick said.

Max didn't reply, but the surge of will he sent at Maverick through their Soulbond was like a wolf snapping its jaws.

"Fine," Maverick huffed. "So you want to go and pop another set of pills, then?"

"I—"

"Oh, Max!" Elena's voice called. "You finally came out of your cave?"

Maybe an hour or two break will help us focus better . . .

Maverick was more than fine with that thought. He was already drifting into unconsciousness. Max sent him a subconscious message that he'd need him to Cultivate with him later. Maverick clearly heard him but decided not to answer. Max bristled at him, but he was already drifting away.

Max turned to Elena.

"Hey, Elena. Yeah, we really needed a break."

Max turned towards Sid's kitchen, and Elena walked beside him.

"You've been doing this Cultivation thing?"

"Yeah," Max said. "It's really been wringing the juice out of me."

"You're working so hard. Did something happen?"

"Yeah," Max said. He just realized he would need to tell people about his situation. He could be putting everyone at risk. "I think it'd be better to save the story for one of Joshua's little ceremonies."

Elena let out a little laugh. "Didn't think you'd ever be one to suggest having one of those."

Max forced a smile out. It didn't fool Elena. "So it *is* serious, then?"

"It's a big deal, yeah," Max muttered. "But we'll get to that. Tell me something positive instead."

"Mike got up," Elena said brightly. That was good news, indeed.

"Nice!" Max said. "I haven't had a chance to talk with him much, but he seems like a good guy."

"He's pretty gruff," Elena said. "I didn't like him much to begin with. Talk about bad judgment. But then again, I was a total mess early on, wasn't I?

"You've come a long way," Max said.

Elena smiled at that.

"Any idea what Level Mike is on?" Max asked. "I think he could use some of those pills I gave you."

"I don't know. I don't keep track of these things," Elena said. "But he already left to scout and hunt. Said a few words about having rested enough and needing to catch up."

"I like that attitude," Max said. They walked past a few friendly faces they had seen around, and Max and Elena waved at them.

"I know you do," Elena said, giving him a strange smile. "I haven't hit Level Fifteen yet, but I have been studying up on those pills."

"Oh?" Max said, suddenly more alert. "What did you learn?"

"Don't get too excited. I won't be able to make them. But I've taken a good look at their structure, and I have an idea of what kind of ingredients could have gone in. It's all guesswork at this point, but better than nothing, right?"

"Bummer," Max said. "But I guess more than that would be too much to expect."

"Studying them gave me something, though."

"Gave you what, exactly?" Max asked.

"Just a bunch of question marks in the System message," Elena said. "Kind of annoying, really. I got pretty excited at first."

"Damn, that could be something very good!" Max said, suddenly feeling less tired.

He gushed on about his story of learning about Mana manipulation and unlocking similar things and urged Elena to get to Level Fifteen as soon as possible. Elena clearly didn't understand the implications of System messages marked (???), but she was drawn in by Max's enthusiasm.

"Hey, Max! Hey, Elena!" Joshua waved a hand. He was standing around Sid's kitchen and talking to him and the other cooks.

"Hey, guys," Max said. "How's the cooking going, Sid?"

"It's all great, bro," the teenager said. "Just got finished with some soup for the wounded. Dude, all these pots, pans, and what's that thing?"

"A cauldron?" Joshua said.

"Yeah, Chief Bro. A cauldron. Max, all this stuff is amazing. I can make so much more food now, and I've Leveled Up a lot of times. I'm at Sixteen already!"

Max, Elena and Joshua all stopped dead in their tracks and stared at Sid.

"Sixteen?!" they all exclaimed in a chorus.

"How?" Elena asked.

"That is amazing, Sid," Joshua said, clapping the boy on the shoulder.

Max produced his purple sack of Cultivation pills. He wasn't sure how Cultivation worked with non-combat specialists, but if it improved the quality of food for the whole camp, it was worth a few more pills.

"Here, Sid," Max said. "Do you have anything I can put these in?"

Joshua picked up a little stone box with a lid and offered it to Max. Max poured a handful of pills inside the container.

"What are these?" Sid asked and picked one of the pills up for inspection. "Spices? Holy shit, bro, did you find us spices?"

Sid was mildly disappointed to learn the pills weren't a spice. Max gave him the CliffsNotes on Cultivation.

"Yeah, I knew about all that," Sid said. "The jellyfish showed up and explained some of it."

"Great," Max said. "What Level of Cultivator are you?"

"Bro, I haven't had time for that. I'm too busy cooking three meals a day for like 150 people. And now with all these ladles and . . . cauldrons, I have all of these recipes I can try."

Max was a little shocked to hear that someone would disregard Cultivating so completely, but then again, did Sid really *need* to do that right now?

Maybe. It was difficult to predict what kind of benefits Cultivating might accrue. Sure, Sid was able to cook pretty well now, but who was to say he couldn't infuse his foods with Spiritual Energy, making them more filling, or maybe even produce recipes for foods that could help others Cultivate?

"I think you should take some time to gain a few Cultivation Levels," Max said.

"I mean, you're wise and all, bro, but I really don't have the energy for it after cooking all day. You know what I mean?"

"Take a day off, Sid," Joshua said. "You've earned it."

"Thanks Chief Bro, but it ain't that simple," Sid said. "Cindy and Peter are cool. They're like Level Ten and they've got the **[Cook]** class too now. But those three over there working with the roots? I can't leave them on their own, or we'll have stubby-fingered cooks and finger soup for lunch, if you get what I mean."

They laughed and Sid blushed a bit. The three apprentice cooks gave a few apologetic looks in their direction before going back to cutting the roots.

"We'll work it out somehow," Joshua said. "We have a lot of panther meat now. Make a big batch of food so all you cooks can take a day off."

"Taking a day off to sit and meditate doesn't sound like my kind of holiday, bro," Sid said. Then he took a quick glance at Max. "But I'll do what I gotta do."

"You don't have to do it all day everyday," Max said.

"Oh, like you've been doing?" Elena smirked.

"Yeah, but I have a thing to tell you all," Max said.

"What thing, bro?"

"Yeah, Max," Joshua said. "What is this thing?"

"I'll tell you about it soon," Max said. "We need to have one of those little gatherings of yours, Joshua."

"Well, then," Joshua said. "Let's grab something to eat and gather folk around. I'm sure they'll be interested in hearing what you have to say."

"I'm sure they will," Max muttered.

CHAPTER FIFTY-SIX

Nightfire Plans

Max talked for a long time. Longer than he intended to. He just let it all pour out—the situation, how he felt, and what he was going to do. Joshua's gathering started with fifteen or so people listening, but by the time he was finished, over one hundred sat around him, still and alert, the crackling of the fire and a few stray whispers the only sounds to be heard other than Max's voice.

He told them about Maverick and what had happened when he'd chosen his Cultivation path. Then he told them about the Tribunal and the ICCB's apex species, masters of their fates, as well as the three other races. Lastly, he told them about the bounty.

Billions of people would attack him on sight. And Max wasn't exactly hard to miss with his giant golden revolver in tow.

"And that's why I think I should leave," Max said, trying to keep his voice from trembling. "It's not safe anywhere for me anymore."

There was some murmuring in the crowd. Max hung his head. They couldn't deny it, of course. Except for Bill, who rose up.

"What the hell are you talking about, Max?" he asked. "You think it's been safe for *anyone* so far?"

Max raised his downcast gaze. Bill smiled and shook his head.

"We wouldn't even be alive without you, Max," Bill said and looked around him. "Everyone here knows that. While you were a fun little rumor before, after that panther attack, you're our hero."

The clapping started slowly but eventually became loud and sustained. Max looked from Joshua, to Elena, to Lily, to Sid, to Marie, and so on. They all smiled in approval.

"You ain't going anywhere, Max," Bill said. "Maybe we're screwed if you stay with us. Maybe. But we'll sure as hell be damned if you leave us."

"Joshua's a good leader," Max said. "He will know—"

"Of course he is," Bill cut in, raising a hand. "But don't ruin the moment."

That drew chuckles from the people around. They all seemed to be in consensus.

Marie, who was sitting nearby, spoke in her soft, mild-mannered voice. "Did we really need all this spectacle for such an obvious thing? Of course you're aren't going anywhere, Max."

Max must have gotten some dust in his eyes. He wiped them on his sleeve and smiled at the crowd in gratitude.

Max, Joshua, Brian, Mike, and, surprisingly, Christie were sitting around the night fire. The time for heartfelt speeches was over; now it was time for some mindful planning.

"Despite everyone being all mushy and grateful to me, we have a problem," Max said. "It's a bad idea for me to stay. The enemy will be looking for me."

"You worry too much, Max," Brian said and offered a tentative smile.

"I worry about these lives I'm trying to protect," Max said. There was a hard edge to his voice that made Brian flinch back.

"These nightly bonfires might be a bad idea too," Max added.

"Been saying that for a while," Mike said, nodding to Max.

"Come now," Joshua said. "It's tells people where to meet up."

"But it can also attract enemies," Mike said.

Brian didn't say anything, maybe because he didn't have his bravado fully back, but he seemed to nod in agreement.

"How many people do you think are still strays by now?" Max asked Joshua.

"Me and my little lambs were strays just a few days ago, darling," Christie said in her throaty voice. "While I think precaution is admirable, I think you're being cold-hearted."

Max regarded Christie for a silent moment. "I suppose I misspoke. I didn't know your story."

"How could you, darling?" Christie said in a tone dancing at the edge of accusation and playfulness. "You never asked."

"I've been busy," Max admitted.

"Tsk tsk," Christie sighed. "So self-centered."

Joshua coughed loudly. "So Brian and Mike are against the nightly fires. I'm for them, as is Christie. What do you think, Max?"

"I think I'm flattered, but you need to stop involving me in these kinds of decisions," Max said, and shook his head. "I'm just an attack dog."

"You're a damn good one at that, I've heard," Mike said. That must have been the longest sentence Max heard come out of the man's mouth.

"One with a bite," Brian said and gave Max a half-smile. "But look, Max, you can't come at me and tell me you call the shots, and then not follow up."

Max scoffed. "Damn it."

Of course Brian was right. Max didn't know where he had put his bravado, but this was a sensible, straightforward man. Max wasn't going to go as far as to say he liked him, but at least he could give him a measure of respect.

Max turned to Joshua. "Fine. The signal fires can stay. But that's twice the reason to train an attack force. How many [**Combatants**] do we have?"

Joshua thought for a moment. "You, Mike, Brian and his lot, William, Nick and Tate, Sarah, and . . . Of course, Christie and her lot."

"You're a [**Combatant**]?" Max asked.

"Surprised, darling?" she said and smirked. "I don't strike you as *dangerous*?"

Max snorted. "In more ways than one."

Christie winked at him, and not too subtly. "I have five fighters in my team, myself included, Joshua."

"Less than twenty," Max said. "And all but me, woefully under-Leveled."

"You could remedy that," Brian said.

"Yes," Christie agreed eagerly. "Take us with you to the Dreadlands."

"I was actually going there anyway," Max said.

"Thought you weren't leaving," Mike said.

"I'm not," Max said. "But I need to visit the dwarves to get an upper hand in Cultivation."

"From what I gather, you already have an upper hand," Brian said.

"Maybe," Max smirked. "But I like to push my advantages."

"Smart guy," Brian said.

"I have a suggestion," Joshua said. He waited for every head to turn. "Since Max took care of the panther situation, I believe it's safe to assume our little community is safe from attacks. For now."

The people gathered around the campfire murmured in agreement. Mike deigned a silent nod as he put more wood to the fire. A few sparks flew off, like fleeting fireflies, before dissipating.

"So I think it would be profitable to form an outpost in the Dreadlands."

"An outpost," Brian stroked his chin. "Another camp?"

"We can hope, eventually," Joshua said and nodded. "It will be rough to start with. I assume there's food to hunt?"

"There's game," Max said. "I think you'll need me to take down the first few."

"Oh, such arrogance," Christie said. "I am sure you won't say that after you've seen me fight, darling."

"Uh huh," Max said. "I'm sure you're great."

That actually made Christie miss a beat, and a micro-expression of surprise flashed across her face. She quickly regained her poise and smiled at Max like a cat with milk.

"Okay, so how do we do this?" Max asked. "I escort most of the **[Combatants]** there, show them how to kill stuff . . . and then what?"

"Good start," Joshua said. "We will also have to get some **[Artisans]** and **[Laborers]** with you. Don't choose by considering Level; choose by considering grit and bravery. Christie, you'll be in charge of that."

"Yes, sir," she said.

"What do you want to do, Mike?" Joshua asked.

"Stay," the man said gruffly.

Joshua looked at him expectantly and Mike grunted.

"The camp will still need protection from the stray panthers," Mike said. "I ain't leaving Sid's cooking for dust and death."

"I suppose you do have a point," Joshua said.

"He does," Max agreed. "A few **[Combatants]** should stay. Mike is a **[Scout]** anyway, right?

"Right," Mike said. "I will keep Leveling as long as I keep scouting around and killing whatever beast I come across."

They all nodded in agreement. That settled that.

"And you, Brian," Joshua said. "I want you to be the leader of that outpost."

"What?" Brian was taken aback. "You would trust me? What about Max?"

Max raised his hands. "Don't give him any ideas, Brian."

They shared a chuckle over that.

Brian looked like he was embarrassed. "Are you sending me away, Joshua?"

Joshua raised an eyebrow. "No. I meant what I said when I said you should take up the **[Leader]** Class."

"It's been . . . stressful out here," Brian said. "I've been doing a lot of thinking these last few days. I got caught up in something silly. Those men of mine got the better of me. They saw me as better than I am, and I believed them. Good men, but not always the wisest."

You sure did get caught up in something silly. I'll wait and see if you make amends, Max thought but decided it best to remain silent.

"A part of me still thinks I'm the better leader," Brian said, letting himself unhunch his shoulders. "But I suppose I should prove it first."

"I will still let Joshua wear the cowboy hat," Max said. "Sorry, dude."

They laughed at that and Christie, who was sitting next to Max, placed a hand on his shoulder as she chuckled in her throaty manner.

"We will see, Brian," Joshua simply said. "But for now, let's focus on the opportunities. We need to take over the Dreadlands. There are more resources out there. More Experience. We could trade with the dwarves, with Max as our liaison. Many possibilities lie ahead for us."

"We will need to make a plan of action," Max said. "I need to leave tomorrow. I could take Brian's group with me and teach them how to kill the [**Vilefiends**]. Maybe find and clear a cave of them to set up a camp."

"I'm coming with you," Christie said.

"You'll need to find people willing to venture into the Dreadlands first," Max said.

"Then I'll do it, darling," she said in a voice that brooked no argument. "I'll have a group ready to leave by breakfast."

Max nodded at that. He had to respect her attitude.

"Alright," Joshua said. "Let's go over the whole plan once more in order of execution. Come tomorrow morning, Max will leave with the [**Combatants**] and Christie's support crew. Then you will . . ."

Maverick woke up from his slumber. He asked Max through their soul link if they were going to Cultivate more tonight. Max shrugged. He wanted to. If they had time, they could squeeze out a pill or two before sleeping another few hours. Maverick agreed. He was ready to go. He asked if it was okay to use time on this negotiation and planning thing. Max said it was. This was important. For the first time, Joshua's camp wasn't huddling together and scraping by. They were forming a plan of attack, and that excited Max.

CHAPTER FIFTY-SEVEN

Branching Out

Max woke up to a nice System notification in the morning.

Leveled Up Quartz-Level Cultivator (greater) to 6
+2 free Attribute points

"Damn, Maverick," Max said as he got up. He was curled up in his hammock, sleeping on the floor of the hut he had taken over. Max felt slightly bad about it, but he'd be back out there tomorrow. Then it would be caves for him. Well, maybe a soft bed in Durum's estate wouldn't exactly be out of the question.

"I was bored, what can I say?" Maverick said with faux nonchalance. Max could sense he was very pleased with himself.

Max whistled. "Without pills or anything. I have to say I'm *actually* impressed this time."

"Stop that," Maverick said. If guns could blush, Max bet he would. "Our dynamic doesn't work like that. You're ruining our good name."

"I'll have to keep up, so you won't decide to change sidekicks."

"Why are you . . . You know? Not irritable and grumpy and all the other great things I like about you?"

"I guess I just woke up on the right side of the bed," Max said.

"I'm not entirely sure I prefer that," Maverick said.

"I think it's because everything is clear again," Max said. "I know what to do. I know where to go. And most importantly, I'm going back out there."

Max could appreciate the importance of Cultivation, and he would need to do it a lot more. The Zoos Collective had told him that it was a big deal. Durum had said that the Framework and all the Levels and Skills somehow merely facilitated Cultivation. But so far, it hadn't been anything more interesting than a way to get extra Stats. They had a total of twelve free Attribute points to use. Not too shabby.

I've been starting to say "we" a lot, haven't I . . . ?

"As well you should," Maverick said smugly from his holster as they left the bunker.

Max had some breakfast and said his goodbyes to Sid. He would be needed here to feed the majority of the whole community. One of his cooks would join their outpost, but she was barely half the Level Sid was. But it was alright. The Dreadlands was a good place to get Levels for everyone. Max wouldn't be surprised if cooking the meat from those big hairy monsters grazing around there would give increased Experience.

After that Max went up to Elena, Marie, and Lily to say his goodbyes. He caught Lily just before she was about to head out to work with clay. Max sneaked a handful of **[Celestial Illumination Pills]** in her pocket and patted her on the shoulder.

Then they headed off. To Max's surprise, Christie had indeed managed to gather up enough **[Laborers]** and **[Artisans]** of a reasonable variety so that they could set up a little camp. She came to announce it to Max triumphantly, flipping her hair and smiling as if to prove he was a fool to doubt her.

"You know, I kind of like her," Maverick said, while she was still within earshot.

Max gave Christie a glance. She was watching.

"Yeah, she's alright," Max admitted. Christie's smirk widened into a smile.

They didn't take many supplies with them—some cups, bowls, utensils, and such, of course, as well as few sheets of cloth that Max had acquired earlier, and a number of other personal things and knickknacks. However, the idea was that they would acquire all that they needed from the Dreadlands. There was plenty of game to hunt, as well as loot boxes to acquire.

Max was also sure that there was more to explore in the Dreadlands. It was clearly a big place. It was meant to be a combat zone between species, and Max hadn't seen anything of that yet. But then again, if you discounted the dwarven lands underground, he hadn't spent that much time in the zone. There were natural treasures and mysterious boons to be had, that was for sure.

Max hadn't had the heart to tell the others about the hot springs, but as soon as he knew he could kill those giant insect demons, he would take this expedition there. He got giddy just thinking about it. He must have had a goofy smile on his face, because as they trekked through the hills towards the strange white bridge, he got a few funny looks. They kept turning their heads and walking close, because they thought Maverick was apparently "funny" and "interesting." They didn't have to deal with his "interesting and funny" remarks all day every day, though . . .

"What's so great about baths?" Maverick asked from Max's holster. "I mean, you totally need one, don't get me wrong."

"They're just great. The warm water . . . Wait, why am I trying to explain baths to you?"

"You like me and want to keep me informed?"

"Shouldn't you hibernate or something?"

"The need for it comes and goes, what can I say?"

"Just for a moment, you could try not saying anything."

Maverick huffed at that but remained blessedly silent for a while. Probably not so much out of respect for Max's wishes. No, Max could clearly sense the gun was sulking again.

Eventually they got to the edge of the Dreadlands. As they did, they all got their achievements.

"Open the boxes later," Max said. "Follow me."

He was their guide now. Fully responsible. While Brian was the leader of this expedition, Max would call the shots for now. He was the unofficial leader, until he wasn't needed anymore. That was at least how Max saw it. He couldn't vouch for others. Brian had a very different air when he looked at Max, than, say, Christie had.

Max didn't care about any of that for now. He was happy to be back out here. Happy to make progress again.

The harshness of the environment held a certain sort of beauty. The dark ash on the ground. The barren, twisted trees. The sulphuric fumes and the ominous volcano ascending the horizon. The rest of the expedition took it all in while Max kept a watchful eye for **[Vilefiends]**. Not because he was afraid they would attack them. He was hoping to find some so he could help the **[Combatants]** out.

Eventually they found a group of eight of the little demons. Max told his compatriots to hide and wait.

"I'll lock down most of them but keep one free for now. You guys attack it. Watch how they move, watch what they do. Once you're done with that, I'll release two. They work in packs, after all. Just be careful. If you get hit hard, use a potion. I assume every one of you **[Combatants]** has at least one. If you don't, share, for Christ's sake."

It went as smoothly as one could have asked, Max supposed. He used a **[Gravity Well]** on the group. They all got sucked into the swirl, but Max tethered one of the **[Vilefiends]**. It snarled and immediately attacked Max.

Max cast **[Alter Gravity]** on himself and used **[Tether]** to zip around and get closer to the Brian's group of **[Combatants]**. As Max had suspected, the **[Vilefiend]** got tired of chasing Max and went for the less-mobile prey. The creature fought hard, but even against lower-Leveled enemies than itself, it was overwhelmed. Some Health points were lost, but no injuries.

It got a little trickier when Max released two of them. The [**Vilefiends**] were vicious when they were in close quarters, and one of Brian's men got a bit of a scratch on his leg. He was a fighter, though, and even when he fell, he grabbed the [**Vilefiend**] and kept it still while the others beat it to death.

Max noticed that, while using [**Gravity Well**] was convenient, it was draining his Mana unnecessarily fast. He released the whole pack and tethered down every demon, except for two of them. Max figured three might get too messy for now.

Christie's fighters had their go at the demon. Max could appreciate the difference between the two group leaders. Brian's men fought like berserkers. They were angry, ferocious, and brutal. Perfect for a vanguard attack, really.

But Christie's little band of men and women were scrappy. They moved fast, using knives to dart in and out, stabbing once or twice before retreating. If one of the [**Vilefiends**] followed the attacker, it was tripped by another fighter, while a third threw a rock at it. They were fast, agile, and surprisingly well organized.

Absolutely not vanguard material, but definitely dangerous if they just got more Levels. When they were done with the group, many people did Level. Max got some negligible Experience, barely worth a mention as far as his Levels went. But he would have been happy to do this a few more times to help the other fighters get the hang of it.

It wasn't much use to him personally, but he needed to help establish the outpost. It would benefit him in the long run, as well. He would have a relatively safer place to sleep and, with the band's help, he could potentially take out threats that he couldn't have done on his own.

While Max was certain he was a powerhouse right now, his fight with the Stranger had gotten him thinking. He had strong control with the gravity spells. That had enabled him to win by the skin of his teeth against the Stranger and his panthers. But if he had had some proper offensive or defensive spells, the fight might not have been so close. Max wasn't sure how he could acquire them, other than Leveling Up. As far as he understood it, it was possible to learn new Skills through experimentation and chance, but so far that had been limited to talents.

They found another group of [**Junior Vilefiends**] and the fight went much the way the first had gone. They were fortunate enough to loot an [**E-grade Supply Box**] from the monsters, which contained three potions in total. They were all initially offered to Max, but he refused it outright. He couldn't resist taking one [**Mana Potion**] for himself, however.

Dwarfmind.

They also passed a couple of those giant yaks, which aroused much curiosity and fear in the group, but Max told them they'd hunt them later. Max wasn't completely certain he could take one of the great beasts on, but he'd be damned if he didn't at least try.

Eventually they got into the inner layer of the Dreadlands, where the worms and the giant insects dwelled. Max told the group to be very quiet and alert. While they had all been enjoying themselves before, all of them now adopted a serious manner. Max liked that. They hadn't come here to play. They had come here to settle.

But first Max would show them what a [**Foulworm**] was.

CHAPTER FIFTY-EIGHT

Clearing Space

They did *not* like the [**Foulworms**]. All of them yelped when it shot out of its cave. Some of them even vomited when they got close to its corpse. Max still received 300 Experience for killing it. He looted 212 **Cosmic Coins** and found himself slightly miffed at having not received a loot box. It was likely they dropped them more often.

Max went over all of his knowledge of the terrible demonic worms. He told the fighters how simple it was to fight them and how to avoid being eaten. He also mentioned the loot boxes with the caveat that he might be wrong about them.

"Regardless," Max said. "We should clear them out if we are going to settle somewhere nearby. They're really easy Experience, so with them and the [**Junior Vilefiends**], everyone should get up to Level Ten at least fairly soon."

"You sure know what you're doing, don't you, darling?" Christie asked as she squatted down to inspect the worm.

"Like I said, they're simple prey if you avoid their surprise attacks."

"I'm not talking about just that, darling. You were amazing with the little demons. I didn't think it was possible to move around like that."

"Lack of imagination," Max said, quirking a smile. "I'm sure you'll learn all the tricks along the way."

Christie turned to look at Max and chuckled. "Well, well, darling. I am sure I will."

Max didn't have anything further to add to this conversation, so Christie decided to continue. She gave him a quick smile before turning back to the creature. "They do smell awful, though."

"You should see the cave," Max said.

"Let's save that for another occasion," Christie quipped.

Max chuckled. "Wise choice."

"So where should we set up a camp, Max?" Brian asked after he was done inspecting the monster. "In one of their caves?"

"There are plenty of caves around here," Max said. "I would not suggest a **[Foulworm]** lair. We will have a really unpleasant afternoon of spring cleaning if we go that route."

Brian nodded. One of his men, the obese one who Max had tethered to a wall, came up to them. "Won't there be monsters in the caves?"

"Maybe," Max said. "But I'd be more worried about the monsters outside if we don't find a cave to huddle inside. If you think **[Vilefiends]** and **[Foulworms]** are as bad as it gets, you haven't seen enough."

"There's more?" another one of Brian's men asked. He had a scraggly beard and a thin, stringy frame.

"There is," Max said, pointing a finger at the horizon. "See those tall, porous formations over there?"

"With the smoke?"

"Yeah. There are some really nasty things in there. That's why I think we should settle somewhere around this area. This is like a transitory space. It's at the edge of scary and safe."

"Agreed," Christie said as she stepped into the conversation.

"We will trust your judgment," Brian said. "We should find a suitable cave. Easily defensible and spacious enough."

"Sounds good to me," Max said.

They cleared a few more caves of their worms and two groups of **[Vilefiends]**, ultimately taking control of the area. To their good fortune, they ended up with two **[E-grade Material Boxes]**. Now they would just need a nice place to set up camp and open the boxes.

It was growing late in the afternoon and the **[Artisans]** were getting tired. The **[Laborers]** had a hearty amount of Constitution, but even some of them were starting to get weary. Stamina drained faster in the Dreadlands.

Max wondered if they could set up a sustainable camp here after all. Maybe people would need builds more focused on Constitution. That wasn't a problem for **[Combatants]** or **[Laborers]**, but **[Leaders]** and **[Artisans]** would have to set up their build sub-optimally. Not that having high Constitution was a bad thing. Accidents could happen at any time and having a cushion of Health points was a surefire way to keep fighting for humanity.

After another hour, they finally found a suitable cave. It had an entrance large enough that Max was surprised there was no worm inhabiting it. Max went in first to make sure there wasn't something even worse dwelling in the darkness. But after a thorough examination, Max declared the cave safe.

It was actually a fortuitous find. The cave had a large opening right at the mouth. It was like stepping into an atrium of sorts. The round "room" of the cave was maybe fifteen yards in span. From that area, two tunnels continued in opposite directions, ever so slightly sloping underground. Max got excited at the possibilities of the [**Laborers**] expanding these tunnels into full rooms. They could get mining tools from Durum and turn this place into an actual base.

"It's going to need work," Max said, his voice echoing off the walls. "The dust will be a problem."

"Yes," one of the support crew said. She was a girl of seventeen or so, short and skinny. Her long blonde hair was in a matted mess behind her back. "We have to make a door. We also need to get a broom or something to sweep away the dust."

"Great idea," Max said. "What's your name?"

"F-Freya," the girl said. She had spoken out almost unthinkingly, but now that she was speaking directly to Max, she blushed a bit. "Nice to meet you."

"You too," Max said and smiled at the girl. He was getting used to people being uncomfortable around him for one reason or another. It was starting to bother him less and less. "I'm sure we'll be working together more now. Brave of you to join us."

"Thanks," Freya said, demurely. "I want to get stronger. I can't stay huddled up in the camp for my whole life."

"I like that attitude, sweetheart," Christie said and wrapped an arm around the girl. "I'll take care of you, don't you worry that pretty head of yours."

While the rest of the expedition started to prepare the cave and its surroundings for their camp, Max excused himself. It was time to channel his inner *Dwarfmind*. He really needed to be selfish now. He was racing against the clock. And by "clock," he meant billions of other people wanting to murder him.

So Max went to the end of one of the tunnels and started setting up his [**Mana Focus Formation (E-grade)**] on the floor of the cave. Pleased with his work, he sat in the middle of it and took out his purple sack of Cultivation pills.

"You awake there?"

"You know I am," Maverick said. "But I had hoped you'd play with your friends a little longer."

"Feeling grumpy?" Max asked.

"Tired," Maverick said with a theatrical sigh.

"Do you . . . feel bodily exhaustion?"

"I'm not tired physically, you nincompoop," Maverick snapped. "I'm tired of your endless foolishness."

"Yikes," Max said. "I am sorry, Your Prickliness."

"It's spiritual exhaustion, I suppose," Maverick finally admitted. "Despite my awesomeness, I seem to have limits. This is devastating to admit."

"I get what you mean," Max said. "The Spiritual Energy uses these veins, right? Like its own channels."

"Yes?"

"I feel like those are strained. It's hard to explain. It's like overworking a muscle."

"Disregarding the fact that you have never in your life overworked anything, much less a muscle, I have to agree."

"I think we should still just keep pushing for advancement."

Maverick said nothing at that. Max could sense the gun's soul was having an internal debate.

"I'm way too lenient with you, but you are my favorite sidekick. So I suppose I must appease your whims sometimes."

That was all Max needed to hear. Max opened his bag and fed Maverick's bullet chambers with **[Celestial Illumination Pills]**. They had almost half a day to Cultivate. Then they would sleep in the cave and make sure the expedition had its shit together. If it did, Max could go visit the dwarves.

Pleased with the way things were going, Max popped a pill, closed his eyes, and prepared for hard work.

CHAPTER FIFTY-NINE

Cave

Max and Maverick Cultivated throughout that night and the next morning while the others were setting up the outpost. Intermittently, Max idly wondered if the others thought he was being a selfish prick, but it couldn't be helped. He only hoped they would understand. But if they didn't, that was their problem, not Max's. He had bigger problems.

But it wasn't all problems. After a morning of strenuous cycling, they finally got that last Level Up they had been hoping for.

Leveled Up Quartz-Level Cultivator (greater) to 9
+2 free Attribute points

Both of them audibly sighed when the System message popped up. There were still ten minutes or so of their pill left, but right now they just couldn't be bothered. Even after using several and handing them out, they still have over eight hundred left.

"Whew. That was one bastard of a stretch," Maverick groaned. "Why do I keep doing these things for you?"

"It's for us," Max said between breaths. "That's eighteen free Attribute points."

"I want . . ." Maverick panted. ". . . Intelligence."

"I know, I know."

With a sluggish mind, Max brought up the menu and spent his free Attribute points. Since he would be spending an extended amount of time in the Dreadlands and Cultivation took a toll on the Stamina as well, Max decided it was prudent to get a little heavy-handed on Constitution. The extra Health certainly wouldn't hurt either. He put a total of ten points into that. One might think it wasn't necessary for him as a ranged fighter with reasonable mobility, but his fight with the Stranger had been too close a shave. Struggling to chug down a **[Health Potion]** in his death throes was not something Max was keen to repeat on a regular basis. With eight points left, he decided to round out Resistance and put the rest in Intelligence to appease his ever-insistent companion.

Name: Max Cromwell
Cultivation stage: Quartz (greater)
Class: Graviturgist
Level: 19
Health: 700/700
Stamina: 700/700
Mana: 900/900
Alliance: Joshua's Group
Stats:
Strength: 14
Dexterity: 16
Constitution: 70
Intelligence: 90
Wisdom: 55
Charisma: 14
Precision: 37
Toughness: 20
Resistance: 30

Max was pleased with his Stats. His Intelligence had become so high that his **[Tethers]** packed a serious punch now, being able to lock down powerful beasts, such as the mutated panthers. Intelligence also expanded his Mana pool. He was very pleased to have been able to use **[Gravity Well]** for an expanded amount of time yesterday during the **[Vilefiend]**exercises.

And of course Maverick's damage (and ego) went up the higher he pumped the Stat. Max still felt like he needed more offensive options, especially against multiple enemies. But at least he was feeling fairly confident that he could approach the idea of taking down larger foes, such as the giant yaks or the demon insect creatures, with the power he had now.

"Let me get this straight, Maximillian. I went through all of this trouble for a mere five points of Intelligence!"

Max shrugged as he got up from the focus circle. "The points are spent. I need the other Stats too. But you can rest assured, Intelligence is mandatory."

"It had better be," Maverick said. "All this nonsense with defensive Stats . . . I cannot fathom why you would need any."

"I can't imagine you could," Max said as he put away his tools and dusted himself off. "You're a gun. You're all about the offense."

"You say that like it's a bad thing," Maverick huffed. "Single-minded focus is a path of sovereign mastery that is forever closed to plebeian sidekicks like you."

"I feel like being an indestructible inorganic construct clouds you from the fact that I might die any day out here."

"Bah. Nothing is clouded from my boundless genius. I am merely suggesting an alternative approach. If you punch the hardest, who will oppose you?"

"We'll continue the great debate another time," Max said as he came out of the tunnel to the main room, Maverick tucked in the holster. "Morning, guys."

"Mornin'."

"Hey."

"You look dead on your feet, darling."

"Good morning, Max."

A group of people were sitting in a semicircle and divvying up breakfast supplies. Max took a piece of meat from a bowl. It was two days old and smelled funky. He shrugged and ate it anyway. Unless someone learned ice magic, there was no refrigeration.

Wait a minute. Someone really should *learn ice magic.*

"For a seemingly simple monkey, you do have good ideas sometimes," Maverick announced out of the blue.

That drew confused looks and Max sighed.

"What idea?" Brian asked.

Max explained what he had thought of and that prompted an excited conversation between the **[Combatants]** and the **[Artisans]** as to who could both generate their own variations of ice magic.

"Did you see how the dwarves used lava to create floors?" one of the support crew, a young man Max's age, said. "Maybe we could do the same!"

"You can't build anything out of ice," Freya said in almost an admonishing tone. "It's best to just have a **[Combatant]** learn ice stuff."

"You can't just have someone with combat skills work as a walking freezer for the camp or the outpost," one of Brian's men said. "They need to be out there fighting."

"Agreed," Max said. All heads turned to him. Max still didn't quite understand why everyone treated him as an expert in every conceivable subject. "Also we don't know if an **[Artisan]** with ice magic could make permanent constructs. It's magic, after all. We have only been thinking in terms of traditional approaches to better our lives, with people picking up Classes like **[Cook]** or **[Carpenter]**. But there could be rare hidden Classes like **[Ice Architect]** or something who could build walls or bridges. Not just fridges."

"Wow . . ." Freya said dreamily. "I—I kind of want to do that now."

"What's your build like?" Max asked before he attacked the meat for another stringy bite. He wondered if putting a few points in Strength would make eating it any easier.

"I'm kind of floating a lot of free points right now . . ." Freya said, a little embarrassed. "I put most in Constitution during the big panther attack . . ."

"That's . . ." Max trailed off. He found himself constantly underestimating people he noticed. "That was a really smart move."

Freya brightened at that and smiled demurely.

"I think if you want to pursue this ice business, you could contact the Zoos and ask about it. You will probably need an Intelligence build for it."

"Oh. I'll try doing that."

"You think that will work, darling?" Christie asked. "Contacting the Zoos?"

"It doesn't hurt to try," Max shrugged. "But I don't know. I could also ask the Dwarf King."

"I think that's a good idea," Brian said. "I don't trust the jellyfishes."

"Well, I'll tell you this much. They're certainly more on our side than any of the other races of the ICCB . . ."

"I still have a hard time imagining you can just choose what you get," the girl from Sid's cooking crew said, hugging her knees pensively. She had brown messy hair that had been cut short crudely with a knife. Long hair and cooking weren't a good match.

"You got the [**Cook**] Class, didn't you?" Max said.

"I suppose so," the girl agreed. "But I was cooking for a while before I got to Level Ten and chose the Class."

"Yeah, I can't promise for sure you'll get an [**Ice**] Class, Freya," Max said. Then he turned his gaze to look at the others. "But I think it's a good idea to try figuring new things out."

There was a murmur of agreement in the circle.

"I know you *can* affect what the Framework gives you," Max said. "It adjusts to your circumstances. So it's intelligent somehow. I wouldn't be terribly surprised if it took into account your personal tendencies and wishes to an extent."

"Wouldn't that be something!" one of Brian's men—the obese one—said in awe.

"We should test it," Max said, excitement growing. "If Freya contacts the Zoos and spends points in Intelligence, we should see if she can affect her Class. What Level are you now, Freya?"

"I'm at Eight," she said.

"Great," Max said. "Probably not a bad idea to uhh . . . Think about icy stuff?"

Freya giggled. "Already working on it, Max."

"Darling, I didn't know you were so full of creative ideas," Christie said in her throaty voice. She took a look at Freya but said nothing. "You and I should make time to discuss how my team should arrange their Classes."

"Sure," Max said. Freya shot a glance at Christie, and not an entirely friendly one. Max was getting uncomfortable. He got up, tossing the last bite of meat into his mouth.

"Okay, next order of business. We'll go hunt a yak for food and materials. Then I'll go see the dwarves. Finish your meals and let's go."

CHAPTER SIXTY

Hunting

Max tried swallowing. It didn't feel nice. His throat was dry. And it wasn't entirely because of the arid and dusty Dreadlands. He was looking at a giant yak idly grazing by a hillside. All of the [**Combatants**] and [**Laborers**] that had come along looked at him with expressions varying from eager expectation to disbelief.

Truth was, Max wasn't sure how this would play out. He knew he could escape the beast if he had to. But he didn't know how hard it was to kill them. How many shots would he need? How many [**Tethers**] to keep it from crushing him? He couldn't just climb a tree, like he had with the bull-monsters long ago. There were trees, sure. But the yak, when angered and pained, would just bulldoze over any one Max decided to climb.

No, this required a more intelligent approach. He sensed a particularly clear sneer coming from Maverick's soul.

Shut up. I'm willing to listen to any smart ideas you have.

Maverick had none, so Max kept watching the beast. It had noticed them, so Max felt there was no need to hide. The great yak seemed to be curious and cautious at the same time. It sometimes turned its massive head towards them and bleated.

If I just start blasting at it, will it attack?

There was only one way to find out.

He turned to the people waiting behind him. "Okay. Don't do anything. I'll be fine."

With that, he carefully approached the great yak. When he was thirty yards away from it, a safe distance from all the other people watching, he started shooting.

The beast took a moment to react, but once it did, it immediately began barreling towards Max, bleating angrily as it did.

He tried tethering the beast with at least seven spells. It did slow it down, allowing Max to get out of the way of its charge, but it wasn't enough to stop it. Max kept shooting at it and arresting its progress with spells. Using **[Alter Gravity]** to make it heavier worked well. Max then tried to use it again on the beast, in an attempt to essentially increase its relative mass to a point where it would be impossible for the muscles to create enough force.

It didn't work. But Max did get a prompt:

Skill upgraded: [Alter Gravity I] -> [Alter Gravity II]

Max didn't have much time to revel in this, as he tethered himself away from another charge. He shot at it a few times, and the creature bleated and then charged again, grazing Max, which cost him sixty Health points. Then he got an idea.

He was still getting off the ground when the beast turned and charged again. Max dodged the charge to the side and used **[Tether]** to latch himself to the side of the great beast.

He immediately got sucked into its long, fluffy fur. It snorted in frustration. The creature bucked around, tossing and turning its head, but it couldn't reach Max. He just hoped the beast didn't have the presence of mind to fall on its side, crushing him. Well, it was too late to worry about that now.

Max started blasting.

It took a lot of shooting point-blank at the great yak's side to finally fell it. It let out a bellowing death rattle before collapsing on its snout. Max released the tethering and then immediately tethered himself a few yards further away, managing to pull himself away from the monster right before it fell onto its side. Max panted, letting the adrenaline wash through him.

"Well, that was a wild ride," Maverick said cheerfully. "You always take me on the most interesting little adventures."

"You know you could sometimes help and give me ideas yourself."

"I could," Maverick said. "But half the fun is watching your mind work towards a solution."

Max grumbled as his people jog towards them and the fallen beast. It had run a good half a mile before finally collapsing.

Christie arrived first. She had long legs and little to carry.

"You win again, darling," she said and flashed a smile.

"I'm beginning to learn," Max said and gave her a wry smile.

She nodded and winked before the others arrived behind her.

"Nice one, Max," Brian said, giving him a formal nod. "Unfortunately, not something we can replicate any time soon."

"This thing has enough meat and bones for us to not need a repeat anytime soon," Max said.

"Fair point," Brian said and turned to look at the beast. He circled it followed by some of the others. It was a great, magnificent beast, Max couldn't deny it.

"It's too bad we can't take this lump to the camp and process there," one of Brian's men said.

"We need to chop it up here. Might even be a good idea to make a fire here and eat our fill," another one said.

Everyone agreed to that, and they got to work. Since most of them were combatants, they were relegated to the menial task of finding firewood. Not a hard task, considering the twisty trees around. Max suspected them to be so dry and brittle that they would make for quick firewood. As for himself, Max considered his portion of the job done, so he set up his focus circle and started to Cultivate to pass the time.

He and Maverick managed to get through one **[Celestial Illumination Pill]**. No new Levels were yielded, but it felt like they were getting close. Max decided not to ingest another pill. Maverick said he wanted one, and Max wasn't going to say no to that. They had enough pills to spare. Maverick was feeling miffed at not having reached another Level, and he muttered something about having to show a good example for the sidekick.

Max smiled at that and joined the others for a meal of hearty, fatty yak meat. They sat down around a little fire they had made, most of their hands bloody and sweaty, but every one of them happy. Max kept an eye on the surroundings to make sure they weren't jumped by a group of **[Vilefiends]**, but he mostly allowed himself to appreciate this small moment of joy and relaxation. He had been valuable once again. That made him proud.

While the humans ate, Maverick managed to push them to Level Nine of **Quartz Cultivator (greater)**. Max complimented him out loud, so that the other people around could hear. He felt Maverick's soul swelling with pride through their connection at that.

After the food, it was time to strip the great yak of anything valuable, which meant pretty much everything, barring some of the organs. Even most of them, however, were just as valuable as the meat itself, especially the heart, tongue, and liver. Of course, they skinned the beast for massive strips of its hide, which could have many uses. Most importantly, they would be used to block the cave entrance to prevent any excess dust and wind from entering. The bones would be useful for the **[Artisans]** later. If nothing else, they would be good Experience, but in an ideal situation, they could carve tools and weapons out of them.

The others decided that Max should watch the carcass. It would take a while for them to carry everything valuable from the beast to the base. The **[Laborers]** were sure to Level Up massively, but the **[Combatants]** would have to help too, or the meat would rot on the bone before it was all taken.

Which meant Max was left sitting there in his focus circle, while people worked on the carcass. If they happened to be attacked, Max knew he could react fast enough to prevent loss of life. Maverick groaned at the prospect of another few hours of Cultivation, but it couldn't be helped. Max wasn't *too* thrilled about it either. He would rather be having an audience with Durum right now, but he had underestimated how long it took to clean a beast weighing several ton of all meat, skin, and bone.

CHAPTER SIXTY-ONE

Dwarfmind Returns

By the time the outpost crew was done, it was late at night. The whole group had been working nonstop for a good ten hours. Sawing, hacking, skinning, carrying. And at the camp, the [**Artisans**], such as the cooks and leather workers, had worked with the materials.

Now they were all sitting in the cave, absolutely exhausted, no one saying so much as a word to one another. Most of them were chewing on pieces of meat, since it was best eaten right away. The cook was still working. She had one of the young boys from Christie's combat crew helping her, most likely out of personal interest, since Max doubted he had many Levels to be gained from it.

Not that Max cared about any of that at this point. After six hours of almost nonstop Cultivation, he was just as weary as the rest of the crew, if not more so. But he and Maverick now sported a healthy Level Twelve in **Quartz-Level (greater)**. Max was still sure he was crushing whatever leaderboard the ICCB must have had. Having Maverick help pull the weight with the pills combined with focus formation made Cultivation straining as hell but manageable. He could only imagine what the other people had to go through.

After Max finished his meal, it was time to curl up next to a cave wall and do his best to sleep. Tomorrow morning, he would show everyone the hot springs. Max had kept that place in mind when selecting a cave to settle in. Unfortunately, they couldn't set up camp too close to the place, as the towering insect monsters roamed there. That would complicate things, as having to gather water from a mile away wasn't exactly ideal. But at least it would keep the [**Laborers**] busy and Leveling if nothing else.

He also needed to check what had happened to his [**Alter Gravity**] spell, now that it had Leveled Up. The effect would most likely be stronger. But it was necessary to see by how much. A part of Max insisted he test it right now, but his exhaustion won.

With that, Max drifted away into a limp dreamless sleep.

Come morning, they ate, as it was important to stuff their faces full while the massive pile of meat was still fresh. After that, Max escorted everyone to the hot springs. It was best for them to have knowledge of its location. Who knew what intestinal parasite could hit the crew from eating undercooked meat? That could leave only one or two people on their feet. So far, they'd been lucky. No one had gotten any sort of infection to speak of. Maybe the Framework had made their bodies more naturally resistant. They had stopped aging, after all. It wasn't out of the realm of imagination that they were also now immune to most pathogens. Seemingly not all, since Mike did get an infection from the panther claws. But that also could have been something other than infection. It could have been his Health going down and his new body reacting in an unforeseen way. The crux of the matter was, they didn't know for certain, and it was best to play it safe.

They killed two [**Foulworms**] on the way there. Max made a point of checking all suspicious cave openings.

When they arrived at the steamy hot springs, the whole crew sighed at the mere sight of it. They didn't need permission from Max to jump right into the pools, moaning and groaning in a cacophony of pure happiness and pleasure as their came into contact with hot water for the first time in weeks.

When she got out of one of the pools, Max couldn't help but steal a look at Christie's lithe, slender frame as her wet jumpsuit clung to her. She noticed his gaze and gave him the most self-satisfied smile he might have ever seen. Max blushed and looked away, cursing himself. Last thing he needed to do was to give this woman encouragement.

Aside from that, everything went on without a hitch, which was a nice change of pace. No giant insect monsters emerged, although their harrowing screeches could be heard from far away in the smog. It startled the young ones every time, and Max couldn't blame them. He had been scared of them at first. The sounds still made him uneasy, but by now he was battle-hardened and Leveled Up enough to know he could handle them.

Since the hot springs were so close to the hidden doors of Durum's kingdom, Max took his leave. He felt a little uneasy not escorting them back to the cave, but the truth was that he couldn't hold their hands forever. He promised to return to take down another yak later, but that wouldn't be needed for a while.

When Max arrived at the doors of the obsidian dwarves' domain, he didn't need to walk far inside before being stopped by two guards pointing spears at his chest. Max bowed to them, and after a brief conversation in their rumbling language, they realized who Max was and let him pass.

Max had to admit that he was a little lost when he entered the tall, narrow corridors of the dwarves' kingdom. A lot of dwarves he passed seemed to recognize him, as they bowed when he walked past, but he had no time to bow to each of them in return, so he gave them courteous nods instead.

It wasn't long until Rulgum appeared beside him, a magical amulet dangling from his thick, black neck. Max, of course, no longer needed it to have the dwarves' language translated for him, thanks to the talent he had received at the Tribunal.

Of course, this wasn't information he felt it wise to disclose even to Durum. Although Max wondered how long it would stay hidden, given Durum seemed to have some sort of mind-reading spell. Max wondered if he could Level Up his Resistance or learn a Skill or a talent to prevent that.

Well, at least Durum was an ally, but his greed and sneakiness could not be underestimated. Max liked him, but the king was one hell of a *Dwarfmind*.

Rulgum bowed and greeted him with a rumble of courteous word to which Max replied in kind, remembering well the bravery that Rulgum had shown in the Ruins. A flash of dark memories passed over Rulgum's face. He nodded at Max. Max nodded back. They had both gone through shared trauma that day, and that would connect them forever in a way.

"The High King has been very busy, of course," Rulgum explained as they walked through the corridors. "But I am sure he will be pleased to see you again."

Max picked up on that. "I apologize for coming unannounced."

Rulgum turned to give him a smile. He was very bad at smiling, but it seemed genuine enough. "I am truly happy to see you. You have been a great beneficiary to our High King. This is something neither I nor the king will forget. I am sure he will find time for an audience."

"Let's hope so," Max said. "I have my own things to take care of, too. Just now I've brought an expedition of my own here to the Dreadlands."

Rulgum regarded the topic with moderate interest, and so they discussed the status of Max's new outpost until they arrived at the High King's estate. It was an extravagant palace, completely dwarfing Durum's previous estates in terms of size and ostentatiousness. Tapestries of scarlet and sky purple were hung here and there with tassels of solid gold and gems studded to the fabric. Black-shelled turtles the size of small ponies waddled around slowly, carrying a treasure of gems and gold studded on their hard backs.

Within every corner was some sculpture, vase, or other sign of stupendous wealth.

Max and Rulgum made their way through the estate. Eventually, Rulgum left him in a room—a beautiful one at that, with all the necessities, the most important being a king-sized bed. Oh, Max would enjoy the hell out of sleeping in a proper bed again. But before that, there were things to discuss. Rulgum had promised to come back within an hour, either to invite Max to an audience or to tell him that the king was busy.

Maverick was hibernating, but Max decided to pop a pill and work an hour on Cultivation.

CHAPTER SIXTY-TWO

Interesting Rumors

Rulgum came back after an hour, telling Max that the High King would see him in another hour. Max had to ask how they kept time, but Rulgum, despite being friendly ever since their experiences together, categorically refused to tell him. *Damn dwarves.* Maverick had a few choice words to say about such secrecy, but Max managed to calm him down before Rulgum got upset.

Even after two hours of cycling with the pills, they didn't reach Level Thirteen in Cultivation. Still, it wasn't a waste. They were inching closer, one pill at a time. Max was pleased to notice that it was getting progressively easier for his mind to settle and do the work when he sat down. Not that his focus-treasure didn't help as well.

When Rulgum returned after another hour had passed, he promptly escorted them to the High King, who was waiting in a room furnished with more gold than Fort Knox. Even the floor was plated with gold! The room was so shiny, it almost made Max feel a bit queasy to look at it. Regardless, he bowed to the High King, who reciprocated the gesture, but only as deeply as fit a king, so as not to tilt his shiny blue crown.

"Max," Durum said and spread his arms. Max gave a quick glance at the amulet on his chest and then bowed again.

"My liege," Max said. "Thank you for having me."

"Ha, of course. You are the hero who facilitated my rise."

"I see you have been prospering."

"That I have," Durum said and smiled. Then he gave Max a sly look. "Now what can I do for you?"

"I need help with all this Cultivation stuff," Max said, dropping the pretense.

The king nodded and it was clear it was the answer he had been looking for. "I, for one, have of course been busy arranging my kingdom, but I have been given the distilled insights of my team of scholars, who have been tirelessly studying the works you brought from the ruins. There have been . . . some developments."

"Would it be possible for you to teach me more?" Max asked.

"Of course!" the High King said, his smile widening. "But I hope I can bother you with a menial task beforehand?"

Of course, Max thought. Then he quickly suppressed any further inner monologue. He wasn't sure if Durum could read his thoughts on a whim, or if some specific spell was required.

Durum's face didn't betray any further insight to Max. He only smiled and said, "I am sure it will be a mutually beneficial venture."

"What do you need?" Max asked.

"The Old Kingdom is still mostly unexplored," Durum said and sat down on one of the golden chairs. He motioned for Max to do the same. Max complied and Durum continued. "It was fortunate that you found useful things there, but as a *Dwarfmind*, you surely understand our will to return there."

Max swallowed. He *really* had not enjoyed his previous visit to the old ruins. Admittedly, he was much more powerful now and would be further still once he'd spent the free Attribute points from Cultivating.

"I do understand," Max said, "But surely you have already sent further expeditions down there, now that we have an idea what lurks below."

"Yes," Durum said as he held a gilded goblet and poured wine into it. "I sent a fortified expedition down there. One hundred and twenty men. They did a fine job of cleaning up the first floor."

"First floor?"

"The Old Kingdom has deep roots. We do not know how deep underground our ancestors dug, but I burn with passion to find out."

"So what about the second floor?"

"I sent the 120 valiant men down there. Most of them even gained some Levels when they had cleared the first floor, not to speak of the few magical weapons we found and equipped this expedition with."

Durum said nothing. Max thought he understood.

"None returned," Max simply said.

"Actually, we were fortunate, if that is the word for it," Durum said. "A handful of them did. We know what was down there. I am sure you will be very interested."

"Well, don't keep me in suspense."

"Sure enough, we found the same deformed ancestors as the ones you fought on the first floor. They were tougher than the ones from there, though. But that wasn't a problem. My men were experienced at fighting the twisted beasts by now."

"What is down there?" Max said, impatience in his voice. He had not forgotten the Siren. "What hell do you want me to delve into this time?"

"My men say there was a group of creatures down there," Durum said, looking pointedly at Max. Max didn't understand what that gaze meant. Right now, he was frustrated and resented the king for speaking so cryptically. "The records say my ancestors dug deep and wide. Just as we have many entrances to our kingdom, so did they."

Wait. Is he saying what I think he is saying?

"They were tall creatures, like yourself," Durum continued, eyes downcast. "Primitively equipped for the most part. Some of them extremely fast. All of them aggressive, shouting and attacking on sight, speaking in a tongue of spits and hisses. Some sort of lizards, maybe. Their skin was gray and green, I was told . . ."

He gave another look at Max, full of meaning. Max was starting to pick up on what he meant. "But there were some interesting details mentioned. First of all, unlike our twisted ancestors or any of the other beasts lurking inside, they did not move with the ease of familiarity. Whether they attacked or ran from my forces, they were wary at every corner. I found that was passing strange. That was before the survivors told me . . ."

"Told you what?" Max whispered.

"They told me these reptilian creatures were wearing jumpsuits."

CHAPTER SIXTY-THREE

Advanced Cultivator

Max shot up from his seat, spilling the wine. "The enemy!"

Durum nodded grimly. "So, what do you say, Max? There are many treasures within the ruins. Would you rather they fall into the hands of this species?"

Max tried to calm himself. The rush of adrenaline was making it hard to think. He needed to stay cool. Durum wanted him to play into his hand, and he had done a good job. But now Max needed to think about what *he* wanted.

"Give me a minute," Max said. "And don't pry into my thoughts."

"I would not dream of such discourtesy," Durum said.

Okay, so what I want is to Cultivate. Durum might give me something for free. I could just take that and go back to defending the outpost. And then what? I can't Level Up when I'm with them. I did what I could, inching out the easy Cultivation Levels. And honestly, I can't just babysit them forever.

Durum poured another glass of wine for himself and Max. Mad nodded distractedly and took a sip of the swill.

But what Durum is saying isn't a lie or a political swindle, is it? There's another species down there. No matter how you look at it, it's bad for humanity. They're looting the place for valuables. And even if there aren't much of those, they must be getting some serious Experience. If I go down there, kill all of them, and Durum's dwarves and I get the loot, that's this zero-sum game stacked that much further for Team Human. Can I do it, though? What Level will they be?

"I'll do it," Max said, setting his jaw. "But I have a condition that you will have to fill beforehand."

"I see," Durum said, emotionlessly. "What condition?"

"You'll need to provide me with resources to advance my Cultivation stage."

"Oh," Durum said, his expression relaxing. "You're looking to advance to the greater Quartz-realm. Your progress is fast."

Max smirked and shook his head. Durum's eyes widened.

"You're already advancing out of the Quartz-realm? It took me—"

Durum controlled himself, pressing his hand to a fist and hissing. "Impressive. It must be this path you have chosen. I am a lucky king to have such a powerful ally in you. Of course you will receive some **[Spirit Coins]**."

"I thank you, my liege," Max said and nodded in respect. "This does not absolve you from my reward, should I come back alive."

Durum chuckled. "I would expect no less from a *Dwarfmind*. What do you want?"

"I need a plan for my Cultivation. And also any tools or upgrades you can give me regarding it. I am still working with the basic cycling technique."

"Yes, that one is not good," Durum agreed. "You will have your supplies and knowledge, Max. You have my word as a king."

"Thank you," Max said. "I was thinking negotiation would be harder with you."

Durum laughed. "We are friends of a sort, I should hope. But I am a king, and my duty is for my people. However, I believe we are in a situation where our interests converge."

"It does seem so."

"How fortuitous," the High King said. "One thing I should tell you about your next stage of advancement, before you leave this room . . ."

"I'm listening."

"When you reach the Amethyst-stage Cultivation, sheer grit will no longer suffice. Sure, you can keep brute-forcing yourself all the way up to Ruby, as I understand it, but it will take years. I have no idea how Diamond and Celestial Crystallization realms work."

"Celestial . . . ?" Max started. "What do you mean about the next stage?"

"To advance faster and further, certain insights are required, for example, a deeper understanding of Spiritual Energy. I can give you some notions of that when you return, but I am not a great expert. I am stuck in the Greater Amethyst-stage myself and do not know how to break into the Sapphire-realm. Maybe it is not possible for us old races . . ."

Max got up and bowed. "Thank you for your guidance. I will ask you more about this when I return."

Durum was about to fall into some dark, pensive place, but Max pulled him out of it. He put down the wine. "Of course. I will have enough **[Spirit Coins]** delivered to your quarters and have an expedition ready within the day."

"A day?" Max asked. "But last time . . ."

Durum grinned. "Last time I wasn't the High King, and we had to scuttle around in secret. Now things are done as I say."

"I like that," Max said and they shared a laugh.

Max sat down with Maverick in his lap, face strained with concentration. They had been going at it for a few hours, and both of them knew they were close. Just a little bit more . . .

Sweat beaded on Max's forehead and slid down his nose. The droplets fell on Maverick, but he was too focused to complain. Max could feel him through their bond. The weapon was doing its damndest. He was scared of the expedition, just like Max. But while Max was afraid of death and failure, he felt Maverick's fear was of a different kind. He feared the oblivion of loneliness. Max felt a pang of rare, true sympathy towards his companion.

Then they were finally released from their purgatory. The prompt they had been waiting for finally came.

Leveled Up Quartz-Level Cultivator (greater) to 15
+2 free Attribute points
Advancement to Amethyst-Level Cultivator (lesser) available

Max didn't waste time. He scooped up the neat pile of **[Spirit Coins]** left on the table next to him. Max didn't know how many there were. The prompt asked for twenty of them, and most of the coins from his hands vanished.

Advanced to Amethyst-Level Cultivator (lesser)
+10 to all Attributes

The surges of cool power enveloping them were stronger this time. It took a while to get over the shivers. But Max felt good. No. Not good. *Amazing*. Like he had never been younger, stronger, smarter—just *better*. It was a feeling of true confidence, true power.

"YESSSSS!" Maverick exclaimed. "I HAVE THE POWERRRRR!"

"How do you even . . . ? Oh right, childhood memories . . ."

"Our road to excellence is paved with my perseverance, grit, and sheer force of will and resourcefulness bordering on peerless genius. You may bow in my presence."

"Sometimes I can't tell if you're being serious or not," Max said and let out a dry chuckle.

Maverick sighed theatrically. "Oh, Maximillian. You should learn to enjoy the little things in life. Like your contributions."

Max shook his head.

Maverick went on for a while, reveling in their—or rather *his*—greatness. Max was very pleased too, truth be told. And Maverick could feel it through their bond. Max was proud of him as well, but the gun insisted on this charade.

Regardless, Max felt content. He was still scared to delve into the ruins again. What if the enemy was stronger than he was? What if they overwhelmed him and the dwarves?

In the end, Max shrugged. It didn't help to dwell on it. Before he had an idea of what they were capable of, he could only use conjecture based on absolutely nothing useful. Max had asked for a more thorough combat report from the survivors, but they had been too scared and hyped up on adrenaline to make an analysis. They had only said that some were fast and some used projectiles.

Max didn't like fast, but projectiles he figured he could deal with. He brought up the Stats screen and thought about where he should spend the points to best prepare for overwhelming numbers, speed, and projectiles.

He had twelve free Attribute points to use. He needed some Toughness. After the fight with the Stranger, he entertained no illusion that he could somehow keep his distance against a well-built melee **[Combatant]**. At least not yet. He really needed to spend his points considering only the upcoming conflict. *More Constitution? Five into that. No Intelligence this time, sorry, Maverick. Five into Toughness and Resistance each. Hell, make it six each. That's all of it spent.*

Name: Max Cromwell
Cultivation stage: Amethyst (lesser)
Class: Graviturgist
Level: 19
Health: 850/850
Stamina: 700/700
Mana: 1000/1000
Alliance: Joshua's Group
Stats:
Strength: 24
Dexterity: 26
Constitution: 85
Intelligence: 100
Wisdom: 65
Charisma: 24
Precision: 47

Toughness: 36
Resistance: 46

Okay, that's the best I can do for now. The Amethyst-stage boost is nice. Will it be enough, though? I suppose we'll just have to see.

"It's going to be enough," Maverick said. "We're finally at one hundred Intelligence. I feel powerful! LET'S GO KILL SOME LIZARDS!"

CHAPTER SIXTY-FOUR

Second Expedition

The expedition was larger and much better prepared than the last one Max had been a part of—sixty dwarves, most of them warriors, but with a few support crew members sprinkled in. They were nervous as they descended. Max couldn't blame them. The enemy had killed over a hundred of them last time, and those had been more experienced, higher-level warriors than they were.

But Max wasn't there the last time. And Max had never been stronger. High King Durum had of course told the dwarves all of that with animated excitement. It clearly had some impact, but it didn't stop the expedition from rumbling to each other fearfully.

They delved deep into the first floor, Max walking at the vanguard. He had no fear of the twisted little things lurking about. They met a few strays, which Max shot with some well-aimed bullets. The +10 he had gotten in Strength and Precision had really improved his natural ability to handle the unwieldy gun.

The floor had been mostly cleaned up of threats and treasures. As far as Durum told him, it had largely been made up of gold and gems, so nothing Max would be interested in. But Max suspected there was a strong possibility that was what Durum knew he wanted to hear.

The corridors were well-lit and free of corpses and rubble. The place looked almost habitable, if it hadn't been for the sense of eeriness that still hung heavily over the ruins.

While the dwarves had been antsy on the first floor, as soon as they reached a massive, wide corridor carved into stony steps leading into an impenetrable darkness, they all halted to a stop.

Max looked down. There was only darkness. The steps weren't steep, but it seemed like they would extend quite far below them. Max exchanged a few words with the aide, and they agreed to stop for a short rest to gather their strength and nerves.

Once they began descending, they saw dead dwarves lying prone on the stairs, clothes crusty with dried blood. It prompted quiet muttering, which one of the High King's aides, Torgukkuminomorrok, quieted. He was nervous too, Max could see, but it seemed like he possessed some poise.

As Max suspected, it took them a while to get to the bottom. The scope of those stairs was massive. Their march echoed through the dark corridor, as they passed more dead bodies of the previous expedition, all lying on their stomachs. They had been running.

After ten or fifteen minutes, the stairs ended. The corridor split into three different directions. Max motioned for them to stop so he could discuss their next plan of action with Torguk.

"Which direction should we go?" Max asked.

"There is no correct answer," Torguk said. Max thought him a curt and proud man, but he was competent and communicative.

"We need to establish a base. A room that is defensible and close enough to these stairs."

"Agreed," Torguk said. "From now on, you watch the back."

Max shook his head. "I'm the strongest here."

"All the more reason to keep the rear safe. You are ranged fighter. No reason to be at the helm."

Max couldn't argue with that. He started moving backwards, and passing dwarves who nodded or bowed to him. They were all stiff and wide-eyed. Max was nervous too. Maverick reassured him through their link, but it was clear his heart wasn't in it.

It's make or break it. We will just have to see how this goes.

Their helm moved twenty yards forward to the corridor straight ahead. They stopped when they heard a tight *snap*.

Some whiff of intuition warned Max. Maybe it was thanks to some movie he had seen. "Look out!"

It was no use. Only Torguk could understand him. There was a rumbling sound and then a crash. Max watched the torches of the two dwarves at the front winking out as a pile of rocks fell upon them.

They were dead, it was clear. Two men lost already. And that was just the appetizer. One trap meant there were others too.

Worse yet, they know we're here now.

It didn't matter if the enemy had heard them. The one who had laid these traps had just gotten Experience.

Max told this to Torguk, and he grunted.

"I'm more worried about more traps."

Max nodded. "It will be mostly tripwire and maybe door traps. Doors will be hard, but tripwire can be dealt with as something as simple as a long stick."

"We have carts," Torguk said. "We can get a stick there."

The carts were made of polished wooden beams, the width of a man's wrist. They were well-made. Max made a mental note of trying to get Durum to teach his people some basic crafting skills. But now was not the time for that.

Torguk barked a few orders and his men leapt off the carts' side railings. Three of them went to the front to poke around with their sticks in the dark like blind men.

It was crude but effective. They sprung a surprisingly large number of traps. Classic tripwire, all of them, like the first one. Someone had made so many that it was clear it had to have helped them Level. Despite their slow pace, and care, six more dwarves fell to the traps before the end of the day. Three got away with injuries, but they were serious enough that another dwarf had to escort them back home.

Max wondered why the traps were killing the dwarves so easily. Not that heavy, falling rocks or a metal spike spearing you wouldn't kill a normal person, but these were warriors that could access the Framework. Max could only guess that the other person had Skills or talents that made his traps more fatal.

That was not what concerned Max the most. The traps were bad news. At least one of the enemies was a trapper, and the closer they got to him, the more traps they would surely face. Bad news, but manageable.

What was truly concerning was where their enemies were. Oh, they heard things skulking around in the darkness. Something was clearly watching them. It was most likely the twisted ancestors of the dwarves. But why weren't they attacking? Were there only so few left?

If that was the case, the enemy had killed scores of them. Max didn't like the idea of that. Depending on how many people had shared that experience, they could have Leveled a lot. Max could only hope his advanced Cultivation was enough to make a difference.

CHAPTER SIXTY-FIVE

First Contact

Max slept well in the darkness, all things considered. It was a curious thing, and Max wasn't sure why. The fear and anxiety were there. Maybe it was the advancement to Amethyst. Something being different was definitely noticeable. But there was more to it.

Yes, he was nervous about finally facing the enemy. But it wasn't fear of death or pain. It really wasn't. He had grown accustomed to that. With the Siren and the Stranger, especially. Once you have a few brushes with death, your perspective changes.

"Well, well, look at you being all tough, Maximilian," Maverick said.

Heh, shut up.

It really had hardened Max. It had given him a calm that was indomitable. He had used that calm to subdue Brian. He had used a seed of that to kill the Stranger. It had made him stronger. He was what he was supposed to be. A weapon of humanity. A fighter at the forefront.

Still, he wouldn't go into battle with foolish overconfidence. But he had cultivated true confidence, and he would make the most of it. He had to. That was it. That was what this whole hellscape was about. Survival. The right to exist. And Max would snuff out every enemy life out here. Without mercy. That excited a savage part of him. And that was where his calm came from: Confidence. Certainty. Without any negotiation or second guessing, *Max knew what to do.*

He was the first of the group to get up. *That* was probably due to his advancement to Amethyst. It had significantly cut down his need for rest, it seemed. Max had some food and drink before waking up Torguk to get this party started.

They had found a nice, spacious room, with only one entrance. He and Torguk exchanged some back and forth about whether one entrance meant easily defensible or death trap. Fortunately, Max won that argument.

While the dwarves were getting ready for their day, Max went ahead to scout. Torguk had protested, but there was nothing he could do about it. Max told the dwarf to wait for his return before they got moving.

Now Max was traversing the dark hallways, gripping the black leather of Maverick's handle as he moved with care. The Amethyst advancement had done wonders for his night vision. He couldn't see as well as one would in the light, but his sight in the total darkness was definitely uncanny. Still, he would have to watch out for traps.

He was five minutes into his scout when he sprung one.

A pile of rocks and rubble fell on him the instant he tripped on a piece of thin rope, half-burying him. As the dust billowed about him, he checked his Health points. Over two hundred lost. More than Max had expected. And that was with his relatively high Toughness. No wonder the dwarves died or got heavily injured.

The trapper must be fairly high-Level. Not only does he have the ability to magically set up the rocks above, but his traps do an inordinate amount of damage. I wonder what kind of a Cultivator he is.

"Max," Maverick whispered. "Do you think it's wise for us to carry on further? With your legendary clumsiness, we only need two more traps and you're mincemeat."

"You have a point," Max said. "Even one trap, followed by an ambush, would do me in."

"Well, you have potions," Maverick said.

"I'd rather not use them. I can return to the dwarves and let my Health naturally regenerate."

"At least you make up for your legendary clumsiness with some elementary foresight."

"Thanks for the vote of confidence, Mav."

"Don't call me that!"

The expedition got moving promptly after Max returned. He stayed to the back and, while his Health regenerated, kept his ears and eyes open. As they progressed, they lost a few more dwarves to the traps. Max cursed to himself every time it happened. The enemy knew they were on the move again.

By the second hour, the expedition halted. Torguk called Max to the front.

"Heard something."

"What was it?" Max asked.

"Just whispers and hisses," Torguk said. "Not far from here."

Max nodded. "I'll scout ahead, then stick to the front for a while.

Torguk clearly didn't like the idea, but he gave Max a curt bow.

Max went ahead, maybe a hundred yards. He crossed over a tripwire and left a chunk of rock next to the thin rope, hoping it was enough to warrant investigation from the dwarves. It didn't take long before he heard voices too. He crept closer, until two fuzzy shapes came into view deeper in the darkness. Max crouched behind a pile of rubble and gave Maverick a mental note to keep quiet. Maverick scoffed through their Soulbond as if to ask if Max thought him completely stupid.

Max didn't know what kind of night vision the enemy had. They were some kind of reptilians, so they might have better sight in darkness. Max *really* hoped that was not the case. It didn't seem to be, as when Max took peeks from behind the pile of rubble, the two shapes didn't react. They were facing each other, hissing and spitting in their language. Max crept closer to stop behind another pile of rubble.

Now he could already see these creatures' shapes. They seemed to indeed be wearing jumpsuits like Max. One had on arm guards and pauldrons made of some crude metal, and the other one was wearing a pointy hat. They clearly had elongated, inhuman faces, like dogs, or well, lizards. That was about as much as Max could see right now, but he could hear them talking from this distance.

"You heard them too?" the one with the pointy hat asked.

"Of course I heard them," the one in armor hissed.

"One of us should go and report," the first one said.

"By 'one of us,' you mean yourself," the second, more aggressive one hissed back. "Slassekhsnas knows already. She says she can sense which traps are sprung."

That's disconcerting. Can they sense it even if we defuse the trap or spring it without anyone getting killed?

"I think she lies," the pointy hatted one said.

The one with the pauldrons slapped him. Max could hear the echo of it travel past him. "Slassekhsnas is your superior officer. You do not doubt them. Besides, you have no Cultivation yet, so how would you know?"

"I'm Level Fourteen," Pointy Hat said. "I will unlock the secrets soon enough."

"You're a fool to think you will unlock anything powerful like that at Fifteen," Pauldrons said. "Slassekhsnas is Level Twenty-One and has gone through a Class evolution. There is a reason why she leads, and you are here standing guard with your stupid hat."

Well, shit. Level Twenty-One? Who knows what you unlock at Twenty?!

"This hat gives me +3 in Constitution and +2 in Wisdom."

"It gives you a foolish look you surely deserve. Now go run off and tell the leaders that the enemy is here."

Pointy Hat took off in a jog. Max waited until the echoes of his footfalls had faded. After that, he snapped into action.

Max wasted no time.

He double tethered himself against the pile of rubble, repelling himself from it towards the enemy. He zoomed through the air, crashing into the lizard, who yelped and hissed, but to no avail. Max had tethered him against the floor. It wasn't as effective as what he was used to, however. The enemy growled and struggled against the pull, slowly but successfully.

But that still gave Max plenty of time to blast six magic bullets into his cranium. The lizard yelled the entire time before going limp.

Defeated Level 16 [Ishkarassi]
You gained 460 Experience points

Max looked down at the corpse. He felt triumphant. Frantic shouts could be heard from where Pointy Hat had gone. They would soon know that not only dwarves were down here. They would hunt him.

And Max would hunt them too. One by one.

CHAPTER SIXTY-SIX

Skirmish

Max ran back to the dwarves. He was halfway through explaining to Torguk that they need to fall back when the arrows started flying. Giant harpoons with fletchings made of giant feathers shot out of the darkness; those unfortunate dwarves they hit flew with the impact. One struck Max on the side and it pushed him back on the floor for two yards. Over one hundred Health lost.

"RUN!" Max yelled, got up, and turned tail. Only the aide could understand him, but maybe that was enough. Every fiber of Max's instinct was telling him to run and hide.

Max had to trust that.

Even when it meant leaving these people to fend for themselves and die. Some old part of his brain told him it was morally wrong and disloyal. It was overridden by new connections in his brain—the ones that ensured survival and victory. And so he ran.

He could hear the war cries of the lizards and dwarves as they crashed into each other. A part of him wanted to observe and learn, and to fight for the dwarves.

But he did not know if he could escape if he stayed to fight. And if he helped, his Abilities would be revealed. It was possible that this was the best chance for him to fight the enemy. But if he was wrong, he would die and that would be that. He had to trust his instincts.

And so Max ran back to the intersection and went right. He moved as fast as he could to avoid running into traps. He found several but not nearly as much as there had been on the straight path going forward.

Max took another right and began to hear the sounds of battle. A little bit closer and he saw the fight. He could separate the shapes of the tall, slender enemies and the stout dwarves. But they were far away, thirty yards or so. Quite a distance for a pistol, no matter how impractically long the barrel. Suddenly, Max was struck by an idea.

"Mav," he whispered. "Can you see them?"

"Don't . . ." The gun sighed. "No, I can't see them. Better. I can *sense* them."

"How does that work?"

"You really think this is the time, dunderhead?" Maverick asked with uncharacteristic seriousness.

"Okay, good point," Max whispered. "I point, you shoot, yeah?"

"Finally, I get to show you how it's done," Maverick said. "Do you know how personally offensive it is to me when you miss an easy shot?"

"Just focus," Max said and hefted up his companion.

Max aimed in the general direction of the enemy, and Maverick let loose. He shot far faster than Max could tap the trigger. Two shots, one right after the other. They both struck their target and took someone down.

Defeated Level 14 [Ishkarassi]
You gained 390 Experience points

Another volley of shots. Two more enemies fell. But there were plenty. At least fifteen. And they were dispatching the dwarves with grisly ease. Max kept shooting. Maverick was way more accurate than he was.

Defeated Level 15 [Ishkarassi]
You gained 420 Experience points

The lizards had noticed Max by now. Two of them sprinted towards him; he aimed at them and let Maverick do his thing. They were running fast. Clearly, these two were physical types. One of them held a mace and another had elaborate brass knuckles with spikes, which he was now pointing at Max. When they got close enough, Max whispered **[Tether]**, and targeted both of their legs when they got close enough. It worked like a charm.

They were running towards him at an unbelievable speed, and they had no way of reacting or anticipating the spell. They tripped, and Max let Maverick's fire sing through the dark corridor.

Defeated Level 16 [Ishkarassi]
You gained 460 Experience points
Defeated Level 17 [Ishkarassi]
You gained 530 Experience points

Max was pleased. He could feel Maverick's excitement and glee too. But they weren't done. Max kept shooting into the darkness at the fighting shapes.

It made the enemy finally back down. Slowly, they trickled out of the intersection, shouting and hissing. A few massive, harpoon-like arrows shot towards the dwarves. The dwarves took all of this as a cue to retreat. Soon the corridor quieted, only a mess of bodies as evidence of a mortal conflict.

Max had to choose. Should he go back to the dwarves or continue alone?

Easy choice. He would go on alone. The enemy would know where the dwarves were. And as wrong as it felt on some level, Max wanted to use the dwarves as bait. He was still an unknown factor to the enemy. Now they would be certain that something dangerous was lurking here.

Most likely they would know Max was part of an enemy species. But they didn't know anything other than that he had a gun. He had kept his Abilities hidden and now that he was on the move again, delving deeper into the ruins, his location was hidden as well.

Max would need to be stealthy from now on. He hated that he didn't have any food on him. He still had almost a full waterskin, so his survival wasn't an immediate concern. He could be hungry for a day or two. A few days would start sapping his energy. He didn't really have all that much fat left to burn. Max wished he could go back to loot and inspect the bodies, but that was too risky. The enemy would also surely return there.

On the one hand, it would be a good place to strike at the enemy again. But on the other, the enemy would be wary of him there. They would expect him to do just that.

And Max would need to be as unpredictable as a ghost. He needed to stay one step ahead and prepare for every eventuality.

If they have a Stealth-based fighter in their group, I'm pretty much screwed, aren't I?

Well, it was what it was. If there was one thing Max had learned, it was that fighting and survival are chaos. And you needed every advantage that you could take on that chaos.

To do that, there was a clear first step to take.

"We need to find out where their base is."

"My thoughts exactly," Maverick said.

CHAPTER SIXTY-SEVEN

He Awakens II

It didn't take long to get a general idea as to where the enemy's camp was located. It was near an intersection a few hundred yards from the spot that the initial conflict had taken place. Max could feel Maverick's nervous energy through their bond. Max was nervous too, but it was the good kind of nervous. He couldn't wait to bring the tension to resolution and win.

Now, he couldn't attack the camp all gun a-blazing. Even though many of them had died, there were still plenty left. And despite Max's confidence, the fact was that those lives he had taken were snuffed out with almost offhanded ease. Max was squishy, outnumbered, and he didn't have the full scope of the enemy's abilities. He was going to win. But he had to be careful.

Max crept along the dark corridor, stopping every few steps to listen and check around for traps. It was slow moving. The increased Dexterity from the Amethyst advancement helped him tread with more careful steps, muffling the echoes of his boots as best he could.

He was creeping along in the darkness to circle behind the enemy camp. As Max watched out for the stray pebbles so as not to kick them and make noise, he heard the sound of faint footsteps somewhere in the darkness ahead. Careful sounds, just like his. Max quickly hid behind a large fallen chunk of wall. The echoes of those footsteps stopped a second or two after Max stopped himself. The enemy had gone still to listen, just as Max had.

Max's heart rate rose. The enemy had heard him. No further sound was to be heard. Max dared to take a tentative step to peek from behind his cover.

A giant harpoon of an arrow whizzed just past his face, so close, he could have licked it. Immediately, he jerked back. Some grace of luck had managed to keep him silent despite the scare. Max smirked.

The enemy had revealed their location.

Well, their direction at least. Max wasn't entirely sure how far away they were. He figured they couldn't shoot such giant arrows from too far away, but who knew what was possible with the help of the Framework?

Max had a dilemma here. He wasn't sure if the enemy knew for certain he was there. If they did, they could either wait for him to come out of cover, or they could run to get help. Max hadn't heard footsteps since, so he was pretty sure the enemy was there, waiting.

That didn't mean they couldn't get reinforcements just by mere chance. It would be better to take this one out. The harpoon-arrow shooter had been one of the most devastating enemies in the previous fight.

Max shuffled behind the fallen slab of stone, and another harpoon struck straight at the piece of wall, sending an explosion of rubble flying above him.

Okay, damn, he definitely knows where I am. They fly so fast that I can't tether them. I need cover to advance.

The next intersection was twelve yards away. Max was fairly certain the arrows were coming from straight ahead. If he could cross that twelve yards, he could almost be at a range to use [**The Maverick**].

Another arrow came, crushing a part of the wall.

Damn it, where does the enemy keep getting those?

Max looked at the piece of wall he was crouching behind. He hadn't done a trick like this, but it would give him enough time.

Max quickly whispered three repelling [**Tethers**] at the piece of wall, connecting it to himself. It catapulted the stone slab towards the darkness ahead. Another harpoon flew past him, cutting the air with a sharp sound, but it missed. Max managed to run behind the corner of the intersection to his left.

If he had gone right, it might have been the end of him.

Immediately from the right, two enemy lizardmen sprang out towards him. Max could hear the shooter running towards the intersection from their position. Max tethered the two sprinters' legs together and ran. He shot behind him blindly, trusting Maverick to hit his mark. Because of the frantic movement and aiming too high, Maverick didn't get more than a few shots in. He expressed frustration through their bond, but Max had no time for that. He had to run.

His relationship with Mana made him feel when the [**Tether**] spell hindering the two sprinters ended, and he could then hear several footsteps approaching. The enemy was fast. Another arrow flew past Max, crashing into the wall. It missed by a wide margin. Max turned another corner to the left as the rubble rained over him. Hisses and angry shouts chased him. He glanced at his status bars. The green one would drain down well before the physical sprinters would exhaust their own. Not to mention they were gaining on him.

Max needed to kill them. He had revealed what kinds of powers he had, and it would be best to prevent that information from spreading. They were close behind, Max could hear that. He pointed Maverick behind him and let the gun do all the work. After a few shots, something filled Maverick with overwhelming glee. That confused Max, as it was clear no enemy had fallen. But now wasn't the time to ask questions.

Max turned another corner. Wrong one. It was a dead end.

Crap!

There were two doors on both sides of the corridor. Presumably leading to rooms. With few options left, Max chose the left door.

Yup. Dead end. In the very literal sense of the word.

His heart was pounding like a hummingbird. A ranged enemy watching at the door while two melee warriors hunted him inside a space the size of a classroom. Yeah, this was a death sentence. The taste of fear in his mouth grew stronger as he backed away from the door, holding onto Maverick with both hands, pointing him towards the room's entrance. He could get a few shots in, but then they would rush at him, and he had nowhere to go. Spells would slow them down, but they wouldn't stop them. There were too many. This was it.

"Toss me outside!" Maverick yelled.

"What?" Max asked, panic rising.

"JUST DO IT!"

Max had to trust him. He was out of options. He lobbed the gun out of the door.

Maverick did something strange. Something that was hard to comprehend. The gun swiveled in the air with jerky moves, shooting in rapid fire impossible for a revolver. The weapon kept turning and whirling in the air, pointing the long barrel this way and that.

Even Maverick's descent was unnaturally slow. Max had the presence of mind to cast [**Alter Gravity**] on his companion in a surge of instinct, which slowed the gun's descent further. Just enough to get a few more shots in.

Defeated Level 17 [Ishkarassi]
You gained 490 Experience points
Defeated Level 17 [Ishkarassi]
You gained 550 Experience points
Defeated Level 19 [Ishkarassi]
You gained 715 Experience points

Max peeked outside. Three bodies lay on the ground. He crept away from the door and picked up [**The Maverick**]. The gun was practically buzzing with glee and excitement.

"What the hell was that?!" Max asked.

CHAPTER SIXTY-EIGHT

Restock

Maverick chuckled. It soon escalated into laughter that soon grew maniacal. Max was too wide-eyed and shocked to even tell him to shut up. He was just breathing. Heavily. The musty air of the dark ruins felt practically as fresh as a meadow after a spring rain. He was . . . *alive?!*

"How . . . ? What . . . ?"

Maverick finally started to calm down. Max could practically imagine him wiping tears of joy from his eyes, if he had had any. "How did you like my new party trick, Maximillian?"

"I . . . Holy shit . . . I loved it."

"It is a shame none of your friends were here to see it," Maverick said, still basking in glee. "You will have to retell the tale. Nay! I shall retell it. But you can be my prop. We have to rehearse. It shall be an epic. You will need to learn to piss your pants on cue!"

"I didn't piss my pants!" Max protested.

"Maybe not," Maverick said dismissively. "But it would make for better drama."

"Screw your high school drama for a minute," Max said, starting to slowly collect himself. "What was that?"

"I'd love to tell you in great detail," Maverick said. "But shouldn't you do your henchman thing and loot these guys and get the hell out of this dead end?"

Maverick was right. Max nodded and got to work. He came up to the first enemy and, to his delight and surprise, it wasn't just **Cosmic Coins** he acquired. There was *a lot* of stuff.

Potions, coins, Items . . .

"Holy crap!" Max exclaimed.

"Half of that is mine," Maverick said. "Nay, two-thirds."

"You want me to put a silly little hat on you?" Max said, smirking. "You should have told me earlier."

"On second thought, you can keep the stuff. But those **Cosmic Coins** are coming to Papa."

"I'm fine with that. As long as you don't refer to yourself as 'Papa'."

"You drive a hard bargain," Maverick said. Max could sense through their bond just how happy he was.

Max hid the bodies in the corner of the room he had huddled in. The enemy would probably find them, but hiding them would probably buy Max more time than it took. After he was done with that, he decided it was time to creep the hell out of there and find some hole in the darkness to rest and regroup. Max didn't need to sleep yet, but he could use an hour or two to just chill out and think.

"So are you going to finally explain how you saved our hides back there?" Max asked when they were sitting in a comfy corner of a room far away from the enemy base.

"Well now," Maverick started, savoring every word, "you are not the only one with the privilege of exclusive Skills and Abilities."

"I'm . . . not?"

"My sweet summer child," Maverick chuckled. "Imagine how bad a look it would be for me if my sidekick were stronger than me."

"Something happened when you were shooting at the enemy when we were escaping," Max said.

"Very clever, Maximilian," Maverick said. "I got a Skill. **[Semi-automatic Firearm]**."

"Cute name," Max said. "Why didn't I get that Skill, though?"

"Don't get too greedy," Maverick huffed. "It's my speciality."

"It used my Mana," Max said. It was true. It wasn't something Max had noticed immediately. He had been too busy being full of wonder at the fact that he was still alive. But now that he had more presence of mind, he'd noticed that Maverick's ability had consumed somewhere between 150 and 200 Mana. Quite a sizable chunk.

"I wonder why it used up so much," Max said.

"It is, of course, due to my Abilities being S-rank super unique power-move ultimate Abilities."

"Of course," Max said dryly.

"You will have to toss me more often," Maverick said.

"I would have pegged you for the 'Nobody-tosses-the-Mav' type."

"I don't get it," Maverick said. "But I don't like your tone."

"I do agree that I should probably do that more, so you can use that ability and Level Up."

"After semi-automatic should come fully automatic, if I presume correctly."

"I think you do," Max said. His mood was growing pensive. Was this why half the ICCB had been up his ass? Was this something they had foreseen or guessed might happen? Max didn't know what kind of evolution was possible for Maverick, but it seemed to have kicked in fast after they had gotten to the Amethyst-stage of Cultivation. That got Max excited. If Maverick went through an evolution like that so fast, it wouldn't be long until Max could add something potentially very interesting to his own arsenal as well.

"Alright," Max said. "I think it's a good idea that I take a little nap at this point. An hour or two."

"Pfft. We are in the nexus of a battle zone, and you want to *nap?*"

Max sighed. "Just an hour or two, enough to keep me going."

"You don't need it," Maverick said. "I can sense you've still got some juice left in you."

"I could use it. It's money in the bank. We won't be sleeping tonight. It's fair to assume our Cultivation is in a more advanced realm than any of the enemy's. Which means we will need less rest than they do."

"Oh . . ." Maverick said. "I see where you're going with this."

Max grinned before he plopped down and produced his hammock from his Inventory. It would work well as a little cushion to rest his head against. "We'll keep the enemy busy tonight."

CHAPTER SIXTY-NINE

Night Raid

After some sleep, during which Maverick had Cultivated, Max got up. No new Levels were gained, but that was to be expected. Durum had told them that Leveling would slow down when brute-forcing Cultivation. Max wondered about the dwarves he had left behind. Did they understand? Would Durum?

Maverick reminded him that what really mattered was his survival and, by extension, that of his species. All of this other stuff, like politics with some old dwarves, was secondary.

That wasn't exactly true, but Max could appreciate the point Maverick was trying to make.

They got moving. As Max traversed the dark maze, he felt a sense of calm, the sort that one experiences when keeping vigil throughout a dark, lonely night. Not a single sound was to be heard. Not the faintest echo, not the smallest click of rubble kicked up by a foot. Simple silence.

The first thing Max did was check on the three bodies. They were still buried under pieces of rubble and broken furniture in the room where Max had left them. Most likely, they had not been found. That was good, although he had reason to suspect the enemy was wary of their comrades not having returned.

It was easy to relocate the enemy camp, due to the contrast of the orange glow against the darkness.

These amateurs. They really have a fire going?

Max approached with care, stepping over a trap before he could crouch and peek behind a corner. He saw two figures hunched around the warmth of a fire. If these were watchmen, they were not giving Max his due respect. They were blind to anything beyond the light the fire gave them. And Max could see them clearly.

Max approached as silently as a spider in the shadows. He clutched Maverick, bringing himself into a hunter mindset. A cool, calm readiness washed over him. The Spiritual Energy coursing within his body gave him poise as he moved forward. And alacrity. There was a tripwire on the ground, probably connected to a piece of thick rope that led up to the darkness above. The ceiling was high.

Max crossed the tripwire almost disdainfully. It was set up well, just before a small set of stairs leading to a lower level of the corridor. But just as Max stepped over it, he realized it was too late.

Double trap!

He stepped dead on the wire, which somehow tangled on his ankle. With a whirring sound, the rope pulled taut and as it sprung up from the ground, it left him dangling in midair.

A spear shot out of the darkness and hit Max straight in the head. A whopping 200 Health lost, and while, by the old rules of physics, it should have taken his head off, it now only left him slinging about in the air, with blurred vision and a splitting headache.

The two figures by the fire got up and laughed. They started getting closer, and a third, larger figure emerged from the darkness to take up the space between them.

She approached with feminine poise, a truly graceful confidence. A smirk was playing across her reptilian features.

"Well, well," she hissed in self-satisfaction. "We finally found the rat."

Then she snapped her fingers, and the other henchman came to wrestle **[The Maverick]** away from him. Max struggled, but the henchman elbowed him in the face. Hard. Max's vision flashed red, and he let go.

"To think it was caught so easily," one of the watchmen said. "Maybe they are less dangerous than we thought."

The other henchman was turning Maverick in his hands with overt greed and nodding absently.

"The patrons said all races have equivalent mental capacity," the woman in the middle said. "But that doesn't mean some individuals aren't smarter than others."

The female reptilian looked at Max with the satisfaction of a victor. Of course she couldn't tell that Max could actually appreciate what she was saying. He glared at her nonetheless.

"Let's kill it," the lizard holding **[The Maverick]** said. He raised the golden revolver towards Max's head, before the female punched him.

"Don't be so hasty, Rasskarash," she said and pressed a finger to her lips as she looked at Max. "If we could interrogate it, it could be very valuable."

"Honored, Slassekhsnas," the other henchman said. "How would we go about that? It does not understand our nuanced language, and we cannot comprehend this thing's brutish grunts."

So, this is Slassekhsnas. Level Twenty-One. Surely the leader of their little group.

"True . . ." Slassekhsnas said. "We have to see if it is worth the time and effort. Tie his hands and legs."

Now that's bad.

Maverick was trying to say something through their link. But the link wasn't verbal in nature. It was more about emotion and intention. Perhaps it was the higher-Level Cultivation they had achieved, however, because it felt like these messages were . . . less muddy than before.

That's a plan.

Max took stock. He was hanging upside down and had lost his weapon. These were temporary issues. Three enemies. The female lizard probably stronger than Max, at least in some respect, due to her higher Level. Level Twenty could bring a big boost, for all Max knew.

The two henchmen closed in on him. Just as they were about to grab him, Max shouted.

"[**Tether**]!"

Three [**Tethers**], head and both shoulders repelling against the dungeon floor. Max bounced upwards towards the roof. He tethered Maverick to his hand and the weapon shot up in the air, following Max. Another tethering, this one attaching him to the roof. A few more. He still had plenty of Mana.

"Nice one," Maverick quipped as they hung upside down from the ceiling.

"No traps on the roof, assholes?" Max hollered down at the snarling lizards.

Then he dropped Maverick and used a few more [**Tethers**] to suspend him in midair. Maverick started twisting and shooting.

Max worked on the knot wrapped tightly at his ankle. It was rather weird working upside down. It didn't budge. He couldn't pry even the slightest opening loose in the knot. Must have been the result of the woman having Levels in [**Trapper**] or something.

Max produced a [**Knife**] from his Inventory and was grateful not to drop it. Maverick laughed like a maniac as he shot at the lizards who had begun escaping back to their camp.

Max cut the rope from his ankle and started running along the ceiling, placing [**Tether**] after [**Tether**] at his feet. Every time he did it, his stomach lurched, but he had no time to waste. Another tethering brought Maverick back to his hand. Max pointed the weapon in the general direction of the camp and let his companion decide when to pull the trigger.

Defeated Level 18 [Ishkarassi]
You gained 630 Experience points

Many shouts poured over each other as the enemy camp woke up in alert. Max looked at his Mana. Still over seven hundred left. Some arrows flew in his general direction, but the enemy couldn't see Max clearly within the deep shadows of the high roof. Max saw them well enough from his vantage point, with the help of the lizards' campfire. Maverick sang his song of battle, and another lizard dropped.

Defeated Level 14 [Ishkarassi]
You gained 440 Experience points

Max switched positions, moving to the other side of the roof and chugged down a [**Potion of Greater Mana Regeneration**]. He didn't have many left, but if there ever was a situation to use one, it was this.

He also consumed a [**Mana Potion**]. That covered the cost of [**Semi-automatic Firearm**].

More arrows and rocks flew around him. An arrow struck him and he yelped. The lizards could still see the muzzle fire and hear where the shots came from. Another arrow struck. A streak of lightning energy struck the ceiling next to him and rubble rained down.

Oh shit, that's not good.

Soon Max was surrounded by a storm of lightning bolts. One of them struck Max straight in the chest and not only did he lose 120 Health Points, but he almost lost control of the [**Tethers**] keeping him glued to the ceiling.

"Mav, they've got a mage," Max said. "Can you see him?"

"They all look like ugly lizards to me."

"There's too many of them," Max said. "I'm going to run out of Mana at this rate."

"Agreed," Maverick said. "Toss me down as a distraction and get down."

Max did just that. He tossed Maverick and tethered him in midair, from which he kept shooting. Max glanced at his blue Mana bar. He noticed something strange. When he wasn't holding Maverick, the bullets didn't cost Mana.

How does that work? Okay, focus. Not a good question right now.

Max got down by tethering himself along the wall and sliding smoothly to the bottom. He was happy to reach the smooth stone floor beneath him. Then he noticed that he had just stepped on a wire.

"Oh shit," was the only thing Max managed to say before a fiery explosion blasted right next to him.

CHAPTER SEVENTY

Separation

The shockwave from the explosion threw Max back a few yards. He lost over 200 Health from that, bringing him to uncomfortably low in the red bar department. Before he had finished sliding on the stone floor, Slassekhsnas was upon him, wrestling him down and hissing profanities at him.

Max knew he was short on time. He cast **[Alter Gravity]** on his foe and kicked her off of him. She attacked again, but Max used **[Tether]** to slide away. Only to hit another trap. This one rigged with falling rocks.

Max got out of the way and started running. Slassekhsnas was still on his tail, and he could hear Maverick's distant shots growing sparser behind him.

Defeated Level 15 [Ishkarassi]
You gained 510 Experience points

Good job, Mav.

With all of her prowess in traps, Slassekhsnas was fast. Maybe a Dexterity-based build. Max had no time to guess, only to dodge the knife attack.

Wait, why am I dodging?

"**[Tether]**."

The knife was pulled to the ground. Almost. Slassekhsnas fought it. It was clearly difficult for her to wield the knife now, as if it had suddenly taken on the weight of a sledgehammer, but she was still in charge of the weapon.

She has decent Resistance.

She snarled and attacked, but Max used another **[Tether]** on the knife and it stuck to the ground. Then he ducked away from a tackle and picked up some rubble. He quickly whispered, "**[Alter Gravity]**" to make them heavier and tethered them to Slassekhsnas's face. The makeshift shrapnel struck the lizard, and she shrieked. Max picked up some more rubble and continued his assault.

A lightning bolt exploded next to Max. He took some damage. All his bars looked dangerously low. Slassekhsnas was panting too. But she had help. Max didn't even have [**The Maverick**] right now. He cursed to himself.

Slassekhsnas backed away as Max kept shooting rubble towards her. Then he cast [**Alter Gravity**] on himself and ran. Another lightning bolt exploded next to him, crackling in the air and sending rubble flying. Max covered his head and hoped he wouldn't spring another trap.

He was lucky. Slassekhsnas had only had time to set up a few. Max turned a few corners before he used [**Tether**] to climb up to the roof, where he huddled in the deepest shadow he could find and waited.

The enemy searched for him for a long time, torches in hand. They seemed to be checking the rooves too, as they weren't complete morons, but Max had found a good spot. On the one hand, he was extremely pleased to have caused such a commotion. Max had a higher Cultivation Level and he had rested before the attack. He could see that some of the lizards were extremely tired. He considered taking them out as they moved in pairs and groups of three.

But on the other hand, Maverick was in the hands of the enemy. Max could feel him faintly. He knew how far away Maverick was now, as well as the direction they'd taken him. But to get him back would be an ordeal. While the enemy couldn't use his trusted revolver against Max, they sure as hell would keep the weapon under lock and key. As far as the lizards were concerned, there wasn't anything more dangerous down here than Max.

Max considered the situation. He thought he had run past a stairway leading down to another floor at one point, but it was impossible to be sure. There could be monsters down there. He could lure them up here and tether himself to the roof. Then the lizards would have to deal with these foes.

Right now, it seemed like the best available plan.

Well, I could go back to the dwarves. I've cut these lizards' numbers down significantly. But I still don't think the dwarves can take them on, even if I support them with spells. The lizards have a lot of ranged fighters, and the dwarves are squishy.

Max tried to gauge how many lizards were left. Around ten sounded about right, but it was hard to say. There were two distinctly dangerous foes: the lightning bolt mage and the [**Trapper**], Slassekhsnas. That combined with the couple of archers and probably a few melee warriors would make trying to get [**The Maverick**] back a suicide mission without some kind of a plan.

Max felt a pulse of emotion through their Soulbond. It was something along the lines of "Goddamn it, Max."

"Agreed . . ." Max whispered.

Another pulse. This one a warning. A mortal one. Maverick thought it would be dangerous to follow him.

Yeah, no shit. That Slassekhsnas is going to set up a thousand traps around the camp in hopes of me coming back for my prized weapon.

Max knew he needed to get an alternative weapon. He could collect some rocks and rubble, but that wouldn't go far. A spear would be great. He could do some serious damage with a spear and **[Tether]**. But the lizards were no fools. They picked up what their comrades left when they died.

Okay, Inventory. Leaving Mav behind is not an option. Need a plan. And a weapon. Going back to the dwarves is useless. I can't go back to Durum for reinforcements. For all I know, the lizards are already ready to pack and head home. If they take Maverick to some camp or town, I'm done for.

That left Max with one option. He needed to delve deeper into the ruins and try to find something useful there.

As Max hung from the ceiling, he listened for the sounds of the lizards patrolling. They had been going at it for a while now. That was good. Every minute they spent searching for Max was a minute they spent not resting. Max wouldn't need rest for a while. But he needed to act fast. So with care, he slid down the wall and made sure to stop himself before hitting the ground. He hadn't seen Slassekhsnas set up anything in this corridor since he'd been hanging from the roof, but you never knew.

After double- and triple-checking for any traps, Max gently placed his feet down. He oriented himself. He had a good idea of where the stairway should be, based on where the enemy camp was. It wasn't far, only two intersections away, if memory served. That was good, but Max needed to be mindful. With silent and steady steps, he hopped from shadow to shadow, stopping to listen every few yards.

Finally, he found the staircase, tucked away into an alcove. After Max looked around himself one last time, he started to descend. After only a few steps down, however, he heard faint gunshots.

Defeated Level 17 [Ishkarassi]
You gained 645 Experience points

Max smirked to himself.
How the hell did you pull that off, Mav?

CHAPTER SEVENTY-ONE

Damn Bugs

It was incredibly dark down in the third level of the dungeon. While Max's eyes had acclimated by now, he still felt uneasy. This was the first time he had been without his weapon buddy since first being bonded to him. He only now realized how much he had come to rely on Maverick. He needed to approach everything differently now.

With much more care and precision. I can't just be happy-go-lucky and shoot everything.

Max gripped a sharp rock in his hand. The rest of the rocks he'd collected were knocking around his makeshift pouch. One of the Items he'd looted from the lizards had been a **[Woolen Shirt of Brawn]**. It had had a nominal amount of Strength and Constitution. While certainly useful for the guys at the camp, Max had needed to repurpose it to make it back to the surface.

So he had made a small pouch that hung from his other shoulder, draping over his chest. The pouch bulging with rocks bounced softly against his hip as he stalked along the corridors.

Throwing rocks with magic was all well and good, but if this floor contained a Boss, Max sure had to hope it was something he could escape from. What he needed was a proper weapon.

As Max stopped to listen for voices in the dark corridors of gray stone, he thought about going back upstairs. He could hunt down one of the lizards and grab a simple weapon to manipulate with **[Tether]**.

That would be risky for a number of reasons, however. Firstly, there was that **[Trapper]**. There would probably be two dozen traps around the camp. The whole enemy group would also just be overall more alert for him. So picking off a single straggler would be hard.

Another issue would be that it would take time. It was impossible for Max to guess whether the lizards wanted to stay and hunt him down and possibly delve deeper into the ruins themselves, or whether they were preparing to leave the place.

I need to be decisive. If I waffle back and forth, I just lose. I'm down here now, and I'm going to find something useful to get Maverick back.

Max went forward, the sharp rock in his hand getting clammy from sweat. He was beginning to feel some degree of exhaustion, but if he acted fast and could attack the enemy within two or three hours, they should be beyond fatigued.

One thing that worried Max was that he heard constant scuttling from each and every direction. Whenever he tried to look around for the source of the skitters, however, he saw nothing.

Those sound like bugs. Please don't let it be bugs. I really, really hate bugs.

There were also strange gusts of wind that blew through the corridors intermittently, like the heavy sighs of some giant creature. Max didn't like that thought.

To his great misfortune, he found more troubling news after some further exploration. It was a corpse—the remains of one of those twisted husks that had once been obsidian dwarves, the monstrous things with lamp-like eyes. It was being *eaten* by some scuttling, skittering, chattering creatures, the size of Coke cans. They had bulbous bodies, each covered by a shell. Their hideous maws each boastedfour large wedges that clamped onto the flesh of the dead [**Twisted Wretch**]. Max could only see the outlines of these horrible creatures, but he could hear the rip and squish of flesh as the swarm of bugs burrowed into the corpse and had their way with it.

"Disgusting," Max whispered to himself. That was a mistake. Immediately all the bugs in the vicinity of the corpse froze. Then they turned to Max as if in unison and charged, their wedged maws snapping.

Max yelped but acted on instinct.

"[**Gravity Well**]!"

All of the bugs got sucked up into the air to swirl around helplessly. All but one. It skittered at Max and attacked his leg. A searing pain ran through him, and he kicked the creature away. It flew against a wall, ripping a piece of flesh from Max's leg as it did. Max limped over to it, bristling with anger and pain. As the bug tried to get off its armored back, Max came up to it and squashed it under his boot.

Defeated Level 8 [Toxicarion]
You gained 95 Experience points

Toxi-what?

Before Max could finish the thought, an angry red pain started radiating from his shin upwards. He checked his bars in the upper right corner of his vision. He had a new status effect, like a green water droplet.

Don't need to be a genius to know what that means . . .

Max was feeling a bit dizzy and he noticed his Health wasn't regenerating and his Stamina ticked down by a point. The green droplet icon seemed to be ticking down slowly as well. It would take twenty or thirty minutes in Max's estimation to flush it out of his system.

Max got up and looked at the swirling bugs in his spell.

"Okay, doesn't look like one bite is lethal. But if you buggers can make this poison stack, you're a real bunch of assholes."

The swirling mass of bugs screeched and hissed incoherently at Max.

"I really wish I had Maverick with me," Max said. "How the hell am I going to kill you buggers?"

Max was acutely aware that he needed to kill the bugs or get the hell away before he released the **[Gravity Well]**. Using the stones in his pouch to shoot at the well seemed like the most obvious idea, but that could have unintended and risky consequences. What if the tethered rocks would blast a bunch of these things free?

Well, since Max had realized he could be the resident Spider-Man with his **[Tether]** combined with his high Intelligence stat and both the power and the Mana pool it provided, he could have a relatively easy escape.

These things don't look like they can climb walls, but I'm just a dumb cowboy with a gun, not an entomologist or whatever.

But if they couldn't walk on walls . . .

Max grinned to himself. Suddenly the bugs didn't look so ugly and horrendous. Suddenly they looked like an opportunity. They looked like that makeshift weapon he had been looking for.

"Let me just see if there's more of you buggers around here," Max said. The bugs collectively decided that the proper answer to such a remark was more screeching and hissing. Max smiled at them. "I think you guys and I could be allies."

CHAPTER SEVENTY-TWO

Counter-Attack

Running across the wall, jumping from [**Tether**] to [**Tether**] was tiring, even with the venom debuff already gone. This little stunt had cost him a [**Greater Mana Regeneration Potion**], [**Mana Potion**], and [**Minor Stamina Potion**].

Looking down, Max decided it was all worth it. A great swarm, like a skittering black sea, churned below him. One screw-up with a [**Tether**] would mean a horrible death of being eaten alive by ravenous bugs.

But the bugs were not great climbers and they were sufficiently single-minded for the plan to work.

Max had been running along the corridors and swinging around the walls for a good hour now. The swarm at his feet was enough to fill a living-room floor. Maybe two or three thousand of those toxic fat beetles were following him. It was hard to say accurately, because it was still very dark.

Max thought it was enough for his plan to work. He would take the enemy by surprise when they were at their most tired.

Max decided it had to be enough. He didn't want to waste time. So now he was making his way back to the stairway to ascend back to the second floor, where he would retrieve Maverick.

It took some effort for the bugs to get up the staircase. The steps weren't steep, but the beetles weren't terrific climbers, either. Their violent hunger seemed to drive them on, and that was good enough for Max.

Now I just need to avoid the traps.

He saw a few immediately. That [**Trapper**] had not gone back to sleep. There was one very close to the staircase. Not a tripwire this time, but a rope trap, half-concealed in rubble. They had suspected Max had gone down.

Or they're just covering their bases.

Max made sure he had enough Mana to play at being Dungeon Spider-Man and hopped onto a wall. The bugs climbed over each other, snapping their ugly maws, but they quickly gave up. As single minded as they were, however they kept following Max. That could be a problem if there were sentries, but it was too late for a Plan B.

Maverick was in his hibernation mode, but Max could still sense where he was. *Not far.* He wasn't moving either, so either they had put him on a table or someone asleep or sitting still was holding onto the gun. It didn't matter. Max would get his little buddy back.

The enemy hadn't moved the camp, but they had the sense to not light a fire this time. Max actually preferred that. Having been so long in the darkness, his eyes had developed a decent measure of night-vision. He could see the outlines of two lizards keeping watch.

They saw Max coming too late.

"The enemy is here!" one of them shouted as the other ran off, probably to make sure everyone was awake.

Max grinned to himself. The remaining lizard pulled two swords out of their scabbards and prepared for Max, who was closing the distance.

Max lightened his body and when he got close enough, he attached a number of pulling [**Tethers**] to himself and the enemy. Max zoomed through the air and landed knee-first on the enemy's head. The lizard yelped and fell. Max figured he had done a fair amount of damage with that move, but he wouldn't stay to finish the job. He didn't have to.

As Max ran forward into the darkness, he could hear the skitter and hiss behind him as the monsterbugs found new, easier prey. The lizard behind Max screamed in horror as the beetles swarmed him.

Max didn't have the presence of mind to attach himself back to the walls, so he ran into a trap. A simple one made of falling rocks. He managed to get out of the way of most of them, but a flash of red confirmed that he'd failed to avoid them all.

He cussed to himself. The fifty-odd Damage he took wasn't the problem. The issue was that the [**Trapper**] had his location now. Max smirked to himself. That problem was greatly mitigated by the swarming wave of monstrous insects attacking their camp. The [**Trapper**] simply wouldn't have time for Max.

Still, Max figured it was best to turn back. First of all, right above the camp would be a great place to hide. Secondly, it would do him well to observe the enemy, so he would know if they survived the attack and how many were left.

The problem was that it was a risky move. Max was mostly out of Mana. He still had a little over 200 left, and while he did have potions, he'd rather not use them. Using [**Tether**] as extensively as he did, Max had noticed that his Mana regenerated quite a bit slower when he had an active spell going.

Eh. Staying and watching is still the best option. If they notice me, I'll drink a [**Mana Potion**] *and escape.*

So Max found a nice spot in the shadows and watched the show. The bugs were relentless, and the lizards were absolutely not prepared for them. Four of the lizards faced a horrible death and went limp after the bugs had finished with them. The smarter lizards ran. Max found himself enjoying his machinations. Then he realized he had pretty much taken a page out of the Stranger's playbook and his mood soured a bit.

If only that rabid fool had used his talents for this . . .

But soon the shouts of the lizards grew more distant. Max listened carefully. A stray scuttle was to be heard here and there; it was the disgusting crunch of flesh being eaten by the bugs sating their predatory instincts.

Most importantly, Max could feel [**The Maverick**] close by, still as pond water. The escaping lizards hadn't grabbed him.

Max dropped down from the wall tentatively. If the bugs happened to decide they were still looking for sport, he vowed to make the world record in using [**Gravity Well**]. Fortunately, it didn't come to that, but Max passed the swarms attached to each corpse he passed with extreme care.

He couldn't help but smile. This had been a total success. It was time to be reunited with his best friend.

CHAPTER SEVENTY-THREE

Reunions

Max made his way into a small room behind a stone door. With a grunt, he pushed it open, and there, on a pile of rock slabs being used for a table, he found his friend waiting.

"Took you long enough!" the weapon chimed. "You look like a whole family of cats pissed on you."

Max chuckled softly. "Nice to see you too, Mav."

"I must say, I do miss being carried," Maverick said. "You get to shoot more stuff when you have a humanoid slave to move you around."

"Since when have I been a slave?"

"Since you abandoned me," Maverick sniffed.

"You seemed to be doing fine," Max said. "You even killed a lizard."

"Hahha! You . . . You should have . . . Hahahahaha . . . You should have seen it," Maverick wheezed. "That idiot lightning mage was trying to get me to work, which of course resulted in nothing. He smelled even worse than you, and I wasn't about to cooperate."

"Yeah?"

"And he . . . Hahahaha!" Maverick had to stop to catch his breath. How that worked for a creature without lungs, Max didn't know. "He actually peered inside my barrel."

Max grinned as he shook his head.

"And I thought humans were stupid," Maverick said.

"I'm glad you've enjoyed yourself," Max said.

"How did you get here?" Maverick asked. "We didn't get any Experience. What happened to the lizards?"

"Some ran off; some met a less-than-savory death."

"Ooooooh, show me."

Max picked up his companion and fitted him inside the holster. He felt full again. As cumbersome and unwieldy as the ridiculously proportioned revolver was, the weapon was a part of him. And not just in the sense that they shared a Cultivation bond. Well, maybe it *was* that. But Maverick had been with him since the start. He could sense his thoughts and emotions. In that moment, Max realized that Maverick was more than a tool, more than a pet, more than a friend. In a way, Maverick was his soulmate.

"Ugh," Maverick said. "You're so icky. Even your fingers are dirty. Say what you will about the lizards, but at least they washed their hands."

Gods above help my soul . . .

They emerged from the room, and Max showed the gun his work as he explained what had happened. Maverick was quite excited at the whole prospect of using the bugs as a weapon.

"Sometimes you surprise me, Max."

"Why? Because I have good ideas?"

"Well, yes."

"And?"

Through their Soulbond, Max could feel as if Maverick had just given him a quizzical look. "And? There is no 'and'."

"Wow, I'm so glad we had this conversation."

"Anyway," Maverick said. "These bugs are creepy and awesome. Do you think we could use them?"

"Use them?" Max wondered. "For what?"

Maverick sighed. "Like you just did when you didn't have me to solve all your problems for you. *To attack enemies.*"

Max thought about it. "Yeah, that sounds good on paper, but we can't maintain a safe distance from them and move in such a way that they won't cause problems. We spend a lot of time huddling and hiding. I won't always have a wall to [**Tether**] to either."

Maverick hummed as Max watched the bugs finishing off a lizard's corpse. It was almost eaten to the bone already. If you ignored the shape of the skull, it was really hard to tell it wasn't a human skeleton . . . "Do you think you could control those bugs if you had the right Class?" Maverick said.

"I already have a Class."

"Not *you* you, you endless dunderhead," Maverick huffed. "Just 'you' in general."

"You'd make an excellent teacher," Max mused. "Patient and gentle."

"Bah," Maverick said. "So, what do you think?"

"You want to do what exactly?" Max asked.

"I don't know," Maverick said. "That's for you to figure out."

"You're suggesting that if someone came down here with an un-upgraded **[Combatant]** Class, they could interact with the bugs and maybe get a Class in that?"

"Yeah, why not?" Maverick said. "You've been saying you can affect what you get by wanting and needing it."

"It's an idea," Max said. "I'll be mildly shocked if anyone wants to come down here to play with toxic flesh-eating bugs, but I'm getting used to crazy. I'll run it by the people at the outpost."

"Don't forget to mention it was my idea," Maverick said, extremely pleased with himself.

"Oh, I wouldn't dream of it."

"Speaking of the outpost, what are we going to do now?" Maverick asked.

"Yeah . . ." Max said. "That's what I've been pondering over."

"Well, think aloud," Maverick demanded. "I can only sense your thoughts when you're actively verbalizing something. I can't get anything but subtle impressions from the gray soup that is your mind."

"Yeah, you really don't do subtle, do you?" Max said and chuckled to himself. Maverick wasn't amused. Max could feel a surge of impatience from their bond. "We could return to the dwarves now and ask Durum to teach us more about Cultivation, as was originally planned."

"But you don't want to do that?"

"I want to know where these lizards are camped," Max said. "Cultivation will make us tougher, but knowing how organized the enemy is, how big a force, and where they're located, and what resources are available to them would almost as useful, if not more so."

"I don't see how knowing all of that is more useful than getting a high Cultivation Level and just crushing those scaly fools."

Max scoffed. He peered around the intersection and chose a corridor.

"Back to the dwarves?" Maverick asked. "So, you do agree with me?"

Max developed his gait into a jog. "We need to go tell them we dealt with the threat and that we've held up our end of the bargain."

Max had come to the decision slowly, and he knew it. If the enemy had escaped straight back up to the Dreadlands, they would have a decent lead on Max. Tracking them would be hard, especially with Max's skills, but he was so tired and hungry that it was hard to think. But it did put a hint of a smile on his face. No, the enemy wouldn't be far. They hadn't slept properly for two days. With their underdeveloped Cultivation, they'd be on their last legs by now.

Reuniting with the dwarfs, Max had a short exchange with them. They weren't exactly thrilled with him for having abandoned them, but fortunately, he had a good rapport with them by now. Also, actually having delivered on his promise of dealing with the threat didn't hurt.

The expedition leader promised to return to Durum immediately and tell him that Max had upheld his bargain. He also made a quick account of what he had seen and experienced on the third floor of the dungeon. Hesitantly, Max told them about his suspicions of the third floor having a big Boss somewhere, but the prospect of monster-bugs was already enough to clearly deter any bravery from the dwarves for now. Max told him to pass the word to Durum that they shouldn't try to take on the third floor without his help. He doubted it would help at all. Durum might have his good qualities, but the High King's greed was unrivaled. Whether another two score dwarves had to die for him to learn that wasn't up to Max.

"Alright!" Maverick exclaimed as they left the dwarves behind. "The dynamic duo is back together! The Master Key and the Monkey Servant adventure again!"

"You really have a way with words, Mav."

"Thanks."

"Not a good way."

"Hmph," Maverick huffed. "At least I have ideas. You just shoot them down."

"Here's an idea," Max said. "Let's go hunt some scaly fools."

"Hell, yeah!"

CHAPTER SEVENTY-FOUR

Hunting Footsteps

The other entrance upwards was close to the lizards' abandoned base. Max doubted the enemy **[Trapper]** had had time to set anything nasty up, but he still went for a balanced approach of speed and care. Fact of the matter was that Max didn't know much at the moment. The enemy could be making a beeline towards their home base, or they could be catching their breath on the upper floor.

But there was only one way to get more information. And that way was going forward.

So Max went up the stairs, all the while gripping Maverick's handle in the holster and listening carefully. There were no lizard bodies on the stairs. That didn't surprise Max, considering the monster-bugs weren't exactly adept climbers.

Max had actually seen a few of them scuttling here and there throughout the corridors. Maverick hated them. Every time Max used **[Tether]** to get up on the wall high enough for the swarms of bugs to lose interest in him, the gun sent an involuntary mental shudder through their bond.

"What?" Max whispered. "Don't like bugs?"

"They are disgusting, wretched creatures from hell."

"Didn't peg you for a sensitive type, Mav."

"It's about being a *sensible* type. Bugs are icky. Any reasonable person would agree with me."

"Icky or not, they were really useful. You'd still be in the lizard-people's claws if it weren't for them."

"I'll write a thank-you letter to the bugs in my memoirs."

"How are you going to write a book?" Max asked, chuckling as he reached for his water flask.

"Dictation, of course!" Maverick said.

The implication wasn't lost on Max. "Of course . . ."

When the two of them got to the dungeon's first floor, they quieted down and dropped their levity. The enemy could be here. Max doubted they were actively waiting for him to follow them, but it wasn't out of the realm of possibility.

Indeed, Max noticed a tripwire fairly close to the stairs. With his enhanced dark-vision from Cultivation and just simply spending days in darkness, combined with getting better and better at noticing traps, he leapt over the tripwire with ease. He had even checked for a double trap.

"You're becoming less of a klutz," Maverick said.

"Shut up," Max hissed.

There weren't any signs of movement, but a few more traps had been laid down. It didn't seem like the enemy had intended to delve into the dungeon any further. That was just perfect for Max. He wanted to know where the enemy would go from that point. With that in mind, he went onwards.

There were dozens of the **[Twisted Wretches]**'s bodies strewn over the ground. The Lizards had made short work of them. Max wasn't surprised. He had managed to kill scores of them with the help of what were basically NPCs. A group of well-organized humans wouldn't have had trouble with these Wretches. The lizards were as formidable a foe as humans were. Actually even more formidable.

They came in here with the strength of twenty **[Combatants]**. *All of them decently high-Level. I don't know what's going on in other human settlements, but as far as I know, humans are WAY behind the eight-ball on combat prowess.*

And combat was ultimately what this exercise for survival was all about. Sure, Joshua's people were reasonably comfortable and productive. You needed a baseline of survival before you could fight. Having them settle an outpost in the caves of the Dreadlands had been a good idea. That would make humans harder and more capable. And that was what was needed.

The Lizards weren't that great at fighting, though. I basically destroyed their group single-handedly. I'll need to find out what they're doing.

On a whim, Max tried looting the **[Twisted Wretches]** piled up in the corridors, but they had been cleaned up. The lizards weren't stupid.

The smell of death was so intense, it almost made Max want to puke. Any undue delicacy had been sheared off him by the new reality, but that didn't make the smell of decay any less unsavory.

It didn't take long for Max to get out of the dungeon. He exited through an open doorway, through which he could see a red light glowing. It was dim, nothing like torchlight. Indeed, it turned out to be a platform of obsidian atop lava.

This has to be part of the old dwarven kingdom. It's abandoned though. The heat is nasty, but we could maybe live here.

A pulse from Maverick stopped him in his tracks. It clearly said STOP! LOOK OUT!

It was a good thing Max did. He was just about to reach for the handle of a stone door leading out of the room when he noticed a wire attached to the handle.

"Shit," Max whispered to himself. "How did you even see that?"

"I don't know," Maverick said. "But that's a problem."

It sure was. The door was trapped. If Max had pushed it open, it would have triggered whatever had been installed there.

"Just use [Tether] on it and let's carry on," Maverick said.

"Yeah . . ." Max muttered. "But then she'll know I'm coming."

"Crap," Maverick said. "Well unless you're going to magically lose fifty pounds, I don't see you squeezing through that slit."

"I could toss you to the other side and—"

"And what, genius? Maybe I'll sprout some hands and disarm it? For all we know disarming it will alert the [Trapper]. Just stop wasting time."

As much as it annoyed Max, Maverick was right. He took a few paces back and used [Tether] to push the door open. A bunch of rocks smashed into the doorway, throwing up a billowing cloud of light, gray dust. A few cracked pieces of rock flew at Max, but they dealt no Damage.

"We have to hurry now," Max said, more to himself, and cast [Alter Gravity] on himself and [The Maverick] so they could run faster.

Having discarded care for speed meant that Max sprung another two traps. The other one lost him forty Health, but with adept use of [Tether] combined with him running straight ahead, he managed to avoid any severe Damage. It was too late to avoid traps. Slassekhsnas knew he was coming to settle the score.

Max actually got lost a few times in the corridors, twice hitting dead ends. What helped him find the right route was actually following the traps that had been left behind for him. Using them as breadcrumbs, Max finally ascended and found another door. From the outside, he could see faint orange sunlight and the acrid smell of the Dreadlands hit him. Without thinking twice, Max used [Tether] to push the doors open. No trap was sprung, but it had still been the right thing to do. Max felt that the door not being trapped was probably a good sign. It meant Slassekhsnas had run out of either time or materials. Preferably the latter.

After so long underground, the light of the outside world nearly blinded Max. He blinked through the tears and tried to look around him. He had emerged into a part of the Dreadlands that was unfamiliar to him. He took a few paces forward and, as he turned to his right, saw the volcano looming in the horizon.

Judging from the distance, I'm probably a few miles away from the outpost. Four miles? Something like that. I think I know what direction I need to go to find them. But it's not time for that now.

There was a path winding down the ashy ground that had been clearly made by footprints walking in haste. You didn't need to be a professional big game hunter to see these tracks. Max followed them. He came up on a hillside, at which point he lost the tracks, but there was enough suspicious rubble on the ground to see where the lizards had landed. Faint marks of another path they had clearly used to run away on could be seen yonder.

Max lifted his gaze and saw a pack of **[Vilefiends]** a few hundred yards away, but that wasn't what was interesting. What *was* interesting was the pack of half-a-dozen lizards about a mile away in the distance. From his vantage point, they were just a speck moving away. Max couldn't tell if they had noticed him or not.

It hardly mattered. Max had taken the Lizards on when it had been twenty to one. Now there were six or seven of the enemy left. The strongest enemy was a **[Trapper]**, and they were in open country.

Max was done hiding and skulking around in the shadows. It was time to hunt.

CHAPTER SEVENTY-FIVE

End of the Line

Max didn't bother to hide himself. It would eventually be impossible anyway. His Stamina was running low as, despite his high Levels of Cultivation, the fatigue was getting to him. But he knew the lizards were more tired. They had seen Max and their slow-but-steady march had turned into a stumbling jog. They were at the end of their rope.

Empowered by this, Max chugged down a **[Stamina Potion]** and took to a jog himself.

"I want to capture one," Max said. "We should be able to make it speak."

"I like that," Maverick exclaimed. "Let me be the bad cop! I'll shoot their kneecaps!"

"Sheesh," Max said between breaths. "I'd rather not get brutal with them."

"They're the enemy," Maverick said. "Don't be such a wussypants."

"There's a difference between a clean death and torture."

"What difference? Is it somewhere between using monster bugs that eat people alive to kill your enemy?"

Max grunted and said nothing at first. He was sure of his victory. The **[Trapper]** was at a massive disadvantage, and Max had certainly faced worse odds. But he didn't quite know what to do if and when he got a prisoner.

"Look," Max finally said. "I don't know how well you understand fear and pain, Mav. I'll just say this. I'll do what I have to in order to help my people. But I would rather not become something I can't respect in the process."

"Yeah, I don't get it. We good guys, they bad guys."

Max got a little annoyed at that. But he controlled himself. How could Maverick understand? "I've only recently started liking myself again. Brutal torture isn't something humans can afford to engage in."

"Maybe what you can't afford to do is to be a wussypants. This is why I should be the bad cop."

Max recast [**Alter Gravity**] and kept on the run. The enemy had maybe a mile on him. He wished he knew where they were running towards, so he would know how much time he had.

"I just don't see what's the big deal," Maverick said. "You're alright with killing them in cold blood."

"That's why you don't get to be the bad cop."

Maverick huffed.

"Look. I have to kill them. I have to hunt them. But I don't have to make them suffer."

"They seemed to be willing to rip you from limb to limb, given the excuse," Maverick reminded him.

"That may be so," Max muttered. "All the more reason to make sure that humans win this game."

"You meatbags are strange creatures."

"We might be," Max admitted. "But who else is going to carry you around?"

"Fair enough," Maverick said. "Besides, we need to catch someone before we can tort—err, interrogate anyone."

"Let's pick up the pace then."

They ran on and made up a decent bit of distance. Max could already see the enemy clearly. They continued on their desperate, stumbling jog towards the edge of Dreadlands. They had less than half a mile to go.

The last of them kept looking back and shouting. Max wasn't in shooting range, and he didn't want to sprint or use [**Tether**] yet to gain the distance.

I'll wait until they're at the cliff. That way, some of them will want to climb up and escape, and some of them will stay. It's still six against one.

"You don't think you can take them on?" Maverick asked.

Max had a sip form his water flask and wiped his mouth. "It's risky."

"It's risky letting them escape."

Max had to agree with that. If he allowed any of them to do so, they would run off to tell their people that the guy with the massive bounty on his head was right there under their nose.

"There is a world where we could use that to our advantage."

Maverick scoffed. "More advantageous than keeping them in the dark?"

"I suppose . . ."

"I think you're just being a tired wussypants," Maverick said. "Just suck it up and kill all but one."

It was Max's turn to scoff. "Fine. I'll show you."

"That's the spirit, Meat-Taxi!"

Max picked up the pace and started using [**Tether**] to gain on the distance. The enemy noticed almost immediately. With alarmed shouts, they picked up their jog-march into a full sprint.

Good, tire yourselves out.

The edge of the valley was maybe 500 yards away from the enemy's position. Max chugged down a **[Potion of Greater Mana Regeneration]**. He didn't like it. That left him with only one left, but this was not a moment to be miserly.

Another **[Tether]** followed another, and soon Max was in shooting distance. It would have been impossible for anyone to aim properly in these conditions, half-running, half-tether-sliding along the bumpy ground while pointing **[The Maverick]** at the enemy, no matter how steady a person's hand was.

Nobody but **[The Maverick]** himself.

The last lizard running yelped in surprise and pain when the first volley of shots landed.

The lizards reacted immediately. They fanned out. Slassekhsnas, taller than the rest, ran at the head of their formation. She was clearly exhausted, but her long legs kept her stride steady. Max pointed Maverick in her general direction, and the gun let loose a few bullets.

Then something unexpected happened. The other lizards turned and stopped. Slassekhsnas kept running.

"No way . . ." Max said between breaths.

"Why are they stopping?" Maverick asked between shots.

"They're sacrificing themselves so Slassekhsnas can escape," Max said.

"Damn, these lizards are smart," Maverick said.

"They're not just smart," Max muttered. "Humans are smart. But this kind of ruthlessness . . ."

"Focus, Max," Maverick said. "That guy's gonna throw a spear."

"I see it. Ready for me to toss you?"

"Baby, I was born ready!"

"Please, never call me baby again," Max muttered as he cast **[Alter Gravity]** on Maverick and chucked him as high and far as he could with his adequate Strength score. Max took a note of his Mana. A moment later, 150 Mana was gone.

While Maverick was still ascending, he started to spin around frantically and to rain hell down on the lizards.

CHAPTER SEVENTY-SIX

Payoff

The lizards came at Max weapons raised, roaring in fear and anger. They were brave, admittedly, but apart from one guy with a sling, they were all melee-based fighters. And all too slow for Max.

He weaved around them using [Tether] while Maverick spun in the air and blasted at the enemy. Whenever one of the lizards got too close, Max used a repelling [Tether] to push them back. One of them fell, and Max received an Experience drop.

The others formed a group to help each other in case they got repelled by Max. That was the mistake Max had been waiting for.

"[Gravity Well]!"

Three of the enemy melee fighters were instantly clumped together in the air—all but one who apparently had enough of a Resistance stat to pull himself away. The slingshot wielder was accurate, and Max took a few hits from him, dropping his Health down to the four-hundreds. It wasn't enough. Now that the melee fighters were caught in a trap, Max would deal with the ranged attacker.

The remaining melee fighter lunged at him with a sharp, black dagger. Max got out of the way, sliding backwards with a [Tether]. Then he used another spell on Maverick and the enemy fighter, and the weapon zoomed through the air and struck the fighter, as he lunged again. That tripped him off balance. Max picked up [The Maverick] and killed him.

After that, Max moved towards the slingshot guy. It wasn't exactly clear where they got that endless supply of rocks from, but it didn't matter. Another one struck Max, and he took a loss of fifty Health points. He glanced at his mana. Over 600 left. Despite it ticking down, it was more than enough to keep the [Gravity Well] going. From the corner of his eye, Max confirmed that the enemy was still struggling. They were trying to push one of their own out of the sphere, but it was hard to push anything when you weren't grounded. Even if they succeeded, it wouldn't be enough.

The slingshotter cast another rock at Max, but it missed. She was so visibly tired, Max almost felt bad for gunning her down. But this was not the time nor the place for sympathy.

Defeated Level 15 [Ishkarassi]
You gained 470 Experience points

One of the three fighters managed to escape from the [Gravity Well]. He only barely stumbled back on his feet before Max killed him. Max could feel Maverick's bloodlust and glee through their bond, but Max felt detached. This was a triumph. His enemies weren't all even dead, but he knew he'd defeat them. It was almost too easy. They were so tired and weak to begin with, it was like fighting a bunch of ten-year-olds.

The second-to-last one didn't even escape from his spell before he finished him. A Level-Sixteen Ishkarassi.

Class upgraded from [Graviturgist] D-grade to [Gravitician] C-grade
Level Up! [Level 20 Gravitician]
You have gained +2 Constitution, +3 Intelligence, +3 Wisdom, +3 free Attribute points
Skill Choice available!
Signature Ability Choice available!

"Wow," Max said to himself, as he released the [Gravity Well]. "That's good stuff. Those Stat boosts are massive. If I can somehow upgrade my [Tether] through this signature ability, I'm all for it."

The last remaining lizard scrambled to his feet and yelled out "Scum!" as he attacked.

Max pinned him to the ground with two [Tethers] in an almost distracted manner and sat on top of him.

"Our signature ability is clearly [Semi-automatic Firearm]!" Maverick declared. "Did you see me? I rained down hellfire on them!"

"I saw you," Max said and smiled. "Good job."

"Hey, that's my line," Maverick huffed. "As per usual, I did most of the work, so I should decide on the signature ability."

"We don't even know what it is yet. Let's just stop, breathe, and think for a second."

"What do you mean?" Maverick asked. Just bring up the Skill upgrades and let's gooooo!"

Max looked at the direction Slassekhsnas had run towards. He didn't even see her anymore. Chasing her would be impossible. Especially with a prisoner. He could kill the prisoner and take his chances, but that didn't seem like the right choice.

"We need to move," Max said.

"What about all the upgrades?" Maverick protested.

"You know they have a bounty on us, right?" Max said. "What do you think happens when Slassekhsnas reaches their base?"

Maverick hummed as if thinking. "I don't like it when you're right about stuff that I overlook."

"Isn't that what being part of a team means?"

Maverick huffed. "Maybe. But I should still outshine you. Fortunately, that's the natural flow of things. I got another Skill!"

Max raised an eyebrow at that and smiled. "You did? What kind?"

"Not telling. You didn't want to discuss the Skill upgrades, remember?"

"You're such a little girl sometimes . . ." Max muttered. Then he got up and released the spells keeping the lizard down.

The enemy immediately bolted. He threw ash at Max's face and took to a sprint in the same direction Slassekhsnas had gone to. Max targeted a [**Tether**] at a single leg and the enemy tumbled to the ground, cursing.

Max went over to him and pistol-whipped him in the face twice. Then Max wagged a finger at him and shook his head. "Play nice."

The lizard seemed to understand his body language well enough and gave him a reluctant nod. Max was worried he would waste his time until reinforcements arrived, but for lack of bravery or guile, Max's disciplinary measures made the enemy more compliant.

That made Max's life significantly easier. He pushed the enemy in the direction he wanted them to go. He looked at Max and growled, but Max flicked him with [**The Maverick**]'s barrel. The enemy clearly wasn't enthusiastic about this march, so his pace wasn't exactly adequate. Max quickly noticed that his prisoner required a steady drip of snappy physical encouragement to stay motivated.

Max knew the general direction they needed to go towards to get to the outpost. He just needed to choose a route that would avoid most of the enemies in the Dreadlands. Especially [**Foulworms**], as those bastards could cause situations which could enable escape.

Maverick was swelling with self-satisfaction. Max smiled to himself. He was pretty pleased with himself as well. He was tired—exhausted, even. It had been a few very long days. But looking back at it, it had been indeed quite a success, as Maverick's mood suggested.

Max had had first contact with the enemy and triumphed. Against overwhelming numbers, to boot. He had killed a score of the enemy fighters, permanently destroying their potential. There was a grim satisfaction to that. He had Leveled Up and gotten a Class upgrade. A High King of the dwarves owed him a favor. And he had a prisoner to interrogate. Things weren't good—they were great! Now all he had to do was to get back home safely.

Max cast one last glance behind him towards the general direction Slassekhsnas had run off to.

They'll come for me.

Maverick barked out a laugh. "Let them."

CHAPTER SEVENTY-SEVEN

Language Barrier

Max really wanted to look at all his cool new upgrades. But there was a glaring problem. A literal glaring problem. Every few seconds, their prisoner gave Max a scathing glance. Maverick sent off a very distinct, urgent wish through their bond to smack the fool in the back of his head every time it happened.

"Keep walking," Max said and shoved the lizard forward.

He grunted and spat.

"It seems he doesn't like you," Maverick said cheerfully. That made the lizard look back at Max in alarm. Max tilted his head and smiled coolly at his prisoner.

"He's just not very happy with his circumstances," Max said.

"Should we interrogate him?" Maverick asked. "I'd like to do something to pass the time."

"And how, pray, should we do that?" Max asked. "He doesn't understand a word I'm saying."

"But you—"

"Wait!" Max snapped. Then he looked at the prisoner. He was walking, looking forward.

"Listen, Maverick," Max started carefully. "Don't talk more yet. I have a suspicion. It could be completely wrong, though."

Maverick uncharacteristically said nothing. Through their bond, he sent a pulse to tell Max to continue.

"You're of this world. Alpha Ludus. You're created by these aliens. If this lizard guy had been the one to originally claim you, you'd be having this banter with him instead, right?"

"Go on," Maverick said. Max could feel through their bond that he already knew where Max was going with this, but Max continued anyway. It was good to talk it out and make his thoughts more clear.

"I have a Skill to understand all the languages," Max said. "There's no way you just popped up into being and started speaking English."

"You're saying—"

"Don't!" Max quickly interjected. "Don't give him information. Yes, I'm saying he might understand you. I'm saying everyone might understand you."

"Hmmm," Maverick thought on that. "Well, I certainly am extremely awesome."

"I need you to do a very uncharacteristic thing, Your Awesomeness," Max muttered. "I need you to be really careful about what you say when he's within earshot."

"We could just—" Maverick started, before he indeed very uncharacteristically trailed off. Instead, he sent a pulse through their bond. It was a simple idea: *Test it.*

"We will," Max said. "But first we need to get to safety and secure the prisoner."

That paused their conversation for now. Max looked around. He had a moderate grasp of the geography of the Dreadlands. They were close. They'd walk past that hill and take a left and—

His musings were stopped by a sudden ambush by a group of **[Junior Vilefiends]**. These creatures had tended to leave him alone recently, most likely because of his high Level, but now they had clearly wandered too close. They came at him with claws extended, screaming as they swiped at him. The prisoner escaped immediately.

Max acted fast. He nailed the **[Vilefiends]** on the ground with **[Tethers]**. Two of them died from the pressure. Max got a menial amount of Experience. He couldn't care less right now.

His prisoner, who was clearly a physical fighter, had used some kind of a movement ability. He almost glided forward, as if on skates, as he attempted his escape. Max used a couple of well-timed **[Tethers]** to skate across the ashen land himself. He tried a **[Tether]** on his prisoner, but his momentum was too great for it to trap him. Max cursed and used more spells to catch up with him. The dry ash billowed into a cloud that followed in the lizard's wake as he ran for his life. When Max got close enough, he managed to use **[Gravity Well]** and lift the prisoner off his feet.

The lizard screamed enraged profanities at Max. Max came up close and dropped the **[Gravity Well]**.

The lizard tumbled to the ground. When he tried to get up, Max smacked him across the face with **[The Maverick]**. His Strength score was low, but the prisoner seemed to understand the message. There was no escape from this situation. Max pointed at his face. "If you don't play nice, there'll be hell to pay."

The lizard spat on the ground.

"That fact that you think I can understand your primitive language is an insult. You have no idea what you're doing. We have a town of over three hundred people. You will not be able slay us all. We'll rip you apart if you try."

Max did his best not to smirk. That was useful to know. A tad terrifying, but useful. They were over double the size of Joshua's settlement. Were there simply more of them, or were they better organized?

Surely humans had more bases somewhere, too. Max hadn't seen many people at all. Then again, he had spent a lot of time underground.

"Don't you think it'll be hard to get him back to the base if you cut his legs off?" Maverick asked suddenly.

Max raised an eyebrow. "I didn't—"

Then he looked at the lizard. His eyes had gone wide, and the dark green shade of his scales grew slightly lighter.

Oh, Maverick, you sly bastard. So he does understand you.

Maverick sent a pulse of the purest glee and self-satisfaction through their bond. Max smiled to himself. Oh, this made things so much easier. If he just got this payload back home, they would get so much information. This lizard was extremely valuable.

"Let's get this golden goose back to the outpost," Max said with a satisfied grin, shoving the prisoner back in the right direction.

"Golden goose?" Maverick asked. "I don't get it."

"Well, you know," Max stammered, "he'll lay us golden eggs of information and—"

Maverick made a sound as if clearing his throat. "You know . . . Maybe it's better if I take care of the interrogation. You seem tired . . ."

"Screw you."

CHAPTER SEVENTY-EIGHT

Haven

When Max returned to the outpost cave, pointing [**The Maverick**] at a tired, angry lizard prisoner, everyone's jaws inside dropped.

"We have returned triumphant, dear peasants and admirers!" Maverick yelled.

"Anyone got a rope?" Max called out.

Christie came over. She was beautiful as ever but clearly tired and emaciated. "You look like hell," she said in her throaty voice, smiling wanly.

"Good to see you, too," Max said. The lizard made an attempt to escape, but Max tripped him with his foot. His prisoner was so tired, that it was all it took. He fell to the ground with an "*Oof!*". Max tethered him to the ground and sat on him, sighing contently.

Brian came up to them with Freya and another young girl.

"I always worry you might not make it back," Brian said. "You always keep proving me wrong."

"One of my finest qualities," Max said and smiled. "Look, if we have rope or something to tie this guy down, that'd be great."

There was a bit of commotion. Brian and two of his men took care to hold the prisoner steady. Freya brought Max a cup of stale water that tasted like metal and dried meat. Max accepted them gratefully.

Christie and a bunch of others tried to chat him up and ask about all that had happened. Max just smiled at them, barely listening. He leaned against the wall of the cave, letting the soft torchlight and the orange evening sun caress him with their warmth. The water tasted pretty bad, but it made him feel better. He hadn't realized how tired he was.

Maverick noticed his state and went on a lengthy and clearly embellished explanation of what had happened. Max closed his eyes and sighed contently. He was safe. He was alive. They had succeeded against all odds. Yes, he had stirred up the hornet's nest. The lizards would be alert and most likely try to actively hunt Max and his friends down. This outpost idea was much more dangerous now.

But they also had a prisoner. They would get all the appropriate information out of him. Max still wasn't comfortable with the idea of torture. He didn't mind killing. In fact, he didn't even bat an eye at the idea. In a combat situation, it was either him or the enemy, and that was fair.

Max opened one eye and looked at Brian. The man was making an effort at reforming himself. It was half-forced, Max thought, but it looked like things were good here at the outpost. He didn't know if Brian or Christie was running the show, but Brian would be the guy to call on to inflict violence on the prisoner, if the lizard didn't want to cooperate.

Maverick sent a pulse through their bond, going something along the lines of "So you admit I'm right?" Max let out a half-hearted scoff and drifted into a well-earned sleep.

When Max woke up, it was early in the morning. Very early. Everyone was sound asleep. The smell of sweat and sulfur was strong in the still air. Max got up and carefully walked over to a bowl of water and had some to drink. A cacophony of soft snores could be heard. Max sighed contently. He felt refreshed. He suspected it was around 4:00 or 5:00 a.m., meaning he must have slept for over ten hours, which was almost preposterous for someone at his high Level.

It was clearly 100 percent needed. I didn't even realize what a zombie I was. It's a small wonder I got here in one piece.

Then Max finally took a look at his notifications. He got the Stats out of the way first. He had gotten a Class upgrade and the Stat boosts weren't minor at all. In fact, they were massive. If he just rose a few more Levels, he'd leave anyone under Level Twenty far behind. After some contemplation, he put all his free points into Constitution. Max would be spending a lot more time in the Dreadlands, often most likely in dangerous combat, and the extra Health and Stamina certainly wouldn't hurt.

Name: Max Cromwell
Cultivation stage: Amethyst (lesser)
Class: Gravitician
Level: 20
Health: 900/900
Stamina: 900/900
Mana: 1030/1030
Alliance: Joshua's Group
Stats:

Strength: 24
Dexterity: 26
Constitution: 90
Intelligence: 103
Wisdom: 68
Charisma: 24
Precision: 47
Toughness: 36
Resistance: 46

Next up, Max looked up his Skill options. He was really hoping one particular Skill was there that he had been waiting to pick up for a while but hadn't been able to for lack of Mana pool.

[Telekinesis I]
Gain the ability to lift an inanimate object within sight in the air and move it around. The weight of the object you are able to lift, and the speed at which you are able to move it in the air, is dependent on your Intelligence.
Cost: 3 or more Mana per second, depending on the weight of the object.

Yes! It's there. Now, if I'm right about my idea, this Skill could be extremely valuable . . . It could provide me with offense, defense, and mobility . . .

[Gravity Pulse I]
Send out a wave of gravitational energy in a cone ten feet wide, throwing back anything in its path and causing damage proportional to your Intelligence modifier. The closer the object(s), the more potent the effect.
Cost: 15 Mana

Yeah, it's solid. But I doubt I'm going to need it honestly. Not with what I have planned with **[Telekinesis]***.*

Max didn't hesitate; he picked **[Telekinesis]**.

The first thing he did was cast it on his boots.

He lifted in the air, struggling to keep his balance. With great effort and wide, fast waves of his arms, he managed to stay relatively still. Just enough to try to propel himself forward in midair. He immediately fell on his back.

A few mumbles could be heard nearby, but fortunately nobody woke up. Max canceled the spell, which dropped his eerily floating legs on the ground. He glanced at his Mana bar.

Damn, that ate up a lot for just a few seconds.

The spell had sucked up over twenty Mana, which meant that he was probably using ten to eleven Mana per second to keep himself afloat.

Well, that wasn't too bad for a first attempt. But hell, yes, I'm going to fly. I'm going to make it work.

Max crept outside and practiced. It didn't go terribly well. He also used **[Telekinesis]** to float a big slab of gray rock next to him. It was wide enough to stand on, and that was exactly what he did. With his new spell, he lifted the rock he was standing on. The Mana expenditure was even larger, but Max did manage to stay on top of the slab. It was wobbly and it was clumsy. But he was technically *flying.* It felt AWESOME!

Max wanted to let out a *whoop* but controlled himself. Though a big goofy smile remained on his face. Over the next forty minutes, Max spent his time and Mana trying out **[Telekinesis]**. He was able to make multiple objects float, noticing that the Mana expenditure was additive. Moving a single object through the air using his mind was simple. Trying to make two objects move was like trying to push and pull a shopping cart at the same time. It actually gave him a bit of a headache.

Most of the time, however, Max kept working at trying to fly. He really wanted to be able to just lift his shoes up, but the balance was an issue.

Maybe I should start dumping points in Dexterity? That might help me move around in the air smoother, anyway.

His best attempt at flying was using **[Telekinesis]** on his arms and feet and soaring a yard above the air like Superman. Well, it wasn't so much soaring as it was awkward tumbling, but it was a start.

Skill upgraded: [Telekinesis I] -> [Telekinesis II]

Wow, that was fast. I suppose I did spam the shit out of it . . .

As the crown jewel in his arsenal, the last thing Max wanted to do before getting to the business of dealing with the prisoner, he brought up the last notification with the red dot:

Signature Ability Choice available!

CHAPTER SEVENTY-NINE

Signature Ability

When Max opened the notification, the Zoos Collective jellyfish popped up in front of him. But rather than its usual large size, this time it was small enough to fit inside a human's palm.

[Greetings. This is a preprogrammed AI. It has some ability to respond to inquiries regarding the subject matter, but its primary function is to explain the Signature Ability.]

"Alright," Max said. "Let's hear it."

[The Signature Ability is a function of the Framework, through which you can define yourself within your Class choice. Maybe you have chosen a Class such as [Ranger] with proficiency in multiple combat styles. Maybe you have chosen a [Leader] Class that maintains a balance between so-called hands-on leadership and administrative skills. The Signature Ability lets you commit to an area of expertise you think is most valuable to you.]

"That sounds . . . good?" Max said. "My Class is pretty singular, so what should I do?"

The jellyfish went still for a while. Then it continued.

[Your classification is Utility Caster. Within the limitations of your Class, you have versatile Abilities that can control the battlefield and provide both offensive and defensive options.]

Max rolled his eyes. "I'm aware of what my Class does. What would the Signature Ability be good for in my case?"

Another beat.

[You have primarily used your Abilities for control and mobility. This is a close-to-optimal approach, considering the advantage with which your primary weapon has provided you. While this one is not permitted to make suggestions, this one will provide you with advice. You could use [Telekinesis] as your Signature Ability to specialize in offensive capabilities, hurling heavy objects at your enemies. Alternatively, you could specialize your most-used Skill, [Tether], to further enhance your mobility.]

Max thought about it. It seemed . . . Interesting. Also, not exactly an easy choice.

"If I were to specialize my **[Tether]** for mobility, would it hinder my ability to use it for controlling enemies?"

[Astute question. This is not how it works. The specialization will simply tilt further growth towards the direction you choose. It will not hinder your current potency, but it will provide distinct advantages towards certain directions you want to build towards as your Stats and Skills continue upgrading. To put it in simple terms, any Intelligence or Cultivation advancement you accrue will have a higher modifier on those aspects of your Abilities that you choose to specialize in.]

"Okay. I need to think."

Max sat down. The choices were limited. While **[Gravity Well]** and **[Alter Gravity]** definitely had their uses, Max didn't really see them as *defining* him. **[Tether]** was the obvious contender. And Max would have just gone for it, were it not for his new Skill. **[Telekinesis]** would potentially be even more versatile an ability than his current trademark Skill.

The problem was, Max was already extremely proficient with **[Tether]**. It had almost limitless uses and thus was his bread and butter. Max could certainly entertain numerous, even outlandish potential uses for **[Telekinesis]**, but it would be a risk.

But I could fly . . .

Damn it. These were important, literally life-changing choices. He needed to be careful and not be swayed by his emotions.

But flying . . .

Was he really doing this? Taking a massive bet on his life and future? The safe bet would be to just enhance **[Tether]**. It was the obvious choice. But taking risks was how Max had gotten this far. He was unique amongst the humans he'd met thus far. Max could only hope there were others like him, bulwarks protecting

the weak. Max had high hopes that people like Christie and her cubs could grow
to take up his mantle, because he needed to be out there, in the fray, behind enemy
lines.

*And to be fair, for that, flying is the obvious answer. Screw it, I want to fly. I don't
care how I justify it.*

[Signature Ability chosen!]
[Telekinesis II] -> [Telekinesis* I]

The tiny jellyfish stirred.

[Reasonable choice. From henceforth your Intelligence modifiers are
enhanced regarding this spell, and the way in which you choose to use it will
give it further distinct advantage. Be mindful of how you use the spell in the
immediate future, when it still doesn't have a speciality. The way you cast
the next hundred spells will be particularly important in calibrating the spell.
If you choose to use [Telekinesis] to hurl sharp rocks at targets, it will most
likely result in increased velocity for the spell when hurling attacks at
enemies.]

"Understood," Max said. He wasn't interested in asking anything more. He
already had a plan. His mind was rushing with excitement. As soon as his Mana
regenerated, he'd come back outside to cast more spells.

After Max told the jellyfish that would be all for now, it blinked out of existence. His eyes immediately drifted up to his Mana bar. He only had 132 Mana
left. With a sigh, Max admitted to himself that it was better to wait. Maybe he
could wring some Mana potions out of Durum later.

The next morning, Max woke to find the prisoner still holed up in one of the
cave's corridors, hands and feet tied, with Brian watching over him, holding a
sword. Judging from the bags underneath his eyes, he had been keeping watch on
the lizard all night.

"How's our new guest behaving?" Max asked.

"He's been very reasonable ever since we wrapped him up," Brian said and
chuckled. "Get any sleep?"

"Just enough. You have no idea how tired I was."

"Meanwhile, we were up late listening to your gun's stories. Even if only half
of what he said was true, I'd still be surprised you were able to wake up this early."

"Feels good to be safe and back with my people."

Brian's mouth tightened slightly at "my people," but then he just shook his
head and gave a tired smile. "So, what's the plan with him?"

"We're going to interrogate him."

"That's going to make for a long day. You're gonna play Pictionary with him?"

"Actually, I have something more sophisticated planned," Max said, grinning.

"I want to see that," Brian said.

"You don't need sleep?"

Brian clearly struggled with that. "Are you going to start now?"

Max shrugged. "How about we wait for a few hours, until everyone is awake, so everyone can contribute ideas."

Brian brightened up. "A few hours is all I need."

"Go sleep," Max said. "I'll sit by him and Cultivate for a few hours."

"Damn, I should have done that . . ." Brian muttered to himself as he waved a hand at Max. "You'll wake me up before you start?"

"Promise."

Brian nodded and went off, leaving Max to sit on a rock and watch the sleeping lizard.

"Mav, you up?"

The weapon stirred in the holster. "Always! What do you need?"

"You want to Cultivate?"

"Let's do it," Maverick said immediately.

Max smiled and produced the sack of **[Celestial Illumination Pills]** from his Inventory. That's exactly what he wanted to do, too.

CHAPTER EIGHTY

New Reality

The morning was turning into day, and everyone who was available was sitting in a circle around the lizard. Max had Maverick in his lap, and Christie and Brian at each of his sides.

"You think the plan will work?" Brian muttered.

"Sure. I'll start with the talking. You two just look menacing."

"I don't know if the broad is all that menacing. No offense." Brian said and shrugged.

Christie's smile twitched. She controlled herself and cocked an eyebrow. Then she got up and punched the lizard prisoner straight in the face. The lizard yowled and she started yelling obscenities at him until he huddled up. She then kicked him until he cried for mercy.

Christie returned to her seat. The lizard wasn't the only one who was shocked. After a while Brian spoke. "Damn."

"Next time you forget my name, it'll be you on the receiving end of my boot." Brian swallowed. "Noted."

Max looked at them, trying to contain his amusement. Then he shook himself out of it and addressed his gun. "You ready, Mav?"

"Oh yeah," Maverick said, all excitement and glee. "Let's do this! Hey. Listen, Lizard-face. I know you understand me."

The lizard simply looked impassively forward.

"The cool thing about me knowing for certain that you understand me," Maverick continued, his voice taking a sly undertone, "is that I can threaten you. You think Christie here hurt you bad? How would you like an extra nostril?"

The lizard played it tough, but he betrayed himself with a badly timed blink.

Max shrugged and got up and lodged **[The Maverick]** against the lizard's nose. It alarmed the prisoner, who started pleading.

"Okay! I understand, please don't hurt me!"

Max could feel Maverick's mounting excitement. He went back into his sly, gleeful interrogation.

"Now that you've decided to be wise, I'll start off by saying that if you lie or tell half-truths, I'll know it. I have a skill called **[Lie Detection]**. And if that happens, there'll be pain for you. Understood?"

"What the hell are you?" the prisoner hissed.

"First question," Maverick said, savoring every word. "What Level was that **[Trapper]** who was leading your party?"

There was a sullen silence. The lizard regarded Max and his weapon carefully. "She was Level Twenty-Five."

Instantly Max looked at Christie and nodded. She shot up and kicked the lizard in the face. He groaned and fell backwards. Brian got up and hoisted him back to a sitting position.

"Why did you lie to us?" Maverick asked. The lizard snarled and said nothing.

He's tougher to crack than we thought. I'd hate to use more violence than necessary. Still, I can't blame him. He knows we're going to have to kill him.

It took a while. And it got ugly. Most of the folks who had been intrigued at first soon decided they had other pressing matters to attend to. Max stayed for most of it. It was grim. Even Maverick exhausted his glee. But they did extract information. The prisoner told them where their settlement was, how many were there, how many of them were warriors, what their average Levels were . . . To the great dismay of everyone listening, it seemed like his settlement was trading and cooperating with two other lizard camps. Max wondered how badly behind the humans were. He could only hope other people were collaborating elsewhere, because Joshua's camp had no standing allies at the moment.

Eventually the questions ran dry. It was hard to look at the prisoner. He was a mess. Scales and teeth were scattered on the ground amongst blood. Brian was good at patient, deliberate violence. Max thought grimly that they needed people like him. When they stopped asking questions, the prisoner's gaze shifted. The fear and anger had been drained out of him. Only a prideful sneer and a knowing look were left.

Between ragged breaths, the lizard delivered his final harrowing words. He looked at Max and smiled through his broken teeth, "You. You are the one who doomed your whole species. We were but ragged tribes fighting over prey. But after we received the bounty on you, we realized that our existence was truly threatened. You united us, Human. All the tribes converged. You made an undefeatable enemy, Gunslinger."

Max froze. He could feel Christie and Brian turning to look at him. Max only had eyes for the lizard. He looked back. There was pain in his expression, but through the pain shone a cruel mirth.

"I didn't . . ." Max said. "I didn't choose any of this."

For whatever reason, Maverick translated it to the lizard. Max sent a pulse of anger at the gun, who only shrugged through their bond.

"Nor did I choose to be captured and wrung for information," the prisoner grinned through bloody teeth. "My tribe is large. And while I may have made their job of hunting you down more difficult, I can die with little shame. They will prevail despite my failure."

The lizard's grin grew almost maniacal. Max could only listen in horror and fascination. "But you, Human, you have singlehandedly doomed your own race. Ishkarassi are a bickering, warlike people, but we are powerful hunters, powerful warriors. It's why we wound up here. We almost destroyed each other. And we almost ended up doing the same again here with our tribal battles."

"But because of me . . ." Max muttered, "you united."

"We have a collective mind, Human," the lizard said. "Like any advanced species, our thoughts and emotions are shared. But it is a murky water, rarely accessible."

"And?" Max said quietly, wondering if the prisoner was lying.

"I have sensed it, as have my leaders," the prisoner said. "All tribes have quit their internal strife. Your actions alone have united the most powerful warrior species.

"Every mother of my glorious species lays two eggs. Two Ishkarassi are always born. Only one Ishkarassi is raised. We are warriors by nature. When united, there is no creature to challenge us."

Max looked at the lizard darkly. "Yet, I came and destroyed your group of adventurers single-handedly."

Maverick translated this, and the lizard prisoner spat a bloody glob on the ground. "A fluke gained by underhanded tactics."

"You misunderstand us, Lizard," Max said. "Humans are not great warriors, like your people. Most of us are petty little cowards. But it wasn't a fluke that destroyed your expedition. It was the human spirit. It will fight through any calamity, clinging to desperate hope."

The lizard gave him a quizzical, suspicious look. Max continued. "While your people were the apex predators of your planet for millions of years, our history is very different. We were small creatures, prey creatures. We were hunted by cats and birds and yes . . . Snakes. Snakes like you. We survived you and conquered you a million years ago. You fight for conquest. Humans fight for the unquenchable will to live. That will is stronger, and your species will lose just as you have lost today. Our right to exist is absolute." Turning to Brian he said, "I'm done with the prisoner. Ask him what you will and kill him afterwards."

With that, Max got up and turned, never casting a backwards glance at the lizard, who was stunned silent along with everyone else. He walked out of the cave and a gaggle of people followed him.

Outside, he was greeted by the same dry air and faint sun he'd come to expect. But the sun's warmth felt a little more potent right now, the dry air more nourishing. Max had left something behind in that cave: doubt. His resolve galvanized in that moment. It became an absolute will to protect the human race. There was no second guessing, no moral gray area. He *would* see to it that humans won this sick game. Something shifted within him in that moment. It wasn't about fighting for humanity's right to exist. The right was absolute. Humans deserved to exist. They *would* exist. They had existed for millions of years before Max, and they would exist for millions of years to come.

The others looked at him expectantly as if he had the answers, clear reverence in their eyes. Max looked back at them with calm clarity. A lot of responsibility lay on Max's shoulders. And Max would bear it. He would protect these people.

About the Author

Wilbur Woods is an entertainer, coffee drinker, and story eater, as well as the author of the Cosmic Games series, originally released on Royal Road. He has loved stories since he was a kid, and when he asked himself what he really wanted to do, the answer was simple: write.

Podium
DISCOVER
STORIES UNBOUND
PodiumAudio.com

9 781039 465701